Hawkwind's Tale

Katherine A Smith

Book One of the Northnest Saga

Available from author Katherine A Smith

<u>The Northnest Saga</u>

Hawkwind's Tale
Hawkwind's Tale (illustrated editions)
The Fledging of Hawkwings*

<u>The Dragonic Voyages</u>

Dragons to Loose
Dragonic Freedom
Dragonic Pride
Dragons to Keep

<u>Children's Books</u>

Otter Twin Magic
Otter Sea Magic*

*Forthcoming

Hawkwind's Tale

Katherine A Smith

Book One of the Northnest Saga

Kasmith Art and Books

Fort Bragg, CA

For everyone who likes griffins
and princesses
and unicorns

and has at some point in their life
wanted to see or be at least one of the above.

Chapters

Chapter 1
The Fall of Northnest

Icy rain soaked into the fur and fine feathers on her back, making her shiver, but it hadn't yet slipped through her overlapping wing feathers. She tucked her head briefly under one wing, and then the other. The four little human fledglings were snuggled into the down of her belly and tucked against the hot bare skin of the apteria under her wings, and still asleep.

She looked back up at the rain. The tree branches, dark against the slightly lighter sky, enclosed her and her slumbering burden and swayed in the whistling wind. The storm the wizards had called up to ground the griffin flights now worked against them. Their rainbow drakes couldn't move through this weather either, and even if they could have, the trees would thwart their sonar, unlike the nearby caves that Hawkwind could have chosen to shelter in. They certainly would have been drier.

One of the children shuddered and twitched in sleep.

"Shh, easy now, you're safe with me," the she-griffin soothed.

"Mama," the boy whimpered. "I want Mama."

Hawkwind tucked him closer against her, struggling against the sharp lump of tears in her own throat. "Shh, sleep now."

The little boy began sobbing. Hawkwind closed her eyes, crooning under her breath, trying to comfort the child as well as she could. She could only imagine the things the boy had seen, before she'd fought her way to the nursery, before she'd snatched him from the claws of the invaders. Hawkwind suppressed a shudder as the fresh memories crowded in on her.

"Fall back to the keep. We've lost the grounds."

Hawkwind and the other castle griffins obeyed the order, trying to dodge the drakes, trying to cover the humans' escape. Northnest had been a small kingdom, and an overlooked one. They had nothing of great value, and no reason to be attacked as far as Hawkwind knew. Even if they'd had, the unique presence of the griffin wings made others wary. Hawkwind couldn't imagine what the invaders were gaining from this beyond a scrap of cold, semi-fertile, rocky mountain land.

She fell back into the main doorway to the keep, between a pair of guardian griffin statues and her flesh and blood companions, Eagleye and Hawkcall. A knot of drakes was forming, getting ready to charge them: their many colors making them look like a ball of shifting rainbows. The three griffins reared up, screaming defiance. The raspy growls of the drakes answered them, promising death.

From behind, the order came. "Fall back, now. The gate is closing."

The drakes charged, just as Hawkwind obeyed, dropping back—but Eagleye and Hawkcall leapt to meet the charge. Hawkwind cried out in denial, skidding to a halt on the rain-slick paving stones and bracing herself to leap forward and join them—but the gate guards swung down the doors, blocking her companions from sight, blocking her from joining them, from dying with them.

Hawkwind's throat choked and she pressed herself to the solid wooden doors. She could faintly hear the fighting outside. They would die. There were dozens if not hundreds of rainbow drakes out there, and Hawkcall and Eagleye couldn't get back in. She dug her claws into the wood, a cry building in her chest.

"Hawkwind."

It was Icefeather, the retired trainer. Hawkwind spun to face her, wanting to hit her and hug her at the same time.

"They made their choice," the trainer said, before she could speak. "You can't save the lost ones. You're needed, come."

The battle surged on, battering against the keep walls like ocean waves against cliffs. With a conventional army, one that moved only on the ground, the keep would have held them off for hours, maybe days, while the aerial griffins could have made strategic counterattacks.

"The drakes will be climbing the walls," Icefeather went on. "The wooden shutters won't keep them out for long."

The enemy wizards had called up a storm. It had kept the griffins from flying up to engage the drakes directly, but it wouldn't keep the agile, bat-winged drakes from climbing the walls of the keep, and slithering in through any window they could.

"We have our hands full," Icefeather was explaining as the dodged among the milling, panicking people. "Some drakes are already inside."

"Already?" Hawkwind exclaimed.

"We don't have enough Feathyrs for every window, and the guards fall quickly to their claws and maws."

By Feathyrs, she meant griffin warriors, and by guards, she meant the humans. Hawkwind was only an apprentice Feathyr; she hadn't even been assigned to a flight yet, but everyone who could fight, even a little, was doing so.

"We must protect the family," Icefeather ordered.

The family: the human family that ruled Northnest. The griffin flights owed them their allegiance, and had sworn it generations ago. Hawkwind had been raised to give every last drop of her lifeblood for them. She would not go back on her vows now: not when that blood was needed, when it was time to honor the allegiance. Even had there been no vow, she had grown up with the people—both human and griffin—here in Northnest. It was her home; she would fight to defend it.

Icefeather led her to the floor above the family's apartments. The drakes were already there. The pair screamed in challenge as they ran to reinforce the guards and Feathyrs already at work on the swarm. Vision narrowed to the nearest drake, with no intention but to shred it with claws and her vicious, hooked bill. She took injuries but hardly felt them. The drakes kept coming. One by one the defenders fell or fell back. Hawkwind fell back with them, being pushed to the stairs.

The remaining forces made a stand at the opening to the stairs, where they had a chance of forming a plug of swords and claws that could hold back the drakes. For a while, it seemed to work. Then, they were hit from behind. Hawkwind didn't know how drakes had gotten below them. Not prepared for an attack from the rear, half the defenders went down immediately, and the defense failed.

The greater swarm of drakes from above pushed Hawkwind and the survivors down the stairs. She stumbled over Icefeather's still body, but there was no time to mourn, and to Hawkwind's churning emotions, the trainer's death was merely another bucketful of pain thrown into the already overflowing whirlpool. The drakes around her were filling her vision with fangs and talons, and she had to flee, dodge, and escape them. The family—would she be in time to save any of them? Was there any hope of doing so, even if she reached them?

The drakes howled at her heels, pushing her into the royal apartments as they pulled down the last of her fellow griffin fighters. It seemed that there had been a defense here, too. The bodies of guards and some Feathyrs were scattered around the rooms, mingled with brightly colored drake bodies, all splattered with blood. Hawkwind knew there were secret passageways out, down, deep into the bowels of the castle, and out through long, dark tunnels. Had the family had a chance to take them?

No—there, the queen mother; she was gutted. Under her lay her husband, the retired king: mutilated, throat ripped into a bloody hole. Hawkwind ran on, fleeing the drakes. In the next room, the reigning queen and king with the crown princess were in a lifeless pile in one corner. A few drakes were still standing over them, tugging at their limbs but not eating them yet. Maybe they had orders not to.

Hawkwind dodged out another door before they could swarm her. Frantic, she slammed the door between her and them, but the lock was already broken and the frame damaged. She turned, reared up unto her hind legs, and leaned her body back against it, as she surveyed the innermost room: the nursery.

Three drakes hissed at her with their spiny crests rising on their heads and necks: a sunset red one, a lime green one, and a pink and purple one. The barbed chains encircling their necks like collars were glowing a magical red.

Hawkwind had known what the policy would be when the attack came. Here, the deepest room in the castle would be where all the children had been sent. Dead, ripped guards and several Feathyrs were heaped about, leaking blood into the thick periwinkle carpet. The children were huddled into a corner, but it seemed the drakes had been pulling children out of the pile, one by one, and—

Hawkwind sobbed in her throat. The poor little corpses were littered about atop their slain protectors. Her eyes sought the remaining children as the drakes from outside began pounding against the door, and she dug her feet in, trying to hold it closed. Although swift and vicious, rainbow drakes did not have high body mass or great muscular strength; she would hold the door against them for a while. There were no more than half a dozen children left, all between the ages of about five and seven, it seemed: all helpless, all with wide, glazed eyes that fixed upon her.

"Hawkwind," cried a little girl in a tremulous voice.

What could she do? She looked to the side, towards the bookshelf that hid the tunnel out. She looked back at the children. How could she hope to get the bookshelf moved and escape with the human fledglings, avoiding the drakes in the room and the ones outside, that would be inside as soon as she left the door? She needed help. She couldn't do this alone. The three drakes in the room were closing in on her.

Then she saw the oldest child, a boy, reach down and pick up a discarded, bloody crossbow. The drakes remained fixated on Hawkwind, and didn't notice the boy's actions. With eerily calm fingers he set a bolt taken from a dead guard. He aimed, and put the shot into the back of the lime green drake. It howled and all of them spun to face the boy, preparing to attack. Hawkwind took the chance and leapt for the bookshelf. With one vicious wrench she tossed it to the floor, scattering books over the bodies.

"Into the tunnel, go," she ordered the children.

Behind her, the other drakes burst through the door. One girl, perhaps six years old, took the hands of two other children, and dragged them, stumbling over the mixed wreckage and remains, towards the tunnel, while the boy with the crossbow fumbled another shot, and hit the red drake with a glancing blow. Hawkwind, with a desperate war cry, leapt, all talons open, into the cluster of drakes, as she saw the crossbow boy slain: a drake ripping his soft throat out in a spray of blood.

Hawkwind's vision went blind with red for a few moments. When she came back to herself, she found the bodies of a few drakes around her, unmoving, and a few others, backing away, injured and regrouping. She was panting, her heart beating as if trying to break out of her chest. The crossbow boy was dead: his eyes open and staring. It was then that Hawkwind recognized the child prince, gone to join his older sister, parents, grandparents, and probably most of his family now. Hawkwind had failed to protect him.

The other children, those that remained, were tumbling into the tunnel. Hawkwind swooped, snatching up the last little one, a blonde boy too terrified to move from the corner, and dove for the tunnel herself. Roughly, she spread her wings, pushing all the children inside, even though it made them fall and scrape themselves. She shoved in after them. The drakes were screaming again, rushing after. Hawkwind shoved and shoved, until the children were rolled out of the way, and did her best not to step on them as she turned about.

She'd been shown this tunnel, along with all the others. She knew how to operate the inside door, which would keep the enemy from following. Heaving with adrenaline-born strength, she swung the heavy iron door into place. Hands shaking, she gripped the wheel that would lock it, and spun it, sending thick bolts home into the stone doorway. Gasping, she tightened and strained until she could push the bolts no farther.

At last, she forced herself to let go of the wheel. She clicked the lever-locks into place, securing the bolts. There was no way to open the door from the other side. They'd have to get a battering ram of some kind, and even that would take hours to break the iron bolts or the stone walls, especially with no room in the nursery to get a good run going. She could only hope there wasn't a magician who could somehow open the door. Northnest had no magic; she didn't know what magic could or couldn't do.

Hawkwind tried to catch her breath, head dizzy. They had a few minutes at least; they had to get moving to get a head start on their enemies. The tunnel was blacker than night, and she could see nothing, not the door nor the wheel nor the children behind her. She wasn't even sure how many she had saved, or whose they were, or what their names were.

"Children," she began.

At her voice, the crying started. Ignoring it and bracing herself against the urge to join in, she searched for the flint and blade kept near the door, and the torch she could light to help them find their way out. She only hoped the external exit had not been discovered by the enemy.

The crying lessened slightly when she lit the torch, and she was able to make a count: four. There were two girls, one about six years old, one about five, she guessed. The two boys were perhaps both five years old, although one was considerably bigger than the other. Hawkwind shrugged to herself; it really didn't matter their ages, and she was a poor judge of the age of human children anyway. They were too young to be much use; she would have to take care of them. Their shining eyes, wide and showing the whites all around, stared up at her from red faces streaked with tears.

"Where's Mommy?" whispered one of the boys.

Hawkwind crouched down. "Come here and listen to me," she said, and the children inched nearer. "We're going to go down this tunnel."

"It's dark," the littlest girl objected.

"We'll use the torch, and you can ride me."

"I," whispered the oldest girl, "I can walk." She reached out to take a handful of Hawkwind's fur. Her whole arm was trembling.

The griffin knelt down onto the floor and swept her wings back out of the way. "Climb onto me, and hold onto my harness."

The three younger children obeyed. Hawkwind was still a youngster herself, and not at her full adult size, but the weight of three human children was bearable even with her injuries. Once they were up, she partly raised her wings to keep them from rolling off her sides. The older girl held gamely to a strap of the harness, and managed the torch in her other hand. Hawkwind tucked the flint and blade into a pouch on her harness, and they started walking.

On Hawkwind's back, the three children became oddly silent. The girl, too, walked with her dark eyes focused straight forward and glinting in the torchlight, not saying a word, but behind all of them loomed the greater darkness of what they'd just witnessed, and the she-griffin guessed they were all somehow resolutely not thinking about it yet.

Hawkwind walked as fast as the girl could keep up. It was tempting to just stay in the tunnel and hide, but the enemy would know now that there were tunnels. They would look for the exits and eventually break into the tunnels from both ends. Hawkwind knew they had to get as far away from the castle as possible, as quickly as possible.

After walking for several minutes, up and down some stairs, past some other tunnels that fed into this one, the exit door came into view and they stopped before it. Hawkwind examined the opening mechanism.

"Can you put the torch out?" she asked the girl.

"Alright," the girl whispered, "but then we can't see."

"We're going to go outside now. It will be dark, and rainy, but I will be able to see. I'll need you to get on my back with the others."

"Alright," she said again.

Hawkwind watched her rub the head of the torch against the damp, gritty floor until she managed to put out the flame. She dropped the torch with a rattling clunk. Hawkwind lowered a wing so the girl could climb up with the others, and winced a little under the extra weight. She tucked the extinguished torch through a strap on her harness.

Under the push of Hawkwind's muscles, the door opened with groans and the scrape of iron against rock. A rush of fresh, rain-washed air entered with the sounds of the storm. Unfortunately, the children were going to get wet. The joints of Hawkwind's shoulders didn't allow her to cross her wings up over her back, but she did her best to raise them enough to shield the children from the wind.

Dusk had arrived, and with the storm above, light was scarce under the trees in the dense undergrowth and up the steep hillsides. Hawkwind pushed out into the forest, moving up the hill, away from the castle and the gentler valley areas where clustered most of the kingdom's towns and villages. There were some caves to the west, but she headed due north. The drakes would have little trouble searching the caves. The forest would present a bigger challenge.

On her back the children remained silent, but she could feel them start to shiver and huddle closer to each other. Hawkwind kept walking. She would walk until her own body gave out. They needed distance, as much as she could get. It was hours later in deepest night, when her own legs began to cramp and tremble and her vision to fade that she started looking for a place to rest.

There: several trees formed a circle, probably around where another tree had once been—their progenitor. When that tree had died, its roots had sprouted up daughter trees, forming a ring. Hawkwind found a wide enough gap between two of the daughter trees and slipped inside. There, on a thick bed of damp leaves and evergreen needles, she let herself sink to the ground. The children slid off her immediately. She lifted her wings and hooked the children closer: pulling them in against her, two on each side. They huddled down readily, too numb and cold to speak, and she tucked her wings down around them, like any griffin, or any bird, sheltering its young.

There they rested, cried, and slept, to wait out the storm.

Chapter 2
Into the Wilderness

Hawkwind wasn't sure how long she'd slept, but it hadn't been deep or comforting. Under her wings, two children on one side were stirring. The other two were completely still. Concerned, she lifted that wing, but they were just sleeping, far more deeply than she herself had. She checked the other side. There, the two girls were snuggling closer to each other for warmth. The older girl looked up.

"Hawkwind?" she asked.

"Oh, you know my name," Hawkwind said, surprised.

"Mother made us learn the names of all the Feathyrs. She said it was important for the family."

The family? Hawkwind stared at the little girl. Her long brown hair was tangled and her face smudged with dirt, tears, and probably blood. She had a long lavender dress on. White lace and beading decorated it finely. It was ripped across one shoulder so it slipped a little down her back, exposing her shoulder blade. There, as clear and obvious as the coming dawn, was a tattoo done in golden ink of a stylized wing. There would be a matching one on her other shoulder blade.

"You're," Hawkwind breathed, trailing off as her chest tightened.

She'd rescued the child princess, the youngest member of the royal family, and so tattooed shortly after birth, as all members of the family were, with wings on her back to symbolize the alliance between the royals of Northnest and the griffin Feathyrs.

"Jessa," the girl murmured.

Jessika, the child princess: she was probably the only surviving member of her family. There had been three children: a teenage princess, a child prince, and a child princess. There was the ruling couple, and their parents, plus a few aunts and uncles and cousins. Hawkwind had seen most of them dead with her own eyes.

"What are we doing now, Hawkwind?" the girl asked.

The griffin tried to adjust the girl's dress to cover her back, ignoring her big, scared eyes. In response to her action, the girl reached up, found the two torn ends and tied them together above her shoulder, shifting how the dress sat on her, but keeping it from falling off.

"We're going up the mountain," Hawkwind said.

"Into the mountains?"

"Yes. Get up."

Hawkwind pushed to her feet, nearly staggering when the pain hit. On the ground, the other children stirred, objecting to the loss of their heat source.

"I'm hungry," said the littlest boy. The others concurred with varying levels of timidity and implied demand: provide food.

Hawkwind clenched her jaw. Human children didn't eat raw meat. She wondered if it would make them sick. It was spring; there would be no berries yet. Her training had never covered how to provide for humans without a camp and a fire—neither of which she had nor could risk making. She looked back in the direction of the castle and strained her ears. All was quiet, for the moment. She didn't pause to allow her imagination to provide images of what might be going on back in her home; she focused on her current situation. Did she dare search for food, leaving the children in the tree-ring, while still this close to the castle? Younglings of any species needed to eat frequently: she knew that. What could she find? What if she were seen? What if drakes found the children while she was away?

"No," she decided. "We have to travel now. I know you're hungry, but you have to wait."

Three of the children immediately voiced their objections.

"Hush now," the child princess commanded, surprising Hawkwind. "Hawkwind is in charge. We have to do as she says. We can't eat yet, but she will take care of us, and we'll eat soon."

The others quieted, pouting.

Hawkwind moved to the northern edge of the tree-ring and poked her head out. A scan of the underbrush revealed nothing obviously dangerous. Looking up, she could see the dim sky through the leaves. Dawn was coming, and the storm had abated. She could think of no better course of action than to get moving, to get as far away from the castle as possible, but to where?

She knelt. "Come get on."

The children tottered over and climbed onto her, holding onto her harness straps again. Her back and legs ached at the weight.

"You're hurt," Jessika, the princess, commented as Hawkwind began moving off into the forest.

"I'll be all right," the griffin assured her.

"See? Hawkwind is taking care of us, even though she's hurt," the girl told the other children. "We have to be good, too."

Hawkwind moved on, into the undergrowth, lifting her wings to shield the children from branches. She climbed steadily up the rising hillside.

"Will they follow us?" whispered the princess.

She, at least, understood something of what had happened to them, Hawkwind reflected.

"They might," the griffin answered truthfully. "I'm not sure if they know how many children were in the nursery with you, and if they'll notice if any are missing, if they do a count."

"But those things," she went on, her voice even quieter, "they saw us get away."

"Rainbow drakes," Hawkwind named them for her. "They can't speak. They won't be able to tell their masters what they saw."

"So they're not like you?"

"Correct. Drakes are nothing like griffins."

"Why did they come here?"

"I don't know, Princess."

"You can call me Jessa, or Jessika."

Hawkwind climbed over a large fallen tree trunk and dropped

down to the other side with a heavy thump. The princess suddenly grabbed at her wing and Hawkwind worried she'd almost knocked the child off, but that wasn't it.

"That looks like snow-celery," she proclaimed.

"What?"

"There. Let me down."

Hawkwind knelt with a stifled groan and lowered her wing so the girl could reach the ground. She ran over on spindly legs and fastened her skinny hands around a bright green, stalked plant.

"Are you certain, Princess?" Hawkwind cautioned. "What if it's poisonous?"

"It looks just the same," she grunted, tugging at the stalks now.

Hawkwind extended her talons and cut the clump away.

"It smells right." The girl took a crunchy bite. "It tastes right."

Another child jumped down, and the princess gave him a stalk.

"It's good," he said.

The other two got down also and within seconds all four were feasting on the juicy plant. Hawkwind furrowed her brows. She had no idea if it was the right plant or not. She ate almost exclusively meat. Sometimes she partook of prepared dishes that included vegetables, but she'd never paid much attention. She'd have to trust the princess.

"All right, eat while I walk," she prodded. "Get back on."

The children, gripping the stalks in their teeth and grubby fists, climbed back up onto her back. The sharp snow-celery scent and the sounds of crunching filled the air.

"I really hope it's the right plant, Princess," she muttered worriedly.

"It is. It's safe. I've seen it bunches of times."

"Where?"

"In the kitchens. They give me extra cookies there."

"I don't like snow-celery," commented another child, "but this is really good."

"That's because you're hungry and thirsty," Hawkwind said.

She was relieved that they'd found something, at least, to put in their stomachs, as long as it didn't make them sick. The sun rose, sending bright spears of light through the misty trees. The drakes could hunt at night or in the day; their sonar and excellent vision made them versatile fliers. The trees would help conceal the escapees, and the variety of textures and shapes might confuse the sonar—or so Hawkwind hoped—but if an intense search was underway, there was a good chance they'd be found.

She tried to quicken her steps, ignoring the pinch of hunger in her own belly, and the sparks and aches of injuries. Keeping part of her attention attuned to listening for danger, she tried to recall maps she'd seen of Northnest and the surrounding countries. She and the children were heading north. There were no countries that the people of Northnest knew of up there. To them, it was a wilderness of rough, untamable mountains that no one but the rare hunting party ventured into.

A memory, a faint voice teased Hawkwind, echoing from her chickhood.

"O'er the rocky breezes flew,
The wild, the flocks of Snow-in-lee,
Free on the wind, my heart will be,
Top o' the world, and home to me."

The princess paused in her snow-celery crunching. "What's that?"

Hawkwind twitched her feathers in embarrassment, realizing she'd sung it out loud.

"Great-grandmother Hawkmoon sang that to me, in the nest, when I was a chick," she explained.

"Your great-grandmother?"

"Yes."

"What does it mean?"

"I'm not sure. Princess, do you know what is north of Northnest?"

"North of Northnest?" she echoed. "Nothing."

"Nothing?" Hawkwind retorted, amused. "Then what are we in now? This is nothing?"

"This is still Northnest, isn't it?"

"I suppose it could be. So the land will soon vanish, when we reach the border?"

"Uh." The girl seemed caught without an answer. "I guess there will be something, but not people."

"Snow-in-lee," Hawkwind murmured.

"Snow-in-lee?"

"Perhaps my people are north of Northnest."

"Griffins?" the bolder boy chimed in. "There are more than just the Feathyrs at home?"

"There were, many generations ago," Hawkwind explained. "The Feathyrs came from them, originally."

"I know the story," the princess put in eagerly. "My great-great-great-great many times great-grandmother saved Featherfire's life, and they made a pact to help each other, and together they called for peace between the people and the griffins, who were all fighting, and in the end, some of the griffins joined Featherfire and chose to live with the people, in the castle, where they would be safe from more griffin wars, and wouldn't have to hunt, and would defend the people in return. Then the other griffins went away."

Hawkwind nodded. "Yes, that's just about right."

The version she'd been told was slightly different, but close enough. The point was that the other griffins, the defeated ones, had gone north, deeper into their remaining territory, and no one had seen any since.

"So what's Snow-in-lee?" the little boy asked.

"It's the griffin city, I think," Hawkwind said. At least, that was what she had always assumed Snow-in-lee was. She supposed it could be something else: a mountain, a forest, a waterfall, just a named rocky outcropping, or a fictional place entirely.

"Is that where we're going?" Jessika asked.

Hawkwind hesitated. She didn't know where they were going, but perhaps the children would feel better if they thought they had a destination.

"Yes," she told them.

"A trip?" the formerly silent littler girl said.

"An adventure," the bold boy corrected her.

Jessika patted Hawkwind on her head. "Teach us the song, the one about Snow-in-lee."

"All right," she agreed, "but you must sing it quietly, or you'll disturb the forest."

It might make it easier for the drakes to find them, if four children were caroling at the tops of their voices. The lungs of young human children were remarkably effective, Hawkwind had observed.

"We will, Hawkwind," Jessika agreed for all of them.

As softly as she could, she began to sing.

"O'er the rocky breezes flew,

The wild, the flocks of Snow-in-lee,

Free on the wind, my heart will be,

Top o' the world, and home to me."

The children quickly picked it up, and Hawkwind walked on into the day, up and up the mountainside, surrounded by the young voices repeating back to her the old song.

They stopped for sleep that night in a gap under a fallen tree. It was at the bottom of a narrow ravine, overhung with branches, through which a trickle of water ran over mossy stones. At one spot, the water collected in a tiny pool among some rocks. Hawkwind directed the children to drink from the pool, and wash their hands and faces downstream of it, where the water cascaded in the most miniature of waterfalls. The children were fussy with hunger, and Hawkwind's empty tummy, too, was no pleasant thing.

They were now nearly two days walk from Northnest. Hawkwind

had seen no sign of pursuers. The camp under the tree, in the ravine, had been a lucky find. She felt safer there than she had in the past three days. Some things needed to be done.

"Princess," she whispered, drawing the girl aside. "Can you make a small, smokeless fire?"

The girl's face pinched with regret. "With what, twigs and branches? I could do it with flint and steel."

Hawkwind pulled the small flint and short, sheathed dagger that she'd taken from the tunnel from the little pack all Feathyrs wore. The girl's face lit up.

"You have them," she exclaimed.

"Only you use them," Hawkwind emphasized. "You're the oldest and should be the best at handling them. I don't want anyone getting carelessly cut. We're all already injured enough."

"I'll be careful, Hawkwind," the princess promised.

"Can I make you the official fire maker?"

"Yes, Hawkwind," she agreed eagerly.

"You must burn only dry wood, with no moss on it, to help the fire stay smokeless. Understand?"

"Yes, Hawkwind," the girl repeated.

"I'll collect some for you. Stay here and make a ring of stones on bare dirt."

The griffin climbed up the ravine walls, trying not to disturb any vegetation or leave any other signs of her passing. Finding dry wood was no easy thing, after the rain of the previous night. Dusk was well underway when Hawkwind returned, burdened with dead branches. The children were shivering and the two youngest were crying weakly.

"See," the princess soothed, "Hawkwind came back, and she brought us wood for a fire, so we'll be warm."

"A small fire," the griffin reiterated. "Keep it under close control."

"Yes, Hawkwind."

"I will be back."

"Where are you going?"

"To hunt," she explained. "I will bring back meat, and you will cook it, to eat."

"Food," caroled the other children.

"Hush," scolded both the princess and Hawkwind.

"I might not return for a few hours. Sleep, be still, keep the fire small and hidden, and wait here for me."

Hawkwind went up the ravine again. She hoped to find a buck deer, eat most of it for herself, and bring back some of the higher quality muscle meat, like a haunch, for the children. She followed the ravine north, away from the castle, and hopefully towards a place where deer were able to make a trail to the water, to drink.

In the end, she didn't find a deer, but did discover a small group of young boar, probably a bachelor group. Boars were dangerous, but she managed to frighten them with her size and aggression so that they tried to flee instead of gore her with their tusks in self-defense. A pounce upon the slowest of the group, crushing it to the ground with her body weight, and a swift severing of the spine with her bill earned her a kill without any injury to herself.

The small boar wasn't as hearty a meal as a deer would have been, but knowing she had starving human younglings to feed, she ate mainly the viscera, removed the head which might upset the children, and brought the rest back to the camp in the ravine. She landed amid drowsy but eager welcomes, and brought the boar to the tidy little campfire the princess had made.

"What an excellent fire," she praised, gaining her a tired smile.

"I put this flat rock by the fire," the girl explained. "I washed it off in the river. We can cook meat on it?"

"That sounds like a great idea," Hawkwind said.

Between her talons and the princess wielding the little dagger, they cut strips and shreds of meat and passed them to the biggest boy, who used sticks to arrange them on the rock and monitor their status. The two littlest children huddled nearby, drooling and stuffing in each bit of cooked meat as fast as the biggest boy could hand them over.

When the littlest ones had bulging tummies and thoroughly grease-smeared faces and hands, and were falling over with weariness, the princess and the oldest boy paused to tuck them into beds made of piled leaves and grasses at the back of the under-tree camp. Then, the two older children devoured most of the rest of the boar, sating the rumbly hunger demons in their bellies, too.

Hawkwind nudged the two of them into their own grassy beds—which they must have constructed while she was out hunting—where they fell asleep immediately. The griffin was still hungry, but knew she could tolerate it better than the little ones, so she found some wide, thick leaves growing over the river, wrapped the remains of the boar in them, and tucked them under the glowing coals of the campfire, hoping the meat would cook by morning.

She noted that the children had arranged the beds in pairs, with the smallest children deeper under the fallen tree nook, and a gap between the pairs just right for her to lie down as she had before, putting two children under one wing, and two under the other. She did so, meaning to stay awake and on guard, but her weariness gripped her too firmly, and she sank into heavy slumber.

Chapter 3
Pursuit

The children woke before she did.

"Wasn't there some meat left?"

"I can smell it a little."

"Maybe it's just the smell from last night?"

"Under the coals," Hawkwind slurred. "Dig it up. Don't burn yourself."

She managed to pry her eyes open to the sounds of focused and efficient excavation, followed by subdued cheers and the crackle of charred leaves.

"It's good. It's cooked."

All four were gathered around the remains, pulling bits of meat off bones and swallowing them down as though they hadn't stuffed themselves like horses at a grain-spill last night. Hawkwind tried to rise, and groaned at the pain. The second day after an injury was always the worst. Her muscles were stiff and cramping.

"Here. We're full."

The princess was offering her a morsel of meat. It wasn't much, as far as griffin appetites go, but Hawkwind wasn't about to decline the kindness. Delicately, she took the scrap from the princess' fragile fingers, and gulped it down.

The princess had a firm gaze. "Do we have to keep going? Today, I mean. Are we going to travel more?"

"Can't we stay?" whispered the littlest girl.

Hawkwind took a moment.

"What's your name?" she asked finally.

The girl pressed both palms to her chest in questioning confirmation.

"Yes, you," Hawkwind nodded gently.

"Kassandra," the girl said.

"And you?" she looked at the older boy.

"Rikah," he answered, "son of Rikan, finest smithy in Northnest."

"I have met your father," Hawkwind told him. "A fine man, strong and honest. And your name?"

The smaller boy looked up from under long, blonde lashes. "Karo," he murmured.

"Karolan," the princess clarified.

"I'm Hawkwind, as you know. I'm a Feathyr of your kingdom. It is my duty to keep you safe."

"We," stuttered Kassandra, staring down at the ground, "can't go home."

"Not right now," Hawkwind said to the teary faces. "Perhaps someday."

They all brightened at that.

"But first you will have to grow up strong and smart and brave, and you can't do that in this ravine. In winter, it will flood."

"And what would we do for clothes?" asked the princess.

"And food," Kassandra agreed.

"We'll need weapons to take back the castle," Rikah said.

"We must keep moving," Hawkwind nodded. "Searchers, enemies, will come. They will find us before we're ready to fight them. I must take you some place safe."

"Snow-in-lee?" the princess guessed.

"Perhaps."

"Are you hurt? Can you even walk?" she asked the griffin.

"I will be fine. Now, wash your hands and faces, and anything else you can but don't get your clothes wet or you'll be cold. Then have a long drink, as much as you can hold."

The children obeyed, even helping each other to wash off grease and dirt from hard to reach places. Hawkwind had decided to follow the ravine. It was going north anyway, and staying near it would provide water. When the children declared themselves ready, they climbed the ravine walls—the fallen tree blocking their passage along the ra-vine floor. The princess Jessika and Rikah the smith's son climbed up by themselves. Hawkwind carried the other two. At the top, she found the adventurous ones searching for both more snow-celery and walk-ing sticks.

Hawkwind began striding on her way, and the two followed, bringing snow-celery and early berries to the other children as they went. She let them wander a little, sometimes ahead of her, sometimes behind, always in sight, always coming back to her after a few min-utes. She kept the river on her right wing, and in that way they walked through the day, taking occasional breaks, but making steady progress up the wooded slope, without any signs of pursuit.

Their evening camp was not as good as the previous. It was a dry sand bank, surrounded by trees and vegetation. It would shield them from view, but not from anything determined to attack them. She'd started watching for a good site starting mid-afternoon. With nightfall imminent, she'd selected the best option available. The children made sleeping nests and a fire while she went hunting. Luck brought her a deer this time, and she ate nearly her fill. It would keep her full now for a cou-ple days. The children, too, had plenty for both dinner and breakfast.

In the morning, Hawkwind began to grudgingly believe that they had avoided pursuit. It seemed the threat that had taken Northnest was behind them. Somehow, they had evaded its net of danger. She led them on that day with a more confident stride, but it didn't last.

"Hawkwind," whispered little Kassandra, tugging at her fur from where she was astride the griffin.

"Kassandra?"

"I think something's out there."

Hawkwind sharpened her eyes and swung her head around, scan-ning the underbrush. "Rikah, Princess," she called, just barely loud enough to reach them.

The two children trotted back obediently, and Hawkwind led them all into the shelter of some large shrubs. Once they were all crouching among the bracken, Hawkwind addressed Kassandra again.

"What did you see?"

"Nothing," the girl said, "I just think there's something there."

Rikah scoffed under his breath, but Hawkwind persisted.

"Why do you think there's something there?"

Before the girl could answer, a painfully sharp, high-pitched squeaking assaulted the griffin's ears, although the children gave no sign they'd heard it.

"Drake sonar," Hawkwind hissed. "Get down. Lie flat. Burrow into the dead leaves."

The children obeyed, scuffling down until they were completely covered. To drake sonar and eye both they would hopefully look only like lumps in the forest floor, and drakes had a sense of smell poorer than even griffins. Hawkwind, however, could not hide so easily.

"Stay here," she ordered. "If a drake comes, if it attacks, you must run all in different directions, as fast as you can. Otherwise, do not move from here until I return."

"What if you don't come back?" the princess asked.

There was little time for discussion, but Hawkwind thought rapidly. Four human children alone would likely not survive the trek into the territories of the wild griffins—if they existed—and would not be welcomed, Hawkwind assumed, even if they did.

"Go due east, the direction where the sun rises, and look for a village in Northnest, and people who will hide you," she instructed. "But I'll be back."

Hawkwind hadn't flown since the battle at the castle, but she partly extended her wings now to make long, light leaps through the forest, which was quieter than running. If a drake found her, she would fight, but she hoped she could find someplace suitable to hide herself before that happened. Several leaps ahead, her keen eyes picked out a fallen tree with a gap below it; that might do.

She never made it—a roar of excitement turned her eyes up, to where a pair of rainbow drakes was streaking down through the canopy. Hawkwind aborted her run, skidding about on the forest floor, shredding ferns and kicking up detritus, as the nearer drake slammed its body full into hers. It darted its long body around her, trying to wrap her in its snake-like coils, and snapped at her neck. Hawkwind scrunched herself down and back, ducking her head, dodging the attack and the wrapping coils, but this drake was too quick. It sunk claws into her wherever it could, latching on gamely.

Then, Hawkwind heard screams of terror from the throats of the children. The second drake: somehow it had found them. She struggled, trying to break out of the drake's hold, adrenaline shooting through her as she kicked and kicked with her back legs like a cat toppled by a larger adversary. Her talons ripped into the drake, making it howl with rage, and she thrashed, sinking in her own hand talons and trying to get a shot at its neck with her wickedly hooked bill. She had to kill it fast and go after the one chasing the children.

The drake writhed and bit into her shoulder as she frantically leaned out of the way of another lunge for her throat. It hurt, but the drake had made itself vulnerable with the move. Now, Hawkwind could seize its neck in her bill, and she did, holding on hard, only needed better footing for the leverage to snap its spine. She had to let go with her talons to get that. The drake didn't realize what she was doing, perhaps because it hadn't felt fangs in its neck, only the pressure of her bill mandibles, and hissed with glee when she nearly released it, but then she re-gripped, rolling the drake under her body, twisting it around with all her strength.

Then, the fight was over. One vicious yank and turn, accompanied by a sickening, wet crackle, and the drake went limp. It might have still been alive, but it wouldn't be running or flying ever again. Hawkwind left it, leaping with all her speed towards where she'd left the children. The commotion in the brush led her easily on, and she tumbled through the trees into a small, ferny clearing where the rainbow drake was wrestling with—

Hawkwind pulled up short, bill agape as she tried to accept what she saw. There was a deer-sized beast fighting the drake. It had one broken drake wing trapped under its hind, hoofed feet. The drake snarled and spat, half-pinned to the ground, lashing at its enemy with its long, sharp-scaled tail, and slashing with claws and jaws whenever the leggy beast thudded back down from its rearing position, trying to crush the drake.

The beast's hide was blue, edged with rust, blotched and speckled along its back and neck with mist grey and moon glow white. Feathery plumes of hair trailed from its hocks and chin. Its mane and tail grew steely, bleaching to silver at the tips. Its tail was long, bare for the first meter from its haunches, but waving long locks from there to beyond the tip. A single, loosely spiraled horn the color of smoke crowned its forehead.

A unicorn: Hawkwind had seen illustrations, but those had made the beast look much like a horse with a horn tacked on. Although four legged and overall equine in build, Hawkwind would never have mistaken this creature for a horse with a horn. Its legs were longer, compared to its body, than a horse's, its head rounder, ears more like a deer's, with hooves cloven like a goat's, but the biggest differences were how it moved and how it behaved.

It was calculating how to destroy the drake. It was moving with more grace, agility, and flexibility than any horse had ever known. It was fighting, having been given no command by a human rider, to defend the child shaking and crying under the ferns behind it.

The unicorn struck the drake's head a cracking blow with a fore hoof, and then reared up high, tucking its chin to its throat, and plunging down to drive its horn through the drake's chest. The rainbow drake shuddered and died. The unicorn stepped off the broken wing, lifted the beast, still impaled upon its horn, and dragged it into the bushes

at the side of the little clearing. As it backed away from the corpse, Hawkwind saw that the drake's barbed tail tip was imbedded in the unicorn's haunch. The barb ripped away, sending a cascade of glistening blood down the unicorn's leg. The area around the wound was starting to turn black. Hawkwind wondered why. None of the unicorn's other wounds, or Hawkwind's own, were blackening.

The unicorn staggered back into the clearing and collapsed onto the gouged dirt and ferns. Hawkwind detected movement beside her and started to spin about, but it was only the princess and Rikah, leading Karo. So the child across the clearing was Kassandra. Hawkwind looked over, and saw the unicorn extending its head and neck towards the little girl.

Kassandra uncurled from her ball and crawled slowly to the unicorn. Hawkwind's breath caught, but her body felt paralyzed, perhaps with shock. Kassandra sat on her knees, nose to nose with the unicorn: its heavy breaths ruffling her filthy black hair. Then, she reached forward with both hands and put them on its face, between nose and horn. Then, she leaned forward, and rested her cheek there, too.

For a moment, all was still. Then, the unicorn took a long, deep breath, as if filling enormous lungs. Kassandra's eyes closed as if with sleep. So closed, too, did the black, weeping wound in the unicorn's haunch.

The little girl was trembling when she sat back up. The unicorn extended its neck, giving her a velvety soft nose-kiss. Then, it arched its neck up, tucking its chin like it had before, and gave a smart, rapid jab of the tip of its horn to the center of Kassandra's forehead. The little girl toppled over with a surprised cry. Hawkwind's strange stillness vanished with a surge of rage and she leapt towards the unicorn, which just as quickly swung its head towards her.

"Peace, Sky-cousin," a rich but hard voice trumpeted inside her skull.

Hawkwind skidded to a halt in the ripped up loam. Kassandra was rolling onto her side. There was no blood: just a small pink mark, shaped rather like a tiny, five petalled flower, on her forehead. Wearily, she smiled at Hawkwind. Then, she snuggled into the tattered ferns and went to sleep.

The unicorn heaved to his feet, blood, dirt, and bits of foliage still clinging to his coat.

"What happened?" Hawkwind asked aloud, not knowing how the unicorn had spoken without using its voice.

It's dark, liquid eyes gazed at her. "We knew there was a lone griffin, with four innocents, in our forest," it rumbled in her head. "I came to watch."

"We?" she asked.

"My clan."

"Why did you fight the drake? What did you do to the girl?"

Dark eyes closed and the beast said nothing.

No sound of rustling brush announced them. Just suddenly, there were two more unicorns behind the battered male. One was fiery red with black points, and the other purest gold dusted with white and umber. None of the beasts gave any indication of speaking with each other, except that the blue male tilted his head a bit towards Kassandra, and the two newcomers glanced at her and spent a few moments looking over the other children, and Hawkwind, too, from a distance. Without another word, the group turned to go.

"Wait," Hawkwind called.

"Please, wait," the princess added.

The unicorns paused, looked over their shoulders, and waited. Princess Jessika walked towards them.

"Thank you for saving Kassandra," she said. "I'm really glad you were here."

The blue male only responded with a slight angling of one ear.

"Um, we're trying to," she stuttered, "is there a?" She trailed off, looking back to Hawkwind for help.

"Might there still be a city of griffins in the mountains, here, in the north?" Hawkwind asked gently. "I need shelter for these children. Our home was destroyed."

"Northnest Feathyr, you seek Snow-in-lee," said the red unicorn without moving its mouth.

The princess nodded, so Hawkwind knew then that the unicorns spoke into everyone's head.

"Be wary," added the gold unicorn.

"Travel seven days at the pace you've gone," resumed the red unicorn. "Follow this river. Go to the right when it splits. They will find you, if you are sure that is what you think you desire."

The unicorns glanced once more at sleeping Kassandra, in eerie unison, and then resumed their retreat, and no words from any of the children, or the griffin, could bring them back.

Hawkwind carried Kassandra, and the child woke at dusk, quiet and dreamy but seeming none the worse for wear. From that day, the small group settled into a pattern. They walked during the day, with the children collecting whatever edible plants they found—Hawkwind forbid them mushrooms since she knew they could be poisonous. They located sleeping spots by dusk. The children set up the camp while Hawkwind hunted, and they cooked and ate whatever she caught for dinner and breakfast. Gradually, even Kassandra and Karo began helping out with the camp making and cooking. Jessika did indeed become an expert fire-maker. Rikah embraced his role as head cook.

Hawkwind's injuries healed. They managed to subsist on the food they found and hunted, and kept up their strength. They encountered no more drakes. The weather got colder the higher up they went, and the children relied more and more on Hawkwind's natural body warmth, having no extra clothing, but summer was gaining strength, most of the snow had melted, and no one froze.

In this way, they passed out of their birth land of Northnest and into the territories still held by the wild griffin clans of the far north.

Chapter 4
A Warm Welcome

A week passed. The children grew leaner, dirtier, and stronger. Their pale castle-skin tanned to match the mud that got smeared on it from time to time. There was no more singing. They labored along the paths, which grew rougher and rockier, up, always up, into the mountains. One afternoon, Hawkwind paused along the trail.

"Break time, Hawkwind?" asked the princess, her voice listless.

"Yes," the griffin confirmed. "Down for a minute, please."

Karo and Kassandra had been dozing on her back. Rikah and Jessika woke them and helped them down, found them marginally comfy spots to lie down and they kept sleeping. Hawkwind, too, lay down on the path, tucking her head under a wing. Her eyes were gritty and sore, her head light. Her limbs trembled and ached. It wasn't from the altitude; she'd flown far higher than this.

The children weren't sleeping well at night, waking up from nightmares a few times a night each. She'd wake up, too, and snuggle them until they fell back into sobbing sleep. Little Kassandra was actually doing the best, remaining quietly sorrowful most of the time, instead of screaming from night terrors. Jessika struggled to keep her jaw clamped on her cries, but her limbs and tear ducts wouldn't obey as easily. Often Karo could not be comforted, and just cried until he became exhausted.

Hawkwind herself was suffering from the endless ache of losing her home and everyone she'd ever known. She was wearier than she'd ever been in her life: mind, body, and heart. One of the children was petting her back. It felt good.

What could have only been a moment later, little hands were shaking her shoulders, but when she opened her eyes, she saw immediately that the sun had moved a considerable amount, making the shadows stretch across the path. How long had she slept? The children were calling her name.

"I don't think they're Feathyrs," the princess was saying. "Stay here."

Then, shadows began passing over the ground. Hawkwind looked up. Five griffins were circling them.

"Children, come here," she ordered, lifting her wings so they could sit down underneath them.

The griffins, dark against the bright sky, continued to circle, making a few more passes, until one changed its path, dropping down onto the trail a few yards ahead. Two more landed behind it. The other two landed on the trail behind Hawkwind. All were fully-grown: half again bigger than she was. Their colors varied from white to grey to brown to black, with patterns that included wing bars, banding, streaking, and spotting.

The one on the trail directly ahead, the leader, so Hawkwind assumed, was counter shaded black and white with bright amber eyes. It took its time examining her, with more of a confused air than an alarmed one. Hawkwind stood, keeping the children safely tucked against her sides and her feathers slicked down submissively.

"State your Aerie," the black griffin demanded finally. "This is South-scree land, and I don't recognize you."

"I don't have one," she answered. "We're—"

"Rogue," hissed a tan and brown griffin behind the leader.

It started to step forward, but the leader flipped out a wing, blocking it.

"Those are humans, aren't they?" the leader snapped.

"I thought humans were bigger," commented the other griffin, a speckled white one, behind the leader.

"My name is Hawkwind," she proclaimed, over the muttering of the others.

"Hawkwind?" repeated the leader. "The Hawk Line is dead."

"We're from Northnest," she went on.

"Northnest is a legend," it spat.

"We need help."

"Help?"

The tan and brown one hissed again, "a rogue asking for help? Trying to get back in when you've been kicked out?"

"Are you from Snow-in-lee?" Hawkwind tried.

The tan one scoffed on a laugh. Over her head, the black and white leader gave a sharp nod to another griffin behind her. She heard the vigorous flapping of wings, suggesting one of them had taken off.

"You seek Snow-in-lee, rogue?" the tan griffin sneered. "You wish to speak with the dead, or perhaps become one of them yourself?"

"I'm just," Hawkwind panted, "we escaped an attack and we need shelter. I will do anything to earn warmth and food for these children."

"You mean they aren't your food?" the white griffin chuckled.

"What do humans taste like?" the tan one asked the white one. "The fairy tales never mentioned that."

The pair began laughing over theories of how humans tasted, but the leader was silent now, watching Hawkwind with narrowed eyes.

"Why is a griffin caring so much about human chicks?" the leader asked slowly.

"I am sworn to protect them," Hawkwind said. "It's my duty, my purpose."

For a few moments the four griffins eyed Hawkwind and she tried to keep her expression genuine and submissive, hiding her fear. The children held tight to her legs and said nothing while the white and tan griffins joked about eating them. Finally, the leader hissed at the pair to be quiet.

Then, there was a raptorial cry and six more griffins landed on the trail. Hawkwind presumed one of them was the one the leader had sent away—to bring reinforcements. One big griffin shouldered its way to the front, facing Hawkwind, standing beside the black and white one, who backed up slightly as if with deference.

"What are these?" asked the big newcomer.

Size alone suggested that this new commander was a female, as adult female griffins were almost always larger than males. She was grey with black wing bars, banding, and eye stripe, except for a white underside, streaked with black, and a white crown, tipped with black. Her eyes were goshawk red, and her bill heavy and steely. Hawkwind also saw that three black stripes had been dyed into the grey fur of her forearms. A check showed that the leader of the first group had two white stripes bleached into its black fur.

"Well?" Three-stripes growled.

"An intruder," provided Two-stripes, "and four small humans, it seems."

"My name is Hawkwind, and we're from Northnest," she repeated. "The castle was attacked, but I managed to escape with four children. The kingdom is overrun with enemies so I have nowhere else to go."

"The Hawks are a dead Line," Three-stripes interrupted. "Ancient, but dead, long ago. Northnest is a chick's nesttime story. You're lying."

"Northnest is eight day's walk from here, straight south," Hawkwind argued. "Surely your widest patrols have seen it."

"You see before you our widest patrols. This is the border of our lands," Three-stripe said. "Being a lying rogue, you know this."

"What?" she objected.

"Why do you have humans with you?"

"I'm taking care of them," she said again.

"Rogues are not allowed to return from exile. You have crossed the border. You will be detained and your fate decided," Three-stripes proclaimed.

"Understood," said Two-stripe from behind, although the black and white griffin looked dubious. "And the small humans?"

"They are mine," Hawkwind declared, tightening her wings around them and trying not to tremble. This wasn't going the way she had expected.

"Humans are little threat," Three-stripe ruminated, "in small numbers."

"They seem to be fledglings," spoke up a griffin from the back, poking its head forward between some others.

"Irrelevant. I suspect an advance scouting party, rogues and humans preparing an invasion of our territory. Detain the humans for questioning."

The circle of griffins was closing in. Hawkwind couldn't fly with all four children, and even if she could have, ten bigger and unburdened adult griffins would have had little trouble catching her. Hawkwind's fur and feathers started standing up, an unconscious reaction to threat, trying to make herself look bigger.

"Hawkwind?" The children were pushing close against her, wrapping skinny arms tighter around her neck and limbs. At least a couple took hold of her battered harness.

"Restraints," muttered Three-stripe to a subordinate.

"Please let me speak and try to understand," Hawkwind tried. "We mean no threat to you. We come for help, help I will pay for with servitude."

"Wrap this up," Three-stripe sighed, waving a hand.

Several griffins jumped on Hawkwind, pinning her down and wrestling for her hands and feet. The children screamed. Karo immediately burst into panicked tears and tried to burrow between Hawkwind's belly and the ground. Rikah had a stick, and stood under Hawkwind's shoulder, poking any other griffin that came within reach.

"Hawkwind?" the princess demanded. "What do we do?"

"Run," she ordered.

Hawkwind hadn't been sure whether she should use her talons and bill, but to distract the attackers and give the children a chance, she snapped out with her head and bit hard into the nearest piece of enemy. From the corner of her eye she saw the princess trying to sneak between griffin legs, holding Kassandra by the hand.

Hawkwind growled through her mouthful of enemy. "Rikah, get Karo."

She twisted and writhed, keeping her hands and feet away from the other griffins, but finally, one snagged a hind leg, jerking it out from under her. To the side, the two girls screamed, and Hawkwind saw them pinned to the ground by the sharp talons of two griffins.

She let go with her bill to shout. "Don't hurt them."

Rikah and Karo went running the opposite direction, trying to dodge swiping hands. Hawkwind struggled towards the two girls, but someone grabbed her other hind leg. She kicked hard, breaking the grip and feeling flesh tear under her claws, but was grabbed again. They pulled her hind feet together, lashing them tight.

Desperate, she thrashed. Three-stripe stepped in front of her as two griffins leapt onto her back, crushing her to the ground. Two more griffins seized her hands. Three-stripe stamped on her head, grinding her bill and throat into the dirt.

"Valiant," she heard the leader say, "but pointless."

After that, she was thoroughly bound: talons, claws, and wings. They made her into a neat bundle, capping it with a leather hood that blocked her vision, hindered her hearing, and made her bill useless both for speaking and fighting. Only a small gap was left, over her cere, to allow her to breathe. She could hear struggling and children crying and arguing, so she hoped that meant they were all alive, although she wished they had been able to escape.

She was picked up, flown through the air, and there was nothing she could do about it. Hawkwind closed her eyes and conserved her strength: waiting for what would happen next.

After a time, the group of griffins landed, and she was set on the ground. Through the hood, she detected the babble of many voices. She was lifted, put on something that moved, maybe a cart, and then dumped back on the ground after a few minutes of travel. She heard the sound of metal clanking, and felt new, tight bands fastened around her wrists and ankles. Another band was fastened around her neck, and another around her whole body, cinching down her wings.

As if that wasn't enough, while she was still firmly bound, unable to do any more than perhaps rock her body with futile wiggling, someone pressed down on her, squishing her against the floor, taking even that slight movement possibility away. She heard the ring of metal shears opening, and wild, panicked realization hit her. Desperately, she tried to thrash, to get away, to dislodge the weight on her, to fight, and escape.

The griffin holding her down was big and strong. Despite her struggles, she hardly budged, but she cried out in denial, voice strangled in her throat because she couldn't open her bill, as the metal shears chopped, and chopped again, and again, and again. Hawkwind felt the reverberations up her body, a frantic message from her nerves, alerting her brain that her feathers were being cut, that she would be unable to fly, that she had to get away, to stop it—right now. The sensation only heightened her cries, and she trembled, sobbing with loss.

Finally, the shearing stopped and the weight of the other griffin left her body. Then, rapidly, the leather thongs holding her legs, arms, and wings were cut, just as someone slipped the hood off her head. As she got her vision, she saw two griffins rapidly backing away, holding the thongs and hood. All around her, her cut flight feathers were scattered, glinting chocolate, caramel, and cream on the slate floor. The cut edges of her wings scraped against her back and sides: rough and raw.

Hawkwind curled up, feeling as helpless and vulnerable as a freshly hatched chick. The metal cuffs and chains on her wrists and ankles ground against the floor. Her limbs each had a chain running to a central point under her body. From there, a thicker chain ran through a ring imbedded in the floor, together restricting how far and how easily she could walk. A belt of fine chain links held her wings tight to her body: not that she would have been able to fly with them, had they not been cinched, but a strike with the wrist joint of a griffin's wing could be a powerful blow, propelled by massively strong flight muscles: the strongest muscles in her body except for her heart. She wasn't muzzled; her bill was now her only unrestricted weapon.

Half hiding her head, she looked around at her surroundings and captors. Two griffins were watching her from a few paces away, and behind them, some others milled. Between her and the watchers, a wall of bars loomed. She was in a dungeon or prison of some kind. She saw only one other captive, chained several yards away, wing cut like her and curled in a ball, head hidden, with no one paying any attention to it.

That seemed like a good policy. She was trembling still, and now moved to hide her head, as if that would let her escape, pretend she hadn't just been—the children!

Hawkwind surged to her feet with such force that the watching griffins all flinched. She started to charge them, remembering only at the last minute that her legs were chained. Narrowly, she avoided falling on her face, instead, planting her feet and lifting her neck feathers: a clear threat-gesture.

"Where are my children?" she demanded.

Her captors looked at her like she was a haunch short of a herd beast.

"There were four human children with me," she stated. "I am their protector. They are no danger to you. You must not harm them. They must be kept warm and fed."

The lack of comprehension on the faces of the jailers made her grind her bill.

"I forbid you to hurt them," she shouted.

"Still screaming?" came a wearied, dry voice from the back of the crowd.

The crowd parted, and Three-stripe stepped through the gap, along with another griffin, who was a dull tan and white, with some faint barring and dark edging to its wings. Hawkwind felt an angry hiss growing in her throat.

"Where are they?" Hawkwind demanded. "If you've hurt them, I'll rip your feathers out."

Three-stripe hacked a short laugh. "A juvenile threat," she rumbled. "How old are you, little one? Fifteen winters yet?"

The defiant hiss wavered and died in her throat, and she swallowed rapidly a lump of fear and despair. She was fourteen winters; she could just barely be considered an adult.

"What Aerie have you been kicked out of, and what was your crime?" Three-stripe went on.

"I have no Aerie," Hawkwind rasped. "I was born and raised in Northnest, like my children, but you don't believe me."

A twitch at the corner of Three-stripe's eye betrayed her impatience.

"I couldn't lie even if I wanted to," Hawkwind babbled. "The only griffin place I've ever heard of is Snow-in-lee."

The dull tan griffin's feathers gave a little flick.

"What am I supposed to say?" she pled.

Three-stripe didn't seem to have a reply to that.

"She does seem rather young to have been expelled from an Aerie," the tan griffin murmured. From the voice, Hawkwind guessed it was a male. He was fairly small, too, which reinforced the guess.

Three-stripe's eye twitched again. "There are those here with skills to get the truth from you."

"Come now, Rocksky," the tan griffin frowned. "You'd send a new fledge to the crying room?"

Three-stripe, proper name of Rocksky, hissed, but made no other response. Hawkwind tried not to bristle. She was not a new fledge; she'd fledged almost a decade ago.

"Even our good detention hall manager would have a pause before following that command. It is contrary to the spirit of the Words."

"Understood," Rocksky spat finally. "What do you suggest, Elder Thornfire?"

The tan griffin looked down on Hawkwind, where she stood panting, arms and legs quivering.

"I think, some food and water," he said. "She looks as though she could use it."

Hawkwind almost wept with relief. "My children," she said, swallowing down a whimper.

"What is this she is going on about?" the elder asked of one of the other griffins standing at attention.

"There were four small humans brought in with her," the griffin answered, before Rocksky could, prompting her to hiss again and turn away.

"I leave this in your hands, Elder," Rocksky said as she departed. To Hawkwind, it sounded almost like a threat.

"I assume," the questioned griffin went on uneasily, "she means them."

"And where are they now?" the elder asked.

Another griffin, a grey one, answered this time. "Not knowing exactly what to do with them, they were placed in a confinement stall in the kennels."

"These humans, they are dangerous?"

The grey griffin shrugged its wings. "They don't appear unduly so, Elder. Some of the commander's flight reported what appeared to be resistance, including strikes from their hands and feet. One of them had a stick, used as a club. They didn't appear to have the strength to do a griffin any serious harm. None of the flight was hurt by them."

The elder nodded. "Kindly bring the four humans here, without hurting them, or letting them hurt you."

The griffin hesitated. "This is on your authority, Elder?"

He frowned. "I suppose it will have to be. You may inform Eldest Skycall. Go now."

Chapter 5
Interrogation

The grey griffin and two others departed, and the tan elder griffin turned back to Hawkwind. She looked up at him, hardly daring to hope. He seemed to be examining her, noting the tattered harness she wore, her injuries, and probably her age and fitness.

"Commander Rocksky is passionate in her duties," the elder remarked, "but not very flexible. She often cannot see the need or possibility of exceptions to her orders."

He stepped closer and took a seat just beyond the bars. Hawkwind's back legs trembled with fatigue, but she forced herself to stay on her feet.

"You're helping me?" she asked.

"It seems you're going to cause me some trouble. Yes."

"Why?"

"Why am I helping you or why will doing so cause me trouble?"

"Both?"

He stared at her again for a long moment. Hawkwind noted the wrinkles in the skin around his eyes, and the stiff dryness of his cere. He wasn't old enough to start showing it much in his feathers, but he was no young griffin.

"You seek Snow-in-lee?" he murmured, apparently ignoring her question.

"That's the only wild griffin place I'd ever heard of, in a song my great-grandmother sang to me."

"Your name is Hawkwind?"

"Yes."

"You are of the Hawk Line?"

She nodded. "Yes. My mother was Hawkbright before becoming the mother. Her mother was Hawkbrave, and—"

"Reciting your lineage will not tell me anything useful." He stopped her with a wave of his hand. "The Hawk Line is but a legend here, an old story. In the story, the Lines split. The Hawk, Falcon, Eagle, Ice, Snow, and Cloud Lines left us, abandoned the homeland."

"Those were the Northnest Lines," Hawkwind said.

"And you claim to have come from Northnest."

"It was my home, and the home of the children I brought with me from there. We were attacked."

He stared deeply at her. "No one here will believe that."

"Why not?" she demanded. "It's true. You could fly down there and see for yourself."

The elder shook his head. "Your ignorance alone at least proves you're not a rogue."

"I don't understand."

"Exactly."

Hawkwind heard a door open, followed by a babble of voices.

"Yes, we're taking you to her."

"Really? I don't trust you."

"She's down here."

"You put her in a hole? Meanies."

"She'd better be alright."

The three griffins who had departed returned. The four children were perched on their backs: the princess, Kassandra, and Rikah holding Karo. It seemed it was Rikah who'd been doing most of the talking.

"Hawkwind," the princess called, hopping down from her mount and running to the bars.

"See, she's alright," one of the griffins said.

"What happened to her wings and tail?" Rikah demanded.

Hawkwind tried to go to the bars, but the shackles held her back. Karo was trying to squeeze between the bars to get to her, and the princess had reached out, until she saw that Hawkwind was chained. The princess turned around, showing Hawkwind her back, and faced the room full of griffins.

"Let her go," the princess ordered.

One or two of the griffins had the conscience to look uncomfortable.

"I'm afraid we cannot, right now," the elder Thornfire said.

Rikah strode up to him and shook a fist at him. "What did you do to her feathers? Let her go, now."

Hawkwind felt she should call the children back, try to make them understand, but seeing them defending her, standing up to beings several times their size, made a new, tender lump rise in her throat. Karo, the smallest, had gotten himself part way through the bars, stretching his hand towards her.

"Let them in," the elder commanded gently, "and leave the door unlocked."

One of the griffin guards obeyed, and Karo immediately disentangled himself from the bars and ran inside. Hawkwind lay down, tucking the chains out of the way, and tried to raise a bound wing as much as possible. Karo huddled under its dubious protection, and she tucked him close like a downy chick. The princess came inside, too, but stood before her.

"They've cut your feathers off?" the girl said, lip trembling.

"They will grow back," Hawkwind told her.

"How long? You have to fly us back down to Northnest, so we can retake our castle."

Her arms were folded and face stern, but Hawkwind could see her swallowing, her narrow chest quaking as she held back tears.

"Hawkwind is a good griffin," Rikah was proclaiming. "Why did you lock her up?"

Kassandra was watching the confrontation, leaning against the cell door frame, big blue eyes calm and curious.

"It wasn't my decision," the elder griffin was telling the boy.

"Then whose decision was it?"

"It was mine."

All heads turned, except Karo's, to the new speaker. Another handful of griffins had entered the central prison area, making it a bit crowded. Thornfire pivoted, putting Rikah slightly behind him. The other griffins reshuffled themselves, too, with the grey griffin who had gone to fetch the children taking a spot near Kassandra, as if to protect her also.

The newcomer was big, probably a female, black on her back with slate grey wings with white wing bars and black banding, and a pristine white underside sparsely streaked with black. She also wore a sort of collar that looked more like clothing than a collar one would hook a leash to, such as on a dog. It was leather, wide and golden, with a few polished stones set into it.

All the griffins in the room except Hawkwind bowed their heads for a breath, and then looked up again.

"Eldest Skycall," the elder Thornfire began.

"Thornfire," she cut across him. "Since when do you now presume to countermand standing orders as to the disposition of rogues and re-lated captives, as well as all the other ways in which you overreach your position? Rocksky reported that you removed her from her position as overseer of this case."

"I did."

"Explain yourself."

"I felt Commander Rocksky's view of the case was too narrow, and she hinted at sending this youngster to the crying room. I see that as a violation of the Words."

"Your interpretation of the Words is broad, and always has been," the Eldest Skycall retorted.

"And Commander Rocksky's has always been narrow," he said in reply.

Eldest Skycall did not respond for a moment, and Hawkwind re-mained still, afraid to speak or act just yet. Rikah, apparently, was not so afraid. He stepped around Thornfire's shielding foreleg and walked up to the big leader griffin.

"You put Hawkwind in there and cut her feathers off?" he accused.

Thornfire reached out, snagging the back of Rikah's tattered shirt, and started to pull him back.

"Let me go," he ordered, trying to twist away.

Kassandra shifted her weight back onto her feet, as if about to do something, and the princess ran back out the open cell door before Hawkwind could grab her. Rikah ducked his head and lifted his arms, slipping out of his shirt, and skidded to a stop again in front of Skycall, his dark little boy skin looking dangerously fragile against the natural weaponry of the griffins.

"Get on me," Hawkwind told Karo, and the little boy obeyed.

She got to her feet, stepping forward as far as her chains would let her.

"What is this?" Skycall asked, looking down at Rikah.

The princess grabbed his arm and held him. Hawkwind lifted her head.

"He is my charge," she called, "and so are the other three: human children I saved from an attack of wizards and rainbow drakes."

"A rather pointless but selfless action for a rogue," Skycall said with a tilt of her head.

"I don't believe she is a rogue, Eldest," Thornfire said.

"Your belief is nothing next to the truth."

"I seek shelter and food," Hawkwind continued. "I will pay with my service, or in any other way you can suggest."

Skycall advanced, and Jessika and Rikah retreated until their backs hit the bars.

"Rogues who return to the territory of any Aerie are executed," Skycall said. "You were told this when you were exiled."

"Look at her, Eldest," Thornfire insisted. "She is hardly fledged. What Aerie would exile such a young one?"

"Hawkwind is our protector," the princess Jessika spoke up. "She saved us. We need her to keep taking care of us."

What is this?

"She thought she could come to Snow-in-lee for help," Rikah added with a tremendous pout. "Now you've locked her up and cut her feathers off. You're no help at all."

Skycall stared down at the two children for a long moment. Then, she walked her rear legs in and sat. "What are your names? Do you have names?"

"I'm Jessika and this is Rikah," the princess said. "Pleased to meet you," she added, although to Hawkwind it didn't sound like she really meant it, and she didn't bow like Hawkwind knew she'd been taught to.

"You aren't afraid of griffins?"

"We lived with griffins. They protected us."

Skycall moved her head a bit closer to the girl and boy. "And what have you heard of Snow-in-lee?"

"Hawkwind sang us a song about it. She said we were going there, because there was nowhere else to go now."

Skycall's gaze transferred to Hawkwind. "Sing," she commanded.

The big leader griffin had icy blue eyes, and Hawkwind's throat suddenly tightened up. She swallowed, trying to force it open, while Skycall's expression began to narrow dangerously.

"O'er the rocky breezes flew," a voice, soft like snow falling, lit upon the air.

"The wild, the flocks of Snow-in-lee,

Free on the wind, my heart will be,

Top o' the world, and home to me."

All eyes had turned to Kassandra. The little girl, gentle eyes fixed in the middle distance, fingers curled lightly around a cell bar, had sung out into the raw and rocky prison the lullaby Hawkwind's great-grandmother had taught to her, that she had taught to the children.

"An old memory, that is," Thornfire said quietly, "and a lovely voice."

Hawkwind could see his eyes roving over the girl, lingering last on the slight, pink flower shape on her forehead, where the unicorn had struck her with his horn. His eyes went next to Hawkwind's, and they seemed to glow from within, with a light like the first crackling of a newly lit flame. Just the sight of it almost lit a glimmer of hope in her eyes, too.

"What is your name?" Skycall demanded, also looking at Hawkwind now.

"Hawkwind," she answered.

"The Hawk Line—"

"Yes, I know you think the Hawk Line is dead," she argued, sick of hearing it, "but it isn't. I am here. I am alive."

"Where are you from?"

"Northnest. My Line has lived there for generations, since the split you all know about but claim to be a legend."

"And what do you think you will do, Hawkdaughter of Northnest, in this Aerie?"

"I don't even know where I am."

"This is South-scree, the most southwesterly of the Aeries. So what will you do here?"

"I will do any task you put me to," she pledged, "as long as the children have food, water, and warmth. They don't eat nearly as much as a griffin."

"And what Line will you ask to take you in? We have five here."

"What Line?"

"The Mothers and Elders council, of which I am the moderator, governs South-scree. We pass direction on to the administrators of each Line, and they distribute duties in accordance with our directives. To be a contributing member of this Aerie, or any Aerie, you will require membership in a Line, Hawkdaughter."

Her rigid bill could not smile, but Hawkwind thought she detected a sly smiling of the skin around Skycall's eyes, and a measure of fury rose in her chest.

"You will petition to be adopted by a Line, then?" the leader went on.

"How does that work?" Hawkwind asked.

"You write a manuscript, detailing your merits and why you wish to join the Line of your choosing. You explain what benefits you will bring them. If the mother of the Line accepts your petition, she will grant you an audience, and set you tasks. If you perform admirably, she may agree to adopt you."

Hawkwind nodded. She could do that. "What kind of tasks?"

"They will be tasks that demonstrate the merits you claimed to have in your petition, such as any number of learned skills like crafting or magic use, or if you possess none of those, then fighting, hunting, speed at message carrying, or the gathering of other foodstuffs from the surrounding areas."

Hawkwind kept nodding.

"Are you a magic user or a master of a craft?"

"I was a guard in training, of a sort, so I can fight, and I know how to hunt."

"Ah," Skycall murmured, tilting her head ever so slightly. "But how will you prove yourself skilled at those, without being able to fly?"

Chapter 6
The Tale of Snow-in-lee

The prison guards had made Hawkwind and the children comfortable, although they hadn't removed her chains, providing some stuffed bags of hay that could be flattened into beds for the children, with blankets to go on top, as well as food and drink for all, though Hawkwind had needed to explain what the little humans could and couldn't eat.

Hawkwind dozed, her belly full of food she'd hardly tasted, while the children finished their quiet supper and lay down to sleep, too. She hadn't known what to say to Skycall. Indeed, how could she demonstrate her fighting ability, or hunting, without being able to fly?

Griffins naturally molted, but over about three months, once a year, usually in late winter, losing one feather one day, and another the next, in a pattern that kept them more or less flight worthy the whole time. To lose all her primaries and secondaries plus her tail feathers at once was a catastrophe. Once she got up the courage to pull out the stubs—a painful but necessary task—her body would replace them as fast as it could, but she would be ground bound for at least a month. If she didn't pull them out, they wouldn't grow back until her next molt.

A noise from the stairwell alerted her and she lifted her head. Around her, the children slept on, and the other prisoner seemed deeply asleep as well, but the elder Thornfire was making his way down the steps. One guard was on duty, the grey one that Hawkwind had learned was named Skymist; she was half asleep herself, lounging on a big leather pillow with a book. Skymist sat up to give a nod to Thornfire.

"Here to continue interrogation of the new prisoner," he said, with a glint in his eye that suggested a measure of sarcasm to his words.

"Of course, Elder," Skymist replied. "Go ahead. You can pretend I'm not here."

Hawkwind carefully disentangled herself from the sleeping children and stepped as close to the bars as she could.

"Without the ability to compete to be accepted into a Line, what am I going to do?" she asked at once. "I can't fly, Elder Thornfire."

"Calm yourself, little hawk," he soothed. "Don't think I'm not aware of that, and we'll find a solution."

"But Eldest Skycall said," she blurted.

"Don't worry about Skycall."

"Isn't she the leader?"

"She's a sort of leader," he allowed. "She certainly likes to think she's the ruler of indeed, the world, not only South-scree, and she can be a difficult adversary."

"So what do I do?" Hawkwind asked again, trying not to let her shoulders droop too much.

"I have some ideas what we will do, little hawk, but you must leave those plans to me if you want an alternative to petitioning to enter a Line and facing the tests without flight." Thornfire eyed her critically. "Do you trust me to handle that? Or would you rather choose to petition?"

Hawkwind held his gaze. "I don't know you. We've only just met. I don't know if I should trust you, or anyone here. I thought I'd find welcome among my own kind. I was wrong. I don't know what to expect anymore."

Behind Thornfire, Skymist shifted on her pillow and glanced up at Hawkwind. "Thornfire is a radical, crazy old wizard too big for his hunter harness, but he has good intentions."

The tan male griffin raised his brows as he speared Skymist with a smoldering gaze. "Is that any way to speak of your elders?" he drawled.

"He'll do his best to help you, if he pledges it, but it's still possible his plans might fall through the ice and get you eaten by a snow-screamer," Skymist concluded. "So that's how much you can trust him, in my opinion."

Hawkwind felt a few fragments of her fear melt under the friendly

SKYMIST

banter of the pair. She dared to hope a little. Thornfire gave Skymist an extra bit of glaring and then turned back to Hawkwind, settling his wings with a raspy shuffle. He flicked some imaginary dust from his forepaw.

"So, will you leave it to me?" he asked again.

"What are you planning?" Hawkwind countered carefully.

Voice low, he murmured, "What do you know of Snow-in-lee?"

"I only know the lullaby," she told him, swallowing her other questions, "and that it was a place where griffins lived."

Thornfire took a seat. "I can tell you the tale of Snow-in-lee. Listen well."

"Long before South-scree and Ice-peak and In-the-wind were founded, most griffins lived in a sheltered dale among the mountain peaks called Snow-in-lee. It was our first city. The wind skipped around it, the morning light bathed it, and the snow fell only lightly there," Thornfire began. "Our homes were carved into the mountain sides and we built a network of towers connected by bridges nestled in the dale itself. There, we flourished. There were libraries, art galleries, crafting houses, and armories, too. What made it all possible were the two Stones, the Moonstone and the Sunstone."

"I have never heard of those things," Hawkwind said.

"I will tell you of them. When griffins began to live together, to form communities, instead of struggling on their own or in small family groups like any animal predator, those of us with magical talent began to meet. Upon meeting, we either fought and died of rivalry, or banded together and shared our knowledge. Those who shared started a place where they kept their secrets. They choose a valley, named it Snow-in-lee, and started a school for young griffins showing magical talent. Together, their talents grew and they discovered new ways to use their magic. They wrote it all down and stored the books and scrolls in libraries there.

"It was there, in that school of concentrated magical talent, that they discovered how to create magic that could be stored in stones. The stones could then be set to run the task done by the magic in the stone, and they would do so eternally, without rest, as long as they periodically received some new energy to keep them going. It was much easier than having a magician repeatedly performing spells for some ongoing desired effect, although magicians did have to set up the stones initially, and keep them powered, and that took great skill: the more complicated the spell, the more skill was required.

"As for the Sunstone and the Moonstone, they were crafted by a pair of quite powerful magicians. Most stones were small, and did simple things like creating light. Such small stones took only a few moments or minutes to make, depending on their size and power of the makers. The Sun and Moon stones however, were as large as melons, and were the work of years for the creators."

"What did they do?" Hawkwind asked eagerly.

"I'm getting to it. Are you aware that the moon we see in the sky pulls on the waters of this world?"

She shook her head. "How does it do that?"

"I'm afraid I don't know that either, but Icecloud knew, somehow, and created the Moonstone to pull more water up through the small spring in Snow-in-lee, until the valley was flooded with it."

"How would that be useful?"

"It wasn't at first, as the spring already provided the small school of magicians with plenty of water, but then Starflight created the Sunstone. Perhaps you can guess what that one does."

"It makes light?" she guessed.

"More than light, the sun heats our world, and so the Sunstone, placed into the waters the Moonstone had called up, created light and heat, made the water warm and then hot, and then steam began to fill the valley. Among these frigid mountains, warmth was a rare thing indeed. Suddenly, everyone wanted to live in Snow-in-lee—griffins and everything else in the mountains. The plant-eaters were no problem, but when ice-lions and snow-screamers and other predators started showing up, the magicians had their hands full. They welcomed other griffins on the condition that they help defend the school. Snow-in-lee boomed and soon most of our population lived there. Our Lines established themselves and we wrote the first Words."

"It sounds ideal," Hawkwind commented. "What went wrong?"

Thornfire sighed heavily. "The coldest winter ever known descended on the mountains. The peaks and mountainsides both were encased in ice. Only Snow-in-lee survived, and even there it was chilly, despite the hot water. The griffins could survive, and they allowed any nonviolent animals to join them."

"But not every animal was nonviolent," Hawkwind surmised.

Thornfire nodded grimly. "Starving and freezing, their watery homes frozen solid, the talis came."

"What's that?" she asked as, behind Thornfire, Skymist hissed.

"The talis are an ancient people, no doubt," the elder allowed quietly, "and usually we have no contact with them, as they are creatures of the water, long-lived, and very slow breeders, but upon that winter they all descended upon Snow-in-lee. They took it from the griffins."

"Took Snow-in-lee, and took our lives as well," Skymist spat.

"We griffins have little defense against a talis," Thornfire confirmed, shoulders shifting with discomfort. "The magicians tried their best, but there were too many. Any conflict with them is mortal for us. Many died."

"Many of us, and few of them," Skymist contributed. "And they're still there now, they say, bathing in the warm waters, eating every beast that dares come near, while our city crumbles around them and they care not."

Hawkwind found herself frowning, staring at the ground. "What do they look like?"

"Pray you never see one," Skymist answered immediately. "See one, and it will be the last one you ever see."

"There are a few drawings and some descriptions around," Thornfire provided, "but they don't really do the beasts justice. Have you ever been captivated by something sparkly?"

Hawkwind ducked her head, a griffin-blush.

"We all have," Thornfire soothed. "We like sparkly, shiny objects, pretty patterns and colors, and even with harmless objects, our natural fascination can be difficult to resist. Talis are finned serpents that can grow large enough to swallow an adult griffin when they unhinge their jaws. They have intricate, glimmering scale patterns, but they also have something more, some sort of magical hypnotic essence that can distract and entrance us, making us slow and hesitant, and easy to catch."

"Is there no defense?"

"Somehow, some few griffins seem to be resistant, but we've found no way to tell which ones they are, until confronted by an actual talis. Then you know. You either can't look away, or you fly away."

"And they have Snow-in-lee?"

"Yes," Thornfire said.

"How do they keep the Moonstone and Sunstone working?" she asked. "You said they require some magic put into them, and how long ago did Snow-in-lee fall?"

"It was many generations ago, more than a griffin has feathers. The Talis are not unintelligent. They have some language and they work some water magic. I suspect they recognized that the Stones were magic. They also may have kept some of the griffins they captured for a while, since they don't need more than a meal or two a year. It's possible they learned of the need to recharge the Stones from the griffins they kept."

"Kept until they got hungry," Skymist mumbled.

"At any rate, all reports indicate that the city is infested now. They have comfortable, unlimited warm water to return to after they go hunting. There's no reason they'd leave. Talis have cold flesh. They are slow until they strike, and they let their venom weaken their prey, so that even if it runs, they can follow at their own slow pace and pick it up later. The warmth, however, makes them faster, and even more deadly."

"They sound horrible," Hawkwind said, hugging her chest with her forelimbs and making her chains scrape against each other.

"After the griffin Lines were driven from Snow-in-lee, they tried to retake it, but failed. The survivors founded other cities instead. Generations later, there was a conflict with the humans, which I expect you are aware of since you come from where you come from. The new griffin cities encroached on human territory." He lowered his voice a little. "Most of the Lines here at South-scree refuse to admit to any wrongdoing, or that any error was made that could have ever incited a conflict with the humans. They blame the fight on the humans alone and refuse to believe that any of the Lines would have a reason to ally with the two-leggers against their own kind. Thus, they deny the existence of Northnest and declared your Line and the others to be extinct."

"But we're not," Hawkwind protested. "Or, well, we weren't, but we might be now," she concluded with a whisper.

"I long suspected the existence of Northnest," Thornfire told her. "It is, however, forbidden to fly beyond the bounds of our territory without council approval."

"As if you ever listen to the council," Skymist muttered.

Thornfire, if he heard her, ignored the comment. "Now you are here, and it is proven. The legend of Northnest and departure of the five Lines is true."

"So you believe me?" Hawkwind asked.

"I believe you completely," he assured her at once. "Your situation is so, well, strange? It's difficult to choose an appropriate word. I can only concede that you are genuinely what you are, and your four human children as well."

Some weight of fear lifted from Hawkwind's heart. "I'm so glad someone believes me."

"I believe you, too," Skymist called. "It's too weird to be fake, but the council probably won't see it that way."

"Leave them to me," Thornfire said without turning around. "And speaking of weird: perhaps, Hawkdaughter, you'd be kind enough to try to befriend the other prisoner we have?"

She looked over towards the other wing cut griffin prisoner. He or she was still curled in a ball, motionless except for some subtle belly movement, indicating breathing.

"I must be on my way. Many things to do, I have," Thornfire went on, getting to his feet. "Oh, but one more thing."

"Yes?"

"Do you have any magical talent?"

Hawkwind shook her head. "I never knew griffins could do magic until I came here and heard you speak of it."

"There were no magicians at Northnest then?"

Hawkwind shivered. "Only the ones that attacked us, and loosed the rainbow drakes upon us."

"They'll not find you here," the elder assured her, voice soft. "The mountains are too cold for drakes. They'll have been turned back by the winds and snow, even if they managed to track you beyond the unicorn glades."

She nodded, swallowing, fighting back resurging memories of fleeing through Northnest, out the tunnel, and through the forest. Her wounds ached and prickled.

"I'll be going then."

Thornfire exited up the stairwell. Hawkwind checked on the children, seeing that they were all still sleeping, huddled together in a ball of skinny arms and legs.

"Do they need anything else?" Skymist asked.

"Not right now," Hawkwind told her. "They have food and a warm place to sleep, which is more than they've had for days. They will need new clothing, as theirs has been quite ruined, but I don't know that South-scree can provide it."

"Hmm, I can talk to some folks," the guard answered. "I'll see what I can do, once I'm off duty."

"That would be very welcome, and I'll repay you when I can. They could also use a bath soon, but it's not critical."

Hawkwind sensed Skymist's hesitation. "I'm supposing they don't dust bathe? How do humans bathe?"

"With a tub of warm water, soap, and some cloth rags to scrub their skin with," Hawkwind explained. "Then they'll need towels to dry off with before they get cold."

"Fascinating. How bizarre to be a human, with such naked skin, no claws, no sharp bill or fangs. How do they survive? Is that why you and the other Northnest griffins were taking care of them?"

"They do well when they have weapons. Their hands are clever and so are their minds. Sometimes I think they are more intelligent than us griffins. They are certainly inventive. What they lack they create: weapons, clothing, housing, cooking, tools, and art."

"But these little ones," Skymist went on. "They are like fledglings?"

"Yes," Hawkwind confirmed. "They are mostly defenseless, but they can be useful in ways other than fighting. Still, they need me to protect them, and I will. I swore it."

Skymist made no reply to that. Hawkwind watched their little fingers twitch in sleep, their closed eyelids fluttering, pink lips slightly parted as they breathed. Rikah was snoring a little through his nose. Through the rips in her dress, Jessika's wing tattoos were slightly visible. Hawkwind adjusted the garment, covering them up. She didn't know if they would mean anything to the South-scree griffins, but she felt an instinctive need to keep the girl's identity secret.

"So, who is the other prisoner?" she asked Skymist, turning around to face the grey griffin.

"We picked him up last week," the guard provided, "but who he is no one can say, for he has not spoken a word."

Skymist shrugged, and Hawkwind strode towards the huddled prisoner, her chains clanking against the floor. She wouldn't be able to reach him, and stopped when she hit the end of her tether. The prisoner's feathers were ragged and dirty, but seemed to be in a pattern of white, grey, and black.

"Hey, hey you, excuse me, you other prisoner," she called out, but the griffin made no response. "Can I talk to you? Are you alright?"

Hawkwind picked up a small clump of mostly clean hay bedding that had just sort of solidified to itself when it got wet. Not sure what else to do—she didn't dare send one of the children to awaken a traumatized griffin—she pitched the hay clump at its head. The prisoner jumped and startled at the impact, even though it hadn't been a heavy blow. His wide eyes stared frantically around as he let out a piercing shriek of fear, struggling against his chains and the mesh that bound his cut wings. Frantically he scrambled backwards until he hit the end of his chains, jerking to halt and falling onto his face.

"It's alright," Hawkwind tried to soothe the panting prisoner.

He'd pushed back to his feet, bill agape and panting, still staring around with panicked eyes.

"He's been sleeping or unconscious most of the time," Skymist contributed dryly. "Whenever we try to awaken him, he does this same song and dance. We leave food for him, but he won't touch it during the day. It's gone by morning though."

To Hawkwind, he seemed quite small, young, and rather skinny. "You don't know his name or where he's from?"

"He won't respond to anyone. He just stares."

Hawkwind took a seat facing the prisoner. He stared blankly at her. She put a hand to her own chest. "I'm Hawkwind," she said.

"We tried that," Skymist sighed.

Perhaps words were not the best choice. Maybe he was deaf? Hawkwind picked up the chains that bound her and shook them. Then she pointed to his chains. She pointed to a wing and showed him that her feathers were cut. Then she pointed to his wings. She pointed to herself with one hand. She pointed to him with the other. She held up her hands together, trying to suggest that they were the same, both her hands and she and him.

Whether he understood or not, she didn't know, but his body relaxed and he continued gazing at her. Suddenly, he sat back on his haunches, too, and held up both his hands, copying Hawkwind's pose. Her face brightened with joy: a response. Now what should she do? She tugged on her chains and stroked her temporarily crippled wings, hunching, cowering, and whimpering with the soft crying chirps that nestlings use to call their parents. Having given the play acting for a few moments she straightened back up to normal and tried to make a gesture that suggested "and you? How do you feel about it?"

The prisoner put his hands down and gazed at her, head tilted and brow furrowed as if thinking hard. At last, he looked over to Skymist and pointed at her, tilting his head farther and giving an expression that conveyed confusion to Hawkwind.

Skymist lifted her hands in defense. "I didn't do anything to him."

"I think he's wondering why you're not chained and wing cut," Hawkwind said. "I think he's deaf maybe."

"We sent messages to the other settlements, with a physical description, asking if anyone is missing him, or exiled him, but no one seems to know him," Skymist supplied. "We wouldn't exile someone for being deaf; that's ridiculous. Something else is going on with him. It seems like everything terrifies him, like he's in fear of his life every moment."

Hawkwind looked back to the prisoner and didn't have an answer for her. She had no idea how to explain it. Her expression of helplessness seemed to communicate something; he put his hand back down and lowered his head in depression, still trembling slightly. At least he seemed calmer now.

"Maybe he can write," Jessika suggested from behind Hawkwind, startling her.

"You're awake," she said. "I suppose his cry awakened you all."

The four grubby children were sitting together on the cushions now, although Karo still looked half asleep.

"If he can't talk, maybe he can write, or draw pictures," she elaborated.

Immediately, Hawkwind brushed the floor clear of hay fragments, leaving a slightly dirty, sandy surface. Skymist got up and came to the bars to watch. The prisoner flinched at her movement, but nothing more. Hawkwind dipped a finger in the water bucket and wrote, "my name is Hawkwind," on the floor.

"What kind of writing is that?" Skymist commented. "You write funny."

"How do you write?" Hawkwind asked her in return.

Skymist dipped a finger, too, and wrote something on the floor, but Hawkwind couldn't read the letters.

"What did you write?" Hawkwind asked.

"My name," Skymist answered. "I assume you wrote your name, too?"

"Our written language diverged," Hawkwind guessed, "after all the time apart, now Northnest griffins and South-scree griffins write differently."

"I'll bet you all learned Northnest writing when you joined with us," Jessika said, walking up to crouch beside Hawkwind, "and forgot your own."

"But we talk the same," Skymist said.

"I think we all always talked the same," Jessika opined.

Hawkwind just shrugged and looked at the prisoner. She pointed to her writing and to Skymist's, before the wet letters dried and vanished. The prisoner shook his head at Hawkwind's writing, but looked longer at Skymist's. Then, with a shaking hand, he reached into his own water bucket, swept aside the hay, and drew some marks on the floor. They made no sense to Hawkwind but Skymist was watching closely.

"The writing is very similar. Rainsoft?" she said. "Your name is Rainsoft?"

The prisoner looked at her uncomprehendingly. He opened his bill, as if to speak, but nothing came out. He coughed, croaked, and managed only a quiet warbling cry.

"He can't talk," Jessika observed, "but he can make the cries and calls like griffins, and falcons and eagles and all can make. Why can't he talk?"

"Talking and calling come from two different places in our bodies," Skymist said.

"She's right," Hawkwind confirmed. Gently she touched the girl's throat with a finger. "We talk from here, just like you, but we make our cries and calls and screams from a place deep in our chest." Hawkwind placed her palm against her own keel, although the actual origin of the cries was much more than skin deep.

The prisoner had put a hand to his own, feathered throat.

"Let me see," Rikah said suddenly, elbowing his way between Jessika and Hawkwind.

Hawkwind tried to grab him, but the boy was already out of range of her shackled hands. "Come back, Rikah," she ordered. "He might not be safe."

The boy ignored her, walking up to the prisoner without fear. At first, the griffin jerked back, but then seemed to decide that the boy was of no threat. With great delicacy in his trembling fingers, the griffin touched the boy's arm, shoulder, and hair. Rikah giggled.

"That tickles," he said. "Now, I'm going to touch you, too."

Hawkwind watched, breath held, as the boy lightly petted Rainsoft's chest, and then the sides of his neck. Then, his little clever fingers worked under the feather-fur of the griffin's throat, lifting up layers of it to look at the skin below. Rainsoft kept his chin lifted, orange eyes watching the boy nervously. Rikah stepped in closer and dug his fingers deeper. Hawkwind quivered. With his sharp bill unfettered, a single bite could instantly kill the boy. Rainsoft, however, didn't move.

Finally, Rikah seemed to find something, and parted the feather-fur with both hands. Hawkwind leaned in against her chains to look at the skin revealed there.

"Oh, Rainsoft," Jessika sighed.

A twisted, ugly, white scar marred his throat.

"He can hear. He just can't speak," the girl went on.

"And I don't think he knows our language," Skymist suggested. "I wonder where he came from."

"I wonder how we could ever ask him," Hawkwind concurred softly.

Hurried footsteps on the stairs interrupted their pondering.

Rainsoft
and
Rikah

Rainsoft jumped, but Rikah put his arms around the prisoner's neck, hugged him close, and whispered, "it's alright."

Jessika ran back to the other two children still lying on the sleeping cushions, and Hawkwind stepped up to face the bars as Skymist returned to her post. Two griffin guards were trotting down the stairs in perfect synch. They stopped, Skymist nodded in salute, and they gave smaller nods back.

"Rogue Hawkwind," one of the newcomers began, "you are called for in the council chambers. You will accompany us."

Jessika, leading Karo and Kassandra by the hands stepped up beside Hawkwind.

"Just you," the guard went on. "The human chicks have not been summoned."

"They are in my care," Hawkwind argued.

"That is not disputed. As their caretaker, you will speak for them before the council. Your fate and theirs is to be decided. Naught will be done with them until then."

"I'll make sure they have everything they need," Skymist spoke up, "until you come back."

Hawkwind looked from Skymist to the children, in pain. How could she possibly leave them here in this place alone?

"You'll come with us, conscious or unconscious," the guard growled. "It would be a shame if the little ones were hurt when the only one called for is you, Prisoner. We'll not lay a claw on them if you come quietly."

Hawkwind swallowed hard, and put a hand on Jessika's shoulder. "Tell Skymist about anything you need, and watch over the others until I return."

"Hawkwind," Karo whined, but Jessika shushed him.

"You'll come back?" the princess whispered.

There was nothing she could say. "I don't know," she admitted. "I will do everything I can to get back to you, unless I must trade myself for your safety, but I'll do everything I can, either way." She stopped, realizing she was babbling.

In silence, Hawkwind patted each child on the head, except for Rikah, who was still clinging to Rainsoft.

"I'm ready," she told the guards.

With long hooks and much jangling of locks and latching and un-latching of chains and doors they fetched out her chains and led her by them out of the cell. She submitted to a band around her bill, to prevent her from biting. Then they led her up several flights of stairs, and she got her first look at South-scree.

They emerged on a south-facing mountainside. The sun showed it to be late morning. From the stone platform Hawkwind and the guards stood on, the city descended down the slope, an expanding collection of structures made of stacked grey stones that had either naturally bro-ken or been chipped into flat paving stone-like shapes. As such, they stacked easily and securely.

Hawkwind looked up, behind her, where the structures continued up the slope. She'd always taken for granted the human-built castle she had lived in. This entire community made by griffins for griffins of in-tricately stacked and interlocking stones was something she hadn't ex-pected. She looked down at her feet, seeing that the platform she stood on, too, was made of the flat sections of stone fitted tightly together.

There were other griffins about. They walked through the paths of the city, on their way to some destination or other, or took short flights from one section to the next. They came in every color Hawkwind had ever seen in griffins, from black to white, from brown to grey, with wing bars, feather banding, tail banding, speckles, stripes, spots, and streaks. A few even had bright patches of rust red or golden yellow. Most were wearing some kind of leather harness with pouches to carry whatever it needed for its trade or current errand.

"The council is waiting," grunted one of the guards, and Hawkwind moved along obediently when he tugged her chain.

They passed along a walkway and down a few flights of stairs, moving down deeper into the densest part of the city. Hawkwind tried not to feel too ashamed when other griffins of the city stared at her with curiosity or confusion. A few even glowered at her. After a walk of several minutes, Hawkwind and her guards approached the largest structure Hawkwind had yet seen in the city. It was round and slightly domed. She could see several skylights from her angle. She noted a rather ornate entrance up some steps, but the guards took her around to a small, modest door instead.

"This is the council hall," one guard told her, as they passed through the door.

They walked down a dark hallway and into a small room, from which a short set of stairs led up into the brightly lit hall. Above, she heard idle conversation. The guards stopped her, and sat, so she did, too. A dark brown griffin glanced briefly down the steps at them, and then flitted away.

"Attention," a voice called out. "Council is resuming session."

The idle chatter died away. Hawkwind's heartbeat sped up and one of the guards slipped off the band that had been holding her bill shut.

"The next matter is the rogue picked up yesterday," the voice continued. "Present her for judgment."

The two guards led Hawkwind up into the hall, taking her to a low walled stone box to one side, where they locked her chains to iron rings set into the floor. They positioned themselves on either side of the box, facing out into the hall. Hawkwind looked around. The room had five large sections and one small, arranged like slices of a pie with a big hole in the middle. Her box was in the hole, along with a few other assorted griffins who were not restrained, but rather sitting in various states of agitation around the edges. She faced the small section directly across from her, where only one griffin sat: Eldest Skycall. The other five large sections contained five griffins each. In each section one of those griffins, a big female, sat in the highest perch, in back of and above the other four griffins, which had lower seats in front of her.

As Hawkwind gazed around, she identified Thornfire in the section directly to her right. She also saw Commander Rocksky, standing in the pit in front of a different section. The commander's sneer of dislike was not imagined. Thornfire, however, gave Hawkwind a brief nod of encouragement.

"Commander Rocksky," Skycall instructed, "please report for this council the manner in which you discovered and apprehended this rogue."

The black, grey, and white griffin took a step forward. "The rogue was seen crossing the southern escarpment with four human children."

Muttering immediately circulated among the gathered griffins, but Rocksky ignored it.

"I was fetched by Starsun's scout when they encountered the rogue. My troop investigated and I questioned the rogue when I was unable to visually identify her. She repeatedly lied about where she was from—"

"No, I didn't," Hawkwind objected loudly. "I never lied."

"Order," demanded Skycall. "You will have your chance to speak. Commander, continue."

"When no clear answer could be attained, my troop subdued her and the children and fetched them here. No one sustained any major injuries, and the rogue fought bravely for the human children."

"Understood, thank you," Skycall praised. "Do you have anything else to add to your report?"

"Only that Elder Thornfire interfered with my authority, preventing me from obtaining more answers from the rogue using other techniques."

Hawkwind saw Thornfire clenching his bill.

"Noted," Skycall said. "You may step down."

The Commander Rocksky stepped back to her position. She didn't look at Hawkwind again.

"Elder Thornfire," Skycall sighed with what seemed long suffering patience, "you have again involved yourself in a minor matter quite obscure to your position, countermanding the true authority of it. Do you have an explanation for your actions?"

The elder straightened, "this fledgling is no rogue, Moderator. She has never even been in a griffin settlement."

"And what proof have you of that?"

"She has no knowledge of our ways," he said, "and is of the Hawk Line."

"So she claims. A clever rogue could easily pretend and lie."

"She came wandering in from territory claimed by no griffin."

"As any rogue would, were she careless or malicious."

"She has human children with her," Thornfire went on.

"So what if she stole them? Perhaps she was exiled for insanity."

"You think she is both insane and capable of pretending and lying, as well as being careless or malicious?"

The Moderator's eyes flashed dangerously. "You question me, Thornfire?"

"What purpose could she possibly have for coming here, except for the story she has told us?"

"A story is all it is," Rocksky barked. "Send her to the crying room. They'll get a real answer from her."

"She is not a criminal," Thornfire shouted back. "She's done nothing wrong, broken no law."

"Except crossing our border," Skycall insisted.

"Did she hurt our border by crossing it?" Thornfire all but sneered. "She came seeking our help, yet there are those among us who would send a fledge to be tortured. This chick came to us asking for aid: injured, exhausted, and trying to care for young ones. Just because we've been having trouble with a tribe of rogues pilfering from us does not make her a rogue. She's nothing like those wild, fierce, cruel exiles."

For a moment the silence rang in Hawkwind's ears.

"She is not exactly a chick. What if she is a plant, a spy, sent by the tribe of rogues," someone suggested. "She could have been sent like this, to get inside our city, to gain our trust."

Murmuring followed this idea, until the room began to buzz.

"Order," Skycall commanded, and the talking died down. "Some time in the crying room might indeed gain us answers," she ruminated. "And while we're at it, we need answers from that other rogue, too. Perhaps he could be motivated to find his words."

"No," Hawkwind objected. "Rainsoft can't speak. His vocal chords were damaged."

"Silence," hissed Skycall.

"How do you know his name?" asked Thornfire urgently.

"We discovered that he could write," Hawkwind explained rapidly, "but only the way you all write, which I can't read. He can't read my writing either. Skymist was able to read what he wrote, though she said some of the letters were a little different. She said he wrote his name, as she wrote hers, so she read that his name was Rainsoft."

"Did he write where he's from?" Thornfire went on, leaning forward urgently, hands clasping the rail in front of him.

"No, the guards interrupted us."

"Silence, now," demanded Skycall: her ear ringing screech echoing through the hall.

Hawkwind and Thornfire both went quiet.

"I have enough trouble," the Moderator growled, "tribes of rogues attacking us, without all this nonsense."

"Eldest Skycall," Thornfire said composedly and calmly, "I agree. The rogue tribes must have the focus of this council."

"For once you speak sense," she spat back at him.

"These two prisoners we have, do they seem anything like the rogue tribe members we have seen? Those griffins are full adults, hardened by a rough life outside a city, in the wild. They were exiled because they were criminals, murderers, and thieves. Such brigands would never take two small, helpless, young griffins such as our prisoners into their tribe.

More likely they would attack and kill them, don't you think? I can only surmise that our two pathetic little captives are something else. If the council will allow it, I will take charge and responsibility for them."

"And what would you do with them?" Skycall demanded at once.

"You think to have them join our Line, Fire?" demanded also the big female in Thornfire's section. "That is not your say."

"No, no," Thornfire quickly assured them. "Thornmother, I would never presume to have that authority, no. Eldest Skycall, my reasons are ones which, if you care not for the prisoners, would even send them to be tortured for information they don't have, perhaps are not even of any interest to you, and might be a burden on this council's time."

Skycall's eyes narrowed. "They cannot walk free in this city. They are not of our Lines. They are not citizens."

"They will not remain in this city," he said simply.

An uneasy rustle passed through the gathered griffins, and Hawkwind stared around in confusion.

"Fire," began the Thornmother, "it is a fool's errand. He is lost."

Energy crackled through Thornfire's feathers. Hawkwind saw it clearly, like tiny threads of white lightning.

"None in this city will aid you, because we all know how hopeless it is," Skycall cried out at him. "So you think to bring prisoners who cannot resist? You think they will walk with you into death because you free them from their cell? For all your learning how has the wisdom to avoid certain doom evaded you?" She thrashed her wings and tail in fury. "How can you be taught this?"

"He is my brother, my full brother, and I will not rest until I know his fate," Thornfire screamed back. "None in this city will aid me in finding a fellow lost citizen." He wheeled towards the Thornmother. "None in my own Line will aid me in discovering where a child of Thorn has gone and why he'll not return. There is no other then, than myself."

"And two prisoners you will try to guilt and coerce into helping you?" Skycall sneered, disgusted.

"And I will promise them," Thornfire declared, "that when we return with my brother or his remains, putting to rest this mystery, that they will be granted citizenship," he looked again at the matriarch of his Line, "and a place in the Thorn Line."

Silence fell again.

"You ask us to promise this?" Thornmother said, "Eldest Skycall and I?"

"Yes."

"Your brother is dead, Fire," she whispered.

"How do you know?"

"You know where he went. We all know. He made no secret of his delusional ambitions. He is dead."

"Then I will bring back whatever is left of him."

"There will be nothing, and you will perish, too," she went on. Her stiff posture melted a little. "Fire, you and he are my half-sibs as well, and my cherished Linemembers. You think I don't care for him and you? You think I wouldn't care to watch you leave for your death as well?"

Thornfire fumbled at his chest, finally lifting a small pendant on a long chain out from where it had been hidden under his feather-fur. It was a small green stone wrapped in silver metal.

"Our sire gave one to both of us," he said. "I'll find the one that belongs to Wing. If it is not still around his neck, then I will know him to be dead. Do I have your word that you will grant Hawkwind and Rainsoft a place in the Line, when we return?"

Thornmother hissed a sigh and turned her face away. "They are outsiders," she objected.

"I forbid it," Skycall exclaimed.

Thornfire turned to her, spine stiff. "Eldest and Moderator you may be, Skycall, but you do not control the membership of the Lines."

"I can reject any griffin from this city," she retorted. "So you seek your brother? We all know where he went. You want these crippled weakling outsiders to be a part of us? Very well. Here are my conditions."

She spun, leaping down from her perch and all but landed atop Hawkwind. Fast, faster than Hawkwind could follow, Skycall had gripped her bill, yanking her head up as the Moderator looked down at her.

"Prove yourself," she said slowly. "Bring me the Sunstone."

Hawkwind jumped in shock, eyes flashing wide and open even further than they had been.

"And tell your tattered little friend Rainsoft to bring me the Moonstone," she went on inexorably.

At last Skycall released her and stepped away, turning to look up at Thornfire.

"You bring back your brother's pendant—with or without him. Do that," she all but laughed, "and we'll see about letting your cannon fodder join us. Now get out of my sight, and out of my city, until all three of you have retrieved your assigned tokens for reentry. This meeting is over."

Without a backward glance, Eldest Skycall took the tunnel out of the hall, and vanished into the city.

Thornfire

Chapter 8
Departure

Despite Hawkwind's half-hysterical concerns that they should leave the city immediately, Thornfire had brushed her off, insisting instead that leaving the next day would plentifully fulfill Skycall's order to get out of the city.

Hawkwind was flopped belly down on a thick leather cushion in front of Thornfire's hearth, where a warming stone cast delightful heat across her back, drying her freshly washed fur. Karo was submerged up to his neck in a barrel filled with water heated also by a warming stone. Rikah was combing the boy's tangled hair. Kassandra and Jessika, already bathed and wrapped in makeshift clothing, were scrubbing down Rainsoft as he sat in a tub, trembling only intermittently.

Thornfire pushed a bowl with chunks of meat in it under Hawkwind's bill, and she stared at it, hunger clenching her belly.

"Eat," he said. "You'll need your strength in the coming days."

She didn't need telling twice. Karo finished his bathing, Rikah helping him to climb out of the barrel and get wrapped in a towel.

"I wish we could provide you with better clothing," Starbright, Thornfire's apprentice remarked, carrying a bowl of cooked meat into the room from the kitchen area. "Griffins don't wear clothing like yours."

"It's alright, Starbright," Jessika assured her from where she was running a wide toothed comb through Rainsoft's fur. "We can maybe learn how to make some."

For the moment, the children were wearing lengths of fabric wrapped around parts of their bodies and tied off. It kept them more or less covered and warm, but certainly wasn't stylish.

"Maybe I can learn how to make some, too," Starbright suggested cheerfully.

"I suggest you spend your free time on studying," Thornfire

grunted.

"Oh, Master," the apprentice complained, "I just don't have the right soul for water magic."

"You cannot be considered even a low-level magician unless you become comfortable with all the elements," Thornfire said, in a tone that suggested he'd told her this many times before. "I will not advance you to mixing elements in your magic until you have mastered those water spells."

"I'm much better at fire," the young griffin confided to Jessika. The princess grinned at her.

"Yes, and your light, earth, and wind spells are admirable as well," Thornfire growled, "but you must have water, too."

"What about dark?" Rikah spoke up.

"Dark?" Thornfire hissed.

"Well, if fire and water are opposites, and wind and earth, wouldn't dark be the opposite of light, so wouldn't you learn that, too?" the boy rattled off, seemingly oblivious of Thornfire's reaction.

Starbright was staring at the ground, and Hawkwind had the feeling that she, too, had asked this question.

"I do not teach dark spells. I do not know dark spells," Thornfire emphasized. "They have no place in life. Starbright, study your water magic."

"Yes, Master," she acquiesced.

Hawkwind finished off her bowl of meat: grateful she'd had the excuse of eating not to talk. "What shall I do with this bowl?" she spoke up.

"Oh, I'll take it," Starbright said at once, and the golden griffin snatched it up and practically fled.

"Rikah, you need to bathe next," Jessika remarked. "I'll get the clothes for Karo."

The children went on with their bathing of themselves and Rainsoft, and Thornfire came to sit by Hawkwind at the hearth.

"Will you tell me," she began quietly. "About what happened at the council, and what's going to happen? Where are we going? How am I supposed to—?"

Thornfire's deep sigh stopped her. "I need your help."

She nodded in silence, examining a floor tile. "What about my children?"

He shifted and eyed the four little humans, and lowered his voice. "Hawkwind, do you really feel the need to take care of them? Why don't we just take them to the edge of a human village and leave them? Surely other humans could look after them better?"

Hawkwind's bill had dropped open. "What? No," she spluttered. "How could you suggest such a thing?" She had to resist jumping to her feet. As it was, her fur and feathers began to lift in reaction.

"They're humans; you're a griffin. You're not related to them. They aren't a part of your Line," Thornfire went on. "They're weak; they couldn't stop you from leaving them somewhere."

A growl tried to surge out of her throat. "If you want me to help you you'd better stop saying things like that."

"We're helping each other," the mage emphasized. "They are an unnecessary complication. Don't you see? There's no reason you have to be burdened with them when there are other solutions, better ones."

"There is every reason," Hawkwind all but hissed.

"Explain them to me," he urged. "I can't understand your devotion, and do stop bristling so."

She tried to force herself to relax, and gazed over at the children as they were finishing their bathing and dressing. "They're all I have," she began, groping after words. "I don't know how to explain it except that they're everything to me. We lived together in Northnest. I promised to protect them. Ever since I was little I knew I was there to protect them—not just these four, they weren't born when I was little. Northnest was my home, our home, and my place in it was to defend it, defend all the people."

"Ah," Thornfire sighed. "You were raised from chickhood to take on this role. I see why you cannot easily abandon it."

"I got them out," Hawkwind went on, having hardly heard him. "They're all that's left, and they need me. I'm all that's left, the only Feathyr remaining. What would I be if I forsook everything the Feathyrs stood for, everything we promised?" She turned her fervent gaze onto Thornfire. "Don't ask me to leave them. If you want me to help you, you must accept that they will be a part of it, too. They are my charge," she whispered. "I decide, so you need to tell me where we're going."

He shook his head. "Much as you wish to be the sole protector and decider of their fate, here in a griffin city or in the wild mountains it cannot be so simple. What if we do not return? What if they die on our journey?"

"I don't even know where we're going," she protested.

"Yes, you do," he murmured to her. "You've suspected it for a while, and came to know it in the council chamber."

"Why are you bringing me into this?"

"Because I can."

"You can't force me."

"No, I can't, but your other option is to leave this city, you and your children, alone, and try to survive out there, somehow, without your flight feathers."

Hawkwind felt her throat clench. "Could I let them stay here, temporarily, while we're gone? Might Starbright be able to take care of them?"

"She could."

"But then what if we don't return?"

Thornfire didn't speak for several heartbeats.

"She would have to hide them, right? They aren't allowed to stay in the city," Hawkwind said. "She couldn't hide them forever, and if discovered, she'd be punished, and they'd be kicked out or killed. She might be exiled. She'd be right in the position I was in. If she tried to fly them, one at a time, to a human city, there's no telling what would become of them—not all places are safe and not all humans take in orphans, rather like griffins, I see—and if she got caught, she'd be punished."

"But where we're going is quite dangerous," Thornfire reminded her. "If they come, they could be killed. They are tiny and defenseless, and we have much to do."

The door to the kitchen area creaked, making Hawkwind and Thornfire look up from their quiet conversation. Starbright eyed them through the gap, and then pushed it the rest of the way open and inched into the room. Thornfire's expression darkened as she slunk down to her belly, feathers and fur totally flat in submission. She laid her head all the way down onto the floor and looked up at her master with pleading eyes.

"Let me come," she begged. "I'll watch the children. I'll take care of them while you all do whatever it is you're going to do."

Hawkwind heard a growl growing in Thornfire's chest.

"You're going to find Uncle Thornwing, aren't you?" she went on. "I want to come. I'll help. I'll do everything you say. I'll make and guard a camp and feed the human chicks, so whenever you take breaks from searching you have a safe spot to come back to. That way, we won't be breaking any rules here, and the human chicks won't be risked travelling with you while you're searching."

Thornfire didn't speak.

"It sounds like a good suggestion to me," Hawkwind offered. "It would be a compromise between all possible negative extremes. The children would be in some danger, but not hiding illegally in the city. Starbright would be in some danger, too, but not doing anything illegal. Thornfire and Rainsoft and I would still be risking our lives, but we'd have a watched camp to return to, where food and safety would await us, and I wouldn't be parted completely from my charges. I vote that Starbright comes."

"There is no voting," Thornfire snapped. "I am in charge. Anyone who doesn't like that is free to leave the griffin territories and never return."

He stood and glared down at Starbright, who remained on her belly, just looking up at him with humble eyes.

"Apprentices," he growled, stalking away towards the kitchen. As he exited, he cast three more words over his shoulder. "You can come."

Starbright beamed at Hawkwind in silent joy.

The warming stones were fading, but they had heated the rock house well, and cuddled up with the four children Hawkwind was pleasantly warm. It had taken a while to get to sleep, as the children had slipped into another spate of weeping as they settled down to bed. Hawkwind had spent some time comforting them and squelching her own urge to mourn.

She knew well enough what had triggered it. They had new clothes, a bath, plentiful food, and a warm place to sleep. After so many days of stress the pressure had finally eased. Life had moved a bit back towards normal. They started to think that life would go on, but everything they associated with a happy normal life was missing. They were having trouble adjusting, and they wouldn't get time to adjust any further, because they would all shortly be back on a trail in the wilds.

Now it was deepest night, but a hollow sound had awakened Hawkwind. She checked the children; all were slumbering well. Thornfire and Starbright had their own little rooms at the back of the house, carved into the mountain itself. Rainsoft was sleeping alone on the other side of the room. Hawkwind stared at him, and after a few moments the mournful sounds came again. He shuddered.

Careful not to wake them, Hawkwind disentangled herself from the children and piled them together on the cushion she'd been sleeping on. They clung to each other in sleep. She adjusted their blankets and walked silently to Rainsoft. His eyes were closed, but his muscles twitched, and he made the sound again, a little louder and longer. Behind her, one of the children whimpered.

Hawkwind lowered herself beside Rainsoft and put a wing around him. Immediately, his whole body jerked and he wiggled towards her, still asleep. He huddled under her wing like a fledgling, and she hugged him close. Now that he was clean, she could see that he was a charcoal black with a white underside streaked with grey. In size he was smaller than her, which wasn't unusual for a male close in age to her. He made the soft chirps nestlings make with their parents, and Hawkwind wondered if perhaps he was younger than she'd thought, and where his parents might be, or what had happened to them. How had he gotten that neck wound, when the rest of him seemed scar and injury-free?

She hugged him a bit tighter and relaxed down to sleep, feeling the pulse of his heart. The last time she'd curled up with another griffin had been the night before the attack on Northnest. Now, her sister Hawkcall and their friend Eagleye were dead, eaten by the drakes. Perhaps she should have died with them, but if she had, she wouldn't have gotten the children out, and she wouldn't now be curled up in warmth and comfort, hearing the heartbeat of another. She wanted to live. Was it cowardly, selfish? Hawkwind didn't know. She strangled her sobs in her throat and drifted off to sleep.

She woke when her subconscious noticed that Rainsoft had stiffened and his heart rate and breathing changed. When she opened her eyes she saw that he was staring at her, orange eyes wide: puzzled, alarmed, and pleased all at once.

"You didn't seem to be sleeping well," she told him gently.

Hawkwind doubted that he understood anything she said, but had decided she'd speak normally to him anyway. Her tone would probably convey some meaning, she hoped. At any rate, he didn't scream or bolt, so she preened his neck feathers gently, a sign of friendship that she hoped he'd recognize. Wherever he came from, maybe it meant the same thing there.

The sun was just starting to rise, softly illuminating the room as Hawkwind looked around. The children were still sleeping, huddled in front of the cold warming stone. Muted clanking and the rustle of canvas turned Hawkwind's attention to the kitchen. Before she could get up to investigate, hesitant tugging on her neck feathers froze her in place. Rainsoft had returned her gesture of friendship, and was preening her in return.

He stopped as she looked down at him. His orange eyes were calmer than she'd yet seen. He lifted a hand and made a movement with his fingers. Hawkwind, puzzled, shook her head, and he repeated it. She watched carefully as he did it again. Nervously, she lifted a hand and tried to mimic it. For the first time, she saw him smile.

"What are you trying to tell me?" she whispered.

He started to write with his finger on the floor, tracing out shapes, letters, but stopped abruptly and looked back up at her, frustrated.

"I know," she sighed. "I can't read your writing, and you can't read mine."

Rainsoft reached out a hand and clasped her upper arm firmly, warmly. He leaned in and briefly nibbled her neck feathers again. Then he smiled again. There were no words, but she knew what he meant, and she smiled back.

Rainsoft curled up again as Hawkwind went to investigate the kitchen.

"Ah, you're up," Thornfire commented.

Eight canvas and leather packs were lined up on the food preparation table. The smallest was no bigger than a melon. The largest was fit for an adult male griffin. Hawkwind assumed Thornfire would be carrying that one. Although females were larger than males, both Starbright and Hawkwind were young, and still smaller than Thornfire. Rainsoft was even smaller.

"We'll have to go on foot, since you and Rainsoft can't fly yet," Thornfire was grumbling. "Damn them and their feather-cutting. It will make this venture much more difficult. I hope you can run."

"Where are we going?" Hawkwind asked timidly.

Thornfire slammed a bundle down on the table and glared at her. "Are you an idiot? We're going to Snow-in-lee. How has that escaped you?"

Starbright glanced apologetically at Hawkwind but kept her bill buttoned and continued filling packs. Hawkwind left the kitchen and returned to where she'd slept. Kassandra was shivering, so she lay down with the children and let them snuggle against her sides, where they slept on, and Hawkwind trembled.

She must have fallen back asleep. When Starbright shook her shoulder, morning light was streaming in through the east window.

"There's food in the kitchen," the apprentice said. "Then we'll be leaving."

Hawkwind made sure the children and Rainsoft ate, although she had trouble forcing the food down herself. After that, they gathered in the living area and Thornfire handed out the packs. Hawkwind ensured that the children's packs all fit comfortably. Of all of them, Rainsoft looked the most dubious. No one could explain to him where they were going. The children had cheered when Hawkwind told them they were finally going to Snow-in-lee.

"It will be dangerous," she corrected them. "Griffins don't live there anymore."

"Then why are we going?" Rikah demanded.

"What does?" Jessika asked instead.

"Large snakes live there," Hawkwind explained. "We are going to find Thornfire's brother, and to get two magic stones."

"Magic stones?" Rikah scoffed.

"If we get them," Hawkwind went on, "we can live here in South-

Starbright

scree. If we don't, the griffins won't let us stay, and we'll have to go search for another home someplace else."

"I don't like snakes," Karo whispered.

"You won't have to see them," she assured him. "You four will be staying with Starbright in the camp we make near Snow-in-lee. You won't be in any danger."

"What about the rainbow drakes?" Karo whimpered.

"They don't live in the mountains. Besides, Starbright will be there to protect you if there's anything threatening."

"That's right, I will," the apprentice chimed in with a grin.

"She's not very big," Rikah grumbled.

"But she can do magic," Hawkwind countered.

"Magic?" Karo whispered.

"When we have time, I'll show you," Starbright said.

Thornfire coughed behind them. "We need to get going now. We'll be walking out of the town today, heading east," Thornfire explained. "To make the best time, I suggest that each child ride one of us griffins."

There was an immediate argument over who would get to ride Hawkwind.

"Here now," Thornfire shouted. "It will be settled by weight: largest child on largest griffin and so on. That means Rikah on me, Jessika on Hawkwind, Karo on Starbright, and Kassandra on Rainsoft."

The children moaned and complained, but soon enough each one was standing by his or her assigned mount. Rainsoft looked puzzled until the children began climbing on. Kassandra put a calm hand on his shoulder.

"Dear Rainsoft," she said softly, "may I ride on your back?"

Although still looking a little puzzled, the dark grey griffin knelt like the others, and the little girl climbed up, hooking her hands and feet under his new leather harness.

"Through the city I will go first. Then Hawkwind, Rainsoft, and Starbright will go last. You all will obey everything I say instantaneously, understood?"

Hawkwind, Starbright, and some of the children looked dubiously at Rainsoft.

"Ah," Thornfire revised. "I realize there may be some communication problems. We will," he paused, "well, we'll deal with it, somehow. Any questions?"

No one spoke.

"Then let's go."

Thornfire led them out of the house they'd spent that one comfy night in, waited until they had all exited, and turned to lock his door. He set a hand on the door frame, frowned and muttered a word, and the stone door frame and wooden door fused together. Hawkwind gasped, blinking and trying to get her eyes to understand what she'd just seen. Rainsoft and the children, too, stared with confusion and awe.

"Someday I'll be able to do that," Starbright confided to Hawkwind.

"Not until you get your water spells under control," Thornfire repeated. "No merging magic until then."

He led them off through the city. Curious griffins walked or flew over for a look at the strange procession. When it became clear that they weren't hostile, the children began waving to the puzzled griffins.

"One more thing before we go," Thornfire announced, stopping in front of what appeared to be a shop of some kind. "Wait here. Young Rikah, please get down for a moment."

The boy slid off his back obediently and stood hugging Hawkwind's foreleg while Thornfire went alone into the shop. There was lettering over the door, but as it was in the written language of South-scree, she couldn't read it.

"Starbright," she ventured, "will you teach me to read and write your language?"

The young golden griffin smiled. "Of course, Hawkwind, I'd love to. We can work on it when we stop to camp for the night."

Thornfire emerged from the shop with a bundle in hand and stuffed it into his pack. "Now, we're ready. We'll be traveling through a relatively safe area initially. It's covered by our patrols daily. Hawkwind and Rainsoft will need to be with Starbright or myself at all times, otherwise there could be confusion about rogues again, and we don't want that. To help ensure your safety, wear these."

Thornfire handed out painted wooden pendants strung on thick cord. Starbright nodded confidently and put hers on without delay. Hawkwind and Rainsoft followed suit. There were even smaller ones for the children to wear.

"These tokens advertise that you are abroad on South-scree business," Thornfire explained. "They should keep you safer. All the other griffin cities recognize them. Don't lose them. Of course, they'll do nothing against predators or talis."

Hawkwind followed Thornfire as he resumed the walk through the city. They reached the edge, passing through a gate in the rocky wall that encircled the settlement, and stepped out onto the wild mountain slopes.

A week passed as Thornfire led the group on foot through the mountains. Their path took them along rocky cliff edges with fatal drops on one or both sides, up or down steep hillsides, and down into small forested valleys. They walked all day with the children sometimes astride their mounts, and sometimes trotting along with them or running about to pick any edible plants they saw. One or two of the griffins would hunt every other day or so. On the seventh night they camped, as they usually did, in one of the forested valleys.

"Head," Kassandra commanded, and Rainsoft quickly patted his own head. "Wing," she said next, and he lifted a wing. "Wings," she modified, and he lifted both of them.

Throughout their travelling, little quiet Kassandra had spent most her time riding Rainsoft and talking to him, teaching him to understand spoken language.

"Stand up," she ordered, and he did it. "Sit, lie down, walk over there, come here, run that way, run to your left, back up."

Hawkwind hid a chuckle. It was comical to see the comparatively big griffin so eagerly taking orders from the tiny girl. Hawkwind could only imagine how excited he must be to be starting to know a little of what his companions were saying.

"Good job," the girl praised him. "You're really doing great."

"So are you, Kassandra," Hawkwind called over to them. "Thanks to you, Rainsoft is learning how to understand us."

Hawkwind twitched as Starbright poked her with her wing wrist. "And you would soon be learning to understand him," she scolded, "if you would pay attention. Now, here is the spelling for 'complicated.'"

Hawkwind obediently returned her attention to the marks she and Starbright had been drawing in the dirt with their claw tips. Frowning a little, she copied the spelling. She'd learned the letters of the wild griffin language, and now she'd advanced to learning how to write words she already knew in one script with a different one.

"I'm ashamed to say that I think Rainsoft is making more progress than I am," she murmured.

"Now write, 'it's too complicated,'" Starbright commanded.

"There has to be a better way to understand him," Hawkwind mused as she followed Starbright's directions. "He knows how to write. He knows language. Someone must have taught it to him, but that person didn't teach him how to understand verbal language. It's strange. There must be something else."

"Now, 'it's too complicated to explain.'"

"Do you think that's it?"

"Do I think what's what?" Starbright asked.

"It's too complicated to explain? His history, where he came from, why he's alone: has anyone asked him in writing?"

Both young females looked over at Rainsoft, where Kassandra was trying to get him to understand a new verbal concept by drawing pictures in the dirt and acting things out. The charcoal grey griffin watched intently, and would give a short nod or shake of his head to indicate his understanding. He also sometimes made a distinctive movement with his hand, which Kassandra apparently understood to mean that he wanted her to play-act the subject again.

"That's it," Hawkwind gasped. "That's what he was doing that night at Thornfire's, and I've seen glimpses of similar things during the trip."

"You've lost me," Starbright admitted.

"He talks with his hands, with gestures."

Hawkwind got up and walked over to the griffin student with his child teacher, interrupting them.

"Rainsoft," she began, and he gave his short little nod. The first thing Kassandra had done was to teach him the spoken names of everybody in the group, including his own. Hawkwind hoped he knew enough spoken language now to understand her. "You," she pointed at him, getting another nod, "talk," another nod, "with your hands." She pointed to them.

His expression in return was a smile, but with hints of both relief and exasperation that it had taken her so long to get it. He nodded.

Hawkwind stared, "teach me." The words were out before she realized it.

His eyes widened. Then he nodded. Starbright came over to sit with them.

"I'd like to learn, too," the apprentice mage said.

"Rainsoft and I are trying to focus," Kassandra said firmly.

"We should take turns," Starbright instructed. "We'll take turns being teachers and students. If we work together, we can all learn."

The princess Jessika walked over then, holding a big leaf cupped like a bowl, filled with pieces of cooked meat that had been pulled off that evening's dinner by master chef Rikah.

"What are you doing now?" she asked.

"Well," Hawkwind began, "some of us are learning to write, and some are learning to listen, and some are learning to watch."

"It's sounds complicated," the girl responded with childish bluntness. "Kassie, I brought you your dinner."

Kassandra took the leaf-bowl into her lap and began eating with her fingers.

"So, can I watch?" Jessika asked.

"Certainly," Hawkwind told her.

The girl scampered off and returned with a bundle. She sat down out the way and continued work on her current project. It seemed that Thornfire had noticed how tender human feet were. The bundle Thornfire had bought on the way out of the city had been full of sections of leather and cords, and some sharp tools that Hawkwind had initially been concerned about. Human skin was remarkably vulnerable to cutting edges. Thornfire had offered the bundle to the children and Jessika had insisted she be allowed to work. Hawkwind had grudgingly given in. Karo already had a pair of sandals made by the girl, and she was hard at work on Kassandra's pair. So far she hadn't cut herself more than a little nick or two.

Kassandra, busy with eating, watched as Hawkwind began trying to learn how to talk with her hands.

"Yes?" she prompted, and made the little head nod that Rainsoft used.

He did it back at her.

"No?"

He gave her the little head-shake, and she copied it. That was easy enough. Humans and griffins all used similar gestures. Hawkwind tried to think of what to ask next.

"Go?"

He gave her a gesture for that, having learned the word from Kassandra already. Starbright and Hawkwind practiced the gesture.

"Stay, eat, wait, come, help, please, stop, sleep," Hawkwind prompted one after another.

"We'd better review what we've learned," Starbright suggested, after several minutes had passed and Kassandra was done with her food.

Rainsoft quizzed them by giving the gesture, and they spoke the word. Then Kassandra said the words aloud, and the two lady griffins gave the gestures. Jessika even tried some, too, although she'd spent most of her time focusing on her sandal making. Starbright quizzed Hawkwind on her writing after that. Kassandra quizzed Rainsoft again. As the last of the food disappeared down human and griffin throats, the evening darkened to true night, and all began to feel ready for sleep.

Hawkwind helped the four children curl up between Starbright and Rainsoft. Thornfire stood alone at the dying fire, and Hawkwind went to stand briefly with him.

"You all are much at work, learning new things I wish I could spend time on, too," he told her as she sat beside him.

"Thank you for helping Karo and Rikah learn to prepare the food, though," she said sincerely.

"They are good young humans," he smiled. "Rikah indeed has the hands and mind of a true crafter. What he will come to make, I can't predict."

"His father was a blacksmith."

"Perhaps he absorbed some talent there, or was born with it."

"And Karo is helping, too?"

"Ah, that one."

"Yes? Is he being obedient? He is a little reserved, but a kind boy."

Thornfire chuckled. "Not to worry. I'm not sure what will become of him."

"Why do you say that? Is something wrong?"

He smiled at her. "There is something about him. It is small and low still, but like the stirring deep within a seed, or the first touch of light on the dawn horizon, I think something much bigger will come of it. Give him time. I will help him."

"What are you saying, Elder Thornfire?"

"He may have power, Hawkwind. It may be that unconscious knowledge of it is making him wary. He may know there is something within, but not what, and he is waiting: knowing it will surely bloom, but not when."

"A magician's power?" she breathed. "Like the kind that brought down the drakes on Northnest?"

"Power is power. Many things can be done with it, including death and destruction, including kindness and creation."

"There were no magicians in Northnest. How could he have that power?"

Thornfire shook his head. "It takes one to make one. Without a teacher, latent power will usually remain latent. Power calls to power. I expect there were humans and griffins both in Northnest with latent power. Without a master to see it and coax it out, it would have faded away."

Hawkwind gulped. "Could I have it, too?"

Thornfire looked critically at her. She got the strange feeling that he was looking inside her. "If there was power in you when you were born, it has faded, Hawkwind. I'm sorry. I can't see any now. It's rare in the first place. I am one of only a handful of mages at South-scree."

Hawkwind squinted down into the fire, not sure what to say. She couldn't be sad to not have something she'd never wanted, but for a moment she'd thought she might have something that would help her situation.

"You should get some rest," Thornfire instructed. "Our path will soon become more difficult."

"Why is that?"

"We must travel on foot, so we cannot pass over the next range of mountains between us and Snow-in-lee. Thus, we shall have to go either around or under. Either way will be difficult for different reasons. I will soon have to make the choice. The path will fork by tomorrow evening. Off to bed with you."

She acquiesced. "Good night."

"Good night, Hawkchild."

The path was sometimes wide enough to walk side by side. When it was, Hawkwind alternated between walking by Starbright, and walking by Rainsoft. She talked with them both, trying to learn whatever she could. It was hard to communicate with gestures while walking, but Kassandra chattered on endlessly at Rainsoft anyway, and Hawkwind supposed it was at least giving him some kind of listening practice.

Jessika, when she was on Hawkwind, had her partly completed sandals in her lap, but still contributed occasional thoughts. Rikah generally ran about on his own legs, gathering plants, sticks, stones, or anything else that looked like it could be eaten, thrown, or broken into bits. Thornfire had taken to having Karo ride him, and sending Starbright up on occasional reconnoitering assignments, more for her own practice than need.

As Thornfire had promised, dusk was upon them when they reached a forking of their path. "We'll stop here for the night," he announced. "There is a good camping site just there."

"The trail splits," Starbright observed.

"Yes, and tomorrow we must take one of the paths to our fate. Can you hunt for us again, Starbright?"

She seemed to clamp her bill shut on whatever else it was she'd wanted to say. "Yes, Master."

Starbright took a short run and leapt off the nearest cliff. Jessika immediately set about making a fire in the pit Thornfire indicated while the other children located the softest bits of ground for them to sleep on. Rainsoft followed the children and began clearing the disused site of any branches or rocks that had taken up residence there.

"So," Hawkwind began tentatively to Thornfire, "what are the two options?"

He didn't seem to mind the question. "The right trail would take us around the highest peaks at a lower altitude. It is longer but has less altitude gain than the left trail, which would take us through a pass between the peaks, and then through a long tunnel under the mountain."

"They're both dangerous, aren't they?" Hawkwind guessed.

The sound he made was not quite a chuckle. "In different ways, yes. Besides that both trails are old and rarely used by griffins, we must consider the terrain, weather, and who the trails are used by. Plus, there is your situation."

"My situation?"

"There are drakes after you, aren't there?"

"You think they'd still be looking for the children and me?"

"How would I know, daughter of Hawk?" he pled. "I've never even seen one, only read of them. You said they were controlled by magicians."

"Yes, that's what I heard, when we were attacked."

"Do the magicians know you and the children escaped?"

She shook her head. "The drakes can't talk, and no one else saw me escape."

"That you know of," he corrected. "The ways of wizards are wide and subtle indeed. Why might these people want you?"

"I don't know," she stuttered. "Only because they wanted to kill everyone and take the castle."

Thornfire gazed off down the trails for a few breaths. "My dear Hawkchild," he sighed. "There is something you're not telling me."

Hawkwind's heart pounded and she felt sweat break out between her toes and across her cere. Her skin tingled with anxiety, as though every feather was being lightly tugged on. When she didn't reply, the mage broke the silence.

"You don't have to tell me now, but I hope someday you will trust me enough to do so. I do ask, if your presence is likely to bring more danger down upon us, make mention. We will have enough danger with what we're walking into already." With the rapid twitch of a raptor, he pointed his bill down the left trail. "I think we'd better go through the passes, and under the mountain. Carry on your teaching and learning, Hawkwind, and you might at some point wish to tell Rainsoft what we're doing out here. I do believe he still has little idea."

Thornfire trotted off down the left trail before Hawkwind could get her bill unstuck enough to say something. What she would have said, she didn't know, but his shadow disappeared around a corner in the trail and she found herself feeling like she should have asked him or told him something else.

Rikah had the fire going. Jessika was fitting her second set of finished sandals onto Kassandra's feet. Karo was staring into the fire, poking it with a stick, and frowning. Rainsoft, too, was staring at the fire, sensitive pupils contracted almost to pinpoints, expression calm and neutral. Hawkwind sat down beside him.

"Rainsoft," she began.

He made a tiny warble of acknowledgement and cocked his head at her.

"Do you know," she began, speaking slowly, "where we're going?"

"That's too hard for him," Kassandra commented.

Hawkwind quashed her annoyance and tried again. "We walk," she said, using the gesture for walk that she'd learned from him the previous evening. Then she pointed, "that way."

He started to get up.

"No, no, no," she corrected. "I'm sorry."

Rainsoft made the gesture for apology. She copied it.

"Problems?" Starbright called as she landed just at the edge of the fire with a bled and dressed buck mountain-deer. "Let's write it out after we eat."

The golden griffin walked into the light carrying one leg of the prey animal. Rikah took it from her and placed it on a wide flat rock in the fire. The children gathered around to wait until it was cooked while the griffins went into the semi-dark to clean up the rest of the carcass. Thornfire even flew in to join them, right on time. Four hungry griffins finished a mountain-deer in under a minute except for the pessimistic picking around the joints for missed shreds. They were hunting every night, one beast split among them. It meant they didn't eat huge meals every few days as they would normally, but it kept them going well enough. After the food, all four rejoined the children around the fire.

"What did you want to ask?" Starbright prompted.

"I think Rainsoft deserves to know where we're going," Hawkwind said.

"Ah," Starbright nodded. She wrote in the dirt, and Hawkwind had learned enough that she could read the words, although she wouldn't have been able to write it herself. "Has anyone told you where we're going?"

Rainsoft shook his head.

"So you don't know?" Starbright wrote and said aloud.

Head shake.

"Have you ever heard of Snow-in-lee?"

Rainsoft stared at what she'd written, and stared some more, and stared some more. It was as if she'd cast some kind of griffin-petrifaction magic on him. Hawkwind watched his visible face-skin around his eyes whiten with fear or shock or something else. He started to tremble.

"We're going there?" he wrote rapidly and messily.

"Yes," Hawkwind said aloud.

He shook his head firmly and repeatedly, and made a sharp and vigorous gesture along with it, over and over.

"Rainsoft," Hawkwind breathed, starting to reach for him, but he was backing away, and she started to worry he was going to bolt.

He started saying something, sitting back on his hind legs, hands working rapidly as he gestured out whatever he wanted to say. Even if his whole body hadn't been shaking, there was no way Hawkwind could have understood a word.

"We can't understand. You're talking too fast," Hawkwind tried to tell him calmly.

"Stop, Rainsoft," Kassandra commanded. "Write."

"Yes, write," Hawkwind agreed, giving him the gesture for it as well, since she knew that one, along with "please."

Rainsoft slapped his hands against the ground in frustration, warbling with impatience. He swept away Starbright's words and began writing rapidly. Starbright leaned in and spoke as he wrote for everyone's ears.

"Why are we going to Snow-in-lee?" he wrote.

"Long explanation," Starbright said as she wrote the reply. "Thornfire," she pointed, "brother missing there," she wrote. "I," she pointed to herself, "helping my master and everyone," she wrote. "Hawkwind," she pointed, "needs Sunstone to be free," she wrote. "Children," she waved her hand at them, "go with Hawkwind."

Starbright paused. She hadn't explained Rainsoft, and he slapped his hand down.

"Why me?" he wrote, gesturing angrily.

"You get the Moonstone, you can stay in South-scree with us forever," Starbright wrote and said.

This didn't seem to impress him. "What is the Moonstone?" he wrote and gestured.

"Long story," Starbright answered. "Magic stone."

"Where is it?" he asked.

"In Snow-in-lee," she told him.

He shivered all over. "No, no, no, no," he repeated again. A strangled cry came from his throat and he lashed his head from side to side. "Death," he wrote finally, giving the gesture for it with his other hand, and repeating it over and over, more and more sloppily, until he fisted his claws on the ground, bent over and trembling.

"Leaving," he scratched out. "Goodbye."

Rainsoft turned to go, but Hawkwind leapt out and grabbed him. "No, don't go," she pled. "Rainsoft, stay."

He didn't try to hurt her, but he did flinch away and try to wiggle out of her grasp, which hurt her in a different way.

"Please," she begged, not sure why she wanted so badly for him to stay, but knowing she wanted to help him, and couldn't bear the thought of him wandering alone in the wilderness. "Stay with us. Tell me. What do you know about Snow-in-lee? Why are you so afraid?"

He finally shook her off, but didn't run. He faced her and made three very clear gestures. One was "speak" and one "fast." Hawkwind assumed the other had been "too" or "you."

She told him "sorry."

Rainsoft slowly faced the fire again. Starbright read out what he wrote next in the dirt. "You mustn't go to Snow-in-lee. You will be imprisoned and killed."

"Imprisoned?" Hawkwind echoed.

Starbright went on reading when Rainsoft had wiped away his

words and continued. "I was born in Snow-in-lee. I lived there. I escaped a little while ago."

"What?" Hawkwind gasped. "There are still griffins there?" She darted a look at Thornfire. "Did you know this?"

The old mage had remained strangely calm through the whole discussion. Now, he gave Hawkwind a languid blink of his eyes. "I knew Rainsoft was from Snow-in-lee," he nodded.

"What? How?"

"He smelled of it, especially when he was first brought in. Since he's been washed, not as much anymore."

"Smelled of it? How do you know what Snow-in-lee smells like? You've been there?"

He nodded, stretching his back and popping his joints. "My brother and I went there several times, but we never went deep into the city. We were never seen or caught, but we came to know the scent all too well. There aren't many things we griffins can smell, but talis are one of them. If anything could be said to be the mortal enemy of griffins, it is they, and our ability to scent them is a vital line of defense."

Starbright was writing and erasing furiously for Rainsoft's benefit.

"When we were near Snow-in-lee, we observed signs that made us suspect some griffins were still there, but we never saw any. I am most curious about the situation. I knew Rainsoft would be immense help if he could get to talking about it. Rainsoft's arrival was the catalyst for my decision to go after my brother now. Your arrival," he gave Hawkwind a nod, "was a convenient coincidence for me. I needed the help, although the human children I admit, do complicate things slightly."

It took another minute for Starbright to finish conveying everything to Rainsoft, but he was already shaking his head.

"If you go," he wrote, "you will die."

"You escaped," Thornfire countered. "How?"

The charcoal grey griffin grunted, writing, "long story."

Thornfire chuckled. "We have time."

Rainsoft had lowered his head. His shoulders were still trembling. Hawkwind extended a wing and put it around him.

"I think that's enough for one night, Elder Thornfire," she tried. "Rainsoft," she called, and he looked at her. "Will you stay?"

He did hesitate, but not for as long as he could have, before he nodded.

"Most excellent," Thornfire said.

Hawkwind had to resist giving him a dirty look. As it was, her neck feathers still rose a little in perturbation, despite her best efforts to keep them flat. Rainsoft had put his head down, curling up under her wing, and she made no move to dislodge him. The children came with their blankets and tucked themselves under Hawkwind's or Rainsoft's outside wings. Starbright smiled with amusement and positioned herself between her master and Hawkwind—a diplomatic move in Hawkwind's opinion—before drifting off to sleep.

Hawkwind stayed awake a while longer, watching the fire die down, and seeing the glowing coals reflected in Thornfire's hooded eyes.

Chapter 10
The Tunnel

"We shall go through the tunnel," Thornfire announced the next morning as they gathered at the fork in the road. "It will keep us away from any drakes that might still be flitting about and looking for Hawkwind and her nestlings."

He led them down the trail.

"What's in there?" Hawkwind called to him.

"Bats, bugs, all manner of little furry critters," he answered lightly.

"What's in there that's dangerous?" Jessika corrected from astride Hawkwind.

"Besides colder temperatures, darkness, cave ins, pits, slippery rocks, things to bump your head on, and plenty of things to trip on, you mean?"

"Yes," the girl dignified with a reply.

He cleared his throat. "Snow-screamers," he admitted. "There's likely a large colony of snow-screamers, and possibly other things like wolves and snow cats and maybe even bears, but they'll probably leave griffins alone. The children will need to stay close."

"What are snow-screamers?" Jessika asked.

"Do you know what a monkey is?" Starbright called from behind them.

The girl twisted in her seat. "I've seen drawings."

"Snow-screamers look like part monkey, and part cat. They're about the size of a large dog, with wide paws like snowshoes, and they usually travel in packs. They have long, grey, white, and light brown fur; big eyes; and very sharp teeth."

"They're dangerous?"

"If they mob a griffin before it can get off the ground, they win," Starbright admitted. "In the tunnels, we probably won't be able to escape them, if they find us."

"Maybe we should go around instead," Hawkwind suggested, unnerved by the description. "What's so dangerous on the other path?"

"Rock dogs, and possibly snow-screamers out there, too," Thornfire answered, feet not faltering in his continued trek down the path through the pass and towards the tunnel.

"What are rock dogs like?" Jessika wanted to know.

"Sort of like wolves," Starbright provided, "but instead of fur they have a thick layer of body fat, and skin so tough that our claws can't get through it. Since we can't fight them, we have to run. If we can't get airborne, they chase us. They have great endurance, so they run their prey to exhaustion. Then they eat. Plus, they aren't afraid of fire because their skin is so thick it doesn't really burn them."

"We'd have to post a watch all night long," Thornfire complained.

"Snow-screamers fear fire?" Hawkwind checked.

"That's right. They don't like bright lights and unknown smells and things," Starbright told her.

"That should make them easier to handle than the rock dogs then."

"Except that they're incredibly territorial," Thornfire said. "If they detect us, they will wait for any opportunity to eat us."

"What if we can't find wood for a fire down in the tunnel?" Jessika asked.

"There are other ways than wood to make warmth and light," Starbright commented. "Thornfire and I are with you; we can handle everything."

"But all you children, stay on your mounts at all times," Thornfire emphasized. "No walking or running or anything on your own feet. You can get down only when we've made camp. You'll also need to stay quiet; snow-screamers have excellent hearing. Understood?"

"Yes, Thornfire."

"Uh-huh."

"Okay."

"I understand."

"Everyone, be watchful," the mage went on. "And try to be silent."

They walked on for a while in that silence, descending for the start between two tumbled walls of rock. The only sound besides their feet was the popping and dragging of Jessika pushing her thick twine through leather as she worked on sandals for Rikah. Above them, their view of the white sky narrowed.

They stopped at midday by a thin waterfall that cascaded down one rock wall. The children were allowed to get down, drink, and see to bodily needs. Thornfire instructed everyone to fill their water skins before going on.

"We will encounter underground streams," he told them. "We'll have to drink from them when we run out of this water, but not every stream will be drinkable, so it's best to take all the water we can."

"What about food?" Hawkwind asked.

"We may have to resort to eating bats or other small animals. If we survive an attack of snow-screamers, we can eat them."

"Ew," Jessika commented under her breath.

"Bats aren't bad," Thornfire said. "I've had them before. Crunchy. Snow-screamers are stringy and tough, but edible except for the guts, which tend to be full of parasites."

"You'll survive," Hawkwind told the girl. "I expect Thornfire and Starbright's magic can cook anything you want to eat."

"Of course it can," Starbright smiled as Karo climbed back onto her. "I'll cook anything you need. I'm good with fire."

"Why have we been making a real fire then, every night?" Hawkwind asked as the group moved off again.

"Magic takes energy. If we don't have to, we don't use it."

The trail was winding now among the peaks, sometimes climbing up steep trails, and other times twisting along little narrow valleys. They group stayed quiet, speaking only in whispers, as all sounds were taken up and bounced around the crags by echoes and the wind. They camped for one more night before entering the tunnels in a shallow cave some yards away from the tunnel entrance. Thornfire forbid them from going to look at it.

"No scent near the tunnel," he said. "We want a comfortable night's sleep don't we? Snow-screamers have an excellent sense of smell, too. It's risky enough without giving them a trail back to us. Now, make camp here. There's wood, so build a fire. Starbright and I will go hunting. Hawkwind, Rainsoft, guard the camp."

Rainsoft nodded with understanding and the two mages went off to hunt on the wing. Jessika presented Rikah with his sandals. The children got the fire going and prepared their blankets. Hawkwind and Rainsoft sat with the fire at their backs, looking out of the cave into the darkness and waiting. Without Starbright to translate, it was difficult to talk, but Hawkwind decided she wouldn't let that stop them.

"Are you all right?" she asked slowly.

Rainsoft eyed her for a moment, and then gave a roll of his head that suggested "somewhat," to her.

Then, he raised his hands and slowly made a few gestures. Hawkwind copied them and made a guess. "Are you all right?" she said, doing the gestures along with them.

Rainsoft smiled and nodded at her. She smiled back, and he asked her in earnest with his hands, if she was all right. Still smiling, she copied his head roll. He gave her some silent laughter in reply. For a few minutes Hawkwind practiced the gestures, memorizing them so she could ask again any time she needed to.

Then, with a combination of words and gestures, she asked, "Are you going to Snow-in-lee?"

His visage turned serious and he made the gesture she'd seen the previous night, the one that meant "death."

"Death," she said, copying it. "You think we'll die."

He nodded, slowly and simply, not breaking his gaze at her. Hawkwind didn't know what to say, but after a few moments he made another statement.

"I will go."

She could only nod, humbled by his bravery. "Thank you," she told him.

His smile, conveyed mainly through his eyes and the lift of his feathers, since griffin bills were rather immobile, was soft, and for the first time since her entire community had been killed, Hawkwind felt like she had an ally, a wing mate. An empty place inside her filled, and anxiety she didn't know she was carrying melted away like a heavy blanket slipping off her back when standing up. Rainsoft's released sigh of a breath suggested to her that maybe he was feeling the same thing.

Thornfire and Starbright landed with a thump in front of them, bearing a big mountain sheep each. Hawkwind's mouth watered instantly.

"Good, nothing attacked," Thornfire commented. "Take a haunch to the little ones and let's eat our fill."

Hawkwind didn't hesitate to obey, ripping off a hind leg and carrying it to Rikah, who was ready with the dagger to hack into it. Hawkwind returned to the others, who had already started eating, and bit hungrily into one of the beasts. With almost a whole half a beast to herself, she could eat nearly her fill. When they'd finished, Starbright carried away the refuse; hopefully anything attracted by the scent would go to the pile of leavings, and not the bloodstain on the trail.

The four griffins rejoined the four children, who were just starting to eat their cooked dinner, and sat down for the evening lessons. Hawkwind pushed herself to memorize more and more. There was so much she wanted to be able to say. Rainsoft seemed no less ruthless. When her head finally felt full to overflowing with new words and gestures, she cuddled down among her four children and let sleep take her. The fire had been banked so it would burn all night, hopefully keeping away any snow-screamers that might be in the area. The morrow would see the group descending into the tunnel; Hawkwind wanted to be well rested.

The wind made a hollow, moaning sound passing across the tunnel entrance. The four griffins with their human riders stood in front of the gaping hole, preparing to enter.

"Who made this?" Hawkwind whispered to Thornfire.

"After our ancestors were driven from Snow-in-lee, attempts were made to retake it. One of those attempts involved digging out this tunnel, allowing the army to approach unseen and bivouac here before attacking," he answered. "That attempt failed and the tunnels were abandoned. Other things moved in."

"How long of a journey is it, to the other side?" Starbright asked.

"Two weeks."

"Two weeks?" Hawkwind gasped.

"We'll be fine. Snow-in-lee isn't going anywhere."

Thornfire straightened up from where he'd been sorting through a pile of rocks at the side of the road. He held four smooth round stones.

"I'll be relying on you children to hold onto these," he said.

Then his brow creased with concentration, and a moment later all four stones were noticeably emitting light. Thornfire passed a stone to each child; the children examined them with wondering curiosity.

"They'll need daily renewing," he commented. "Starbright or I can handle it."

"I can do this someday?" Karo whispered.

"Not too long from now, I expect, with training," Thornfire nodded. "We should get going. Stay alert. This place is a warren of tunnels, both ones our ancestors dug, and new ones dug by all manner of creatures. I know the way, so follow me, and try to be silent."

Hawkwind watched Thornfire and Karo move into the darkness, only Karo's magic stone pushing back the gloom. Starbright and Rikah followed. The boy had a hard, straight stick he had peeled of bark and taken to carrying around. He brandished it like a sword, prepared to defend against the dangers of the darkness. Hawkwind stepped aside and let a dubious Rainsoft go ahead of her.

"We'll be all right," Jessika whispered to Hawkwind.

Hawkwind smiled reassuringly. "Yes, we will."

She followed the others into the tunnel.

Hawkwind couldn't say how many hours they had been walking. She wasn't exhausted yet, but she guessed they'd been travelling through the tunnels for most of the day. Thornfire led them on in near silence. Kassandra was leaning forward, lying on Rainsoft's back, and whispering into his ear. Rikah and Starbright, too, seemed to be chatting. Hawkwind couldn't see far enough ahead to be sure, but she imagined Thornfire might be lecturing Karo about magic. Princess Jessika, on Hawkwind's back was somehow managing to juggle the light stone and her leather working; she still had to finish a set of sandals for herself, and she was determinedly working without talking or looking up.

The tunnels so far clearly looked to have been carved, but since the time they'd been fresh cut stone, slimes and algae and phosphorescent moss had come to coat many of the rough surfaces. The floor was well trodden, mostly dry except in certain patches, and clean except for dirt, a few stones here and there, and occasional bone fragments. At least the bones were white and brittle: clearly old remains. They hadn't seen anything larger than bats and rats so far—which all the griffins made a point of snatching and swallowing when they could.

Their steps echoed slightly, more when they passed a side tunnel. From time to time, Hawkwind heard drops of water hit the floor somewhere out of sight. The light from the magic stones gave them all long, black shadows that stretched out from them and merged with the deep shadows of the tunnels. Being last in line, Hawkwind's fur and feathers were constantly prickling, and she had to fight the urge to be always watching over her shoulder. She didn't see or hear anything following them, but that logic couldn't stop her brain from inventing all kinds of beasts and enemies that could be following them anyway.

When they finally stopped to sleep, Hawkwind's shoulders and back were a mess of muscle knots. Jessika got to the ground, immediately starting to try on her finished sandals, and Hawkwind stretched, arching and curving her back and extending all limbs. She checked on her wing feather re-growth progress at the same time. During the evening she'd spent in Thornfire's house, she and Rainsoft had received the favor of the others checking their wings to be sure they'd found all the cut feather stubs and pulled them out. New feathers were starting to grow in, but they were only about twenty percent emerged from the sheath. Not that there was anywhere to fly in the tunnels anyway, but she estimated it would still be at least two weeks before even brief fluttering falls would be a possibility.

Thornfire had picked a good camping site, in a short tunnel off of the main tunnel they'd been traveling. A large stone was already in place in the center of the room and Starbright was standing over it, making it emit light and heat. A jog in the side tunnel meant light would be at least partly blocked from reaching the main tunnel. The children were already pulling out their blankets.

"I will check the trash area," Thornfire announced. "Hawkwind, will you watch my back?"

"Of course," she assured him.

Hawkwind followed Thornfire back out into the main tunnel.

"I noticed you took the tail," he whispered.

"I didn't want to risk Rainsoft just deserting us," she said.

"And you wanted to protect him."

"What do you mean?"

"Don't get all defensive," Thornfire replied, and Hawkwind thought she detected a teasing tone to his quiet words. "It's perfectly natural."

She didn't say anything in response, but found herself perturbed and wondered why. The trash area Thornfire had mentioned wasn't far away. A narrow side tunnel went off the main tunnel, ending in a small room with a pit on one side. There was no smell currently, but

Hawkwind could see why it was called a trash room. Old refuse and waste filled the pit, most noticeably old bones.

"There's nothing dangerous around," Thornfire proclaimed after a brief investigation. "We can come here in pairs or trios before sleep, and we'll have to do all our eating here, or in the tunnel leading to this room," Thornfire explained. "Anything smelly that might attract animals needs to be kept away from where we sleep."

They headed back to the campsite and Thornfire watched over it while Hawkwind showed Rainsoft and two of the children the way to the trash room. When they returned, Thornfire took Starbright, who looked exhausted from having powered up the big heat and light stone, and the two other children. After that, Thornfire took Rainsoft to go hunting in the caves. With Starbright already nearly unconscious, Hawkwind stayed behind to guard the camp.

Thornfire came to let them know when the hunt was done, and they again ate in two teams in the tunnel before the trash room. Rainsoft and Thornfire had only managed to collect a bag of bats, but the mage had used his magic to roast a few of them so the children could have cooked meat. Hawkwind still wasn't sure if they would ever be able to safely eat raw meat; she'd never heard of humans doing that.

"Are there a lot of these camps with trash rooms along the tunnel to the other side?" Hawkwind asked Thornfire after they'd all gathered back in the camp.

"There are, and hopefully they will be as unoccupied and safe as this first one," he told her.

"I can't believe armies moved through here."

"You will see, when we get towards the exit, rooms and rooms carved out where they rested. Last I was here, most of those rooms had families of snow-screamers living in them."

"What will we do when we get there?"

"We'll have to sneak past. Don't worry about it now. Get some rest. There are many days yet to travel."

Chapter 11
The Darkness

It was the third night. Hawkwind noticed that Karo had become very quiet, clinging to Thornfire, staring around at the dark walls with wide eyes. The other children, too, were subdued. They ate their meal of roasted bats gloomily but without vocal protest.

"How long will we be in here?" Karo whispered to Jessika as they cuddled up on their blankets.

"I don't know," she said. Her big eyes sought Hawkwind's.

"I want to get out," Rikah complained. "It's always dark."

"I'm scared," Karo added.

Kassandra said nothing, but her knuckles were white where she clutched her blanket.

"When will we get out?" Jessika asked.

Hawkwind debated. She didn't want to lie to them.

"They heard just as well as anyone when I said how long it would take," Thornfire said.

"Human children have a different perception when it comes to time," Hawkwind informed him. "They can't always conceptualize something like 'two weeks.' To them, it might as well be never or now, especially when they're stressed and scared."

Karo started crying. Jessika hugged him as his tears set off Kassandra and Rikah, too. Hawkwind lay down beside them, covering them all with her wings, but that turned out to be the wrong choice. Karo batted away the arms and wings trying to encircle him. His sobbing increased in volume. Thornfire winced.

"Can you quiet him? He'll bring down enemies upon us."

"It's dark," he cried out. "I'm scared."

Kassandra huddled against Hawkwind's side: her hands clenched, teeth chattering, as tears slid silently down her cheeks. Jessika didn't seem to know what to do. She'd pulled up her knees and hugged them with her arms. Her eyes would dart around their cave camp and then back to Hawkwind, over and over.

"I want to go home," Rikah demanded of Thornfire. The little boy's wet face screwed up into a trembling-chinned glare of defiance.

"You can't," Thornfire spat bluntly. "We're going through these caves until we come out on the other side."

"No," howled Karo. "Out, now."

Starbright, who was on watch at the cave entrance hissed back at them, feathers flat with fear. "Quiet," she scolded. "Master Thornfire's right. Sounds echo. You'll bring them down on us."

"I'll increase the light," Thornfire told her. "Maybe it will keep them away."

"Karo," Jessika tried to command. "Come here."

She held out her skinny arms and the little boy tumbled into them, his shaking legs giving way. She snuggled him as he cried, and his voice was muffled a little against her chest.

"Rikah," Hawkwind said firmly and calmly. "You must be brave."

The older boy turned to her, his expression struggling to collapse into sobs while he fought to make it threatening.

"We can't leave now," she went on. "You know how far we've walked. It's a long way. We have to sleep here and keep going. We will get out."

"Master, Hawkwind, Rainsoft," called Starbright. "Here, now. Something's coming."

The three griffins spun about and converged on Starbright, filling the gaps around her and blocking the cave entrance.

"What is it?" Hawkwind asked.

"Shush, let me listen," Thornfire hissed before Starbright could answer.

The light shone bright around their black shadows into the tunnel beyond theirs. Hawkwind heard scratching on the ground and the panting of many breaths. Her neck feathers prickled and her heart rate doubled. An eerie crying whine bounced through the tunnels, echoed by several other cries.

"Snow-screamers," Thornfire rasped. "They're just beyond our light and sight. If the light fails, they'll attack."

"I won't be able to sleep, knowing those things are out there," Starbright shivered.

"When we leave after sleeping, they'll still be waiting. They might brave the light of the small stones," Thornfire grumbled.

"They'd attack from the front and back, wouldn't they?" Hawkwind hazarded.

"Indeed. We're better suited to fighting them right now."

Starbright and Hawkwind stared at him, but Rainsoft didn't seem to have picked up on his subtext.

"Now?" Hawkwind repeated.

"I can dim the light," he shrugged. "We'd eat well."

"Unless they overran us."

He gave her a somber look. "Now that they are so fixated and attracted to us, they will try to overrun us, now, or tomorrow. You've already pointed out the problem with fighting them tomorrow."

A cold weight settled in her chest. She'd felt true battle only a few times before: when Northnest had been attacked, and facing the drakes in the forest. Before that, it had been sparring matches and war games using figures and maps, with the occasional hunting trip, if that counted. All over her body, Hawkwind's feathers lifted, a subconscious response to threat.

"Now is better," she admitted reluctantly.

Rainsoft looked at her questioning.

"Enemies," she told him, "out there. Thornfire will put out the light. They will come. We will kill them."

His jaw tightened. His body quivered. Hawkwind wondered how much fighting experience he had; they hadn't talked about that yet. She still knew very little of his past. Mostly, they had spent time acquiring language so that such things could eventually be talked about.

"How many?" he asked with a gesture.

"How many?" she repeated towards Thornfire.

"Could be dozens, but in close quarters, we'll only have a half a dozen at us at once," he said.

She frowned. How was she supposed to convey that?

"Many," she said helplessly.

Rainsoft reflected her frown and gave a short, nervous nod. Thornfire seemed to take their silence for consent. He looked over at the bright stone and concentrated. The light began to dim, and the children started crying louder.

"That will bring them," he said grimly.

A piercing howl echoed through the tunnels. Dozens of others answered it until the stone halls rang with the chorus. Eyes glimmered in the darkness and Hawkwind began to be able to discern long limbed bodies with matted grey fur. They came closer, into the faint light: their maws open to reveal their needle-like teeth.

Hawkwind extended her claws and gaped her bill in challenge. They others did the same, starting to hiss a threat cry. It didn't seem to impress the snow-screamers. More filed into the tunnel: making a block of slowly weaving enemies.

"Aim for the eyes," Thornfire advised. "Don't break ranks. If even one gets through, the human children will not survive."

The mass of snow-screamers inched closer. One darted out and made a passing slash. Starbright flinched back out of the way, but immediately retaliated, gouging through its fur and flesh to leave a bloody gash in its arm. It shrieked with fury and danced back. As a whole, the pack snarled and retreated a couple steps before milling about and advancing again. They were cautious now, advancing in pairs or trios.

"When they come, whoever is closest, grab it," Thornfire ordered. "The others kill it."

No sooner had he spoken than a pair of beasts lunged in. Hawkwind grabbed the swiping paw that came for her and yanked. The screamer, feeling itself caught, squalled in fear and tried to jerk away. Rainsoft leaned forward and slashed its face, making it shriek. Hawkwind had its paw still, so she pulled it closer and stepped down on its upper arm, pinning it to the floor. Rainsoft darted out his head and bit down on its neck. Griffins could crush the neck vertebrae of deer; these snow-screamers weren't much larger. With a crunching, crackling sound, the screamer went limp. Rainsoft and Hawkwind dropped it. The whole skirmish had happened in only a couple seconds. Hawkwind checked on Starbright and Thornfire. They'd dispatched the other screamer, too.

"Well done," Thornfire praised, panting a little.

Hawkwind had only a second to share a pleased expression with Rainsoft before four more angry snow-screamers jumped at them. Each griffin had to take care of a whole beast alone this time. Hawkwind tried to grab hers, but ended up exchanging swipes instead. Starbright snared hers, breaking its neck. Rainsoft saw success next, ripping out a throat, and then immediately clawing Hawkwind's beast to distract it, so she could slash its eyes.

The fight went on, with new snow-screamers jumping in to fill the place of the fallen, as dead snow-screamer bodies began to pile up. All the griffins took minor injuries, mostly on their hands and forearms. Sticky blood coated the floor. Eventually, the screamers became hesitant, thinned out and intimidated. They milled uncertainly just beyond the remaining light and the snarls and shrieks of battle faded into dark echoes, vanishing at last, so that Hawkwind just heard her pounding heart and the heavy breathing of the griffins around her. The children had gone completely silent. The few remaining snow-screamers glared over the dead bodies, and then turned as one and retreated into the darkness.

Thornfire slumped, panting hard. Starbright waved a hand and the light from their campfire stone brightened back to the usual normal.

"Come on, back around the stone," Hawkwind encouraged them.

"Who's hurt?"

Thornfire lowered himself down to the floor. Rainsoft and Starbright sat, too.

"Not had a fight like that," Thornfire panted, "for some years now."

"Never had a fight like that," Starbright said.

He waved a hand, chuckling, "you've seen nothing, child."

"Are you all right?" Hawkwind asked Rainsoft with voice and hands.

He nodded, but rotated his arms, showing off his scratches. She examined them. None of them were bleeding profusely.

"I think they're fine," she said.

"Snow-screamers are filthy," Thornfire spoke up strongly. "The wounds may be slight, but we're all likely to get infections from them. Starbright, I've taught you to cauterize, right?"

"Yes, Master," she breathed.

Hawkwind gulped. "This is going to be painful, isn't it?"

"You'll live," he grunted, reaching out to grab Rainsoft's nearest arm. "We'll burn out any contamination. The scars will be worse, but you won't get wound rotting and fever and die. I'd consider herbal poultices if we could go collect the ingredients, but we can't, and the small amount of dried herbs I brought should be saved in case the children get hurt. I think cauterizing them would be too traumatic for them."

"I'll practice on myself first," Starbright whispered.

"Dangerous wounds," Hawkwind told Rainsoft, as Thornfire got ready to start. "Thornfire will fix them. It will hurt."

"I understand," he signaled back.

Starbright was already strangling her own whimpers as Hawkwind went to check on the children. They had huddled together in a ball of skinny arms and legs, heads hidden.

"Jessika, Rikah, Karo, Kassandra," she called gently, "it's over."

The princess lifted her head. "We're safe?"

"For now. Sleep if you can. There may be more food soon."

Under Thornfire's direction, Hawkwind took a brightly glowing stone in her bill, and started dragging the carcasses to the trash cave. It was usually dangerous to go alone, but Thornfire said the fight would have the screamers intimidated for a while, so it would be safe enough. When she'd finished and returned to the main cave, Starbright was working on Thornfire's wounds, Rainsoft was curled up, shaking a little, and Thornfire gestured her over, so he could begin cleaning and sealing her wounds.

"This is a variation on creating fire," Thornfire explained conversationally. "We just make the fire very tiny and very hot, right at the tips of our fingers. It hurts just as much as getting burned by real fire does. You'll just have to bear it."

Hawkwind endured it, impressed by Thornfire's ability to be treated by Starbright and maintain enough concentration through the pain to use his magic on Hawkwind and talk at the same time. He had to switch arms when Starbright finished with one, but it didn't break his stride.

"We'll go cook a few snow-screamers after this," he continued. "They're so filthy, they're safer cooked, or we'd all have belly aches tomorrow."

"Especially the children," Hawkwind agreed.

"They would probably make the children deathly ill," Thornfire agreed, "without thorough cooking. Starbright and I will be exhausted. We will probably have a long sleep here, but at least we have faced the first threat of the tunnels now. We have the respect and wariness of the snow-screamers."

"The first threat?" Hawkwind repeated.

"You wish to know how many more there are?"

"I'm not sure," she admitted, scared of the answer.

"I'll let you know how many we encountered, of the total, when we are safely through to the other side," he teased.

The next several days went quietly. Most nights they ate bats or other cave creatures. They occasionally encountered snow-screamers. Sometimes the screamers ran away. Other times they fought. They re-filled their water skins at underground streams that Thornfire said were safe. They slept in the caves he chose.

Hawkwind came to long for the sun almost as much as the children did. She continued to take the tail of the party, but the feeling of being followed and watched never abated, and she began to sleep poorly. If it was snow-screamers following them, the beasts never revealed themselves from behind, but Hawkwind wondered if it might be something else, one of the other threats of the tunnels.

On the sixth day, Thornfire suddenly halted them before a bricked archway. It was a unique find, as most of the tunnels had been rough and moldy thus far, the only structures being wooden timbers to brace the ceilings, but Hawkwind didn't quite have the energy to appreciate it. She heard a noise like a foot scraping on the rocky floor and glanced behind. There was nothing to see there except the black tunnel vanishing out of sight.

"What is it, Master?" she heard Starbright ask.

Thornfire motioned them closer, and Hawkwind pushed up beside Rainsoft.

"We've reached the halfway point," he said, voice hushed but tense. "Through this archway is a short tunnel and then a large, open cavern. Once we cross that, there will be another tunnel, and then a bridge over a chasm."

Hawkwind's neck feathers prickled and she whipped her head around. There was nothing there.

"Hawkwind?" Thornfire queried.

"I'm sorry," she apologized. "I'm very jumpy. I didn't sleep well."

"Do you think there's something following us?"

Her bill dropped open a little. Was he serious or mocking her?

"I mean it. Do you think there's something following us?"

The others were looking at her, too, now.

"I think I'm just nervous," she said. "I haven't seen anything. Sometimes I think I hear things, or I feel like there's something there, but there never is."

His brows lowered. "It concerns me. It's always possible it isn't just your nerves. The light keeps most things away down here, but there is one thing it will attract. To cross through this cavern safely, we must cover the light stones."

"What's in there?" several people whispered.

Thornfire took his time before answering. "I don't want to frighten you unduly, but extreme caution and even a little fear is merited."

Karo cowered down on the mage's back. Kassandra looked as unmoved as usual. Rikah seemed to be trying to keep a fearless and determined countenance, but Hawkwind saw his hands whiten against Starbright's feathers. Jessika's hands, too, began tightening against Hawkwind's back.

"In the war against the talis, the one that utilized this tunnel, many griffins were killed. Others were entranced by the talis, but not killed due to rescue or the talis getting distracted, or other such good fortune, if you can call it good," Thornfire explained. "Sometimes, when a talis entrances, if it is just briefly, no harm is done. When the spell is broken, the affected griffin can just shake it off. Other times, if the entrancement lasts too long, or if a griffin's will is completely broken by it, there is lasting damage. Some such griffins cannot recover."

"What kind of damage?" Hawkwind asked.

Thornfire continued as if he hadn't heard her. "Of course, our people would not leave any injured behind. Some mind-wounded griffins were brought back here. This cavern was the recovery area for the wounded. Our people thought that the dark and quiet would be soothing, but I can't say if that was the best thing they could have done. Some of the mind-wounded ones recovered eventually. Some died." He took a deep breath. "Others changed."

"What happened?" Kassandra asked in a breathless whisper.

"They went mad. They became afraid of everything, or attacked their friends and family, or both. You can imagine that our ancestors couldn't imagine slaying their former companions and loved ones, their Linemembers, no matter how sick they seemed. Maybe some were put to rest, but others escaped, ran into the depths of the tunnels, but without light they were nearly helpless. The army moved on. The lost ones remained. The descendants of those griffins make their main colony here, but they are no longer like us. They are no longer griffins."

Thornfire stared intently at all of them. "If they detect us, they will attack. We can only hope that if we move silently and stay to the darkest shadows, that we might go unnoticed."

Hawkwind shivered. She wanted to know what these not-griffin creatures were, at the same time afraid of seeing them.

"Their eyes have become extremely light sensitive; they see very well in the dark. High on the wall to the right is a small hole that lets in the slightest bit of light. To be illuminated by that light is fatal. We must cover all the stones, and I would like the children to wrap up in their blankets, which are darker than their clothes and skin. Please prepare."

Hawkwind turned to Rainsoft while the children got ready.

"Did you understand?" she asked with words and hands, hoping she knew enough gestures now to convey anything he hadn't gotten from Thornfire's brisk explanation.

"Mostly," he replied, keeping his gestures clear and slow so Hawkwind could understand. "Dangerous animals?"

Close enough. "If they see us, hear us, they attack us. No light."

Rainsoft was watching the children hide the light stones and cover their pale skin, although Rikah was rather browner than the others, and seemed to understand. He sagged his dark grey wings to hide his lighter underside. Of all of them, Rainsoft had the coloration most suited to going undetected here: if he stood still and kept his belly covered, he would almost blend into the rocks. Thornfire's tan, Starbright's gold, and Hawkwind's coloration which was merely a bit browner than Starbright's, were all light enough to readily reflect light.

"Are we ready?" Thornfire asked. "Follow me. We will go very slowly. Children, hold on tight. If we are spotted, we will run for the exit on the far side and make for the bridge. Now come, and be careful with your foot steps."

Thornfire went first. Starbright followed him. Hawkwind let Rainsoft go next. Now in the near total darkness, Hawkwind strained her ears and focused on placing and lifting her feet silently. Something rustled behind her and she looked back. She thought she saw a darker shape in the darkness. Was it just a feature of the tunnel walls? Had it been there before but not visible because of the light stones? It didn't move, and after a moment, she continued following Rainsoft down the turning tunnel, through the archway, and into the big cavern.

Despite all of their best efforts to keep their footsteps silent, it seemed to Hawkwind that every step echoed with the crushing of fine grit. She followed the faint outline of Rainsoft and tried to still her racing heart. She could see the pinprick of light high above, so high that she wondered just how tall the ceiling was. Faint dust motes danced in the light. To her left, the cavern vanished into deepest black. She couldn't see the back wall, but she thought she faintly detected the wall to her right.

They passed behind a pillar wider than her whole body. It was roughly carved but clearly solid and functional. There were some old, grey bones piled at the base of it; she could only see them because compared to the blackness of the cavern, they glowed. Hawkwind moved on, passing between the pillar and the next one, still in slow, steady silence except for the faint grating of the dirty floor under their feet.

Hawkwind glanced behind, noting the grey bones still seeming to glow in the darkness. Then they vanished. Her breath caught. A second later, they reappeared. Had something moved between her and them, blocking her view?

She looked around frantically for anything else she could see, anything else that something might cross in front of, revealing a moving object. Something rustled in the darkness, like dry feathers. She felt Jessika tremble on her back; the girl had heard it, too. Hawkwind walked on, trying to follow the dark shadow that was Rainsoft.

Then she saw three dark shadows ahead of her. Rainsoft was the one in the middle—she hoped—and what were the other two? They seemed to mirror Rainsoft's movements, pacing him on either side. Had he seen them? They couldn't be just Thornfire and Starbright, could they? Had they fallen back to walk beside him? What were the dark shadows? Were her eyes playing tricks on her?

Trying to restrain her racing heart, Hawkwind looked ahead, searching the blackness for what she assumed would be the deeper blackness of the exit. She couldn't find it yet. One of the dark shadows ahead of her began separating towards the right. Was that one Rainsoft?

Hawkwind's mouth went dry. She couldn't tell which one was he. She passed another pillar with a larger pile of bones around it. She heard crushing from ahead, like brittle bones breaking underfoot. That must be Thornfire. Hawkwind headed towards the sound, following the middle shadow. She glanced to her right and thought she saw a deeper darkness moving, paralleling her.

The dry, dusty blackness settled over her like a spidery blanket. Suddenly, she wasn't sure where her companions were or what she was following. Frightened, she halted. Jessika shifted silently on her back, probably concerned. Feathery whispers drifted around her. Hawkwind tried to make out the next pillar, thought she saw the glowing bones at its base, and started moving towards it.

A dark shape passed in front of the bones and away again.

Hawkwind strained her ears for the sounds of the others' footsteps. They seemed to be coming from in front of her, steadily, slowly moving away. Almost shivering, eyes stretched wide, Hawkwind continued on towards the next pillar. She thought she saw dark shapes moving all around her, beyond the reach of her limited vision. She envied Jessika, who could just hide under the blanket, waiting for someone else to get her out of the fear, never having to try to look and listen to the emptiness.

A sudden scrape followed by a scratch followed by a dull thud came from ahead to her right and Hawkwind clenched her body, refusing to jump in surprise. Footsteps shuffled on the floor. Someone grunted. Hawkwind heard panting from behind to her right. No one was supposed to be behind her.

Adrenaline flooded her body, telling her to run, fly, escape, but she didn't know where to run. She couldn't see the exit yet. Slowly, as silently as possible, she worked her way to the next pillar and searched for the following one.

She heard footsteps behind her.

Hawkwind's fear spiked and she turned her body, putting the pillar, festooned with bones, behind her. She looked left and right, searching for the owner of the footsteps, but they had gone silent.

She felt Jessika's fingers run through her back fur, soothing. No doubt the girl could feel Hawkwind's racing heart. Hawkwind waited, listening. She didn't hear anything anymore. Though her hearing probed the room, it was more silent than snowfall, as if she was now alone in the big cavern, but she dared not move. Who or what was all around her?

Her held breath began to burn in her lungs. She had to move, had to breathe. Perhaps the others were already at the other side, waiting for her. Hawkwind turned again, stepping towards the next pillar. Never in all her life had she been prey. Always she had been the one stooping down, winged death. Was this how it felt to be hunted?

She reached the next pillar, all the while trying to stop the bone fragments under her feet from crunching. Behind her, more crunching footsteps echoed. Panic rose higher inside her like a swelling tide. She wanted to run, and her body trembled with the effort of keeping to a slow walk. Any second she expected to feel claws in her back, or rather in Jessika. She imagined the girl's scream of terror, at the same time that acidic guilt chewed at her for feeling relieved that she might be protected by the girl's body.

Sharp cracking, as though someone had crushed a dry skull underfoot, echoed from Hawkwind's right. Hawkwind choked on a gasp and barely restrained a startled jump. She kept walking smoothly, at least that was her intention; her arms and legs trembled with every step. To her left, someone walked sloppily through a pile of bones, scattering them with the sound of dry laughter slithering across the floor. More gritty footsteps came from behind her.

Jessika hugged her tighter. "They're all around us," Hawkwind heard the girl say in the slightest, barest of voices.

The next rough footstep, like sandpaper on steel, came from Hawkwind's right, much closer than before. She stared into the darkness, barely detecting a blacker shape moving just out of reach. Hawkwind came to the next pillar and didn't stop. Looking ahead, she thought she saw Rainsoft's back, with his human bundle on top. She hoped it was Rainsoft.

Behind her something kicked a pile of bones she'd very carefully stepped over. She felt some of them knock harmlessly into her hind legs and she wrenched down hard on a budding scream in her throat. Jessika was trembling on her back. She passed another pillar. Out in the pit of the cavern, something hissed. It was sharper and higher than a griffin's hiss, but close enough in sound that it sent shivers dancing over Hawkwind's skin like prickling fire sparks.

The hiss resonated through the cave, and then was repeated from a different location, ahead to the right, and then from directly behind, and to the left, and again and again until the hissing rasped like icy rain, wearing away what little sanity remained. Jessika had been right: they were all around, whatever they were.

As Hawkwind passed more pillars, not daring to run, the hissing and gritty footsteps and tinkling scattering of cracked up bones came closer and closer on either side. She stared straight ahead, but with her peripheral vision saw only a moving mass of deeper darkness on either side. She could no longer guess how much she was imagining and how many of the sights and sounds around her were real. The possibility that a horde of misshapen not-griffins were about to leap on her and tear her to bits was something her mind couldn't quite get a hold of, like the one time she'd tried fishing with Eagleye and Hawkcall and hadn't been able to get the knack of gripping those scaly, slippery fish. Hawkcall had laughed at her fumbling.

A darker shape appeared ahead, beyond a final, paler pillar, like a clearing in the midst of storm-tossed forest below: the archway exit and safety. With all her will, Hawkwind resisted the dancing urging of her adrenaline, but couldn't stop her feet from hurrying. The scratchy hissing rose in volume around her. On her back, Jessika was shaking like she was sobbing. Hawkwind thought the dark shapes around her were moving in, ready to snare her with prickly claws like blackberry vines.

She passed the final pillar. The dark shape in front of her, hopefully Rainsoft, moved into the archway blackness and vanished. Hawkwind followed to the accompaniment of dozens of screeching hisses, expecting an attack at the last moment.

She saw the edges of the stone doorway clearly as she passed through. Below her, the stone changed from planed flat rock to uneven laid stones. An easy glance left and right showed her the floor dropping off into blackness only a yard away on each side. She'd reached the bridge. Behind her, the final shrieking chorus of hisses died away. The dark shape in front of her stopped, and she did, too.

"They let us pass," Thornfire whispered from the front of the line.

Hawkwind's body shook as her dying adrenaline burned in her like acid.

"You didn't say they'd do that," she stuttered, "that they'd surround us and follow us and hiss."

"They never did that when I've passed through before," he replied. "Let's keep moving and get across this bridge. Then we'll rest and talk."

Hawkwind followed, still in darkness, hearing now only the muffled crying of the children and the steady tread of four sets of griffin feet across the old bridge. She was too wearied to even fear the open chasm below her, forgetting that her wings were not yet fully feathered again and, if she fell, she would plummet to the bottom. The archway on the other side, leading to more tunnels, with stone walls closing back around her, gave a sense of security.

"Let's stop here a moment," Thornfire said. "Children, you can reveal the light stones again."

Hawkwind had a moment of irrational panic. She'd only heard Thornfire speak, not Rainsoft or Starbright. What if they had been silently snatched, and it was two not-griffins walking along with them? What if the light revealed not her friends' faces, but the sightless eyes and pale feathers of the hissing monsters from the cave behind them?

Four blankets were tossed back and four children sat up, holding four glowing stones. Hawkwind's heart stumbled like a stag run into the ground and she swayed on her feet, clumsily sitting, panting for breath. It was they: Rainsoft, Starbright, and Thornfire, all shaken, but safe. The children, too, looked terrified, with dirty tear streaks on their cheeks, but unhurt.

"What happened in there?" Starbright asked, and Hawkwind was secretly relieved that the apprentice's voice reflected as much terror as Hawkwind herself felt.

"I have before passed through that cavern without being noticed," Thornfire murmured. "The first time, my brother and I were attacked and we had to run; we were more cautious after that and eventually decided to travel to and from Snow-in-lee only when the weather was good, so we could fly. I've never witnessed what happened this time. They noticed us, but didn't attack us."

"Because there were four of us?" Starbright suggested.

"Bright, there were dozens of them," he shook his head.

Hawkwind raised her brows; she'd never heard Thornfire refer to his apprentice so informally before, but she kept any comment about it to herself. Usually only Linemembers called each other by their shortened name.

"I'm glad we're all safe," he went on, and in the dim light Hawkwind saw the tips of his feathers trembling. "They could have killed us all. I think something was making them too unsure to attack. I can only assume it was the presence of the children. They might not be so indecisive next time."

The group sat for a few more minutes in silence, huddled around the light. The children dismounted and went to Hawkwind for comforting hugs. All four griffins shared reassuring preening of feathers with each other. In time, the dregs of the terror passed, and Thornfire got to his feet.

"We should choose a campsite as far away from that cavern as we can. Let's get moving, and then we'll have a long rest," he said.

The children remounted, the griffins stood, and they resumed their trek through the tunnels.

"The rest of the trip should be less difficult, or at least only as difficult as the caves on the other side of the big cavern were," Thornfire told them the next time they woke up. "We near Snow-in-lee. The presence of the talis there keeps other big predators away."

"Do they come into these caves?" Hawkwind rushed to ask.

"No. I have never seen one here. Snow-in-lee will still be a walk of a few days beyond the tunnel exit. We will still encounter snow-screamers, as I mentioned before, but these ones, like the others, fear light. We will pass swiftly and silently through their territories. Keep the light stones visible. Now, let's get ready to go."

The tunnel floors and walls passed around them as they made their way, following Thornfire's lead. They ate mostly bats and blind, cave-crawling rodents, although they did encounter a few packs of snow-screamers and feasted on them, after the flesh was cooked and their own wounds cauterized.

It had been over a week underground and the children especially, became weak and slightly ill, spending most of their time sleeping. Jessika had finished making sandals for all of them, and she, too, mainly dozed, only rousing for eating. There were dozens of caves in this section of tunnels, where the great griffin armies had rested, and even with snow-screamers taking up many caves, finding places to sleep was not difficult. No one had energy for teaching or learning new words, even though it would have been a wise way to use time.

Hawkwind had no way of counting just how many days had passed, but some several sleeps after the big cavern with the not-griffins, she noticed a change in how well she could see her companions. The light of the small stones the children carried never wavered; Thornfire and Starbright renewed them after every sleep. Hawkwind had the thought that perhaps her own eyes were just getting better. Maybe she was becoming a not-griffin, too.

After yet another turn in the tunnel, after hundreds of turns in the tunnels, however, she noticed that she could see more colors in the rocks and the shadows were different, cast in new directions. Ahead, Thornfire stopped. Starbright almost bumped into him, and Rainsoft into her. The mage turned his head back at them.

"We're near the exit." Even he sounded baffled, as if leaving the maze of tunnels had become a fantasy never expected to come true for him, too.

As one, the children sat up.

"Hurry, let's go," Rikah demanded.

"Patience," Thornfire countered. "We do not know what might wait outside, and our eyes will take time to adjust to daylight again. There is still the chance of running into more snow-screamers at any moment."

He began leading them off, but Hawkwind could tell that his steps were quicker. The brightness in the tunnels grew until she was nearly blinded. Within only a few more turns, the group stepped out into the open air.

Moonlight: it was only moonlight soft as a flower and clear as a river that bathed the mountainside where they emerged. It turned the grass silver and the dirt black, the mountain white and their feathers pewter and onyx and ivory. The children tumbled to the ground and walked aimlessly around with their palms upraised as if bathing in rain, laughing and crying at the same time.

The full moon was too bright to let the stars show, and not a single cloud fought it for a piece of the sky. Under that bare iron dome, against the naked mountain, Hawkwind felt exposed to the eyes of anything that might be passing, but no one made move to seek shelter. After the confinement of the tunnels, the vaulted air was both searing and freeing, and she took deeper breaths than she felt she'd taken in weeks, as if trying to suck in all the space she now had to spread her wings, and hold it inside her.

The others, too, were stretching their wings wide, worshipping the night, and Hawkwind noticed that Rainsoft's new feathers were coming in nicely. A check confirmed that hers were the same. They'd both be borderline flight worthy in a few days. The open air and hope of flight infected her with a double freedom that bore her to the ground until she stretched out on the cold grass, rolling to her back and opening her eyes wide to the endless sky and its icy moon. Without meaning to let it, sleep snuck up and took her deep under her dreams.

The morning dawned bright and crystal yellow glowing around the mountains, turning the sky fresh white and chasing off the night's solemnity. Hawkwind awoke feeling like a chick again, both fragile and full of untarnished wonder, all fear and sadness like a foreign thing she'd never felt.

Her companions were scattered across the little field by the tunnel exit. Karo was surprisingly clinging to Thornfire. Starbright had curled up near her master: looking so flattened she seemed very young. Rikah, Kassandra, and Jessika had collapsed near each other, holding hands or with heads pillowed on other body parts. Hawkwind was most startled to find that Rainsoft was tucked against herself, back to back, but she didn't mind.

They hadn't built a fire before sleeping, and no one was on watch. Anything could have attacked them, and for a moment, Hawkwind's heart pounded—but nothing had, and she calmed again. Her stomach rumbled, loudly enough that Rainsoft awoke behind her.

"Sorry," she told him.

"It's all right, good morning," he gestured to her, and then stretched, ran, and leapt up onto one of the boulders surrounding their little field with a burst of vigor, wings half open like a cormorant drying off after a dive.

The rising sun brought out some deeply hidden notes of umber in his charcoal feathers and frosted his white chest with gold. Hawkwind jumped up to join him, squinting against the light.

"I'm hungry, too," he said with his hands.

"Rainsoft," she began hesitantly. She touched his throat with a gentle finger, indicating the scar below his fur. "Why? Why can't you speak?"

He rolled his shoulders in a minor shrug; brow furrowed, and folded his wings. "Always," he told her. "Everyone. No speaking."

"Someone hurt you, on purpose?"

Rainsoft tilted his head, and then signed, "I don't understand."

Hawkwind searched for a way to explain. They hadn't yet covered how to talk about intentional versus accidental. She pointed again at his throat. "Your parents, too?"

He nodded.

"Who hurt you?"

His jaw clenched along with his claws. After a moment he let out a breath and hesitantly gestured something, but Hawkwind didn't know the words.

"I don't understand," she apologized.

Rainsoft nodded as though he had expected as much.

"When did it happen?"

"I don't remember. I was a chick."

She didn't want to press any further. Somehow, she was feeling like she was asking things that were far too personal, and yet, talking about it with him made her feel closer to him.

"Thank you for telling me," she said.

The tension was gone from his face when he glanced at her, smiling a little, even, and then leaned in to preen her neck feathers. She returned the favor.

"Hawkwind, Rainsoft," called Starbright from below. "Let's go hunting."

Hawkwind jumped back down to the little field. Everyone was

awake and squinting at the sun.

"Is it safe to hunt here?" she asked. "Aren't we close to Snow-in-lee?"

"We're getting there," Thornfire confirmed. "Since I know the area, perhaps I should lead, taking just one of you, so two others can watch over the children."

The three young griffins looked around at each other.

"Perhaps it would be best if Starbright went. You two can't fly yet," he went on.

Hawkwind resisted a sigh. She extended her wings and flapped, but it was immediately evident that her feathers hadn't grown in enough yet, although the vanes were unfurling. Thornfire nodded at her.

"Soon enough," he assured her. "Starbright, let's go."

Hawkwind and Rainsoft retreated to the huddle of sleepy children as the two flighted griffins took off. The children got up to hug Hawkwind, and then went on to hug Rainsoft, too, clearly surprising him, but he seemed to take it with good grace.

"We're so happy to be out of the caves," Jessika beamed.

"Yeah, now the hard part starts," Hawkwind groaned, but when the children's faces fell she regretted her comment. "Not for a while yet, and you'll all be safe here with Starbright. Jessika, maybe you can get a fire ready."

They hunted for downed wood in the general vicinity while Jessika built a small fire pit against a rocky wall. By the time they'd accumulated a pile of twigs and branches, Thornfire and Starbright were sailing over with a bled mountain-deer. Starbright lit the fire, a chunk of deer was ripped off for the children, and the four griffins took the rest of the animal a short ways away to fill their stomachs with the best food they'd had in weeks.

"There is a camp we're heading towards," Thornfire explained after they'd eaten and while they waited for the children to have their meal. "I've used it before, and its location makes it very difficult for talis to get to. We'll use it again. Starbright and the children should be safe there. It's still two nights away, however, and the territory between here and there is not safe. We must be extremely cautious."

Once the children had eaten, they mounted up. Starbright extinguished the fire with a thought, and Thornfire led them off, down a narrow trail, ever closer to Snow-in-lee.

Two days passed with a few sightings and skirmishes with snow-screamers and a far away spotting of a pair of ice-lions, but no sign of talis. As noon approached, three days out from the tunnel exit, they topped a rise that gave them their first view of Snow-in-lee. White towers stuck up above the rim of peaks that surrounded the valley. No flags flew from them. No griffins wheeled in the air above them. Steam, however, rose steadily out of the valley, drifting gently upward among the spires, and seemed to have inspired moss and lichens to grow in any crack or crevice on the towers, making them look lined with green and orange.

Rainsoft made a whimpering noise, and when Hawkwind looked over she saw that he was half crouched, as if cowering, feathers and fur slicked flat with anxiety. She looked back at the white towers. They were going there, and she had little idea of what they would encounter. Rainsoft was tasked with fetching back the Moonstone. Would he be capable of it?

"Let's keep moving," Thornfire said. "We'll be seeing plenty more of that place."

A shiver ran over Hawkwind's skin and she went to Rainsoft, giving him a gentle nudge of encouragement. He responded, standing up faster that she had expected and leaning into her, butting his forehead against her neck. Uneasiness swam through her.

"Let's go, Rainsoft," she urged him.

When she walked off, Rainsoft following, she saw Thornfire watching her with a blank glare, and she chilled.

"What's his problem?" she remarked to Starbright, who was a little

ahead.

"What?" she replied, appearing baffled.

"Thornfire," Hawkwind indicated with her chin.

Starbright paused. "I didn't notice anything. Is something wrong?"

Hawkwind clenched her bill. "Never mind."

Starbright gave her a confused glance and trotted into her place in line. Thornfire leapt to the head of the group and took them onward, along a narrow, rocky path with a sheer drop on one side and a vertical cliff on the other. It wound upwards, becoming more broken and unsteady until the griffins were taking long hops between outcroppings. They had to open their wings slightly for precision landing, and Hawkwind was gratified to feel that her wings were now supporting her; her feathers were recovered enough that she could probably fly again. At last, they alit on a gravel-choked landing in a gap in the cliff, and passed through into a slanted but spacious little plateau among the jagged peaks.

"This is the camp," Thornfire announced. "The only other way up is by flying. This is the safest place close to Snow-in-lee. It would be all but impossible for a talis to get up here."

The spears of mountain rock all around enclosed the camp, helping to keep out the wind, but it was still rather cold. The ground was rocky, but in places it seemed the rock had been planed smooth. Lichens subsisted in most of the sheltered spots. There was a deep fire pit, well blackened, with a big stone in the center that Hawkwind suspected was for magical light and warmth when wood was not available, but there was a pile of old, weathered wood in one corner of the camp that she supposed had been flown up by previous occupants.

Another corner of the camp appeared to be the refuse pile, devoid of all but some bone fragments. The third corner had rocks piled up in a way to make a private spot that Hawkwind assumed was for personal disposal of waste. In other places along the walls, rocks had been piled to create separate rooms. Old disintegrating pieces of leather on the floors and walls might have once been roofs.

"It's not the warmest place," Thornfire admitted, "but we'll make it work. With luck, we'll only be here a few days."

Hawkwind winced and turned away. She didn't even want to talk about how the scouting of Snow-in-lee would start.

"Children, let's choose a spot for you to camp in," she called, and the four little ones clambered down off their mounts.

She insisted they claim the smallest of the rock rooms for themselves and that they sleep together. Their shared body warmth would be a big benefit on the cold mountain. Hawkwind's pack had been mostly full of blankets for the children and they managed to make a fairly comfortable nest. Since the mages could make the stone produce heat and light, Hawkwind took the weathered pieces of wood and made a sort of roof over the children's room to help keep out the wind. She even managed to add some old pieces of leather that weren't completely disintegrating yet.

"The biggest problem with this spot is lack of water," Thornfire was saying as Hawkwind rejoined him and the others around the now magically lit campfire. "Starbright, you'll need to fly down to refill the water bags most days. Of course, you'll also have to hunt, for all of us, if you can. You may also want to gather boughs of greenery for roofing the rooms and cushioning our nests. This is a secure camp. Even snow-screamers and ice-lions can't make the climb up here, much less the talis, so the children will be safe while you're gone."

"Don't worry," Starbright asserted. "I'll take good care of the children and the camp." She nodded at Hawkwind. "I can put a warm stone in their bedding at night so they won't be cold."

"For now, let's settle in," Thornfire concluded. "Then, perhaps Hawkwind and Rainsoft will be ready to accompany me on a little flight over the area and a hunt."

Thornfire walked off to claim a spot to sleep, leaving Hawkwind gaping behind him. She sure hoped her wings were ready.

Hawkwind had taken the room beside the children's. Starbright was on their other side, with Thornfire on her other side. Rainsoft had taken the room on Hawkwind's other side. Bedding, such as there was, had been set up. It was now past noon. If a scouting flight was to be done, it had to be started soon.

Hawkwind watched Thornfire stride out to the magical campfire. He wore only his tough leather harness with its pouches and loops full of tools and weapons and other supplies. Hawkwind had never asked what he kept in the bags; mage stuff, she assumed. She and Rainsoft had unburdened themselves, too, and now wore only their harnesses: old but still functional ones borrowed from Starbright and Thornfire.

Thornfire looked around and motioned for Hawkwind and Rainsoft to join him. The pair exchanged glances over the half crumbled wall between their rooms, got to their feet, and walked out to stand with him. The mage gave them both a look over.

"Can you fly?" he said simply. "Show me."

Hawkwind stepped away to give herself some room. Rainsoft did the same, perhaps copying her or perhaps understanding what Thornfire had said; Hawkwind still wasn't sure of how much he understood.

"Fly, Hawkwind, fly," cried Rikah from the entry to the children's room.

"You can do it," Jessika agreed, smiling.

Hawkwind opened her wings, taking a close look at her flight feathers. They were bright, unmarked and crisp like the petals of a flower opening for the first time. It seemed that the vanes had all unfurled completely. Her flight muscles would be a little weak from nearly a month of not using them, but otherwise, she should be flight worthy.

"Looks good," she muttered.

Thornfire nodded. "Up you go," he said, giving her little shooing motions with a hand.

She crouched; launching up from the ground was difficult. Then she remembered the entrance to the camp. Beyond it were wide-open air and a fall of hundreds of feet. She turned, facing the path.

"Follow me," she told Rainsoft. He gave her a nod.

Wings half furled, Hawkwind ran. She kicked up pebbles as she struggled to get as much speed as possible over the short runway. The edge approached, she reached it, launched off it with a vigorous thrust of her hind legs, and snapped out her wings, falling into the void. She dropped several feet before her wings did their job, catching her on the winds and kicking her up towards the sky.

She could fly again, and joy surged through her chest in waves of heat. She glanced at each slotted wing, feathers stretched and bending up at the dark tips, just as she had seen them do hundreds of times before. Her muscles held them level, pressed hard against the air. She was airborne, exactly where a griffin was meant to be.

Hawkwind turned, looking behind to see Rainsoft launching off the same place she had. His dark grey wings reached out and caught the wind as surely as hers had: beautiful. He flapped hard, bringing himself up to her, and paced her. She caught his thrilled gaze and grinned at him.

He made a few gestures. "I'm happy. I love flying."

"Me, too," she replied in the same way.

"Last year," he went on, as they circled, "I flew—" he followed with a few more gestures she hadn't learned yet and she had to shake her head in confusion. He frowned briefly, but then smiled again and said, "It's all right. Later."

Thornfire caught up to them, his dull tan plumage reflecting the sun flatly.

"Fall in and follow me," he called out.

Hawkwind and Rainsoft took positions to the side and slightly behind each of his wings, matching his flight path as he led them across the mountains. Flight: it had only been a month, but to be denied what Hawkwind felt was her right as a griffin, a month had been far too long, and to get to fly again made the world feel right. The joy that lit her up from within was almost overwhelming, and seemed to be reaching through vacant rooms inside her, lighting lamps and opening shutters, revitalizing places that hadn't been used for weeks, and even discovering new places that Hawkwind hadn't known existed.

She retained enough focus to follow Thornfire's right wing tip, but any need to observe the landscape or watch for roving talis dissolved into the barest pretense as Hawkwind instead watched inside herself with awe as her body lit with life and heat. The desire to fly faster gripped her, and she had to throttle it down so she didn't go zipping off at high speed. She wanted to race, to hunt, to—she wasn't even sure what she wanted.

Her vision went fuzzy as she failed to focus. Her muscles burned, as if her body was feeding them too much energy, and she was ordering them not to use it. A cry of frustration backed up in her throat when she clamped her bill shut on it. What was wrong with her? Flying had never felt like this before.

Thornfire was shouting something into the wind, maybe her name, calling for her attention, but his command just made her growl. She didn't want to follow his orders. She didn't even want to be flying with him. In fact, she almost felt like trying to smack him, not truly hurt him, but just give him a little whack and knock him out of the sky, make him tumble, make him fly away from her.

"Hawkwind," Thornfire was calling, "let's go back."

Go back? Go back now, when what she wanted was to fly, fly faster, fly farther, and outstrip the wind? Her vision and hearing returned enough that she was able to look at him and read his expression. He looked concerned. He was looking at her like she was ill or injured. She? Indisposed? And what did he know about it?

Hawkwind swerved, flashing her claws at him, a threat gesture, and he expertly slid out of the way, almost as if he'd expected it. Well, fine then: Hawkwind bolted. Her restraint vanished and the fire in her muscles leapt up with glee, shooting her ahead with rapid pumps of her wings. She didn't know where she was going, and she didn't care, as long as Thornfire didn't follow her.

Several strokes ahead, she glanced back, but the mage hadn't made chase; he was flying in a tight circle, holding his former position. Rainsoft, however, was in rapid pursuit. Terrified ecstasy sunk claws deep into her and more energy flooded her flight muscles. She was flying faster than she ever had before, so that the ground blurred by below her. Her heart pounded at an unsustainable rate.

She looked back; Rainsoft was, somehow, keeping pace. She pushed harder, making rapid turns, gaining speed on dives to send her dashing into brief climbs. A forest was below her now; she didn't even know where she was, but it didn't matter. Her breath was starting to burn her lungs and the tingling in her muscles told her they were soon to stop working: a little farther. She looked back; Rainsoft was gaining on her, had almost caught up.

There: a break in the tree canopy showed a tiny meadow. Three young buck deer went scrambling for the trees as she arrowed down through the opening at breakneck speed, half tumbling into the ground and tearing up some of the grass and flowers. Rainsoft landed practically on top of her, wings and arms and legs and tails tangling, and his panting breath a twin to hers. He bit her on the neck. It didn't hurt but she shrieked at him. He did it again, with a strange sort of trilling rumble coming from his chest, and Hawkwind felt his whole weight shift onto her back.

They engaged in a novel sort of subdued struggle then, and Hawkwind didn't understand what was happening until a few minutes later, when it became clear, and then after several more blurry but sharp shattering minutes of straining bodies and exploratory exclamations, when a resolution had been achieved. Rainsoft flopped to the ground beside her. She felt his thudding heartbeat reverberating in her own bones. Except for that, and Hawkwind's own raspy breath, there was sudden quiet.

A sort of white noise invaded Hawkwind's head and she stared straight off, not truly seeing. She felt awash with sensations she'd never felt before—not even hints of. They were feelings she didn't know she could feel. She thought it should have scared her, but they were good feelings so, foreign though they might be, she didn't fight them. Nor could she deny what had happened.

"We mated," she breathed in wonder, but even if he'd heard and understood the words, Rainsoft didn't respond. "But only matriarchs mate."

Why? Why, why, why? Like a mouse trying to escape the shadow of a plunging hawk, her mind ran around in little circles while her body finally recovered, heart and breath slowing to normal. She had no need to get up, and no thought of her human charges, or the camp, or talis, or Snow-in-lee. In a half an hour it had all vanished.

Drained, Hawkwind put her head down and half slept until she felt Rainsoft climbing onto her again, and then afterwards, her same confused mouse of a mind ran in circles and got nowhere until she went back to drifting in the sea of satiation the sensations of her body provided.

The rest of the afternoon vanished in that repeating pattern and sunset crept upon them: nestled under the canopy without a care for the vulnerable position they'd spent several hours in. The growing darkness among the trees finally made Hawkwind sit up, and a measure of her customary sanity returned. She stared down at the sleeping Rainsoft, facing the fact that she'd let him—be honest—invited him to mate with her, and she'd loved every second of it.

She was no ignorant child. Although she'd never observed a matriarch mating, which was always a private thing, she'd seen the beasts of the field and forest, the farm animals, the dogs in the kennels, and she knew how mating went, but why had it happened to her? And now, Rainsoft was different; she'd mated with him.

Quivers of embarrassment and anxiety wormed their way over Hawkwind's skin. The waiting was worse; impatiently, she poked him awake. With a trilling rumble, he stretched and sat up. Facing his orange eyes, Hawkwind didn't know what to say. Even if she had been fluent in a form of communication with him, she wouldn't have known what to say. He didn't look quite as uncomfortable as she, but he still flicked his feathers too much to imply serenity. Seeming on an impulse, he reached out and preened her neck feathers.

"Are you all right?" she asked finally, with words and gesture.

"Yes," he answered, "are you?"

"Yes," she said, and then realized she didn't have a good word for how she was feeling, so just shrugged, rolled her wings and ducked her head.

He nibbled her feathers again. The edge of his bill grazed her neck, sending a resurgence of heat through her and Hawkwind leaned into him, biting his neck in return. The conclusion was inevitable. The sun was nearly down when they again resurfaced from that ocean of connection.

"We must go back," she tried to convey. "It's getting dark."

Rainsoft nodded agreement and the pair leapt off from the ground, struggling into the sky, gaining altitude, and then trying to retrace their flight and find the camp again.

Chapter 14
Future and Past

The sun had set by the time Hawkwind and Rainsoft stumbled to a landing through the entrance of the camp. It seemed Starbright and Thornfire had gone hunting. There were the remains of a fresh kill, and a whole additional beast left cooling on a boulder at the edge of camp.

"That's for you two," Thornfire said even before they could give greetings. "Eat."

Hawkwind didn't need telling twice. Ravenous, she ripped into the offering, and Rainsoft let her have all the best bits. Once they'd preened the blood off of each other, Rainsoft walked to his chosen room and curled up with his back to the common area: clearly wanting to sleep and be left alone. Perhaps he was as uncomfortable as she.

Starbright was already sleeping in her room, and the children likewise. Thornfire stood over the magic stone in the campfire pit giving Hawkwind a glare that commanded her to come and talk and broached no possibility for dissent. She wanted to disobey him anyway, but another force brought her to him. He was an elder; he might have answers to her questions; it was clear he already knew what had happened.

Hawkwind walked up to him, sat primly a couple feet away, and braced herself.

"Don't be embarrassed. It's perfectly normal and if your story was indeed true, I expected it from the beginning," he said with a shrug. "I'm just glad you didn't try to rip my feathers out."

"What happened?" she asked helplessly. "Why did this happen?"

He chuckled and then seemed to restrain himself, as if noticing that Hawkwind's distress was genuine. "My dear Hawkchild, you told me your home was destroyed, your entire settlement wiped out, correct? Except for yourself?"

"Yes," she confirmed.

"You are the last of the Hawk Line. Your matriarch was killed. There are no other females of your Line alive. Of course you would wake up. There is no other female Hawk in dominance over you, so it's your turn."

"What are you saying?" she demanded.

"You are the new matriarch of the Hawk Line," Thornfire said simply. "Your body woke up and told you to mate. That's not a command a matriarch can easily ignore. If Rainsoft hadn't been here, you might have even gone for me."

Hawkwind could help but make a sound of disgust, and Thornfire laughed out loud.

"I knew you'd take him, and it's one of the reasons I wanted him along," the mage continued. "I didn't expect it quite so soon, but I think getting to fly again after such a long period of frustration must have acted as a catalyst on the situation."

Hawkwind stared at the glowing firestone, unsure how to feel about this new development.

"I'm afraid, other than isolating yourself from males, that there's little you can do about this. It's possible you could ask to fight another matriarch, back at South-scree, and if she is able to thoroughly beat you, and you join her Line, you might go back to sleep, but without a close blood tie to her, it might not work."

"So I'm going to feel like this all the time?" Hawkwind pled.

"No, certainly not, only when you're ready to conceive."

"Conceive?" she gasped.

"What do you think matriarchs do? You're not aware that matriarchs are the only female members of a Line that have chicks?"

"Of course I know that, but," she trailed off.

"You might not conceive this first time," Thornfire said gently. "It was rushed early, triggered by the flight, and you are young for a matriarch."

"I'm fourteen winters," she whispered.

Hawkwind shivered. She might have a chick, and Rainsoft would be the sire.

"Even if you do, you won't be able to tell for a month or more, and it won't bother you for another month or two after that. It would be about eight months before the birth. If you don't conceive, then you'll keep having heats for a day or so once every month or two until you do."

A low keen built in her throat. "I don't know if I want this," she said.

"Should I have told you sooner?" Thornfire asked.

She darted a glance at him, but he looked honestly contrite, and even a little uncomfortable.

"It's not normal for a male to be telling a new matriarch about all this, even though males know it, and share it with younger males, when they become mature, although I don't know if anyone told Rainsoft anything. Usually, the retiring matriarch passes on this sort of thing and more to her successor."

"All males mate?" Hawkwind asked.

"Possibly," he answered, now looking even more uncomfortable in his turn. "It depends on if they are chosen by a matriarch they like. Sometimes matriarchs have particular favorites, or, very rarely, just one favorite, but it's not healthy for the Line if all offspring have the same sire. It's best for a matriarch to choose many different males, including ones from other Aeries if ever visiting."

"And males come into heat, too?"

"Males get interested in mating if there's a matriarch around who is in heat. We can tell, and it affects us. We behave differently depending on our age and personality and if we like that matriarch. If we don't like her, we just stay out of the way until she has chosen someone else and recovered. Even if we do like her, we have to be careful. If she doesn't want a particular male, but he's pushy anyway, she might claw him up to make her point."

Hawkwind clenched her hands on the rocks around the campfire.

"It doesn't overwhelm you and control you and make you lose your mind?"

He smiled a little. "Not until it's clear the matriarch has chosen and the flight comes to its end. You know, it may be disconcerting now, but some would consider you lucky. I don't think you can say this situation is all unpleasant."

Hawkwind looked back at the firestone, still not knowing how to feel.

"Starbright is my daughter," he said suddenly, and Hawkwind gaped at him. "Don't tell her. She doesn't know."

Hawkwind nodded agreement. She'd suspected their relationship was close and wondered about it, but hadn't suspected that the mage had sired his apprentice. Their colorations were somewhat similar, however, and now that Hawkwind knew, she could think of more ways they were similar, too. She suspected that he'd passed on his magical abilities to her if that was the way it worked.

It was normal that a griffin wouldn't know its sire. Hawkwind didn't know who hers had been although she'd had a suspicion: not that it mattered anymore. There were reasons why chicks weren't told. Sires always came from other Lines, and regardless of a chick's sex, its duty was to be loyal to its birth Line. Withholding the information could also prevent bullying or teasing in some situations. It was also sometimes the case that a matriarch would mate with more than one male during her heat and wouldn't know which was the father of the chick.

Male chicks found mentors among the older males of their own Line. Both females and males were almost never raised by their mother, getting passed to other members of the Line, so it wasn't like either of their birth parents played a major role in their lives. Hawkwind had been raised by her grandmother. To her, Hawkbrave had been her most important family member, closer to her than her actual mother, who had been busy with leading the Line and having more chicks anyway.

"Starkind, her mother—retired now of course—is a particularly good friend of mine, and we made a couple other Starchicks, too, but only Bright inherited my magic. Mages are always popular and I never rejected other matriarchs either. So, I've been through what you're going through, in a way," Thornfire continued. "Yet you also have so much more to deal with. I want to help you, Hawkwind, but it won't be easy. You are now the matriarch of the Hawk Line. If you embrace that, it will give you power and purpose, even more than you had when you took on the goal of seeing those human children to safety.

"We have a task here. I will find my brother. You and Rainsoft will retrieve the Sun and Moonstones. If Rainsoft did indeed come from Snow-in-lee, there may be even more we accomplish. His past, whatever it may be, waits down there in that city full of talis. If we can get through all this, we will go back to South-scree with whatever and whomever we find. Then I will do everything in my power to help you find a home, where you and your children—both human and griffin—can be safe."

Hawkwind awoke curled up with Rainsoft in his room. The wind had whistled all night long, covering any sound of their companionship. She should have been exhausted, having gotten only intermittent sleep, but somehow she strode to the sunrise side of camp feeling alert and ready. Her spirit had settled and now waited patiently for the right moment to leap to action. Today the investigation of fabled Snow-in-lee would begin.

She felt a touch on her shoulder and turned, expecting Rainsoft, but it was Jessika: shivering slightly and with sleep-grit still stuck to her umber eyelashes.

"Did you sleep well, Princess?" Hawkwind asked, softly enough that no one else would hear.

The girl ran her fingers through Hawkwind's fur. "I'm not a princess anymore, Hawkwind," she objected, eyes on the rocky dirt.

"Sure you are," Hawkwind smiled. "You're my princess, the Princess of Northnest, and I am your Feathyr, sworn to protect you. Don't forget it."

Jessika's face twisted up for a moment, about to cry, but then the girl forced herself to take a shaky breath and calm the tears away.

"You're going to Snow-in-lee today?" the girl asked.

"I think so. We'll at least investigate around it. We might not go in."

Jessika hugged her foreleg. "Be careful. You're my Feathyr. I need you to protect me, like you said."

"I'll be careful," Hawkwind assured her. "I need you to take care of Rikah and the others, and do what Starbright says, all right?"

"We will. I'll see you later, then?"

"Of course," Hawkwind smiled.

The girl ran back to the room she shared with the other children. Rainsoft and Starbright were both emerging from their rooms with much stretching and groaning. Thornfire strode out of his nest, giving a nod of good morning to Hawkwind, and took a look over the gravel entryway, towards Snow-in-lee. Hawkwind caught Rainsoft's eye and gestured, "good morning" to him. He returned it and they both trotted over to join Thornfire.

"I trust you both will stay with me today," the mage said, "and not go flying off. Things should have settled down by now, hmm, Hawkwind?"

She only blushed a little as she nodded. Indeed, the roiling passion of the previous half-day had all but vanished, and she felt calm and ready now: back to her old self.

"Rainsoft," Thornfire summoned, "you lived in Snow-in-lee?"

The grey griffin nodded in confirmation. "It's all I remember," he gestured, and Hawkwind translated aloud.

"Your mother, father?" Thornfire questioned.

"They were there," he confirmed, brows lowering like rain clouds.

"Thornfire," Hawkwind interrupted, "you could write your questions in the dirt, and Rainsoft can read them and answer them fluently

You're my
Feathyr.

the same way."

"A good idea," the mage agreed, sweeping away an area of gravel and extending a claw for writing.

"But say everything aloud, if you don't mind," she went on. "I want to know everything, too, and I can't read quickly yet."

"What was life like there?" Thornfire said, as he wrote in the dirt. Rainsoft scratched out a reply and Thornfire read it. "We lived in one big room," the mage reported. "We never left it. We were fed. Meat was dropped in through a hole near the roof. There was also a door, but it rarely opened. There was a window, too, high in the wall, and narrow. We could see only a stone wall through it."

"You were prisoners?" Hawkwind commented, stunned.

"We could not leave the room," Thornfire went on reading as Rainsoft wrote. "I was born there. I never flew more than a flapping hop. I can't speak. My parents and siblings can't speak either."

"Why not?" Thornfire asked.

Rainsoft touched his throat and wrote with his other hand. Thornfire read, "I saw, when my little sister was born. The—I don't know this word: brakil?" Thornfire pointed to it, and Rainsoft made a gesture that Hawkwind assumed was the sign language for the word, but it didn't mean anything to her. Thornfire kept reading. "The brakil came into the room after she was born. I was terrified. I had never seen them before that I remember. I was only a few years old. My parents let them take my sister. They cut into her throat. She screamed. They kept cutting until she couldn't scream anymore. Then they left."

Rainsoft stopped writing. His wings were trembling and Hawkwind wrapped one of hers around him. "Thornfire, let's stop," she whispered.

"No," he refused. "I need this information. I have to know what the situation is down there." He brushed away Rainsoft's writing and scratched his own. "Draw a brakil, please."

In the blank area below the command, Rainsoft started sketching with a claw. A long, round body with no limbs but spiny fins along its length and around its head emerged. It looked like some sort of snake. It had the first quarter of its body reared up, much like a snake. Rainsoft drew a quick sort of scale pattern along some of its back. "Big," he wrote beside it; Hawkwind could read that word. "Sharp," he went on, drawing an arrow to indicate its pointed, barb-like tail.

"That is a talis," Thornfire said softly. "As I suspected, they are keeping some of our people captive."

"Why?" Hawkwind asked, shivering.

"They need them to keep the Sun and Moonstones running," he said briefly. "Rainsoft," he began writing again. "How did you escape?" Rainsoft started writing, and Thornfire continued to read out his words. "The brakil, talis, came again, years later, and took my older brother. My parents didn't stop them; they just stood still. My brother, too, just stopped, and let himself be taken. I wasn't as scared this time, but didn't know what to do, so I just stood and watched, too. I didn't know why no one tried to stop the talis. I never saw my brother again. A few years later, they came again. They came for me."

"Why?" Hawkwind asked. "Why did they take you and your brother?"

"Later," Thornfire told her. "What happened when they tried to take you?" he wrote for Rainsoft.

"My parents stood still, like times before," Rainsoft wrote for Thornfire to read aloud. "When they had taken my brother, they wrapped him up in their coils and dragged him out the door that way. They approached me. The door was still open."

Rainsoft stopped writing and stared at the ground, as if thinking hard. He swept away the words and slowly and deliberately, starting writing again.

"My parents taught me to read, write, and speak with my hands," he wrote. "We had some books. The room we lived in was big enough to walk and run around in. The ceiling was high and we flapped and hopped but never flew. Most of the time we read or slept or told stories. My parents told us hundreds of stories, mostly about the talis. They said the talis were powerful beings that ruled over us. They didn't seem to fear them, but rather they thought that the talis were caring for us."

His brow furrowed and he wiped away the words in the dirt so he could keep going, the strokes of his claw getting more vigorous. "They said the talis had brought them together, and kept them safe, and fed them. They told me that when my brother was taken, it was so he could be given to his fated mate, to be with forever and have a family with. They told me that I would be taken, too, for the same thing, that it was a day I could look forward to, and not something to fear."

Rainsoft cleared his slate again, with a furious swipe. "I could not accept what they said. They comforted me and assured me that some-day I would understand. I did not know why they so calmly accepted the situation. I was curious. I wanted to know what was outside the room, where the talis were. The meat we received looked like another kind of creature to me, and I wondered what it was, where it lived, what it ate. I did not want to live the same life my parents had lived. I did not know why they never resisted the talis, but I decided that I would, when the talis came for me."

This time, after he rubbed away his words, Rainsoft sat for a while, staring at the ground, Hawkwind retracted her wing from around him, now that he seemed less traumatized. He noticed, looked up, gave her a smile, and briefly preened her neck feathers.

"I didn't want to cause a problem around my parents or sister," he wrote for Thornfire to read. "When the talis came, I stood quietly and let them wrap me in their coils. My parents didn't even bid me farewell. My brother hadn't told them goodbye, so I didn't either. They took me out of the room I had spent my whole life in and into a long narrow room. I now know it is called a hallway. They took me down the hall-way a long way, to another door. I looked around. The hallway turned. I had no idea what was beyond it. The talis put me down to open the door. I ran."

Hawkwind stared at him, an intense sensation of pride making her chest tremble like a newborn butterfly's wings. Rainsoft cleared his writing again.

"At first, they didn't notice. They weren't paying attention to me. Then I heard them hiss with anger. I had never heard them make a sound before. I ran, and I was sure they would catch me. I got tired right away; I had never run so much. I didn't know where to go. I got lost in so many hallways. I ran up and down stairs searching for a safe place. I was surprised I outran the talis. I found an exit to the building I was in. I saw the sky."

It was Thornfire's voice saying the words, and he was using an even and measured tone, but looking at Rainsoft's face gave all the intonation needed. His orange eyes lit up much like a clearing sky.

"I tried to fly," he wrote, "but I could hardly even hop, so I ran. I saw a few more talis, but they couldn't catch me. It took me hours to find a way out of the city. I located a warm river. There were talis along it, and they were faster than the others had been. I was exhausted, but the talis were mean, trying to bite me and stab me with their tails, so I dared not stop. I knew then that they were not our gods, or not any gods worth living forever in a single room for. I ran and I kept running. I had no idea where I was going, or what this world was. I didn't know how I would survive or what dangers I would face out in the world, beyond some old legends my parents had recited."

"Your journey is remarkable," Thornfire said, writing it at the same time. "I see why you were so confused and scared when you were captured and wing cut and locked up in South-scree."

"I learned to hunt and learned to fly," Rainsoft wrote. "I almost died of hunger before I managed to catch my first prey. I never saw other griffins until your people caught me. I am afraid to go back, but I also want to save my parents, and brother and sister. I don't see why the talis have the right or power to keep us captive."

Thornfire quickly cleared away his words and started explaining. "Rainsoft, you are special. The talis, brakil, hypnotize griffins. Most griffins can't stop staring at them, and lose their ability to think, move, or resist. Very few griffins are immune to that. The reason you were able to escape is because you are. Your parents and siblings were helpless against the talis. That is probably why your parents learned to accept their fate and love the talis. There was nothing they could do."

Rainsoft's jaw muscles were bulging. He wrote curtly, "I didn't know."

"They hypnotize me, too," Thornfire admitted. "That is the biggest danger to us. You have a unique immunity."

Hawkwind wondered if she would be immune, too, but expected she wouldn't be at the same time she hoped she'd never have to find out.

"Do you have any idea how many griffins are in Snow-in-lee?" Thornfire asked.

Rainsoft shook his head. "And I don't know how to find them. I got lost getting away. I don't think I'd be able to find the room I lived in again."

Thornfire straightened. "Well, today we'll just fly over. The talis can't hurt us from the ground, and they have poor distance vision. They probably wouldn't be able to see us, even if they looked up."

Hawkwind filed away that morsel of information and nodded her agreement. "Are we ready then?"

"Let's have a nice flight," Thornfire smiled. "Rainsoft," he said fervently. "Thank you."

Rainsoft nodded and gestured, "you're welcome. It felt good to be able to tell someone." Hawkwind translated his signing.

The three of them launched, one after the other, off the gravel entryway. Wings stretched to catch the air, they took up the formation they'd briefly had the previous day, and Thornfire led them over the mountain peaks towards the steaming valley of Snow-in-lee.

Chapter 15
Snow-in-lee

The trio landed on a rocky peak above the ancient city. It was nearing sunset and the white towers were made bloody, the plant life black, and the swirling steam petal pink by the red sun. They had spent the rest of the day, after hearing Rainsoft's story, flying over the city, first from a distance and then as closely as they dared, looking for ways in and signs of life. Now, they clung to the spire above the city and looked down upon it. Thornfire pointed.

"There below us, the warm river Rainsoft found when he escaped," the mage spoke, slowly, perhaps hoping Rainsoft would be able to follow. "It exits the city through several metal grates at the base of the southern walls and winds away from the city until it plunges into a hole in the rocks and vanishes from sight. Did you see the great gates on the western side? The talis never bothered to shut them when they won the city. Probably they couldn't figure out the mechanism. I expect Rainsoft exited through those gates.

"There are also two back ways. You saw where the city touches the surrounding mountains on the northern and eastern sides, I expect. There are tunnels through the rock that open into the buildings that abut them. One of those tunnels is how my brother and I used to visit the city."

"Will we use those tunnels for getting in?" Hawkwind asked.

"Probably. They will have to be scouted to see if the talis hang around them. They're higher up in the city. The talis tend to stay to the lower areas, nearer the hot water, and I've never seen talis there before, but it's best to be cautious. Let's check them tomorrow."

Hawkwind saw Rainsoft give a firm nod from the corner of her eye, and she wondered again how much he was coming to understand spoken language.

"Thornfire," she began nervously, "how are we going to do this?

The Stones are deep in there, aren't they? And we have no idea where your brother is, do we? There are sure to be talis around. How many? How can we just wander through the place searching?"

"Calm yourself, Hawkwind," Thornfire soothed. "I've wandered the place before. There are ways; we just have to be careful. I will grant you," he gave her a dubious look, "I have never seen the Stones."

"How do you know they even exist? They're just a story."

"It's not just a story. It's in our history."

"Not all history is true," she told him, thinking of all the things she'd read and heard people claim. "Most of the griffins at South-scree even consider Northnest and its creation a myth."

"History may be falsified and bent to reflect the writer's preferences, true, but the hot water is still there," he countered. "The Stones must be there. Perhaps tomorrow we can get a glimpse of them. It's getting late. Let's go back to camp now. The talis will be leaving the city with their store of heat in their bodies to hunt. We mustn't be caught out in the open."

Hawkwind spent that night in her own room. She still valued Rainsoft as a dear friend and companion, possibly more than any griffin she'd ever known except her grandmother and sister, but the irresistible urge to be with him had faded. Her heat was over, and it relieved her. Something like that would only get in the way of her focusing on sneaking through an ancient city full of giant finned snakes capable of hypnotizing her to retrieve a magic rock.

When she woke up after a night of half sleeping and shivering, however, she wished she'd slept with Rainsoft simply for the benefit of sharing his body heat. She resolved to ask to curl up with him at night from then on, as long as they were on the mountain. She didn't think he'd have any reason to refuse.

"Perhaps you should sleep with Thornfire, or the children," Hawkwind suggested to Starbright as the golden griffin emerged from her own room yawning. "It would be warmer."

"Good idea," Starbright replied.

Hawkwind covertly eyed the young female. It didn't seem that Starbright had cared about or even noticed that Hawkwind had awakened as a matriarch and had a tryst with Rainsoft. She supposed that was natural. Hawkwind herself had never paid any attention to the habits of matriarchs. Males had been totally uninteresting except as platonic companions before two days ago. Perhaps Starbright truly had been oblivious. Hawkwind wondered if Starbright would ever earn the place of matriarch for the Star Line back at South-scree.

There were no remains from the previous night's dinner except what had been cooked and hidden under gravel by the campfire stone for the children. Hawkwind still felt full, however, so it was no hardship to get up and going without something to eat. Thornfire and Rainsoft were sitting by the campfire stone, writing things to each other.

"Rainsoft says that during his escape, he estimates he saw about a dozen talis," Thornfire shared. "Of course he never encountered the hot pool at the base of the city, and that is where most of the talis are likely to be."

"Do we have any chance of killing a talis?" Hawkwind asked, sitting down with them.

"I don't think their scales are immune to our bills or claws. If we could avoid being hypnotized, there's a chance."

"No one has come up with a way to do it?"

"You fancy fighting one of those beasts with your eyes closed?" Thornfire countered. "They strike as quickly as any serpent, when they're warm. That is a hopeless battle. Perhaps Rainsoft could do it, if he were very careful and fast, facing only one of them. The odds would improve if the talis were cold. They're slow when they're cold."

"What defenses do we have then?"

"The smell," Thornfire reminded her. "Talis have a strong, musky scent, although I suspect that Rainsoft may not be able to detect it, since he spent his whole life among them." Thornfire started writing in the dirt again. "What do talis smell like?"

Rainsoft shook his head. "I never noticed a smell," he wrote.

"So you and I, Hawkwind, will have be aware of the scents around us."

Starbright, perhaps wanting to feel useful, started writing down everything that was being said.

"Talis also have poor distance vision, as I mentioned, but they still have an uncanny ability to detect other creatures. I confess that I don't know how they do it, if it is by scent or hearing, or vibrations through the ground, or something else. At any rate, we must move silently and as light of foot as possible. Our scent, unfortunately, we can do little about."

"Have you ever fought one?" Hawkwind asked.

"Any time one showed a hint of detecting me, I fled. I've never faced one in battle."

Rainsoft gestured, "I will fight."

"They are strong, and they strike rapidly," Thornfire said slowly, giving Rainsoft a firm glare. "Fighting is dangerous. I don't want you to die, and I cannot help you. I must not look at them."

Rainsoft nodded reluctantly.

"Maybe I will be immune, too," Hawkwind hoped, "and then we can fight together."

He gave her a little smile and she returned it.

"We should get going," Thornfire suggested. "We'll scout the upper areas today, and see if we can get a glimpse of the hot pool and the Stones. Tomorrow we will leave early in the morning, at the coldest time of day, after the talis have spent their warmth hunting and are at their weakest. Hopefully we won't encounter any talis today, and we'll formulate a plan how to approach the situation tomorrow."

"The camp will be ready for you when you return," Starbright said cheerfully. "Be careful, all of you, and come back safe."

"All right, let's go," the mage instructed, and led them to the sky.

"It's open; that's not a good sign," Thornfire observed in a whisper.

A thick wooden door, nearly bleached of its color by however many winters and summers, was propped open against the rock wall, leaning crookedly from old hinges.

"Wing and I always shut it when we left, for security. The talis aren't good with doors," he went on.

"Why did you and your brother come out here anyway?" Hawkwind breathed.

"I sought the libraries," he answered. "Magic lore lost for centuries may be preserved here somewhere. My brother has an uncanny ability to commune with animals, understand them, and control them. He had the idea that he could do something about the talis. We were both young, especially Wing; we had the crazy idea that we might find a way to take back Snow-in-lee."

Thornfire shook his head, like an old horse swaying in its pasture. "We were fools. I realized it eventually, and gave up, but he never did. I refused to keep returning with him. One time, he never came back."

"Do you think he's alive?"

"I don't know. If he is, I expect he is a prisoner of the talis now. Let's move forward. Keep scenting for talis. I will regularly flick my tail. If I stop moving, and stop flicking, it may indicate that I've seen a talis. If that happens, get ready to run, and dig your bill or claws into me. A sharp pain can break the hypnotic effect."

They crept around the doorjamb and into the dank tunnel. With silent, slow steps they moved forward. The tunnel was only slightly larger than a full-grown griffin. If they did encounter a talis, it would be difficult to turn around and run, even if they weren't hypnotized by it.

The tunnel was not long, and shortly they came up to another door, this one only partly open, wide enough for a griffin to squeeze through. Hawkwind and Rainsoft waited while Thornfire cautiously peered through the gap, tail slowly flicking up and down. He cautiously looked around the back of the door, and then moved into the room beyond. Hawkwind and Rainsoft followed.

"Hawkwind, do you smell it? It's faint now. It will be much stronger if a talis is near."

She took a deep breath and caught it, a rich musk of sweat and clay earth and something else that stank sourly.

"I smell it, I think," she answered softly.

"Good," Thornfire murmured. "If it ever rolls over you in waves like to make you sick, you are far too close to a talis. This room is unchanged from the last time I saw it."

The room had no door into the rest of the building, or if there had once been one, it was long disintegrated. Hawkwind glanced out the doorway, seeing an empty hallway except for some moss and grasses growing up between the stones. She crossed the room in about six strides. It too was mostly empty but for debris of old rocks, boards, and sacks slowly rotting in the corners. Mushrooms grew up from the piles in a few places. The room was lit only by light coming in through the door-less doorway.

"Let's keep moving," Thornfire told them.

He led them into the hallway. Occasional doorways opened into more rooms on each side. Thornfire stuck his head into them, checking them, and Hawkwind followed suit. They looked much like the first room had, but sometimes with more wreckage of things that might have once been furniture. The rooms had windows also, all unglazed, but Thornfire didn't lead them into any of the rooms to look through the windows until they came to a turn in the hallway, where a ramp led downwards.

"Wing and I thought this was probably a residential area, possibly for those who defended the city: sentries, guards, and the like, since it's near an entrance," Thornfire explained. "The ramp leads down to more floors of rooms like these, and to a large hall. We think that was where guests and traders who entered this way would be received and occupy stalls for sale of their goods. Before we go that way, come take a look here."

The group clustered at one of the windows.

"You can see part of the hot pool, and there, Hawkwind, your first look at a talis," he said. "You're far enough away, here, that it can't entrance you."

It looked bigger than she'd expected, even from such a distance. It was lying at the edge of the pool with the water lapping over its long, scaled body. At the moment, it looked quite peaceful.

"Are they all blue and brown?" she asked.

"It looks that way now, from this angle, with this light," Thornfire explained. "As it moves, the light will play over its scales and its color will shift. Even though we're far away, you probably shouldn't look too long."

Hawkwind moved her gaze away from it and shook her head. Had she been slightly hypnotized, or just curious at seeing one for the first time? She couldn't be sure. She didn't want to believe that she was vulnerable to talis enchantment, even though she knew it was very likely. Griffins such as Rainsoft were exceedingly rare, according to Thornfire.

"Onward," Thornfire prodded, leading them back out the room.

They went down the ramp to the bottom and cautiously into the big hall.

"Wing and I have already picked through all this wreckage," Thornfire whispered.

Indeed, there were piles of wood, canvas, stone, broken pottery, bits of metal, and other materials scattered all around the room. Hawkwind tested the air. The scent of talis was slightly stronger, but not enough for her to fear there was one nearby.

"I am walking the path that Wing and I usually used. If he had to flee and was killed during his escape, I'd expect his body first to be along this path, if the talis didn't eat him, which they probably would have," Thornfire explained. "Still, there might be signs of a struggle. We'll go next to the balcony where he often observed the talis."

"Thornfire," Hawkwind called in a whisper, "was your brother immune to the talis' hypnotism?"

"Very much so," he replied. "It's one reason he felt more comfortable here than I did. This way."

They took a narrow staircase up a tight round tower, emerging onto a snug balcony. Below them, the hot pool was clearly visible, but a portion of it vanished back among more buildings.

"We can't see the Sun or Moonstones from here," Hawkwind murmured.

"I've never seen them," Thornfire confessed. "They're deeper into the city, at the center. We'll have to find our way there without getting caught."

"And then find a way to steal the Stones and make it out without getting caught," Hawkwind added. "How heavy will they be?"

"I can't tell you. I don't know what kind of rock they were carved from, a heavy type or a light type."

The talis were soaking lazily in the pool below, their long finned bodies waving gently. From here, closer, Hawkwind could observe the ever-shifting colors of their scales. There had been times, back at Northnest, when she'd seen the wastewater the kitchens threw out. Often she saw a film on the water, like liquid rainbows ever shifting and shining. There was an aspect of that when she looked at the talis, combined with the flutter of a thousand autumn leaves in the wind flashing gold and ochre and rust and butter yellow against the bright blue of a midday sky. She wanted to watch forever.

"Don't look too long, Hawkwind," Thornfire warned sharply, but quietly.

Hawkwind tore her gaze away from them.

"There is no evidence of my brother here. Let's keep moving."

The trio descended the tower, checking for scents and the sound of movement with every step, but this, too, seemed to be an area of the city that the talis had found no use for, and did not occupy.

"We'll go to the library," Thornfire whispered.

They moved into another building and up some stairs. The scent of talis diminished. Thornfire led them now to a grand doorway. The doors, made of some kind of metal that had tarnished over the years, stood slightly ajar, just enough for the griffins to slip inside. Hawkwind stopped and stared in awe.

"I've never seen such a room," she remarked, "even in Northnest, and there were large rooms there."

"This was the mages' library," Thornfire said, neck arched and wings slightly mantled, as though he somehow took credit for it.

It was a long room, stretching along one side of the building, with wide windows all along it. The ceiling was high, looking down on the wreckage of shelves and desks.

"Generations of mages stored their research here, though I do expect that they also kept some spells to themselves, written only in their own grimoires," Thornfire went on.

"Even though this was supposed to be a place of education and sharing?"

Thornfire offered her a smile. "No mage gives away all his secrets. For example, despite all my reading here, I've never found the book that explains the Stones."

He walked into the depths of the room. Hawkwind and Rainsoft followed, watching as the elder lifted heavy layers of canvas, glancing at the piles of books hidden under them.

"You emptied all the shelves?" Hawkwind wondered, noticing that among the disintegrating bookcases was not a single book.

"I have done my best to save them," he answered. "Being on the shelves, exposed to light, air, and any rain or snow that blew in, they were fast deteriorating. There are far too many for me to move back to South-scree, even in a lifetime, and even if I had some place to put them. Piling them up in the darkest, most protected corners, and covering them was the best I could do. I did take a few. Perhaps someday," he didn't finish his thought.

Thornfire flicked his wings to resettle them. "At any rate, there is no sign of my brother here either. I thought, if he expected to die, and wished to leave his pendant for me to find, he might have left it here, knowing it was my favorite place in Snow-in-lee, but I don't see it anywhere."

The mage sat and beckoned Rainsoft and Hawkwind closer.

"And now, the easy places are exhausted," he said. "From here, the only other places I have explored, I did so with great risk, as they are areas I or my brother have encountered the talis in. There are other areas of course that we never ventured into, either because they were true talis territory, or because they looked structurally unsound, or just uninteresting. Most of the upper area of the city is nothing but empty rooms with bits of wreckage, like you've seen, and most of the lower area the talis live in."

Rainsoft raised his hands and gestured. "My family: I want to find them."

Hawkwind translated aloud for Thornfire.

"I hope we can rescue them," Thornfire nodded seriously. "I need to search for my brother in deeper areas of the city, too. The problem is all the talis around. We need a way to get them out of the city or at least distracted."

"They're here because of the hot water the Stones make," Hawkwind affirmed. "We have to steals the Stones first, don't we?"

"You have summed it up nicely," Thornfire praised.

"The talis will know," Rainsoft countered, with Hawkwind again as interpreter, "someone took the Stones."

"They aren't that bright," Thornfire said cheerfully. "If we can get out without getting caught or seen, they will be confused, yes, maybe even angry, but they won't know what to do about it. It will take them a long time to formulate the thought that someone stole them. It would take even longer for them to come up with the idea that if they investigate and search that they might be able to find the thief and take back the Stones. Such a thing would probably never occur to them. They will simply observe that the Stones are gone, that the water is draining and no longer so hot, and thus Snow-in-lee becomes of no more particular use to them than any other location in the mountains. A few might remain, but they won't congregate here any more."

Hawkwind shrugged, "we have to steal the Stones at some point anyway," she agreed grudgingly.

Thornfire flexed his pectorals. "Let's see if we can find a safe part of the city from which we can see the Stones, and get as close to them as possible."

According to Thornfire, he'd never explored this part of the city. For a few hours now, Hawkwind, Rainsoft, and Thornfire had been clinging to the roofs, jumping across spaces between buildings, and scaling walls. The architecture of the city surrounded them like a stone forest, and they leapt from branch to branch like rather large winged squirrels. They had decided moving about on the exteriors of the buildings—where the talis had little hope of climbing—would be safer than sneaking through rooms and hallways where they might encounter a talis at any moment. Now the trio crouched together on a gutter cloaked with steam and looked where Thornfire pointed.

"Down there," he whispered. "This looks like the source of the water: the original spring. I think those are the Stones."

A few stories down was a circular pool made of stone blocks that merged almost seamlessly with the natural stone they were set on. From the pool, spouts on four sides let the water drain into series of connected pools that wound away among the buildings, including into a rather large main pool. From the center of the source pool bubbled up fresh, hot water that sent steam up in warm, wet clouds carrying the scent of sulfur. Directly above that roiling center hung two stones the size of melons, one above the other. The bottom one was half submerged in the water itself. Both Stones were dark, like black seeds in the midst of all the white water and mist, so they could be discerned even through the veil of steam.

"How are we going to get them?" Hawkwind mused.

"See? They are suspended there by long lines, chains, I think," Thornfire said. "If we find where the chains are tied off, we just pull them up."

Hawkwind followed the lines with her eyes. There were four, suspending both Stones in a sort of two-storied harness.

"Four lines, and three of us," she remarked.

"We won't be able to pull them all up at once. We pull three, some-one goes and pulls the fourth, then repeat," he said.

A variety of potential problems ran through Hawkwind's mind, but they wouldn't be able to tell if any of them were likely to occur until they actually tried it.

"Let's do it," Rainsoft gestured, jabbing his bill towards the pool confidently.

"I'm ready, too," Hawkwind murmured.

"Up we go then," Thornfire led them off.

They climbed up, following the lines until they found where they were attached to metal brackets clamped to stone pillars. It was a few stories higher yet, at an altitude where the Stones had become diffi-cult to see. There was a ledge to stand on, although it was thickly cov-ered with moss and other tiny plants growing in the gaps between the stones. There was nothing to wrap the lines around to hold them as the griffins pulled up the Stones.

The buildings kept going up higher another few stories above them to where some kind of bridge crossed over the gap. From there, Hawkwind also saw an array of heavy chains dangling down in the cen-ter of the steam chimney and ending at about eye level. They had heavy, wicked looking hooks on their ends and seemed to be coated with rust.

"The two of us just pulling up a single line each may be able to manage," she said, "but the third that has to run back and forth be-tween two lines won't be able to do it. There's nothing to hold the line once it's pulled up so he or she can let go to go to the other line."

"That's a problem," Thornfire agreed. "I worry about the Stones slipping out of their harnesses if we are only able to pull up three lines, and can't keep the balance exactly right."

"What about those hooks? Can we lower them and hook the Stones, and pull them up?"

"Let's go up there and see what the setup is," Thornfire agreed, "but those hooks may not be well suited to grabbing the Stones."

The three griffins climbed up to the bridge that crossed over the steam chimney, from which the hooked chains dangled like wind chimes. As she pulled herself over the edge and got her feet under her, Hawkwind felt her feathers starting to prickle. She glanced around quickly, but saw no danger. As she walked out onto the bridge, her unease grew.

Most of the city was covered with moss and lichens, but here, a bare trail led to the bridge, as if it was used perhaps not frequently, but from time to time, enough to keep all but the most stubborn of lichens from growing on it. She followed the path with her eyes, back to an open doorway. When she reached the place where the chains were crudely wound around the bridge, she saw that the stones in that area were dark, as if permanently stained with shadow.

"Thornfire, what are these chains for?" she blurted.

He, too, was staring at the setup, feathers slicked. "I don't know," he confessed.

Rainsoft was as still as a statue beside her, as if he'd stopped breathing.

"I have a bad feeling," Hawkwind stuttered. "I don't like this place."

"What you are feeling is an echo that lives in the rocks and metal here," Thornfire explained slowly. "I can feel it clearly, for it is a type of magic, just as I can feel the magic in Stones down there. The magic of the Stones is bright and steady in my mind, like a lantern flame in calm air. This, however, is sharp and aching and laced with the fear of the dark. What you feel are layers of pain and death. It burns me inside to be near it, for it is not a type of power I am attuned to drawing upon. You two it will make uneasy and ill and frightened."

"Pain," Rainsoft gestured, "death: whose?"

Thornfire's eyes closed as though he watched an innocent who had been safely hidden step into a battle, and he could do nothing to save him.

"Griffins', many griffins' deaths," he answered, although Hawkwind felt like she hadn't needed to hear it said. She'd already known, only she hadn't wanted to see it.

"That's why they keep the griffins here," she whispered. "Death magic will power the Stones?"

"We griffins are slightly magical by nature. I doubt very much that's how the original griffin mages did it, and I don't know how the Stones work, but I think it plausible."

That's why the Stones were dark. That's what had stained the bridge. That's what had created such a thick coat of what she'd thought was rust on the chains. That's why the hooks were so big and wickedly pointed. She wondered: did the talis kill the griffins before they ran the hooks through their bones and hung them to bleed out? The horror of having the thought and the visions it created almost made Hawkwind lose her last meal. She purposefully did not look at Rainsoft.

"I don't think these hooks will aid us in getting the Stones," Thornfire was saying, although a buzzing in Hawkwind's ears made it hard to hear him. "I have another idea. Let's go back to the mossy ledge."

She numbly followed Thornfire off the bridge, and they waited until Rainsoft had spent some moments in stillness, staring at the stain, and joined them. He didn't say anything. They fluttered back down to the ledge and avoided looking at the hooks.

"It's risky to pull up the Stones without the fourth line while the lines are aligned like this, sort of north, south, east, and west," Thornfire explained, pointing, and Hawkwind focused on his words to dispel her lingering nausea. "No matter what three lines we choose, one side will have no support and the Stones could tip easily, but if we can break one line off from its bracket, we could pull up the lines in a sort of north, west, and southeast configuration, for example, and be much more stable."

Hawkwind nodded, and Rainsoft was nodding, too.

"Once the Stones are level with this ledge," Thornfire went on, "one of us pulls while the other two let out slack, until the puller has brought the Stones to the ledge."

"I think it could work," Hawkwind agreed.

The confused tilt of Rainsoft's head led Hawkwind to try to translate with word, gestures, and drawings clawed into the moss, while Thornfire searched for the weakest looking line and bracket. Eventually, the young griffin seemed to understand, and they sat in uncomfortable silence for a few moments, waiting for Thornfire. Hawkwind's eyes were drawn to the rusty hooks, and she fought away the vision of Rainsoft impaled on them, struggling and dying, as soon as it inevitably assaulted her mind.

Impulsively, she leaned over and preened his neck feathers. He made a sound like a nervous nestling and returned the favor. The moment ended as Thornfire hopped back over to them.

"They're all pretty solid," he said. "I'll have to use some magic, see if I can melt the links. It'll take a while, so wait a bit."

The mage went to the nearest line, crouched down, and extended a finger to hover just above the spot where the line attached to the bracket.

"I'd like you both to come hold the line," he instructed.

Hawkwind and Rainsoft huddled down with Thornfire, holding tight to the line, while he worked his magic. She looked down at the steamy pool below. It seemed devoid of talis, and she wondered if perhaps it was too hot for them, or maybe they, too, avoided this place of death, although they didn't seem to have had a problem with creating this place of death. At least it meant that the griffin trio wasn't likely to be discovered, unless the talis came out to execute a captive griffin while they were there.

"Hold tight, it's almost through," Thornfire announced, and Hawkwind tightened her grip.

She could feel the new unsteadiness in the line, and when it broke the sudden partial weight of the Stones hit her arm, but it wasn't that much: three lines still held it.

"Hawkwind, Rainsoft, who shall hold this line?"

The shift in his posture, although subtle, immediately informed Hawkwind of Rainsoft's intent, and Thornfire nodded.

"It is yours then, Rainsoft. Do not drop it. I will do the pulling. It's magic; I'm magic. I'm best suited to handling the Stones until we know how safe it is. Hawkwind, let's get in position."

Hawkwind glanced back as she walked off, watching Rainsoft adjust his line so it was equidistant from two others. She claimed one of those two, and Thornfire claimed the other. Her hands were shaking as she gripped the line. If the Stones fell, they would plunge deep into the hot spring. Although the lack of magic input would mean they'd eventually stop working—someday achieving the goal of helping to disperse the talis—the spring had been natural to begin with, just smaller with lower water flow, and Hawkwind imagined it would remain active. There was no telling how deep it was. The Stones would probably be impossible to retrieve. Gone with them would be her chance of having a safe place to live with her human wards at South-scree. Hawkwind clenched her jaw. This had to work.

Through the mist the three griffins made eye contact and balanced back on their hind legs with wings and tails extended and bracing for balance against the ledge and walls. Purposefully exaggeratedly, Thornfire lifted an arm and lowered it to the line. Hawkwind copied him and matched his slow pull. A quick glance confirmed that Rainsoft was doing the same. Far below, the Stones shivered in their harness as they moved a fraction skyward. Hawkwind fixed her gaze on Thornfire then and synchronized herself with him: hand over hand, pulling steadily. The loose line she gathered, she trapped under a hind leg.

Silent but for the subtle rumbling bubble of the spring below and the soft scratching of the fine chain between claws and mossy rock, the procedure continued until the Stones in their harness stood taut and level with the ledge the griffins perched on. Hawkwind looked out at them, almost close enough to touch. The darkness stained on them was rusty and curdled: old blood that the mist had not been able to wash off.

Thornfire jingled his section of slack line to attract attention and made another exaggerated pulling motion, this time horizontally. Hawkwind and Rainsoft nodded and stood ready to release line as he would pull, moving the Stones across the chimney and to his ledge. With enough slack now, Hawkwind was also able to adjust her positioning slightly, and Rainsoft did the same, making three equal angles around the central Stones, and keeping them equal as Thornfire drew the Stones to his ledge.

After several more cautious minutes, Hawkwind saw Thornfire close his hand around the line adjacent to the harness the Stones sat in. Then he backed up and set them down on the mossy ledge. Hawkwind released breath she hadn't known she was holding, let her line loosen, and rushed to his side. Rainsoft arrived not a second later.

Thornfire looked up at them, face shining with delight and awe. "These are the most magical artifacts I have ever encountered, items of legend thought lost to us forever. Hawkwind, Rainsoft, it is thanks to your help and all our caution and bravery that they have been recovered."

One, the one that had been lower in the harness and sitting partially in the water, was mostly clean, although the bottom half along with the harness appeared encrusted with some kind of mineral. Heat radiated from the Stone.

"That's the Sunstone," Thornfire confirmed. "It will be hot to the touch so be careful Hawkwind."

The Moonstone was thickly coated with blood, especially on the topside, but had no other remarkable feature.

"If you pass your hands near it, you may feel a strange sensation," Thornfire said. "I think it's harmless. It pulls things to it. Solid things aren't affected much, but air and water—and blood—will be drawn close and stick to it if they can. Rainsoft, you can probably safely carry it in your hands, but I do have bags."

Thornfire took off his pack and drew out two leather sacks. He handed one to each of his companions. Hawkwind stared down at the Sunstone. She could feel the heat from it beating on her, even through her fur and feathers, making her need to blink more to keep her eyes moist. Below the Sunstone, the moss it sat on was already browning.

"I can't believe someone made something so powerful," she murmured. "This must be something like a hundred times hotter than the ones you and Starbright make."

"And self-sustaining for a hundred times longer," the mage agreed. "Whatever craft was used to make these Stones is long lost. What remains is merely a shadow of what our mages once knew."

She lifted the Stone by its fine, metal chain and spread out the leather bag below it, then lowered it into place.

"Hopefully, the bag won't burn," Thornfire said.

"I'll keep an eye on it as we fly. We are flying back now, aren't we?"

"I suppose we should. The Stone should be safe at camp."

Rainsoft had his bagged, too. They crouched to leap—and then a wave of stench washed over them. Thornfire crouched, wings slightly spread and trembling. Hesitantly, Hawkwind mimicked him.

"Talis," he breathed. "Don't look around, Hawkwind. Listen for the sound of its scales on the stone."

Rainsoft hadn't crouched, but instead cast his gaze around. Hawkwind kept her eyes down, on the bag holding the Sunstone, but even without looking noted that the steam had started to clear. She could no longer hear the subtle bubbling of the spring below. Had the talis noticed the difference in their water already, and come to investigate?

Rainsoft lowered himself into her line of view. "Below," he gestured. "Two."

"Against the wall, everyone," Thornfire said, voice barely audible.

The ledge was not very wide. If the talis looked up, they might be able to see a bit of griffin. The trio edged sideways with as much silent care as possible, flattening themselves against the wall. Hawkwind heard a hiss from below, and the sound of water splashing. The stink continued, growing a little stronger. After some minutes, the splashing stopped and Hawkwind thought she detected the faint scraping of scales on stones. She wasn't sure, as she'd never heard such a sound before. The smell began to lessen.

"They're moving away," Thornfire whispered. "I expect they'll investigate further. We need to leave."

"They're gone," Rainsoft gestured, looking cautiously down at the spring.

"Come on."

Thornfire hopped upward, climbing swiftly up the wall, with sweeps of his wings for additional lift. Hawkwind and Rainsoft buckled their leather bags through belts on their harnesses, tugging them to be sure they were secured, and followed. The weight of the Stones pulled down on them, but it was not grounding. They joined Thornfire on the bridge and Hawkwind looked down below at the spring. The water moved only slightly, a few ripples coming forth, and the steam was now only the lightest veil.

"It's time to go anyway," Thornfire said. "Sunset will be soon enough. Can you both fly with those Stones?"

"I think so," Hawkwind answered, and Rainsoft nodded his agreement.

The breeze brought them another whiff of talis scent and Hawkwind looked down at the bridge below her feet, fixing her eyes there despite the surge of need to look around for the enemy.

"Where is it?" Thornfire asked.

In front of their faces, Rainsoft gestured, "many below."

"They noticed more quickly than I had expected," Thornfire

muttered.

"Will they see us up here?"

"If they come up here, they will. I don't see why they would think to investigate the bridge unless they could somehow guess that griffins had stolen the Stones, but logic is not something talis always ascribe to."

A chorus of hissing and raspy growling came from below.

"Do you think they're talking?" Hawkwind murmured.

"They must communicate somehow, I suppose," the mage answered. "They do have some organization to their society, and they came up with a way to power the Stones. Thornwing might know more, if I ever find him."

Rainsoft made a series of nearly violent gestures. "They aren't worth knowing about, except how to kill them," he said.

"I'm inclined to agree," Thornfire grunted.

"More," Rainsoft suddenly added. "More below."

The reek of them grew and Hawkwind's skin prickled. The sound of their scales scraping over stone buzzed like a steady waterfall of sand.

"They are angry," Rainsoft told them.

"How heavy are the Stones? Can you take off with an upward leap?" Thornfire asked.

"I'd rather run into it or leap off something," Hawkwind confessed.

"Let's try climbing that tower."

Thornfire led them off at a crawl, past the shadow of old blood on the bridge and the crusted chains, towards a doorway into a square tower. The stench of the talis grew until Hawkwind began to feel nauseated by it. She kept her eyes on the ground, letting Rainsoft do the visual scanning; she had no idea how close the talis might be now. They could be searching the area, about to discover the trio at any moment. It certainly smelled like they must be close.

They reached the doorway and Thornfire took a cautious look inside. He ducked back out immediately.

"Not this way, up the outside," he ordered.

"What's in there?" Hawkwind gulped.

"Skins: it seems a popular place for the talis to come to shed. You can look if you want, but briefly."

Hawkwind took a quick glance inside. It seemed that the stairway going up had partly crumbled, leaving lots of irregularly shaped rocks scattered around the room, as well as a remaining stub of several steps. The floor was coated with old, stinking fragments and flakes of talis-skin, packed down into a rotting mat that broke up in places into clumps. It looked like the talis might use the irregularly shaped stones to rub against for removing their old skin.

"Let's go," Thornfire summoned.

Hawkwind started to pull back out when a distinct scraping came from the other doorway into the tower. A long, dark shape began to emerge from the deeper darkness of the door. Her brain abruptly stopped communicating with her body, and she got one dazzling glance at the talis before someone yanked her back and slapped her across the bill. She stumbled, dazed, and shook her head.

Rainsoft screeched in her face, and the message was clear: climb. Thornfire was already halfway up the tower and not looking back. Hawkwind followed as a cry somewhere between a hiss and a shriek boomed from within the tower. Rainsoft was right on her tail as she propelled herself up the rough tower. Below, she heard a furious rasp of scales over stone and a hiss of fury, but she didn't dare look back.

The brief glimpse she'd gotten was burned into her brain. The talis' head had been long and triangular, wide jawed, with iridescent spiny fins blossoming from the base of the skull all around. The eyes were small, too small to see iris or white, if they had any. The head had risen from a long, muscular neck further festooned with rigid fins along the spine. That neck had transitioned smoothly into a long, thick body in heavy curves along the floor. The whole body had glimmered like oil on water, rainbows shining and shifting across it. Hawkwind hadn't been

TALIS

able to look away. It seemed there would be no immunity for her from the hypnotism of the talis.

The cries of the frustrated talis bounced up to her as she climbed as quickly as she could. Between the sheer tower walls and the destroyed stairway within, the top of the tower should be safe for them. From there, they could do a dropping leap to get airborne, and leave the city behind for another day, but now the talis would know there were free griffins poking around. They might even make the conclusion that griffins had stolen the Stones, Hawkwind supposed.

Thornfire was waiting when she climbed over the edge. Rainsoft heaved himself up less than half a breath behind her.

"Not the best thing that could have happened," Thornfire panted, "but we're all alive. Hawkwind are you all right?"

"Just a little shaken," she admitted. "I couldn't look away. Rainsoft saved me."

She almost stumbled as the dark griffin nudged up against her, pressing into her body. He nibbled her neck feathers and crooned at her. Seized by a sudden fluttering panic at his actions, Hawkwind stepped away, flicking her feathers. She glared at Thornfire when she caught him smothering a chortle.

"We should go before they find a way up here," the mage said prudently. "Don't look down. We fly for the camp."

He launched off without another word, and Hawkwind followed him close enough to nip his tail. The Stone was a burden, but she'd carried heavier weight in the past, and with strong strokes of her wings she made height and followed Thornfire in a wide loop around the city and back towards the cliffs where their camp lay. Rainsoft followed her.

Chapter 17
Rescue Mission

"It's so warm," Kassandra exclaimed, holding her hands out to the Sunstone.

"It will burn you," Thornfire warned. "Don't touch it."

The children, chilled on the mountain despite their layers of clothing, had gathered around the Stone, as close as they could get without singeing their eyebrows, as soon as Hawkwind had revealed it and placed it in the depression where they had the campfire.

"The other one doesn't do anything," Rikah complained.

"It does do something," Thornfire corrected.

"Yeah, it does," little Karo agreed, "you just can't feel it."

"Like you can," Rikah retorted.

Karo didn't argue back, but his wronged expression told Hawkwind that he clearly could feel it, and she thought back again on what Thornfire had said about the boy's latent magical potential. She put a gentle hand on his shoulder.

"Don't mess about with it, Karo," she cautioned softly.

"I'm not," he protested. "I'm just trying to figure it out."

"Hawkwind, Rainsoft," Thornfire summoned. "Let's eat and talk about tomorrow."

"Starbright, thank you for the meal," Hawkwind called as she turned to follow the mage.

"No problem," the golden griffin grinned back. "I know I've got the easy job."

Hawkwind caught Rainsoft gesturing his thanks as well, and saw Starbright reply the same way. Behind them, Rikah was starting to lay bits of meat on top of the now clean Sunstone to cook. Thornfire led the way to two still-warm prey bodies at the edge of the camp and the three griffins dug in, sharing out the best bits between them. Once the bones had been picked clean and gnawed for good measure, the trio sat

KARO
AND THE
MOONSTONE

together and preened the blood off of each other's feathers. Although Hawkwind tried to be neat, ripping into a carcass was never the tidiest thing and having companions around to clean up with was always a big help.

"How are we going to find your brother now?" Hawkwind asked as soon as her bill was free of feathers.

"How will we free my family?" Rainsoft added by hands.

"We made the talis angry today," Thornfire rumbled, "and they saw us, so they know exactly who took the Stones. It wasn't what I'd hoped would happen. They'll be on their guard now. It will be much harder to accomplish anything down there."

"We shouldn't leave should we?" Hawkwind asked timidly. "There is still hope?"

"The talis' source of hot water will be drying up. They won't need their captive griffins to sacrifice to keep the Stones running anymore. They might not have figured that out just yet, but it won't take them long. You do realize what will happen when they make the connection."

It felt like a cold weight dropped into Hawkwind's belly. "They'll start eating their prisoners."

"I think so, too," Thornfire sighed.

"No," Rainsoft gestured emphatically. "We have to save them before that happens."

"I agree. It's hard to say how quickly they will start doing it, but there's no doubt they will."

"What do we do?" Hawkwind pled.

Thornfire's claws contracted into the gravel with a sound like an icy hiss. "We go at the coldest, darkest hour before dawn and try to free the prisoners."

Hawkwind and Rainsoft stared.

"You're not serious. We'll be caught and killed."

"At the coldest hour the talis will congregate in the pools," Thornfire explained. "In darkness we are less susceptible to being hypnotized because we won't be able to see their scale patterns."

"We won't be able to see anything, you mean," Hawkwind corrected.

"We'll have to move silently, and use our ears. Rainsoft, you know how to open the doors to the rooms where the griffins are kept?"

"A little," he gestured. "It looked like a pulley system. I only saw briefly."

"As long as we don't need to find keys, we can figure it out."

"You're really serious?" Hawkwind interrupted. "You want us to go back."

The mage gave her a firm look. "I thought I made that clear, Hawkwind. I've helped you fetch the Sunstone. You'll help me discover my brother's fate and save Rainsoft's family, and the others."

"But," she trailed off.

A shadow echo of the moment when she'd suddenly been at peace, happy even, floating in a fuzzy sea of soft sunlight and dandelion fluff, wafted through her body and mind. When she'd seen the talis, all had faded: her fears, her worries, her joys, and her thoughts. Contentment unlike she'd ever felt had stolen over her like a pond swallowing a dropped stone. She couldn't have fought it any more than the stone could have floated back to the surface of the pond.

When Rainsoft touched her shoulder, she returned to herself, sitting there on the mountain with him and Thornfire, night breezes whispering around the peaks, as rapidly as if he'd slapped her. Hawkwind noted her legs trembling and her heart racing. Thornfire was regarding her coolly.

"I can't go back," she whispered. "What if I see a talis again?"

Thornfire nodded. "If you see a talis again, the same thing will happen. You will swim in a serenity that will linger even as it swallows you. The same thing will happen to me." He leaned forward. "But if it is dark, you can't see it. In the hallways, at night, you will not be able to see enough to be hypnotized. Look up, Hawkwind. The moon is hidden tonight."

She shook her head. "The darkness is another fear. The talis could be hiding in the dark, and we can't see them, but if we did see them, we'd be helpless. If we fight them, we have to fight something we can't see. What if they can see us in the dark?"

"This is our best chance, tonight, in the cold dark, while they squabble over the last of the hot water," Thornfire said. "I need your help."

Hawkwind clenched her bill and claws.

"Be brave," Rainsoft gestured. "Face your fears. Help me find my family, please."

How could she say no? But how could she bear to go back there?

"I'll go," she managed to gulp out.

"Thank you," Thornfire told her. "Get some sleep. I'll wake you when it's time to leave."

Rainsoft headed for his room, while Thornfire headed back towards the camp center. Hawkwind followed Rainsoft and joined him in his room without asking, but the charcoal griffin gave no sign of objection. He curled around her and held her while she trembled herself into shallow sleep, which lasted until Thornfire woke them in the deepest, blackest pit of pre-dawn morning.

The sky was only a single shade lighter than black, and the mountain rocks were only a shade or two lighter than that. Even the wind had died down, so the night felt like a hollow, cold cave, coated with icy dust that hadn't been touched since the infancy of the oldest trees. Hawkwind and Rainsoft stood silently together with Thornfire before they launched off in turn, catching the frigid air under their feathers and following the mage down to the broken rooftops of the city.

They dropped down onto a balcony and slipped into a building, quieter than falling leaves. Hawkwind's eyes were as wide as possible, trying to suck in light so she could detect the slightest movement. The trio wound down through hallways and staircases, descending into a labyrinth that Hawkwind wondered how she'd ever find her way out of again. She didn't know what they were looking for; only Rainsoft did.

When Rainsoft finally touched her haunch, and she touched Thornfire's so he'd stop too, it occurred to her that they had a plan, of a sort, for finding the captive griffins, but no plan for getting them out safely. She suspected this must be a cell; that Rainsoft had stopped them because they'd reached one, and now she didn't know what they would do. Too late, Rainsoft was opening the door by feel, and he and Thornfire were pulling it open just enough for them to slip through. She followed, not knowing what else to do.

Once inside, Thornfire immediately created the dimmest light she'd ever seen. Four sets of eyes shone back at them, from four griffins curled up together in a nest of old blankets, cushions, and feathers. The room was fairly large, and had a rickety old bookcase with a bunch of books on it; a table; some stones that appeared to have been chipped or worn into spheres; a pile of bones, horns, and antlers that looked to have been carved into a variety of shapes like tools and toys; and a pit in one corner that Hawkwind suspected was the privy. The scent of waste and unwashed griffin mingled with the reek of talis. A barred window high on the wall let in the least bit of nighttime light. There also seemed to be a hatch up near the ceiling, and directly below it on the floor sat a big stone basin as black as pitch.

Rainsoft strode forward confidently, and Thornfire paced him, as if they'd worked it out in advance. The mage lit up the former captive's hands, and Rainsoft began speaking rapidly. Hawkwind had a moment of panic that all the captive griffins might not speak the same hand language. How could isolated families manage to make a language they all spoke?

The prisoners, however, began gesturing back after a few minutes, and the conversation seemed to go on. There were two adults and two juveniles in the nest. Luckily, the smallest juvenile was fledged, although whether any of them would be able to fly in escape was unlikely, based on Rainsoft's history. Hawkwind eyed the group more carefully and noted their skinny chests. Unlike herself and all the other griffins she'd ever known, who had round, barrel-like chests, these ones had narrow, sharp chests with jutting keel bones. They didn't have the pectoral muscles necessary for flight. A glance at Rainsoft showed that he had developed a fair set of muscles there, although he was not as filled out as Thornfire.

"This is taking a long time," Thornfire muttered as the conversation went on.

Before Hawkwind could respond, one of the adult prisoners suddenly stood and nodded. He or she prodded the other adult and nudged the juveniles. Rainsoft turned to Hawkwind and Thornfire.

"They'll come," he gestured.

"Your family?" Hawkwind asked by hand.

"No," he answered. "Maybe the next room."

"We're just going to collect a bunch of griffins?" Hawkwind whispered to Thornfire as the mage put out the light. "We're going to somehow lead them out, dozens of them, maybe more, among hundreds of sleeping talis, in the dark, when we don't even know the way out from here?"

"Yes," he told her simply, turning to lead them all out the door.

They stopped to shut the door and moved on down the hallway. At least the darkness would prevent the freed griffins from having sensory overload, Hawkwind supposed. The next door was not far, and they repeated the procedure, but the griffins in that room went along more quickly, perhaps because of the presence of other prisoners. Over the next hour, they worked their way down the hallway, visiting more than a dozen rooms, and collecting about forty griffins so that the hallway was filled with them.

"There must be another hallway," Thornfire hissed. "Your family?"

Hawkwind could just barely see Rainsoft shake his head.

"My brother isn't here either," the mage went on. "Let's take these griffins up into higher rooms, where they'll be safer, leave them there, and continue. We have some more time before sunrise."

Hawkwind didn't argue, although she wondered how the prisoners would feel about being left in a strange place by griffins they didn't know or fully trust yet. When at last they were installed in a big room with windows that they looked out of at the black mountains in awe, Thornfire turned to Hawkwind.

"I need you to stay with them," he said. "Rainsoft and I will finish and bring the other prisoners here."

"What? No," she retorted without thinking. "What if you don't come back?"

"Then you lead these griffins back to camp, and then back to South-scree," he said.

"I don't know the way," she argued.

"You and Starbright can find the way, but don't worry. We'll be back. Rainsoft, let's go."

In the darkness it was hard to tell, but she thought the charcoal griffin gave her a long, lingering look before he and Thornfire disappeared into the darkness of the stairwell. When she turned around, helpless and afraid, around forty sets of eyes were glimmering at her. There was slightly more light here than down in the hallways, but everything was still a mass of dark shapes except for the slightly lighter rectangles of the windows.

"Don't worry," she said with her hands, making the gestures big in the hopes that the prisoners could all see. "We will wait. They will come back. They will bring more griffins. We will all leave together."

Hawkwind couldn't tell if her words had calmed them; they seemed remarkably calm already. Perhaps this experience was so overwhelming that they had mostly shut down mentally, and were just following with the flock. Gradually, the griffins began to talk among themselves, and then begin to move about hesitantly, followed by sudden short spurts of movement and soft rumbles and coos of happiness.

"They're finding their lost family members," she breathed, "the children and siblings that were taken away."

Silently, Hawkwind waited, watching the sky and watching the door. Many of the griffins cuddled up together and the gentle breathing of sleep filled the room. The sky began to lighten almost imperceptibly. Hawkwind wondered if an hour had passed. She could feel it creeping up on her. Dawn was coming and Thornfire and Rainsoft weren't back. Unable to sit still, she started pacing.

She stopped pacing when one of the former captives approached her.

"You are," the captive hesitated, as if not sure how to word it, "from not-here?"

Hawkwind nodded. "Yes. I can only speak a little with my hands."

"I heard you speak from here." The captive touched her throat. "We can't."

"I learned to speak with my hands from Rainsoft," Hawkwind explained, "but I'm still learning."

"Rainsoft is your mate?"

Hawkwind choked, instinctively making the gesture Rainsoft used when he couldn't or didn't want to answer a question, something like a shrug and a wince and a suppressive wave combined. The lady prisoner did not press her query.

"Rainsoft and the other, will come back soon?"

"I hope so."

"It's dangerous?"

"The talis will kill us," Hawkwind said. "They will kill you all. They keep you so they can kill you when they want." She sighed. "It's more complicated than that. I can't explain."

"I am Icemoon," the ex-prisoner said readily, again judiciously not pressing her questions. "I will go with you. Let's find them."

Hawkwind caught her breath. "If I am caught, no one can lead your people to safety."

Icemoon turned her head, looking out towards the windows. "We have seen mountains, only spoken of in legends. To have seen mountains, it is all right if we die here now."

The sky was perceptibly lighter now. She didn't intend to let all the newly freed griffins die, but Hawkwind made her choice in an instant.

"Let's go."

Chapter 18
The Lost Brother

Hawkwind and Icemoon retraced their steps. Down in the hallways it was still dark as night, but like a night with a moon now; some of the early dawn was managing to filter down. Together they had finished one whole hallway and Hawkwind didn't know where Thornfire and Rainsoft might have gone next, but from the landing of the stairs a short and narrow corridor led away opposite the finished hallway and Hawkwind went down it with Icemoon right behind her.

The corridor opened into another hallway with locking doors along it, just like the raided one. Hawkwind could only imagine that Thornfire and Rainsoft had come this way and freed the occupants, but she had to be sure. It was possible they'd turned off the stairs before reaching the bottom. When she went to the first door, Icemoon followed along, helping her open it. She stuck her head inside, expecting to see an empty nest—but it was full.

Hawkwind's jaw dropped as she saw two adult griffins looking back at her. When she squeezed through the doorway, Icemoon followed her in. Had Thornfire and Rainsoft not made it here, or had these griffins refused to come? Hawkwind had no magic to create light, but Icemoon stood in the faint glow coming through the open door and the barred window high above and began gesturing hurriedly. After a few minutes, the griffins in the nest began talking back and glancing at each other. In another couple minutes, they stood and joined Hawkwind and Icemoon.

Hawkwind hid a groan. While ecstatic to be rescuing more griffins, she now had more to take care of. Once outside the room, with the door shut again, they moved down the hallway to the next door and repeated the process. A half an hour on, the walls of the hallway were becoming visible and Hawkwind had a couple dozen more griffins trailing her. There were still more doors. She hadn't found Thornfire and Rainsoft like she'd wanted to. She feared running into awakening talis at any moment.

They kept going. Wisely, Icemoon described to the prisoners how to reach the room where the others were waiting, and sent groups of them off in that direction. It kept the hallway population down as they pushed on. Every closed door meant more helpless griffins destined to die having never flown, never hunted, and never seen the world, so every door had to be opened.

Hawkwind paid close attention to the scents in the air. Everything smelled like talis but she hadn't yet been swamped by a wave of stench that would indicate one nearby. Her nerves tightened with the rising light and she resisted the urge to pick at her feathers as the freed griffins took the time to convince new prisoners to join them in every room she opened.

At last, only one closed door remained before the next narrow, door-less corridor. Icemoon sent another group of prisoners towards the gathering room several floors up, except for a few who apparently chose to stay. In the morning light, Hawkwind could see her colors now. Icemoon was a light, delicate grey with lots of white markings. Her eyes were blue. She looked older than Hawkwind had expected, but nowhere near elderly. Icemoon gave her a nervous smile and nodded at the final door.

They took hold of the chains and pulled, lifting the heavy latch so they could push it open. Hawkwind stuck her head inside to see a single adult griffin curled up in its nest. Rusty red, black, and soft brown feathers and fur rose and fell with sleeping breaths, but then the griffin stirred and lifted its head.

"Well," he said, "and who have we here?"

A chirping trill came from the nest and a skinny grey and black animal scampered up to sit on the griffin's head. Hawkwind's heart thudded and her skin shivered.

"Are you Thornwing?" Hawkwind demanded.

"I believe I asked first," he countered with a wry tilt to his head. "Let's hurry. The sun is up. You play a dangerous game."

The rusty red griffin leapt from the nest, his animal companion hanging onto his fur. Then the wave of scent hit them. Rank and foul, the reek rolled over them like choking gas.

"Close your eyes," the freshly freed prisoner ordered.

That now-familiar screeching hiss grated on Hawkwind's ears. She stared firmly down at the ground and tried to discern the direction the talis was coming from. They'd made it out the room's door, but now she had no idea where to go.

"Left, left, go left," her new companion instructed.

A shove to her shoulder confirmed the direction. Hawkwind tried to obey, and bumped into Icemoon. Gambling that there were no talis in the direction she faced now, Hawkwind looked up to see the lady griffin staring blankly over Hawkwind's shoulder. The other three griffins with them were the same. Behind her, the rusty red prisoner screamed a battle cry. Along with it, she heard the furious chattering scolding of the little animal that had been with him.

Gritting her bill, Hawkwind slapped Icemoon hard across the face, making her stumble. Hawkwind seized her bill before she could look back up and pointed her head away from the talis.

"Go," Hawkwind heard from behind her.

Hawkwind shoved Icemoon, trying to get her moving, and smacked the next entranced prisoner, repeating the same process of grabbing his bill and pointing him away. She screeched at them all, shoving and slapping, while the sound of the newly freed male prisoner fighting the talis echoed through the hallway. It surely couldn't have been more than several seconds, but it seemed like forever to get the group moving.

"Hurry," he cried. "There's too many. I can't hold them off. Run!"

Hawkwind screeched again, slapping any haunch that wasn't moving fast enough, getting the prisoners to run along the hallway as quick

Thornwing

as they could. Then the new prisoner cried out in pain and fear, and Hawkwind paused.

"Keep going," he ordered. "Get away. Leave me."

"I can't," Hawkwind shouted back. "We came here for you."

The running group vanished into the corridor ahead. The new prisoner had fought the talis, so they clearly hadn't hypnotized him. He also spoke aloud. Hawkwind could think of no other possibility than that he was Thornwing, Thornfire's brother. She couldn't leave him behind. Hawkwind closed her eyes tight, turned, and threw herself, claws extended, into whatever battle was going on behind her.

She was betting that Thornwing was down, so she struck high. She hit scaled flesh, the dry, slippery feel of it making her skin crawl, but the angry hisses of the talis encouraged her, and she struck out again.

"My eyes are shut," she panted, "stay out of my way."

"Move to your left," he instructed. "I'll fight on the right. We retreat slowly. I'll tell you what to do, just keep striking out as fast as you can."

"Are you all right?"

"I'm hurt, but I can make it if I don't get hit again."

Hawkwind slowly backed up, tottering on her hind legs, wings partly open for balance, trying to keep slashing in an irregular pattern.

"Reinforcements are coming," Thornwing bemoaned. "The hallway is filling with talis behind these ones. Where are we going?"

"Through the narrow corridor behind us, then up the stairs. We freed all the prisoners, I think."

"There are too many talis. The prisoners will just be hypnotized."

They fought on for several more steps. Hawkwind grunted as something impacted her right forearm, but she stubbornly kept her eyes shut. The wound didn't feel disabling, only bruising.

"What do we do?" she asked breathlessly.

"We die bravely," Thornwing panted back. "Thank you for freeing me, so I can die on my feet."

"No," she objected. "Your brother came for you. Thornfire is here. We came to save you."

"Thornfire," he repeated, like a prayer. "Where is he?"

"We got separated."

"Fall back, fall back," he ordered suddenly, and Hawkwind scrambled to obey.

A heavy weight hit her face, but her bill took most of the blow, and her eyes were shut, so she didn't feel like she got hurt. Hawkwind snapped at whatever it had been and managed to rip into a bit of talis flesh, earning her a hiss of pain from the beast. Beside her, Thornwing grunted.

"You're hurt?" she demanded.

"What's your name?" he asked instead, voice tight.

"Hawkwind."

"Thank you, Hawkwind, for getting me out. Run now. Tell my brother I love him."

"No," she cried back at him.

"You can't help me," he pled. "Go now."

Hawkwind heard a commotion behind her.

"Get down!" a voice trumpeted.

Hawkwind flung herself back and down, bruising her body on the hard flagstone floor. Her skin suddenly sharpened and prickled with cold, as if she'd fallen into an icy snow bank. A sound she'd never heard before, a crackling, hissing sort of ongoing squeak shivered through the air, and when she drew a breath it chilled her lungs like the darkest pit of winter.

"Rainsoft, go," the thunderous voice commanded, and Hawkwind's heart leapt.

He was here, and that other was Thornfire, giving orders. Her eyes still shut; she only sensed a body leaping over her. The dismayed shrieking of the talis, however, she heard clearly. She could guess what had happened. Thornfire had used his magic, sucking the heat out of the air and the talis, dramatically dropping their temperature and slowing them down. The warm-blooded griffins had not been so badly affected, giving them an advantage.

"Hawkwind, pull back," she heard Thornwing order. "We've got this, but don't look yet."

She got to her feet and scrambled back until she hit a warm body, opening her eyes to see dull tan legs before her.

"Thornfire," she greeted. "It's Thornwing, that's Thornwing back there. I found him."

Hawkwind looked up at him so she could see his expression, although he was still pointed back at the conflict so his eyes were shut. All that was missing were the tears, and they came a moment later, turning to ice crystals almost immediately, like silver jewelry on his cheek feathers.

Rainsoft and Thornwing ran up beside them, Thornwing limping and dripping blood. His slender little grey animal friend still clung to his shoulder, hissing through bared tiny fangs. Hawkwind supposed the beastie had been fighting, too. It panted like it was exhausted and was smeared with blood.

"Let's go," Thornwing said. "They're drawing back for now."

The four griffins fled back down the hallway, into the corridor, up the stairs to the top room where Hawkwind had left the first prisoners they'd freed. The room was packed now. Hawkwind guessed there must be around a hundred and fifty griffins: adults, juveniles, fledglings, and even a few tiny chicks clinging to their parents' backs. She supposed there must be pregnant females, too, but didn't take the time to start examining the griffins around her for signs.

Thornwing and Thornfire were embracing, only pausing for Thornfire to run his cauterizing magic over his younger brother's wounds. "Wing, you're bitten?" Thornfire was murmuring. "Let me burn it out of you, so you can run."

Rainsoft had immediately posted himself as lookout at the top of the stairs and Hawkwind went to him. She could have stopped herself, but she chose not to. Pressing up against him and burying her bill in his neck feathers felt like the most important and rewarding thing she could do, so she did it. His trill of welcome and his wing encircling her confirmed that her choice was indeed the absolute best thing she could have done, and they got to stay that way for a couple minutes.

"We need to get moving," Thornfire's voice threw a rock into the pool of contentment Hawkwind had sunken into.

She sighed only a little over the hollow left inside her when she had to pull away from Rainsoft.

"The talis won't be held back for long," Thornwing added. "We must get out of the city. This way."

Rainsoft translated to the group at large, and most of them looked willingly to Thornwing, who waded through them to the doorway on the other side of the room.

"We won't be flying," Thornfire reminded his brother, following him through the crowd.

"I know how to get to an exit on foot from here."

The crowd began to move, and Hawkwind let them go before her. Rainsoft stayed in place, probably intending to be the rear guard. It took some time for all the griffins to move out of the room and the Thorn brothers had disappeared into the mass of griffins. Hawkwind went with the last few of them, and Rainsoft followed her, glancing frequently over his shoulder.

The talis didn't catch up until some minutes later. Rainsoft's screech of warning alerted the group.

"Thornfire!" Hawkwind yelled, hoping he would hear, wherever he was in the moving column.

As Rainsoft engaged the talis, Hawkwind kept the former prisoners from looking back, and slapped and screamed at them whenever they turned around to look, but she couldn't get to them all— some fell behind. Thornfire and Thornwing came shoving through the crowd to get back to them.

"Rainsoft, get away," Thornwing commanded, and then to his brother, once Rainsoft was clear, "now, Fire."

Hawkwind's skin tightened with cold again, and Thornwing moved past her. The hissing and impact of claws on scaled flesh told her that he and Rainsoft were maiming and killing as many cold-disabled talis as they could. The column of prisoners kept moving, but more slowly without a leader who knew where to go.

"Hawkwind, go to the front," Thornwing commanded. "Keep going down the hall they're on, then take the staircase up four levels and go straight until the next staircase, go down one level and straight again. If I'm not with you by that time, just keep going wherever you can."

She obeyed, although leaving them was painful, and she could only assume the worst for the prisoners that she hadn't been able to keep from looking back at the talis. The crowd of griffins let her pass through and when she reached the front of the column, she followed Thornwing's directions. The staircase wasn't far, but she had to resist dallying; she was afraid they would run into more talis from the front. Regardless, Hawkwind led as swiftly as she could, but the captives seemed to have a hard time keeping up, already panting. She supposed if she had spent every day of her life sitting in a room without exercise, she would tire rapidly, too, so she tried to keep her patience.

As she neared the end of Thornwing's directions, he came pushing through the flock, breathing heavily and wincing with pain.

"Everyone alright?" she asked.

"I'm afraid we lost a few of the prisoners. There was nothing we could do: too many talis and the prisoners hypnotized and immobile. I think their suffering was brief." Thornwing paused, shaking his head. "Fire's getting tired," he told her. "It's a good thing we're fighting in these narrow hallways. By ourselves we drove the talis back, but Rainsoft and I were both injured. Fire had to heal us. With all the magic he's been throwing around, he'll be exhausted soon. We should be beyond the reach of the talis shortly, though. This way."

Thornwing took over leading and Hawkwind was relieved to be able to drop back into the first ranks of the running griffins. She soon recognized a hallway they ran through as one Thornfire had shown her and Rainsoft on their first foray in the city. The exit wasn't far away, and a good thing, too; the griffins were flagging.

Some hallways and corners and corridors and stairways later, Thornwing stepped aside and waved the crowd past into the final rooms before the exit. Hawkwind stopped beside him and stood clutching a stitch in her side. Running up and down dozens of stairways was not exactly the exercise griffins were most suited for. Around her, exhausted captives were collapsing to the floor.

"We're lucky the talis aren't brighter," Thornwing said. "They can come up with solutions to problems, but it takes them time. They aren't as quick as us in making snap decisions and planning quick strategies. If they were, they would have found a way to flank us and cut us off, but they can't think ahead, so they just tried to chase us."

The last of the train of griffins squeezed into the final rooms. Rainsoft and Thornfire staggered up along with them. Hawkwind stepped beside Rainsoft and they leaned against each other.

"It's still a long way to go," Thornfire grimaced.

"Do you think it's safe to rest here a few minutes?" Hawkwind asked. "Some of them won't make it up the trails without a breather."

"A short few minutes," the mage grunted as he lowered himself to the floor. "I need a rest, too."

"Do you want to fly up to the camp and send down Starbright?" Hawkwind suggested.

"I can make it. I don't want to risk her in a fight with talis. She isn't ready for that."

Hawkwind didn't argue. "How many griffins did we lose?"

"Probably about a dozen," Thornfire winced.

"Did the talis recapture them?"

"Killed them outright," the mage said. "The talis are furious."

Hawkwind lowered herself to the floor. "Where did you go? I went to find you and discovered the other half of the hallway on the first floor, but where were you and Rainsoft?"

"We emptied the rooms on the second floor, both sides of the stairwell. We'd checked the other levels above them, but they didn't have rooms of captives. We were coming down to do your section. Luckily, you'd already cleaned it out," he explained. "If you hadn't, we wouldn't have finished before the talis came."

"I would still be imprisoned?" Thornwing remarked.

"Yes."

"You told her to stay behind?"

"With the ones we'd already freed," she confirmed. "Then dawn started coming and I got worried, so I went to look for them."

"I'm grateful you did," he smiled at her.

A nervous little flutter went through Hawkwind's belly, but she didn't pause to examine why. A warm flush of pride at a lucky job well done washed the flutter away.

"I'm grateful, too," Thornfire added. "I hadn't realized there would be so many griffins to free, or that it would take so long."

Hawkwind looked over the gathered griffins. They huddled together, peering about with caution and curiosity. Most of them were young. In fact, Hawkwind didn't see any old ones, and she knew why. Once the pairs got old enough that they stopped reproducing the talis would have taken them for sacrificing on the rusty hooks.

Thornfire got to his feet after a few more breaths. "We should keep moving."

They went out through the door Thornfire had first shown Hawkwind as the way in. The freed griffins stared at dirt and grass in wonder. It was sometimes hard to keep moving, as they would stop to gaze at plants and stones along the path or the clouds and mountains in the distance. They learned quickly not to stare directly at the sun. The talis, at least, did not pursue them, so it seemed their lack of speed would not invite disaster this time, and Hawkwind finally felt safe for the first time since entering Snow-in-lee hours ago.

She set her mind instead to wondering if they would all fit in the high mountain camp, and how they would all be fed. One by one, the huge group filed into the camp, crowding in closer and closer. When it was Hawkwind's turn, she passed a stunned Starbright with a nervous Karo clinging to her back.

"Hi," Hawkwind greeted, and it took a moment before Starbright responded.

"Hi," she murmured dreamily. "Where did they all come from?"

"Snow-in-lee. They were the prisoners the talis were keeping, like Rainsoft."

"How are we going to feed them? I only caught one buck this morning, and I was going to share it with the children. How did the talis feed them?"

"The prisoners never did much exercise," Hawkwind surmised. "I don't suppose they needed to eat every day. The talis just fed them enough to stay alive. It will be a problem now though, especially since none of them know how to hunt."

"They have to learn," Starbright demanded, still staring around dazed at the crowd.

"Where are Jessika and the others?" Hawkwind asked, noting that only Karo was with her.

"They're somewhere among the griffins. Kassandra walked right up to the first new one and started talking to it with her hands."

Thornwing stepped up to them. "I guess none of these griffins can speak?"

"Not aloud," Hawkwind confirmed. "They talk with hand gestures."

He nodded towards Rainsoft, who was wandering among the milling griffins. "So does he? I haven't heard him speak."

"Rainsoft was a prisoner, too, but he can resist the talis entrancement, like you can, and he escaped. South-scree caught him. He knows how to write the same language you in South-scree use, so eventually we started finding ways to communicate. I've been learning how to speak with my hands and write your way, and he's been learning to understand our spoken language, but he'll never be able to speak, and nor will these others. According to Rainsoft, the talis destroyed their vocal cords when they were chicks."

"I see," Thornwing frowned. "Where are you from then? You speak of South-scree as if it isn't your home. Your name is Hawkwind but there is no Hawk Line anymore. And, is that a human child on your back? And you're Starbright, right? You've grown."

"It's not, and he is," Hawkwind confirmed, as Starbright nodded, saying, "I am."

"I'm Karo," the little boy whispered.

"The human children are mine," Hawkwind went on explaining. "We're from Northnest."

"Northnest," Thornwing echoed, "is not a myth?"

"Not a myth," she nodded. "I'll tell you all about it later."

Thornfire came up to the group. "That's all of them. They're quite packed in, aren't they?"

The freed griffins had started settling down on the bare stone in their family groups, but the families were crowded so closely together that they could hardly be told apart. The camp wasn't that big, and a hundred and thirty-something griffins filled it to capacity.

"At least they shouldn't be cold, packed so tightly together," Hawkwind mused. "Are we staying here overnight?"

"We should get moving as quickly as we can, but a night here wouldn't hurt," Thornfire shrugged. "They've already had a lot of trauma for one day, and we need rest."

"Then we go back to South-scree?" Thornwing asked. "Where do you expect to put this many new arrivals? This is almost the population of an Aerie."

"Will they even be welcomed?" Hawkwind remarked darkly.

Thornfire gritted his bill. "You both make excellent points," he ground out. "I will handle it."

"It's like we need a new settlement for them. Too bad they couldn't safely live in Snow-in-lee," Starbright shrugged.

"After what they've been through, I'm not sure how they would feel about that, if it were even possible. With the talis there, I think it would be impossible," Thornfire shook his head. "Even without the Sun and Moonstones, the original spring will remain and the talis might continue to use it; they are water-dwellers. We might someday drive out the talis, but I suspect a population of them will remain there for now."

Hawkwind noticed a few of the griffins poking at the buck Starbright had deposited on the rocks at one side of the camp. The golden griffin growled when Hawkwind pointed it out.

"You handle who eats it. I'll go catch more," the apprentice grumped.

Karo took the hint, sliding down from her back and then clambering up onto Hawkwind's. In a few bounds Starbright was airborne and circling away. Many of the freed griffins followed her with looks of awe and longing in their eyes, succeeded by rapid and silent hand communication among themselves. Hawkwind strode over to the buck, making the curious griffins around it look up guiltily.

"Hungry?" she asked them by hand.

They made the deflecting, suppressive gestures Hawkwind had used herself that morning when speaking with Icemoon.

"Who is hungriest?" Hawkwind went on.

One dark brown griffin looked her squarely in the eyes. "The chicks should eat it," he told her.

Other nearby griffins nodded in agreement.

"Jessika, Kassandra, Rikah," Hawkwind called—an easy thing to do since the gathered griffins were mostly silent, despite their numbers and ongoing conversations.

The human children came running through the crowd, startling griffins who hadn't seen them yet.

"You brought so many griffins," Jessika exclaimed. "Kassandra has been helping us meet them all."

"I'm glad you're enjoying it," Hawkwind smiled at them. "So tell me, have you all eaten this morning?"

"Not yet," they answered, shaking their heads.

Hawkwind turned to the buck and sawed a ragged, bloody steak out of one haunch. Rikah lifted up his hands for it and she passed it over.

"I'll cook it," the boy assured her, trotting it over to the Sunstone.

"Kassandra, will you tell everyone that the rest of this buck is to be shared among the littlest chicks, and invite them to come over?" Hawkwind asked.

The dark haired girl nodded seriously and began wandering among the griffins, gesturing and pointing. Being so little, it was easy for her to wind her way between them. She even boldly tugged on fur or feathers to get their attention. The news rapidly spread as bewildered griffins told their neighbors.

"They don't know what to make of her," Thornwing said from behind Hawkwind. "I've never seen a human either, but I've at least heard of them. Are they all this small?"

"These are human fledglings," she assured him with a weary smile. "They'll get bigger, up to twice their current height."

"You can talk," Jessika said to Thornwing. "Are you Thornfire's brother?"

"I am," he answered, eyes crinkling with mirth. "What has he been saying about me?"

"Mostly that he really wanted to find you," the girl told him.

"And who are you?"

"I'm Jessika, from Northnest. Hawkwind is taking care of me and the others."

"I gathered that. I hope to hear your whole story soon."

"All right," she said, but Hawkwind read her expression as doubtful and evasive, although it was unlikely that Thornwing—seeing humans for the first time—would be able to read the subtleties of her expression. The girl was already grasping the idea that she should be careful about telling all the facts of her story. None of the South-scree griffins knew yet that she was the only living heir of Northnest. Hawkwind couldn't decide whether they would even care, but had chosen to keep it secret just in case.

"Have you seen Rainsoft?" Hawkwind asked before the girl could scamper off to get some cooked strips of meat that Rikah was now handing to Karo and Kassandra.

She pointed. "Over there, with that black griffin and the grey one and the black and grey one and them."

Hawkwind looked, finally spotting Rainsoft huddled in a tight mutual preening group with four or five other griffins.

"That must be his family," Hawkwind murmured. "Thanks, Jessika. Go ahead and get some food."

The girl ran off, dodging fearlessly between sharp bills and claws until she skidded to a stop by the Sunstone. The gathered griffins began shifting about as parents led or carried their littlest chicks over to the buck. Some were still coated with down on their heads and wings.

Once all were gathered, they seemed to discuss the disposition of the meat and then began tearing off bits to feed to the shrill, piping baby mouths.

"I would go bring another kill," Thornwing spoke up, "but I'm afraid I am too weak. I wasn't fed much and lost a lot of weight."

"How did they catch you?" Hawkwind asked him.

"Arrogance," he answered grimly. "I observed them a long time. I thought I'd begun to understand some of their language. I finally thought I would try to communicate with them. They surrounded me, ignoring all my attempts at diplomacy. I tried to fight, to get away, but it was too late. I was overwhelmed by sheer numbers. They tossed me in that room. I don't know what their eventual plans were for me, but they kept feeding me."

"You know what they were doing to the prisoners?" Hawkwind checked.

"I do. I saw it." His bill clamped shut for a moment. "I thought I could talk to them, eventually convince them to stop it. I couldn't bear seeing and hearing another sacrifice." A shudder ran the length of his body and he re-tucked his wings. "They didn't kill the sacrifices before they put them on the hooks. They just ran the point of the hook under the ribs, lowered them over the Stones, and left them hanging."

"I don't want to hear this," Hawkwind said weakly, her imagination creating vivid visions of what that would have looked and sounded like.

"Sorry. I suppose they would have tried to sacrifice me, too, but I was too difficult to handle, because they couldn't hypnotize me. It seems like each room held a family group. I wonder if they would have eventually put a female in with me, but then I suppose I would have caused problems when they came to hurt my chicks, if I made any. I suppose I might have declined doing that."

Hawkwind flicked her feathers in a shrug.

"This is another problem, isn't it," Thornwing went on. "There is no matriarch here. All these females are mothers with a single mate, and their bodies are not likely to go back to sleep, except maybe daughters whose mothers are still alive and awakened. You were right to wonder if South-scree would welcome them."

Hawkwind tried to hide her discomfort at that. She was now an awakened female, too. She had no chicks but she assumed that any matriarch would be able to detect her condition somehow. They probably wouldn't want her in South-scree, much less somewhere around forty actively breeding females.

"What do we do with them?" she wondered aloud.

"I don't know," he admitted. "The more immediate problem is how we're going to feed them."

"We can't stay here. This is too crowded. I can't think about it right now," Hawkwind shook her head: the many questions and unknowns pressing on her like a stormy sky.

"It will work out," Thornwing soothed automatically.

Hawkwind looked up as a shadow passed over: Starbright bringing another kill. She set it down near the other one, in one of the few remaining spots not occupied by dazed griffins. Hawkwind and Thornwing pushed their way over to it.

"For the pregnant females and older chicks, I suppose," Thornwing sighed.

Hawkwind nodded in agreement and managed to communicate it to the freed griffins around her until the message was running through the gathering. There was more shuffling as certain griffins made their way to the kill, adult females and bigger chicks that could move about by themselves. Again an amicable discussion ensued and they divided up the buck on their own.

"At least they're peaceable," Starbright remarked.

"They've never had reason to fight and they're all still too shocked," Thornwing suggested. "I'm sure they'll start causing all sorts of wonderful problems once they start to recover."

He looked over to where Thornfire was still sleeping.

"I think I'll rest a while, unless you need me," he said.

"All of you rest," Starbright nodded. "I'll stay on watch, and wake you if there's any problem. You, too, Hawkwind: you look ready to drop."

Hawkwind was staring over towards Rainsoft as Thornwing walked to his brother to lie down. A strange sensation had fallen into her chest, like cold worms only slightly wiggling.

"He's with his family again," she muttered.

"So?" Starbright asked.

Hawkwind had to remind herself that Starbright wouldn't understand, couldn't understand. Hawkwind wasn't even sure that she understood, herself. In fact, she wasn't sure what she was even supposed to be understanding. Was she jealous, or envious?

"I'll sleep," she agreed. "Here is as good as anywhere. There are folks in my room."

"All right," the golden griffin shrugged, without asking any more about Hawkwind's strange behavior, although the glance she gave her suggested that indeed, strange was the correct word.

Hawkwind curled up on the gravel: brows furrowed and face tight around her shuttered eyes.

"I mated with him," she grumbled to herself, under her breath, "but so what? It wasn't our faults. He was the only male around besides Thornfire, and there's no way I'd, uh, no, I just wouldn't, no, not with him. It's just something griffin bodies do. It didn't mean anything."

Matriarchs had lots of different mates; Hawkwind knew that perfectly well. None of them meant much beyond a day of procreative exercise, although certainly they might be friends and allies. The males also might mate with a variety of matriarchs, if they were lucky, and that didn't mean anything either, except that by doing so they kept the Lines healthy and flowing with new blood.

"I don't even know if I want to be a matriarch," she groaned softly.

And she had no one to talk to about it. There was no retiring mother to discuss it with, to get advice from. Plus, there wasn't even anywhere for her to go be a matriarch in. Northnest was gone, taken, in the hands of hostile strangers, and there was little hope now of living in South-scree.

Hawkwind curled up as tightly as she could, tucking her head far under her wing, unable to quash or even consciously acknowledge that she wanted Rainsoft curled around her. She didn't even have the excuse of being in heat, as she knew she wasn't. That wouldn't happen for some more weeks, if she weren't pregnant already.

That thought scared her so much she failed to fight back a fit of trembling. How could she possibly raise a chick alone when she already had four human children and no Line to support her? As a random, lone griffin she would have had a chance to join a Line at South-scree. Now, the reality of her situation gripped her with icy claws. Again, she had nowhere to go; she was right back where she'd started when she'd escaped Northnest, except now it was worse. Now, she might be going to have a chick, and she was even marginally responsible for a whole bunch of helpless griffins that couldn't speak aloud on top of that.

Her heart raced as her anxious thoughts beat down on her sanity and it was all she could do to not jump up and fly away, far away.

Then, someone tugged gently on one of her wing feathers, a preening nibble. Hawkwind peeked out between her primaries and saw charcoal grey fur: Rainsoft. Without waiting for an invitation he lay down and curled around her, still nibbling her feathers. He must have felt her pounding heart; he trilled gently, a sound used to sooth frightened fledglings. It worked.

Snuggled together, Hawkwind slept.

Chapter 20
Moving Day

Afternoon sun warmed fur and feathers all around as everyone turned their eyes onto the unlikely pair perched on a ledge above the camp. Kassandra and Rainsoft were in the middle of a lesson. The gathered griffins were learning the spoken names of their rescuers and basic, essential spoken words. Kassandra was doing the talking and Rainsoft the translating: his hands moving so quickly that Hawkwind could hardly follow half of it. It seemed he was explaining a lot more than just the meaning of each word Kassandra felt was important for them to know. There was a lot of pointing and miming going on among the freed griffins as they were given directions to test their understanding.

Starbright was oblivious, sleeping now that Hawkwind and the others were awake again, after she'd fetched a couple more prey animals for everybody to get a nibble of. Thornfire and Thornwing were seated side by side, watching the lesson and talking intently but quietly together at the same time. The other three children were sitting with or on Hawkwind, chattering among themselves in hushed voices, mostly about the proceedings and how cute the griffin chicks were. Hawkwind hoped that all the parent griffins had firmly explained to their chicks that the little humans were not food. Chicks were likely to take a peck at anything that moved, and their bills might be smaller than an adult's, but they were still wickedly sharp.

Hawkwind let her gaze wander over the group, spending a lot of time looking at Rainsoft's family. His father was a light grey griffin, with some black in his wings, and was just a little bigger than Rainsoft. His mother was almost all black, but with white wing bars and edging to her tail feathers and white on her belly. Rainsoft's little sister looked a lot like her mother, but her fur lightened to a rich grey on her head and feet. His older brother was a much paler grey, with stronger black markings and a white underside. It seemed he had been mated to a tawny female with chocolate brown feathers banded with black. There were no chicks yet.

Rainsoft had pointed them all out from a distance. He hadn't offered an introduction yet. Hawkwind wasn't sure why, but even as he'd informed her who they were, he'd looked like he just wanted to get it over with, and had found an excuse to talk about something else immediately afterwards. Hawkwind hadn't felt the courage to go introduce herself. Somehow she knew Rainsoft wouldn't have wanted that.

As Kassandra and Rainsoft finished their lesson, Thornfire and Thornwing hopped up to join them and the gathering rustled with sharpened interest. The mage said something to Rainsoft, who nodded in reply.

"We must leave this place," Thornfire began aloud, slowly. Rainsoft, it seemed, was going to translate. "We will walk to a safer place where there is more food. You will all learn to fly and hunt."

A ripple of excited movement erupted. From what Hawkwind could tell, everyone was eagerly commenting about learning to fly.

"We will all learn to talk together," Thornfire went on, bringing their attention back to the front. "We from South-scree will learn better to talk with our hands, and you will learn to understand our voices."

That also got an interested response, although not as great as one as when he'd said they'd be learning to fly.

"We will leave tomorrow. For tonight, rest here. Any questions?"

Hawkwind was a little surprised to see that there weren't any. All the griffins were turning to each other, talking about things.

"I guess that's all then," Thornfire grumbled, hopping back down from the perch.

Hawkwind, the Thorn brothers, Starbright, and the children had claimed the area near the Sun and Moonstones as theirs. The children were vulnerable to the cold, and Thornfire's group had been the one to steal the Stones after all, so Hawkwind felt it was a rightful place for them.

"We might as well relax too, enjoy our evening," Thornfire said as he came up to Hawkwind, Thornwing trailing him.

"Where do you intend to take them?" Hawkwind asked.

"To the nearer end of the tunnel, where all the caves that the ancient armies sheltered in are," the mage answered readily. "There, each family can have its own cave. We can get everyone educated in flying, fighting, hunting, and listening. We'll stay there for at least a few weeks, I expect."

Hawkwind hadn't thought of the caves. "What about the snow-screamers?"

"If there are any, we'll have to take the caves away from them," Thornfire shrugged. "It can be done. It will be fighting, hunting practice, and food source all in one."

The next day, the group moved.

"At least they aren't very noisy," Hawkwind commented to Thornwing, who was walking beside her.

The risk from talis was not gone, now that they were out of the safe camp high on the mountain. Rainsoft and Thornwing were the most aggressively vigilant, being the only ones who could hope to fight talis if they appeared. Rainsoft was currently the aerial scout, while Thornwing was on guard on the ground.

"I think most of the adults understand that we need to stay together," Thornwing replied, "but I can't imagine how difficult that is for them. They've never seen grass or flowers or trees, or all these other things that we just pass by without giving any undue notice."

"And some of them are scared of the new things, and others want to go run out to touch everything."

"Once we're closer to the tunnel it will be safer," Thornwing sighed, "but we'll have a few nights in the open before that."

Hawkwind and Thornwing jerked to a halt as an ungainly chick barely old enough to run came loping across their path, giggling and lunging for a red and black butterfly. Its parent rushed after it, hissing in consternation. The adult caught the baby and tucked it up under its wing. It made a one-handed apology as it hopped on three legs back into line, the chick wriggling and complaining with both voices.

"I hadn't thought of that," Hawkwind gasped. "Some of the chicks, the youngest ones, still have their speaking voice. They'll be able to learn to talk."

"The talis hadn't gotten to them yet, I suppose," Thornwing mused. "We'll have to teach them."

The adventurous chick wiggled free of its parent's imprisoning wing, tumbling to the ground in a tangle of arms, legs, and wings just starting to show pin feathers.

"They're awfully cute," Hawkwind admitted softly. "I'm so glad we could free them."

Thornwing eyed her slyly. "You want some of your own?" he murmured after a moment of hesitation.

Hawkwind felt her nares heat with a blush of blood and she fought to control the lay of her feathers from giving her away.

"I would take care of chicks someday," she deflected, "happily. I never got to back at Northnest; I was too young."

They walked a few more steps in silence, but Hawkwind's skin was prickling, sensing that Thornwing hadn't accepted that answer.

"You smell like all the other adult females here," he whispered finally, "like a matriarch, like a mother. You've awakened. It makes sense, doesn't it, if your story is true. You are the last of your Line."

Hawkwind swallowed hard, forcibly stilling the trembling of her wings. "You can tell?" she asked reluctantly.

"If there is anything a male griffin can smell, other than talis, it is the difference between a sleeping female and an awakened one," he said. "I wonder what the males here think of Starbright. She is mature enough, but sleeping still, and they can surely smell that she is different. I wonder if they know what it means. They were all placed with a female to be their mate. Do they remember how her scent changed?"

Hawkwind didn't know what to say. All she could think was that Rainsoft might have noticed. He might be doing some heavy thinking, wondering why she and Starbright were different, although close in age. Rainsoft hadn't really been told much about griffin society beyond Snow-in-lee. Perhaps he had grown up thinking it was one male to one female and all were fertile. Maybe he was confused. Maybe that was why he hadn't directly introduced Hawkwind to his family.

"So what do you plan to do about it?" Thornwing asked a few minutes later.

"Do about it?" she echoed.

"How do you expect to be welcomed at South-scree? Do you think you can make a home there?"

"How are all these paired griffins going to make a home there?" she countered. "Where is there a place for dozens more Lines?"

"You think they will adopt the idea of having Lines?"

"They won't be able to help it, if the females stay anywhere near their mothers," Hawkwind reminded him. "They won't awaken and the males won't be interested in mating with them. Unless they scatter to great distances or isolate themselves from their mothers they'll keep sleeping."

"Yes, you're right," he nodded. "And that's a good thing. If all females were fertile, we'd be so overpopulated we'd eat the prey to nothing, and then we'd all die."

"It'll be hard enough feeding all these mouths. Plus, the awakened females might have more chicks."

"And so might you," Thornwing remarked, throwing another sly glance at her.

She hissed.

"You don't want to have chicks?"

"I don't know," she growled at him.

"Going to try to wait?"

Hawkwind sidestepped away from him. "Why are you so interested?" she spat, trying to keep her voice down. "I'm not in heat."

"Not yet. Some of these other, freed griffins are. You haven't noticed the tensions?"

"That's why," she said. "Your blood is all up."

"Is my company bothering you?"

"A little," she admitted.

"You'd prefer Rainsoft's company. I can switch with him."

"Why would you say that?"

"You've got him doing some heavy thinking, and you curled up with him last night. I'm assuming he didn't know how to give you a chick, or was holding back for some reason."

Hawkwind's ruff rose in confusion and anger. "What are you talking about?" she gritted out.

Thornwing's playful teasing faded away to be replaced with a heavy sincerity. "When we get back to South-scree, you should have a chat with a matriarch; I can ask Thornmother to talk to you. There's a lot you need to know."

"Maybe you could explain what you're talking about right now?"

"I don't know it the way a mother knows it. I only know what the older males have told me."

He wouldn't say anything more, and Hawkwind was left burning with embarrassed curiosity. Before she could get up the courage to press him for more details, Starbright swung back to the group, carrying another prey. She landed, causing all the griffins to come surround her. Hawkwind elbowed her way to the center.

"Chicks again?" she asked aloud and with gestures.

Most of the other immediately agreed, and those that didn't subsided with only the slightest signs of displeasure.

"I'll go get another one," Starbright panted, stretching her wings first.

"No, I'll go," Thornfire volunteered. "You've done enough for a while. Walk with the group and be ready to defend them should anything happen."

The relieved breath Starbright let out clearly indicated her acceptance of that bargain. Thornfire took off in a flurry of feathers.

"I should go to the front," Thornwing remarked. "I probably know the way better than anyone else."

Jessika, who had run up beside Hawkwind, put a hand on her furry shoulder.

"We're hungry," the girl whispered, sounding apologetic.

"Don't be sorry," Hawkwind replied immediately, and walked without hesitation towards the prey animal slowly being ripped into bits for feeding piping chicks.

"I need some for my chicks," she gestured, indicating her four human children, not having a gestural word for children.

The parents around the food paused to look plainly at the featherless, furless little ones. They tilted their heads with curiosity, but nodded agreeably. Hawkwind sawed off a piece. The four children together ate only about as much as one hungry chick, so it was no great loss for the others.

"What are they?" one griffin asked after tapping Hawkwind to get her attention.

"There isn't a word for them with hands," she explained, and then said aloud, "humans."

Hawkwind startled as Rainsoft landed beside her. Hands moving quickly, he communicated something to the interested griffins, but it was too fast for Hawkwind to catch more than a few words. Those watching, however, seemed to nod in understanding. Hawkwind led the four kids away to a place where she could safely pull out the Sunstone she still carried in a well-wrapped bundle. Rikah took the bloody meat from her and began shredding it for cooking on the Stone.

Kassandra tugged on one of Hawkwind's feathers. "We want fruit and vegetables," the girl said.

"And bread," Karo whispered. "And cookies."

Hawkwind ground her bill. She knew the children needed more than just meat, but she didn't know to get it to them.

"As soon as we can I'll take you all down into the forest. You can look for other things you can eat," she said.

Kassandra nodded silently, but Hawkwind suspected the girl wasn't very pleased, and she didn't know what else to do to help them. Hawkwind turned to face out from the group, standing on guard while everyone finished the food. Rainsoft came to stand silently beside her. Neither of them spoke. When at last the body was picked down to bones, and the smaller bones had been crunched up and swallowed, the group began moving again. Rainsoft resumed his guard from the air.

A while later they stopped again when Thornfire brought them another kill. This time older chicks and pregnant females got to eat. Thornwing volunteered to be the next hunter, which allowed the adults to get a swallow or two of food when he returned in the later afternoon, and the group moved on through the day until they picked a fairly defensible spot in a curve made by the mountainside and camped to sleep.

Chapter 21
Field Trip

"Thornfire, I have a request," Hawkwind approached him first thing in the morning.

"I don't expect you to ask for something unreasonable, so I'm sure we can accommodate it," he answered, in the midst of stretching out his back like a house cat, with wings pointed straight up to the sky.

"The children need more than meat to stay healthy. I need to take them into the forest to forage for other foods, like plants."

"We should be able to do without you for a while. So far, we haven't had any problems. I suppose even talis would hesitate before attacking such a large group of us, and we haven't seen or scented any."

"But it will be more dangerous for me, with four defenseless human children. I'd like to take another griffin along for protection."

Thornfire stood up and wrinkled his brow with thought. "I'd send Rainsoft, but he's the only one who can really communicate with the others. Will Wing be all right? If the talis attack you, he'll be able to fight them."

Thornwing wasn't her first choice after all the uncomfortable questions he'd asked her the day before, but she supposed Thornfire was right; Rainsoft was an essential intermediary, and Thornwing would be able to defend her from talis should they take the more tempting bait of a pair of griffins on their own.

"All right," Hawkwind agreed, keeping her voice carefully neutral. "We'll be careful, and join back up with the group later today."

She found Thornwing finishing his morning preening, with his grey animal companion stretched out in the sun beside him, and conveyed her goal and what Thornfire had said. He gave his agreement without any further comment and the pair of them with four skipping children in toe departed the group and headed for the trees.

"Don't run too far," Hawkwind instructed. "Keep one of us in sight at all times."

She might as well have been talking to the wind, telling it not to rustle the leaves. The children vanished into the undergrowth, chatting at high speed, except for Kassandra, who was her usual quiet self. Hawkwind and Thornwing ran after them, and Thornwing's animal friend scampered off with obvious jubilation.

"What is that beast?" Hawkwind took the occasion to ask him.

"Ferrie, you mean?" Thornwing replied. "He's a mountain-ferret, been with me for years. We get along. I even considered sending him back to South-scree to tell Thornfire I'd been captured by the talis, but I was afraid he wouldn't be able to find his way. He's not that skilled at big picture ideas; he lives more in the moment."

"He's cute, I guess," Hawkwind said.

"Your human chicks like him. They've been playing together for some time now."

"And he's safe? He won't bite them?"

"He won't bite unless they hurt him first. I told them to be gentle with him, and once he saw that they were my friends and were going to be kind, he understood that he shouldn't hurt them."

"Thornfire said something about you being good with animals, and that's why you thought you could talk to the talis," Hawkwind remarked.

"I have always been talented in understanding what animals are feeling, and I can somehow communicate to them what I'm feeling with my posture and sounds," he shrugged. "I do it naturally, sort of like how Fire does magic naturally. I thought maybe I could befriend the talis. I was stupid."

Within minutes the children had located more wild snow-celery and, clutching a stalk in each hand, had found perches on a mossy, fallen log to sit and crunch on the juicy vegetable.

"I wish there were more berries," Rikah commented, "but it's the wrong season. We only found a few wild strawberries."

"I want a cookie," Karo requested.

"What's that?" Thornwing asked.

Karo put his snow-celery stalk in his mouth, tucking the spare one under his questionably clean arm, and held his hands out to show the shape and size, while talking around the snow-celery stalk. "They're about this big," he slurred. "Sort of like bread, but sweet."

"What's sweet?" the South-scree griffin pressed.

"It's a flavor," Hawkwind explained for him. "We can't taste it."

"But what's it like?"

"I've never been able to conceptualize it," she admitted. "No human has ever been able to explain it well enough for me."

Jessika elbowed Karo gently. "That's right, Karo. Remember, griffins can't taste sweet."

"I still want one," the boy pouted.

"My favorite are apple cookies," Rikah said.

"I like almond," Kassandra murmured.

"The closest I can think is that it must be the opposite of bitter," Hawkwind shrugged.

"Bizarre," Thornwing mused, brows furrowed.

"That's really not fair," Jessika commented. "You can taste bitter but not sweet. Who wants to taste bitter? Yuck."

"Toxic, poisonous things are often bitter," Hawkwind explained. "Being able to taste bitter means we can spit out deadly things in time; it helps keep us all healthy."

"My mom likes bitter tea," Rikah provided automatically.

Then all the children went still, and Hawkwind, too, catching her breath like she'd poked herself on a stick. Karo's face began to crumple and Kassandra lowered her snow-celery to her lap, hands shaking. Rikah's lip was trembling. Hawkwind could see Jessika biting her cheek to try to stop the tears that were building up in her eyes.

Hawkwind stepped forward and encircled the children with her wings. Weakly, Kassandra and Karo fell against her, starting to sob.

Jessika and Rikah sat stiff and straight, sniffing and keeping their eyes open to stop the tears from escaping, but they, too, broke down after a brief struggle.

Hawkwind felt her own chest clenching, but she twisted down the cry in her own throat so she could comfort the children, holding them close against her body—no substitute for the arms of their own parents, but all she could offer, and all they had. She turned her head briefly to look at Thornwing, but he had pivoted, facing away, guarding them and giving them privacy.

Hawkwind let them cry for a few minutes. She didn't know how much grieving human children needed, but she didn't see a reason to restrict them, to tell them to not be sad; she just tried to care for them as well as she could. It was Jessika who sat up first, drying her face on Hawkwind's furry shoulder.

"We need to look for more food," she managed to get out between diminishing sobs. "We have to eat. Finish your snow-celery, everyone."

"I'm almost done," Rikah declared, hiccoughing only a little as he gamely took another bite. "I bet you can't finish before me, Karo."

Hawkwind backed off a little as the children finished, giving an extra pet to Kassandra's messy black hair. Jessika hugged the smaller girl against her side until they'd both eaten up their snow-celery.

"We might be able to find some more wild strawberries," Jessika proclaimed. "Let's look over there."

A new focus in mind, the children crawled off, staring at the ground and poking around under the greenery. Thornwing walked gingerly up beside Hawkwind.

"They got reminded that their parents died," she said, forestalling any questions.

"I heard a brief version of the story from my brother," he replied softly. "You and they are the only survivors?"

"That we know of. It may be others were left alive, but when I fled the castle with those four, everyone left was fighting for their lives, and most everyone else was dead already. The rainbow drakes killed everyone they caught. I was alone when I got these children out."

"And you came to South-scree?"

"Only by accident," she said. "I had heard old tales of griffins that lived in the north. I found them, or rather, they found me. Eldest Skycall said she wouldn't drive me out of South-scree if I brought her the Sunstone from Snow-in-lee, and likewise Rainsoft could stay if he brought the Moonstone."

"I found a strawberry," Rikah caroled out. "There's more here."

The other three children ran to join him at a sunny patch of the wild berries.

Thornwing was shaking his head. "Hawkwind, have you been listening? Skycall will never allow you to live in South-scree now. That would mean adding a new Line to the city."

"Thornfire said he'd handle the situation, that he'd make sure my children and I would have a place to live."

"My brother is a mage and an elder and has a lot of power, for a male, but unless he has some extra leverage I don't know about, I can't see how he'll do it."

Karo ran up to Hawkwind, shoving a few final berries into his mouth. "These are good, but I want bread."

"Bread doesn't grow in the forest, Karo," she told him. "I'm sorry."

"How far is the nearest human settlement?" Thornwing asked.

"From here? I'm not sure where I am. I don't know how far, and going into a town would be too dangerous," Hawkwind replied.

"We could fly down the mountain and take a look."

She stared at him. "No, we couldn't. Leave the children here?"

"They could ride us."

"No, they couldn't. What if they fell?"

The other kids had gathered around them now. Rikah's eyes were shining. "I want to ride you," he whispered. "I want to fly."

"No," Hawkwind said firmly. "Your feet stay on the ground. Wasn't that a rule at Northnest? No griffin ever carries a human except in a life or death emergency."

"But we're little," Rikah argued. "We're not heavy."

"Let's do it," Thornwing urged. "By wing, we could find a town and steal some food."

Karo took hold of Hawkwind's neck. "I'm hungry. I want bread," he whined.

"There are straps on our harnesses," Thornwing went on. "We can tie the children on, so they won't fall."

"Yes, Hawkwind, please," begged Rikah.

"This is a bad idea; I can feel it," Hawkwind stated.

"It'll be all right," Thornwing soothed.

She glared at him. "Who got captured by talis? You are not known for having the best ideas. You're reckless. I am not. I have to keep these children safe."

Thornwing eyed her narrowly. "You need to know where there are human settlements. What if these children get sick? And what about providing proper food for them right now? If you don't, they will get sick, and you'll have to go there anyway."

Hawkwind ground her bill. He had a small point.

"We'll hold on, Hawkwind," Jessika said softly, fingers twined in the griffin's fur, big eyes looking up pleadingly. "We need something else to eat besides meat."

Like releasing a dearly caught prey to another who claimed it as theirs when it wasn't, Hawkwind surrendered.

"Are you strong enough to carry two children?" she asked Thornwing seriously. Around her the children bounced on their toes with muffled excitement.

"I've been flying a lot the past couple days, and I kept doing exercises during my confinement," he replied with a flexing of his pectorals. "I can carry them."

"Rikah, you will hold on tight to Thornwing and to Karo,

understand?"

The boy nodded solemnly.

"And Jessika, Kassandra, you will hold onto me and each other, right?"

"Yes, Hawkwind," the two girls murmured.

"Thornwing, let's strap them on."

Although every movement felt like walking ever closer to a cliff edge, Hawkwind helped secure the boys to Thornwing's harness, and he did the same for the girls to hers. The load was heavy, but not as much as a big prey animal; Hawkwind would be able to fly well enough. Thornwing whistled, and his pet Ferrie came running through the brush, jumping up and grabbing onto him. He led the way to a nearby boulder that jutted out over a small valley. He climbed it, and took to the air with a leap. Hawkwind followed.

The girls yelped with fear and gripped tightly onto her back, but they didn't scream or cry, and after several wing strokes, Hawkwind looked back at them. Kassandra's face was open and humbled with wonder as she stared at the unfolding sky. The wind tossed back her curly bangs: revealing the pink mark on her forehead and making her eyelids flutter in response to the air on her eyes. Jessika was watching below as the ground passed, mouth open as if drawing in all the wind of their passing.

From above, the Earth spread out below like a map, showing forests and rivers and peaks and valleys; it was a view the children would have never had before. In the distance, Hawkwind could see level brown and green land. Tiny strands of grey smoke rising from it, visible only to her raptorial eyes, indicated that it was probably a human settlement. It would take a few hours to fly there—a day or more to walk there.

Thornwing and Hawkwind kept to a fairly low altitude, even though it meant more flapping and less catching of warm updrafts to jet upwards followed by gliding. The human children weren't used to the thin air of the upper sky, and lower altitudes were warmer. It was a sunny day and they had warm-blooded beasts to ride, but Hawkwind could still feel the girls shivering slightly as the wind blew steadily over them. Soon enough they were hunkered down, snuggled as deeply into her back fur as they could get, eyes glazed as they watched the passing land and sky.

As Hawkwind and Thornwing approached the town, they dropped their altitude further, almost skimming the treetops with their wings as they tried to shield themselves from view. Most settlements had sentries; some even had an elevated guard tower; big settlements might have a keep, but this town didn't. The griffins didn't want to be spotted, and as soon as Thornwing found a break in the canopy, he swerved down into it, and Hawkwind circled around and followed him.

"So that is a human settlement," the male griffin commented, "both like and unlike our own."

The children were fidgeting with eagerness. Ferrie jumped right off of Thornwing and zipped away into the underbrush on some unknown ferret business of his own.

"We must approach slowly, and stay hidden," Hawkwind reminded them all.

She led them into the undergrowth, moving silently, watching for the first signs of habitation; some of the homes might spill over into the woods. From the brief look Hawkwind had gotten, the town didn't appear to have more than a low stone wall, and a road ran through it from west to east. They were approaching from the north, towards some of the more straggly homes at the western edge.

They crouched down among some bushes edging a stream. On the other side of the stream began a small patchwork field of various early spring crops, attached to a house. A few goats grazed in an enclosed area with chickens pecking around them. A clothesline was hung with dull linens flapping wetly in the intermittent breeze. Fruit trees dotted the empty spots around the house and outbuildings, just starting to flower and leaf out.

"Looks like a nice home," Hawkwind whispered. "It's in good repair, the animals look healthy, the trees are leafy, and the field is full of vegetables."

"Are we going to steal from them?" Jessika asked, tone of voice clearly indicating that she didn't want to.

"They look prosperous enough that they could afford an involuntary donation to four hungry children," Hawkwind suggested gently. "What would you like to do?"

The creak of a door made them all look up. An older girl, probably approaching marriageable age, had stepped out of the back door and down the steps with another basket of laundry. She was dressed for chores, but in clean and sturdy clothes, no patches or worn spots. She sang to herself as she added some undergarments to a half-barrel with a washing board sticking out of it.

"We could see what they would trade for a whole buck deer," Thornwing suggested.

"Talk to them?" Hawkwind gaped.

"Not us, the children," he said.

"It's too risky," she countered at once. "What if they try to detain the children? What if they report them to somebody?"

A second woman emerged from the house, this one much older, with grey streaking her brown hair. She knelt down next to the young woman and started helping her with the washing, joining in to the singing. The griffins and children watched and listened as the two women began a call-and-response song, singing different parts. The smiles between them showed well enough that they were cheerful people.

"Rikah should go," Jessika said. "They won't be as likely to want to keep a boy. Boys are more allowed to run around and live in the woods and do independent things."

Hawkwind and Jessika shared a glance; the girl was afraid she might be recognized if she went. The griffin wasn't sure if this was still Northnest or not—she was a little lost over the geography—but the royal family hadn't secluded themselves; they were well known and might indeed be recognized.

"Rikah, can you do this?" Hawkwind asked.

The boy nodded grimly, chewing his lip and scowling at the house across the creek. "A deer for food and supplies," he said. "A trade, no questions asked, right?"

Hawkwind smiled sadly down on him; a boy his age shouldn't have had to grow up so fast and take on such mature matters.

"If they try to grab me, I run away," he went on.

"And if they do grab you and you can't run away, we'll come get you," Thornwing said, almost a growl, before making a soft whistle. A moment later Ferrie reappeared on his shoulder and he rumbled something low at the little beast. "Ferrie will go along. If anyone tries to grab Rikah, Ferrie will encourage them to let go."

Hawkwind wasn't going to ask how Ferrie would do that, or how Thornwing had told him to do that; she just nodded. "How will we make the trade?" she brought up. "Rikah can't exactly carry the deer over there."

"We'll leave it on the bank here," Thornwing said. "We should be able to sling it out there without being seen. They can come retrieve the deer and leave the traded supplies in its place."

"All right," Hawkwind nodded. "Go get the deer?"

"I'm on it." Thornwing vanished into the undergrowth and Ferrie ran off in the opposite direction, towards the house.

"Rikah, are you ready?" she prodded.

"Ready, but what do we ask for?"

"Food, cloth or clothing," Hawkwind started listing.

"Teeth scrubbers," Kassandra put in, "and hairbrushes."

"Knives, forks, and spoons," Jessika added, "and bowls."

"Cookies," Karo said in a small voice.

"Good, I'm going to go," Rikah announced.

Hawkwind's stomach started flipping over and over as she watched the boy cross the stream by hopping across on some rocks and then walk steadily towards the house and the two women. She heard him call "excuse me" and saw the women stand up with surprise, but after that their voices were too soft to hear. Rikah stood with his arms crossed and feet planted confidently, and neither of the two women tried to grab him, although their postures displayed their concern.

Hawkwind ducked down as the boy briefly turned to point towards the spot on the bank by the creek. When she looked again she thought the younger woman had started feeling suspicious and overly curious, but as she started asking questions more pointedly, the older women patted her shoulder reassuringly. Hawkwind guessed the older woman was the mother of the younger one. She crouched down to be on Rikah's level and talked to him some more. The younger woman stepped back then, still looking dubiously at the boy, and no longer speaking. Hawkwind wished she could hear what they were saying.

After another minute the older woman said something to the younger one, making the latter go back into the house. She came back out quickly enough, holding an object wrapped in a corn husk, which she passed to Rikah. The older woman held out a hand to shake, and Rikah tentatively shook, while Hawkwind held her breath, afraid the woman was about to yank him into her arms and carry him away. She didn't, releasing the boy's hand and standing up. Rikah turned and made his way back around the patchwork field to the stream. Once he'd crossed and pushed through the bushes to reunite with Hawkwind and the other children, he revealed what he'd received to a chorus of muffled squeals of excitement.

"They aren't cookies," he apologized, "but she said she'd baked some cornmeal cakes."

He held out the four small but heavy cakes on the corn husk, thick and slightly greasy, probably from being cooked with lots of butter and possibly lard. Karo's hand shot out towards one, but he pulled it back guiltily.

"Can we have one?" he asked politely, as if remembering his manners.

"Of course," Hawkwind said, "but eat slowly and savor it."

The four cakes were taken up with gusto, one to each child, while Hawkwind questioned Rikah.

"What did they say?" she asked. "Did they agree to the trade?"

"They asked me lots of questions at first, who I was, where I came from," he winced. "I didn't want to lie, so I just told them that I couldn't tell them. The girl didn't like that, but her mom said it was all right. They didn't believe me at first, that a deer would be there on the stream bank. That made the girl angry. Finally the mom asked me if I was telling the truth. I said yes, and she agreed. She asked me what I wanted in trade, and I told her. She said she would do her best to get me everything, but she couldn't promise. She said she would give me enough things to equal the deer."

"You did wonderfully, Rikah," Hawkwind praised.

"The corn cakes were a gift, she said," he went on. "She said she didn't have any cookies, but that she'd try to trade for some with her neighbors, if she could."

Rikah looked down at the corn cake making his hands greasy. He seemed to swallow his next mouthful with difficulty.

"She said I could stay with her, live there," he mumbled.

The other children stopped mid-chew and looked at him.

"I didn't say there were four of us," he added.

Hawkwind's chest hurt. Maybe it would be better if they went back to live with other humans, as Thornfire had once said. Maybe they could vanish into the populace and no one would know they were survivors of Northnest.

"I'm staying with Hawkwind," Kassandra announced firmly.

"Me, too," Jessika echoed only a heartbeat later.

Rikah and Karo didn't say anything.

"Karo," Hawkwind said gently, "you can go live with that family, if you want to. It's all right. I want you to be safe and happy."

After a moment, the boy took a big bite of corn cake, chewed slowly, and swallowed. "Thornfire is going to teach me magic," he whispered. "I'll stay with you, too."

"I'll stay also," Rikah said.

"You can change your mind," Hawkwind felt she had to say. "Anytime you want, we can come back."

A commotion behind them made them startle. Thornwing was dragging a young buck deer through the undergrowth.

"I had to go a ways," he reported, dropping the beast. "Looks like this village does a bit of hunting in the area."

"Then they'll be even more grateful," Hawkwind nodded, "if deer are scarce around here."

"I'll toss it out, provided the deal has been made?"

"It has. Let's toss it out and go back a ways so the people can make the exchange."

Trying to show themselves as little as possible, Hawkwind and Thornwing got the deer onto the stream bank and then the whole group retreated back into the trees, finding a spot to relax where the children could finish their corn cakes and lick the grease from their fingers. Hawkwind and Thornwing sat in a small clearing and preened their flight feathers while the children perched on the curving roots of a grandfather tree. After a few more minutes, Ferrie came dashing through the forest and took his perch on Thornwing's shoulder. He chattered something that sounded happy to Hawkwind.

"Ferrie saw nothing upsetting. So," Thornwing mumbled through a mouthful of feathers, "it was a good idea, wasn't it?"

"What was?" Hawkwind countered.

"The children are getting good food and more because we carried them on our backs and flew them to a human settlement."

Hawkwind stifled a growl. "I'll admit it's working so far, but we haven't got the stuff yet."

"It'll work," Thornwing sighed with a soft smile. "I always have the best ideas."

"Like going to try to talk to talis, yes, the very best ideas."

"All right, that one wasn't the very best, but it might have worked. I had to give it a try."

Hawkwind snorted.

The sun found its way past the leaves above, bringing out the gold color in Hawkwind's feathers and warming her through. She found herself laying her head down onto the clover and dandelions for just a few moments.

She startled awake, the size of the shadows informing her immediately that time had passed while she'd inadvertently slept. The girls were making crowns of flowers and the boys were having sword fights with sticks. Ferrie was licking the grease from the corn husks.

"It's only mid-afternoon."

She looked up at Thornwing, sitting comfortably, leaning against her back.

"I stayed awake," he went on. "Don't worry, I've been watching them."

"Hawkwind," Jessika greeted with a grin.

The girl ran over and placed a dandelion crown on Hawkwind's head. Jessika and Kassandra both wore crowns, too, the bright yellow flowers reflected on their skin.

"We'll make one for Thornwing next," Jessika announced.

"Hold off, there," the male griffin laughed. "It's probably time to go collect your spoils."

"Our what?" Karo asked, pausing in his battle with Rikah.

"The results of your trade," Thornwing rephrased. "Let's see if they've been left on the stream bank for you."

Ferrie ran over and stole Hawkwind's crown; then sat on Thornwing's head, eating it to the laughter of the children. The group crept back towards the creek, approaching slowly in case watchers or

traps had been left behind, too. Hawkwind peered at the house across the stream and fields, but no one was outside. The deer carcass was nowhere to be seen. The bank sand had been raked to clear the blood away, and two bundles were sitting in its place. The two griffins snuck out their long arms to snag the bags and yank them in, and then the group ran back to the clearing where they'd rested.

Eager hands pulled open the bags. The first held food wrapped in corn husks or rough paper: bread, rounds of cheese, fresh green vegetables, carrots, potatoes, various squash, a small bag of salt, dried beans and peas, and a few tiny bags of spices and herbs. The second bag held the inedible items: some wooden spoons and forks, an eating knife, a pair of wooden cups and bowls nestled inside a battered but functional metal cooking pot, a comb, a tooth cleaning brush with the tooth powder it was usually used with, and a bigger knife that might be used for butchering animals. At first Hawkwind thought that the fabric it was all wrapped in was just random scraps, but then Jessika exclaimed.

"Clothes, it's clothing."

The children began laying out the pieces. There were several undergarments, a few shirts and trousers, socks, and a few heavier garments made of knitted wool—jackets, scarves, and hats. Then Kassandra found one more little bundle among the layers and plucked it out. She handed it to Jessika when she saw what it was.

"Sewing thread and pins and needles," the older girl gasped.

Rikah took a look at the items. "I'm surprised she gave us those. My dad wasn't skilled enough to make pins and needles. They're really difficult to make, so they're expensive. These must have cost her a lot."

Jessika held the little bundle close to her heart. "With these, and using this clothing as a guide, I can make us all more clothes. We'll need more as we get bigger."

She trembled, and Hawkwind feared another crying spate coming on. The griffin patted Jessika's back in as encouraging a fashion as she could manage, and the girl sniffed, bit her lip, and straightened up with a firm, tear-denying face.

"There's also this," Karo said, holding something up. "I can't read it, I haven't learned yet."

There had been a letter tucked in among the items in the second sack. Hawkwind took it from him and read aloud.

"To the brave, mysterious young man," she read, "I hope these supplies will aid you on your journey. I wish I could help you more. If you ever need anything and are passing through again, come by my house and I will help you. If you ever wish to have a home, my home is yours. Do not be afraid to visit. Your friends—which I assume you have—are welcome, too. Best of luck, Judit Rania."

Hawkwind winked at Rikah. "I think she likes you."

The boy went red and then spluttered, "but she's old. She's like a granny, besides, I don't like girls."

"You say that now," Thornwing grinned, and then sombered curiously, "actually, how does human mating work?" he asked.

"Later," Hawkwind grunted supressively. "We should get going. Let's pack everything back up," Hawkwind urged.

The weight was greater now, with the big bulky bags, so getting in the air was no easy thing, but once up, the group retraced their wing beats back up the mountainside. Jessika and Kassandra, on Hawkwind's back again, chatted with each other about what they would be able to do with all the things they'd gotten, instead of looking at the scenery this time. As the sun was getting old in the sky Thornwing sighted the group of freed griffins making camp in a spot where the trail dipped into a small valley. Hawkwind followed him down and rejoined the group with a much happier set of human children.

Rainsoft studiously ignored her the evening of their return to the group. He couldn't have missed her flying back in, and he seemed to greet Kassandra with genuine happiness when the girl trotted over to chat with him about her adventure. Did he look Hawkwind's way even once? No. She did, however, catch him sending ambiguous glares at Thornwing's turned back.

As night fell, after the children had devoured most of the most perishable food in the sacks, abstaining from a slice of the kills Starbright had made, Hawkwind found herself and Thornfire sitting and staring blankly at the Sunstone as others were settling down to sleep. He broke his gaze and looked over at her.

"Troubled mind, little Hawk?" he rumbled congenially. "My brother was not uncouth on your journey today, was he?"

"No, he wasn't," she said, "but there is a lot on my mind."

"If there's anything you feel comfortable sharing with an old vulture like me, my ears are open."

"Rainsoft is ignoring me," she confessed.

"That displeases you?"

"I thought we were friends."

The mage rolled his shoulders. "As expected, you and he are both caught in different but related pinches. You're aware of it; you shouldn't be surprised."

"I guess he didn't like that I went off with Thornwing, not him."

"You're not in heat, you said Wing didn't behave inappropriately."

"I'm not and he didn't, but Rainsoft still didn't like it."

"He's also been reunited with his family. His focus may be elsewhere," Thornfire suggested.

"And I don't think he knows what to tell his family about me, because he doesn't know what kind of relationship he and I have, and neither do I. I don't even know what I want," she pled softly, for what seemed like the hundredth time.

"Hawkwind, my dear little lost one," Thornfire murmured, "regardless of what you want, I can tell you plainly what you will have, and it's best you accept it, especially as you probably know this truth deep down. You will be Hawkmother, a matriarch, and you will have chicks eventually. There is just no way you are getting out of that, short of death. If you don't want to have many chicks, try to avoid conceiving as much as possible and pass on the mantle to your oldest daughter as soon as she's ready, but your nature—the nature of an awakened griffiness—is not something you can fight and win."

Hawkwind swallowed with difficulty, gazing sightlessly at the Sunstone as she absorbed his words.

"That's how it will be if you remain in society," he went on.

Numbly, she nodded.

"All you get to decide is if you love Rainsoft and want to exclusively pair-bond to him."

Hawkwind choked on her next breath and turned to stare at Thornfire, who just shrugged.

"We both know how rare a true love pair-bond is. If you think you have that with Rainsoft then your path is clear. Go and relieve him of his anxiety. If not, then your path is more discomfiting."

She shook her head slightly. "I like him. I'm happy to be with him; it's comforting. I don't know what a love-bond would feel like, but—"

"You'd know," Thornfire interrupted at once. "There would be no doubt for either of you. You wouldn't leave each other. You'd never consider another, ever. Even if there were times you had arguments or disagreements, you'd still be paired, and you'd get through them. At least, that's what I have read about the situation, having never experienced it myself."

"What if he feels that way?" she wondered.

"I think he's considerably confused. It's not natural for griffins to live in pairs like these Snow-in-lee griffins do. Certainly they aren't all true love-bonded, if any, yet they know no other way. It's what he grew up with: being taught he'd have a fated mate. Then he meets you, who grew up in a Line where nobody pairs exclusively. Your expectations are completely different."

Thornfire sighed heavily and stretched out on the ground into a more comfortable position. "All that's coming, Hawkwind, is the moment when you and he have to have the talk where you sort it all out and potentially hurt each other's feelings and ruin your friendship. That's what you're dreading."

She kneaded the dirt with her claws. "I think you're right."

Thornfire had lowered his head now, eyes closed in the dim glow from the Sunstone. "Anything else bothering you?"

Indeed, there were things she wanted to ask about: things Thornwing had said she should ask a matriarch. Thornfire looked about ready to fall asleep, though, and she didn't feel comfortable asking in the first place.

"Nothing I want to talk about right now," she whispered.

A sleepy mumble was her only answer.

"Good night, Thornfire," she murmured in reply, giving a quick little preen to his neck feathers.

Then Hawkwind, too, sought the land of dreams.

It was several days later that the group reached the mouth to the tunnel under the mountains. The pace of the freed griffins had improved with time, but they still weren't bringing in quite enough food for everyone, so the adults were hungry and a little weak: never mind being unused to walking long distances.

"Finally," Thornfire grunted. "Now we can find a cave for every family, make a proper long-term camp, and the business of learning to hunt and fly and communicate can begin in earnest."

"There may be snow-screamers in the way first," Thornwing reminded them all with a grim growl.

"We will take the caves away from them," Thornfire promised, "and eat them. Let's get this organized: no reason not to start today."

Between Thornfire and Rainsoft, the whole group was informed of the situation. The announcement that they would all be expected to fight was met with much deflective feather preening, as if most of the griffins were saying, "please don't choose me." Rainsoft screeched to regain their attention, and asked for volunteers. About a dozen came to the front.

"That's enough," Thornwing declared. "No more than that will fit in the tunnels anyway."

"As we go, the others will come in behind us, taking over the caves. We'll keep teams of fighters always on the advancing fronts," his mage brother agreed. "Hawkwind, will you and the children organize the distribution of families into the repossessed caves and begin any cleaning necessary? You and the children are second best at hand-speaking."

"I can do that," she agreed, both annoyed and relieved that she wouldn't have to be fighting the snow-screamers.

Thornfire and Rainsoft began organizing their task force of adult male and female griffins and moving towards the tunnel opening.

"Kassandra, will you ask the others to separate into small groups that they want to live with?" Hawkwind asked the girl.

"All right," the girl said, and began walking into the gathering, talking with her hands as she went.

Rainsoft had already explained a lot, but Hawkwind sat back on her haunches and raised her hands. "Who wants the first caves, near the door?" she asked with the best words she knew.

A few groups raised their hands and Hawkwind gestured for them to follow her. Thornfire and the fighters had already disappeared into the tunnel, so she assumed the first caves were safe. She noted that Thornfire, Rainsoft, and Starbright had dropped their things in the first cave she stuck her head into; that one was claimed. Leaving the cave across the hall from it empty, Hawkwind dropped her packs, including the Sunstone and the new sacks the children had received, in the next cave in, beside the one Thornfire and the others had claimed. Having a buffer of a pair of mages and a fighter between her children and the open mountainside felt like a good idea.

"Who wants this cave?" Hawkwind asked the griffins who had followed her, indicating the cave across the hall from Thornfire's.

After a moment, someone raised a hand and Hawkwind nodded in acknowledgement. A pair of young griffins without chicks claimed the carved rock room. Hawkwind led the others on to the next caves, finding tenants as she went. When the tunnel branched, she headed down one, finding another half dozen empty caves before a dead end, and then turned around. By then, the initial volunteers had been sorted and Hawkwind went deeper by herself to see how the cleansing crew was doing. She found them down another branch with a tumble of snow-screamer corpses underfoot.

"Let's drag these out," Thornfire was saying. "Who ever takes these caves will need to do a little cleaning first."

A glance into the nearest showed Hawkwind piles of refuse: bones, fur, and droppings. The stink wasn't pleasant either.

"If possible, we won't use these ones, then," she said.

She helped them drag out the bodies, which, although stinky on the outside, still had edible meat on the inside—not the best, but they couldn't afford to be picky. They did, however, discard the digestive organs to avoid picking up internal parasites. Once the bodies were outside, the other griffins ripped into them readily enough once Starbright had roasted the meat as an added precaution, and Hawkwind invited another group to join her in selecting semi-permanent cave homes.

By evening, the cleanup crew had gone deep enough into the cave system to clear out enough caves that each family could lay claim to one. The volunteer fighters were the last to choose, and were given the ones at the edge of the cleared area. Even the fighters actually weren't more than a few minutes' walk from the entrance. Most of the now-claimed caves were along branching paths that ran parallel to the mountainside, which allowed for air shafts down into many of them. Those that did not have such shafts had horizontal shafts to neighboring caves. Combined, the shafts allowed airflow through the caves, but they also carried sound, so keeping secrets from neighbors wouldn't be possible unless those secrets were conveyed with whispers. Luckily for the Snow-in-lee griffins, they could communicate silently with their hands.

Enough snow-screamers had been evicted and slain that everyone had been able to eat, and they spent the rest of the evening cleaning up their caves: moving out rubble and moving in arm loads of grass or leafy boughs for bedding. If they stayed long enough they might be able to cure hides and stuff them for cushions, but temporarily they would have to make do. They'd been sleeping on the ground for the past week, so they'd started getting used to rougher conditions than the rooms they'd had back in Snow-in-lee, and having anything at all as a cushion was welcome.

Hawkwind spent the last bits of daylight gathering materials for her children to sleep on, as they didn't do as well as griffins at sleeping on rock. The big sacks they'd gotten from the woman in the village had been emptied and filled with the grasses to make a pair of mattresses. Additionally, most of the caves had included a patch of sand or pea gravel. With the mattresses on top of that, on either side of Hawkwind, the children would sleep better than they had in a long while, Hawkwind hoped.

Conveniently, Hawkwind was also still in possession of the Sunstone, which both warmed her cave and gave off some light. Starbright and Thornfire went around to all the other caves to enchant stones with light and then trooped back to their own cave, exhausted from the effort. Thornwing stopped by Hawkwind's cave to say good night, but Hawkwind saw not a sign of Rainsoft. She assumed he had gone to sleep in the cave his parents had claimed. The children fell asleep over the last of their dinner, and Hawkwind moved them onto their stuffed sacks. She crossed three arching branches over the Sunstone, leaving a plentiful gap between them and the hot Stone, and cast another scrap of cloth over them to dim the light for sleeping. Tired but satisfied, Hawkwind snuggled down between the children for the night.

Chapter 23
Snow-in-lee Hawks

Days passed and a week out saw Hawkwind watching proudly as her students began lifting themselves into the air on their own wings. It had taken days of concentrated exercise to strengthen their flight muscles enough that they could do that much—flapping energetically and lifting a few feet off the ground. They landed with cries of joy, sounding rather like excited fledglings, as they turned to each other, gesturing rapidly.

"They'll be swooping about in no time," Thornfire said from behind her.

"As it should be," she nodded back proudly.

"You've done a great job."

"All I really did was give a few pointers and encourage them," she shrugged. "Like any griffin, their passion for the winds did the rest. There's none of us that can sit on the ground and not want to be in the sky."

"And a good thing, too," Starbright grumbled. "The fitter they get, the better they'll be able to catch their own food. The prey is getting thin, and it's too far to fly several times a day to find enough meat for everyone."

"Hunting lessons will follow graduation from flight class," Thornfire affirmed.

He turned his head to look over at another class in progress. A dozen fledglings that still had their speaking voices surrounded the four human children. The children were trying to teach the little griffins to talk. Adults and juveniles that had already been mutilated by the talis looked over at them with pained expressions, watching the little ones fumble through the first baby-steps of a skill they could never have.

Other griffins that weren't in class at the moment hauled rocks, sand, branches, or bundles of grasses for improving their cave homes.

Thornwing had led yet another group deeper into the cave system to thin the number of snow-screamers there and provide food at the same time. A few griffins that were not employed in any of those ways lay on rocks, sunbathing and preening themselves or each other.

"We're safe and surviving here," Hawkwind ventured. "Everyone is getting stronger. When will we tell South-scree about what's happened?"

The muscles at the corners of Thornfire's bill bunched and his brows lowered.

"We are going to tell them, right?" Hawkwind asked, by dint of will alone keeping it from being an order or demand. "You promised," she added in a weak voice.

"You have to leave this to me, Hawkwind," he said. "I know the mothers and elders of South-scree. You don't. I know how and when it's best to handle them. You're safe now. You and the children have a suitable place to sleep and enough food and water. I must ask you to be patient and content with that."

"Yes, sir," she responded.

Without another word, she turned and waded into the sea of fledglings. The children scooted out of the way for her, and she took a seat among them.

"Hawkwind," said Kassandra, pointing at her.

Immediately, the chortling chicks shouted a dozen different, half-formed versions of her name at her. The human children kept repeating her name, too, urging the little ones to keep trying until they got closer and closer to saying it correctly. Once most of them were getting really close, Kassandra stood and clapped her hands vigorously until everyone fell silent.

"Let's introduce ourselves," the girl said with words and hands.

The fledglings chorused their agreement with chirps, squeals, hands, and happy vocal yeses. Kassandra pointed at the first one, a dusty yellow female with black and white markings.

"Skystrong," she said.

"Nice to meet you, Skystrong," Hawkwind smiled at her.

The little one trilled happily. Kassandra pointed at the next.

"Eaglesong," she whispered breathlessly.

Hawkwind stared, so stunned her breath had caught, forgetting to greet her, and making her start to whimper with worry. Hurriedly, Hawkwind rectified her carelessness, preening the little one's feathers to apologize, but hearing the name had been as shocking as a kick to the bill.

"Are you all right, Hawkwind?" Jessika asked.

"Do you remember Eaglesong from Northnest?" Hawkwind asked weakly. "Maybe you never met him. And there was Eagleye, my friend, and more Eagles."

"I don't," the girl winced.

"It's all right, don't worry," Hawkwind assured her. "I should have realized it when I met Icemoon back in Snow-in-lee. I thought the Falcon, Eagle, Ice, Snow, and Cloud Lines were ended, because they all died at Northnest, but they all came from Snow-in-lee. All the griffin Lines came from Snow-in-lee, and they might still be alive here."

She gasped again, sharply, and leapt to her feet. "There might be more Hawks—more of my Line, here, alive. I might not be the last."

She stared all around, at the chicks, at the adults, as if she'd be able to spot them by sight alone. She hadn't met all the griffins by name by any estimation. Names weren't as easy to translate from hand gesture to words, so often she'd learned only the hand gesture, if there had been any exchange of names at all. She hadn't yet met a griffin who used the same gesture for "hawk" that Rainsoft used for her name, but that didn't mean there wasn't one.

"And if there's an older female who is still having chicks," Hawkwind panted, seized with the need to find such a female right then. "I wouldn't have to," she trailed off breathlessly. Might her body go back to sleep? Maybe she would return to being just a normal, infertile female griffin, a mere supporter of her Line, and not the progenitor of it.

"Are there any Hawks?" she asked her children urgently. "Have you met any Hawks?"

"There are no little Hawks here," Jessika said, indicating her students.

"I met some," Kassandra offered. "Did you want to meet them?"

"Yes," Hawkwind answered. "Why didn't you tell me before?"

The girl wilted under Hawkwind's emphasis. "I didn't know."

"Kassie doesn't really understand yet, how the griffin Lines work," Jessika stood up.

Hawkwind forced herself to lower her fluffed feathers. "I'm sorry, Kassandra. I didn't mean to shout. I got too excited."

The girl got up and hugged Hawkwind's foreleg. "It's all right," she whispered. "I'll take you to them now."

"Later, then," Hawkwind soothed, patting the girl's black hair. "Let's finish introducing all the chicks here."

Hawkwind waited patiently, biting down on her anticipation, as she greeted the rest of the chicks, meeting another Sky, a Rock, a Snow, a Rain that she assumed was a cousin to Rainsoft, a Stone, a Storm, two Winds, and a Fire. She continued to wait patiently as the children wrapped up the class and encouraged the chicks to return to their parents, most of whom actually dropped what they were doing to come pick up their babies as they noticed that the class was over. Then, Kassandra tugged on Hawkwind's feathers and led her to a griffin who was sunbathing on a rock. He looked up congenially when Kassandra tapped him.

"I know you," he signed. "You rescued us."

"Are you a Hawk?" Hawkwind asked.

"I am." He gave his name but Hawkwind didn't know the word for the second half of it. Once they got him to write it down, scratching it out in the dust, she was able to read it.

"Hawkdash," she said. "I'm Hawkwind."

"I know," he smiled at her.

"So, you're in my Line," she went on.

"Line?" he repeated.

"You don't remember Lines? We both share a female ancestor of the Hawk name," she managed to say.

"Yes, I suppose we did, a very long time ago."

"So we're in the same Line. All griffins in the same Line are supposed to live together and help each other."

His expression became uneasy. Hawkwind startled when another griffin suddenly trotted over to join them, and Hawkdash looked up at the newcomer with what seemed to be relief. It was a female, and Hawkwind could smell right away that she was awakened.

Hawkdash gestured awkwardly, "my mate, Snowstar. This is Hawkwind."

"Yes, you rescued us," Snowstar nodded.

"I was looking for other members of my Line," Hawkwind explained, "other Hawks."

"Oh? Why?" she asked.

"I thought I was the last. My home was destroyed and all the other Hawks there were killed."

"I'm sorry to hear that," Snowstar said gently.

"Where I came from, all members of a Line, who share the same ancestral mother, live together, and help each other. I thought I could find other Hawks, and live like that again."

"Hawkdash lives with me and our chicks," Snowstar gestured, and Hawkwind detected just the slightest hint of warning.

"Of course," Hawkwind agreed. "I'm sorry to have bothered you."

"Go talk to my older sister," Hawkdash suggested. "Hawkswift: she's over there learning to fly right now."

There was an older sister? Perfect. "Thank you very much."

"I'm sorry we couldn't help. It was nice meeting you," Snowstar gestured hurriedly, and somewhat apologetically.

"You, too," Hawkwind replied.

She turned away, a private, wry expression on her face. Snowstar had thought Hawkwind was after Hawkdash for a mate, but she didn't understand; as Hawkwind had been raised, she would never have been interested in mating with a male from her own Line. She did want him, but as a protector, provider, and supporter for the Hawk Line. Males in a Line defended it and brought food for the chicks of the Line—their nieces and nephews. Non-mother females did that, too, although more often they were the direct daily caretakers of chicks: keeping them warm and clean, feeding them bits of the prey the males brought, and educating them.

Hawkwind looked around at the griffins struggling through flight class. She identified a few females, and spotted a large one with coloring similar to Hawkdash. When that griffin seemed to be taking a breather, Hawkwind walked up to her.

"Pardon me, are you Hawkswift?" she asked.

The griffin smiled at her. "Hawkwind? Yes, I am. I've wanted to meet you personally."

As Hawkwind got closer, her hopes fell. Hawkswift no longer smelled like she was awakened. Hawkwind noticed details like the dullness to her feathers, the thinness of her fur in certain areas, and the wrinkles on her visible skin. She was too old; her body had decided it would have no more chicks. Hawkswift must have noticed Hawkwind's disappointment. She tilted her head with concern.

"What's wrong?" she asked.

"I was looking for members of my Line," Hawkwind began to explain. "Where I came from, all the other Hawks were killed."

"I have begun to get the sense that the griffins not from Snow-in-lee are quite different from we that are," Hawkswift said shrewdly. "I noticed the female with you, who is your age, Starbright, who still smells like a fledgling, unlike you, and yet you seem to have no mate and no chicks, despite there being males with you, and those males traveling without their mates. I don't know that everyone else is taking the time to observe these things—they are very busy with their own families—but I am not, and I have noticed."

She'd spoken slowly with her hands, and Kassandra—who was much better at Snow-in-lee sign language—translated for Hawkwind, although she did it with some confusion, as she didn't seem to understand the significance behind much of what Hawkswift was saying. Hawkwind didn't expect a five year-old girl, even one so wise and toughened now as Kassandra, to understand the social aspects of mature griffins.

"You are right," Hawkwind replied. "Outside Snow-in-lee, all griffins live with their Line. That is, all the Hawks live together, all the Stars, all the Thorns, and so on. Only one female has chicks, and the others take care of them. The males mate with females from other Lines. There are no mated pairs."

"Your Line," Hawkswift picked up, "was killed except you? So you are the last."

"The last female, so I turned into the matriarch, the mother, the one that has chicks," she twitched her feathers as she admitted it, like blushing. "I don't want to be the one. I realized I could find other Hawks now, from Snow-in-lee, that maybe my body would go back to sleep, and I would not be the Hawkmother."

Hawkswift nodded in understanding and brushed her gently with a wing. "I have passed my days as a mother," she said. "My mate has gone to the," she stopped, flinching and seeming to wrestle with something internally. "My mate was taken and killed by the talis," she gestured out, "not to serve the talis king as we were told, I know now. My brother has Snowchicks, not Hawk. I had two sons who have been placed with mates, Eagle and Wind. I do have a daughter."

Hawkwind perked up, but Hawkswift squashed her hope quickly enough.

"She was my last child, and fledged last year." Hawkswift gestured to the side, and Hawkwind saw a small juvenile female practicing at flapping and hovering some yards away. "She won't be mature enough to awake, as you put it, for several years."

"Are there any other Hawks?"

Hawkswift shook her head. "I'm sorry, Hawkwind."

The weight of her new position settled upon her again; there would be no escape. Hawkswift touched her shoulder, and she looked back up.

"I can't take your burden from you," the older female said, "but I would help you bear it."

Hawkwind made a gesture of confusion.

"You say that in the world now griffins live together with others of their Line. My mate and my sons are gone to their varied destinies now, but for myself, and more for my daughter, I wish to be a part of the world of griffins, and not cling to a vestige of how we lived in Snow-in-lee. You will have to teach us a lot, but if you will have us, we would join you and be a part of the Hawk Line."

Hawkwind stared, stunned. For her part, Hawkswift stood tall, but also humble in her request. The implications of this were profound. Hawkwind would not be the only, would not be the last Hawk. She would gain an immediate heir-presumptive in Hawkswift's daughter. She would gain a mentor and guide in Hawkswift herself, with her experience and maturity an ideal resource. Hawkswift could tell Hawkwind all the things she needed to know about mating and birthing and raising chicks.

As Hawkswift had said, the older female would gain a place in griffin society by being a part of a Line, instead of a stubborn member of a randomly matched mated pair, who would be rejected by all Aeries. She would save her daughter from that fate, too. Her daughter would have the potential to rise up in rank and become Hawkmother, leader of a Line, with all the power and respect attached to the position. Even if she didn't, she would still be a respected and valued member of a Line, and one of its first elders.

All three of them would benefit. It still did not relieve Hawkwind of the—to her—burden of being the mother, but if there indeed were no other choice it might make it bearable, and it would increase her status and influence. Having griffins in her Line would legitimize her position. Having a chick would secure it; she would have to do that as soon as possible. With Hawkswift and her daughter around, especially once they became competent hunters, raising a chick and caring for her human children would no longer be all but impossible.

"Yes," she said and gestured firmly to Hawkswift, unable to hide her growing delight. "Yes, you and your daughter are welcome in my Line. You are Hawks. We belong together."

Hawkswift's burgeoning delight overflowed into quivers all along her skin and through her fur as her every feather lifted with elation. Hawkwind trembled herself as she felt a new and sudden pulse of connection swell inside her. This griffin, this was her griffin, her Hawk, a member of her Line. No matter how distant or lost in the mists of Time, she shared with Hawkswift the blood of a common mother, and it linked them.

Hawkswift called for her daughter, who glided over with hardly a bobble in her flight, and rapidly explained the situation. Hawkwind had a brief fear that perhaps the juvenile wouldn't like what her mother had done. Perhaps she had been looking forward to having her own exclusive mate like her parents had and her brothers now had. Hawkwind eyed her, watching for her reaction, and what she saw made her anxiety flow away like water from an upturned bucket.

Within moments of the explanation, the juvenile's nervous feathers slicked down with relief, and then Hawkwind was startled again to feel a second, new pulse of connection to the young one. Hawkswift's daughter had immediately and naturally slipped right into the role she was supposed to take: obedient and loyal Hawkdaughter. She turned bright and happy eyes onto Hawkwind, smiling as she gave a little bow.

"This is Hawkjoy," Hawkswift introduced.

"Nice to meet you," Hawkjoy gestured. "Should I call you Hawkmother?"

Hawkwind shook her head. "Not until I've had a chick," she explained. "Only then will I truly be the mother. We won't be an official Line until I do, although Swift could still be considered the Hawkmother, actually. We could say that we are in transition between mothers."

Swift shook her head a little. "I don't know how to be a Hawkmother. I'm sure you will have a chick eventually, if you keep trying. If you don't, in some years perhaps Joy will awaken, and she will have a chick instead. We will stay together until one or the other of those things happens and we become official, as you say, and then we will still stay together."

Swift extended her wings to touch both Hawkwind and Joy lightly across their backs, and Hawkwind reflected that Swift was acting and saying things rather like a mother, even if she declined the title. Her mere presence would be inspiration and guide to Hawkwind.

Hawkwind took half a step and then choked it back. She had the urge to snuggle up and preen her new Linemembers, but she didn't know if they'd like it. Her bond to them was tugging, making her want the physical closeness to cement it. Swift acted instead, reaching out to preen Hawkwind's cheek feathers, and then Joy did, too, and Hawkwind stepped up close to them, and they all crowded up against each other, bills full of each other's feathers and fervent trills rumbling in their chests.

Hawkwind had a glimpse of Kassandra standing confused and silent, and she realized she needed to introduce the rest of her family, although Swift and Joy probably already knew their names and had met them at least cursorily. After a minute, Hawkwind put an end to the group preening and called over the children.

Hawkswift and Hawkjoy

The children knew about Lines, of course, even if they didn't know all the details. With a proper introduction, even Kassandra's anxiety appeared to melt away, and Joy looked giddy at the chance to meet the little humans directly and talk to them and ask them questions. Hawkwind, with the children to help translate and contribute bits, ended up retelling her entire story to Swift and Joy. By the evening time they were found circled around the Sunstone in Hawkwind's cave, sharing stories and other conversation.

Hawkwind helped the children to bed, and then fell asleep snuggled against one side of Swift, with Joy sleeping soundly on the other.

Chapter 24
Frolic

Hawkwind awoke early the next morning, with Swift and Joy still sleeping. The children, too, were huddled up and slumbering deeply. She stood without waking the others and strode to the door of their cave, tail twitching and wondering what had awakened her. She felt restless and nervous and desirous of being in the air, despite the steady warmth inside her from finding two new members of her Line.

As her wandering thoughts flitted urgently to images of Rainsoft, a second part of her mind supplied her with the answer. How could it be? Had that much time passed since she'd regained her flight and led Rainsoft on a chase through the sky? That second part of her mind chimed in with the information that no, it hadn't been quite a month yet, but her acquisition of new Line members that would make raising a chick possible and her realization that having a chick would be critical to cementing her Line's legitimacy and her own power and status had probably triggered her body to hurriedly prepare for another attempt.

Her feet acted on their own, taking her down the tunnels to where Rainsoft's family now lived. She paused outside the door, which was shielded with a wooden frame of woven reeds, for privacy. She heard only the sound of sleeping griffins, and couldn't bear to touch the door, much less move it aside, stick her head in, and call for Rainsoft. His whole family was in there.

Perhaps there was someone else? She shut her eyes with a muffled hiss. Yes. Thornwing. He'd suggested Rainsoft didn't know how to give her a chick and implied that he, Thornwing, did. Her body commented that it was a fantastic idea but Hawkwind shook her head. No. She wouldn't go to him. She knew that matriarchs sometimes did go seek out a particular male and demand his services, rather than waiting for interested males who happened to be nearby to come solicit them, but Thornwing was older than Hawkwind, and she didn't have the confidence to go and demand him. If she tried, it would look like she was enamored or begging. That would give him the appearance of power over her, and already her Linemother instinct knew to never do anything that suggested any other griffin had more power than she did.

As she was wrestling with herself and about to just turn away, fly off into the forest, and wait out the heat until it subsided—if it even would without mating activity—the door slid aside with hardly a rustle, and Rainsoft poked his head out. She knew she didn't have to tell him why she was there.

"Will you come?" she gestured.

A nice thing about talking with hands, there was no need to try to whisper. He nodded as he replaced the door, and Hawkwind turned immediately to head for the cave exit. Rainsoft followed as she passed other cave homes in the near darkness. When they reached the exit, Hawkwind leapt into a run and flapped into the pre-dawn sky. She saw no reason to lead Rainsoft on a chase this time; she let him keep up until she settled on a bit of cliff poking out over a valley a good ways away from the caves. Trees and bushes surrounded the bare promontory, and she pushed into them until she located a hollow just big enough for two that was shielded from view from above by tree branches.

Hawkwind didn't feel the need to say anything, and it seemed that neither did Rainsoft. It was with trembling desire that she accepted him, and with sated exhaustion that she collapsed below him when it was over. As she lay panting, his warm weight against her, Hawkwind tried to analyze his technique. What more was needed to make a chick? What had he not done? It had certainly felt fulfilling and he appeared to have concluded correctly. Or had Thornwing been lying, hoping it would trick Hawkwind into asking for him when the time came again?

She groaned and flexed her claws. No, reckless and a bit brash he might be, but Hawkwind didn't think Thornwing was a liar. Beside her, Rainsoft groaned, too, nudged against her, and then climbed back onto her. She would have to hope that this worked anyway. Maybe Rainsoft was doing everything the right way and she hadn't kindled the previous time for another reason. Maybe there was just always some chance it wouldn't work.

Or maybe she should have awakened Swift and asked her about it before sneaking out of the cave this morning. Some older griffin advice for her and for Rainsoft would probably have helped a lot. Or maybe Rainsoft's father had already given him advice? Maybe he'd learned what to do and what he was doing was correct? It felt right at least.

They alternated napping and mating as the sun rose higher until its bright beams drenched them in green twilight under the canopy. Finally, Rainsoft sat up and nibbled her cheek feathers to get her attention. Hawkwind gave him a little smile as she rolled over to look at him.

"Thank you for coming to get me," he gestured. "You could have chosen other males if you wanted, but you came for me."

"I like you," she said, truthfully.

"I like you, too," he signed back, and then looked down, "but you don't want to be my mate."

It was time for the talk. Hawkwind stifled all her possible groans, grunts, and sighs and faced him head on, touching his bill to get him to look back up so he could see her hands.

"Rainsoft, listen to me," she began with both hands and soft voice. "We come from places with different cultures. I am going to be a matriarch." She had to stop, shaken a little by finally admitting it out loud and with conviction. "To have the power to protect my human children, I need status, and I am the only Hawk alive that can do it. I will start the rebuilding of the Hawk Line."

He nodded at her, not happily.

"If you want a mate, one on one," she continued bravely, even as she fought a throat tight with emotion, "you will have to choose someone else who also wants that. I hope, however, that you will join someone else's Line, maybe Thornfire's, and take your place in my culture.

You would always be my favorite. You could mate only with me, if you wanted to."

"But you will mate with other males," he gestured rapidly.

There was no point in hiding it from him. "I will. My Line, like all Lines, needs varied blood. You should also see the value that you have. I don't know if the Rain Line still exists outside of the Snow-in-lee survivors. You might be one of the last of them. Many Lines could be strengthened with your blood. If you talk to your little sister about it, she could become Rainmother of the Line."

Rainsoft stood up, walked away a few paces, hesitated, faced her again, and sat down. "I don't know how to feel about this. I don't know what I want. I want to be a part of the world, not Snow-in-lee, but I have always thought I would have one mate, and once you invited me to mate with you, I thought it would be you, but I see. I have talked to my parents and a little to Thornfire. I see why you invited me."

"I still like you," Hawkwind interrupted. "I like you a lot. I don't want to hurt you, but I—"

"I know," he soothed quickly. "I know." Rainsoft dropped his hands.

"I don't know what else to tell you," she said. "I can't run away to be just with you. I have my children to care for. I have met Hawkswift and Hawkjoy, from Snow-in-lee, and they have joined my Line." She took a deep breath. "I hope I will have your chick, to add to my Line."

Rainsoft gave no reaction. Briefly, but not overly rudely, he gestured, "I'll hunt and come back."

Hawkwind flopped back down on the tangled leaves and grasses as he stalked off into the underbrush. The talk was done. She didn't feel bad and she didn't feel good. She'd been honest. She'd tried to be gentle. It was the most she could do. Hawkwind closed her eyes and dozed as the sun crept across the sky.

It was afternoon when crunching through the trees and the sharp scent of blood alerted her to Rainsoft's return. He'd brought her half his kill, having obviously eaten part of it already. He offered, she thanked him, and ate hungrily. They preened the blood off of each other, and that led to more mating and napping until the sky began to show signs of dusk. At last, Rainsoft stood up and flicked his wings.

"I want to go back to the caves," he gestured.

Hawkwind nodded. "If you see my children or Hawkswift or Hawkjoy, please tell them not to worry about me. I'll sleep out here tonight and come back tomorrow morning."

"You won't come back now?" he asked.

"It's not over yet," she explained. "I don't want to be mobbed."

He seemed to realize what she meant, and leaned down to nibble her feathers. "You'll be safe out here tonight? I'll see you tomorrow? You won't be lonely? Should I stay?"

"I'll be fine," she said reassuringly, "and thank you."

He started to go, and then paused. "I hope you have my chick, too," he signed rapidly. Then he dashed from the hollow and she heard him take flight from the cliff edge.

That settled it then. Either he was doing everything right, or he didn't know what he wasn't doing. Maybe Thornfire and his parents hadn't told him that, or maybe he hadn't asked, or maybe they'd assumed he knew somehow. Hawkwind settled herself more comfortably and drifted off to sleep again as the sun sank and the stars and moon lit the sky above the tree branches.

Hawkwind didn't know what time it was, but it was still dark. She got up to take care of the necessary demands of nature, and then walked to the cliff edge to look at the dark dome of the sky. The moon was nearly full, the sky clear, and the brightest stars competing with the moon's glow. It was a beautiful night for flying, but Hawkwind sensed that vigorous exercise like running or flying would not be conducive to conception. There was only one kind of exercise she wanted: a pity Rainsoft had left.

For a while longer she sat and absorbed the night, listening to the hunting calls of nighttime predators—only little ones, big ones had the sense to stay away from a griffin—and the faintest rustle of their furtive prey. She heard, too, the sound of wings, big wings. A dark spot against the lighter sky, a griffin was flying towards her. Perhaps Rainsoft had decided to return, but no, this griffin was larger, with a wider wingspan, and it was coming straight towards her.

There wasn't much of the cliff bare of greenery, so he landed fairly close, and Hawkwind identified him even in the darkness.

"I thought I scented you in my dreams this morning, and when both you and Rainsoft were gone for most of the day, and then he returned covered with your scent, it was no challenge to understand the situation," Thornwing said. "I'm glad I found you. I just wanted to..." he trailed off.

Hawkwind didn't move so much as a single feather, staring at him.

"I didn't come to try to force you," he resumed quietly. "I just came to offer."

"Offer?" she repeated in a bare whisper, even as her body clamored at her to grab him, yank him, manhandle him; order, command, threaten, coerce him, whatever, until he satisfied her hunger.

"I noticed you have two new members of your Line," he remarked, a bit more confidently. "You really will become Hawkmother. You need a chick for that."

"How do you know that Rainsoft isn't doing it right?" she demanded. "Why do you think I need you?"

"You tell me. Did you feel the chick-pain?"

"The what?"

"It can't all be pleasure if you want a chick. I don't know exactly what it feels like, naturally," he coughed, "but I know how to make it happen, and I know you don't get a chick without it."

"There's supposed to be pain? That doesn't sound right at all," she refuted.

"It only lasts for a few seconds, so I hear, and I think you'd know it if it had happened."

Hawkwind regarded him icily despite the blistering fire inside. Surely he couldn't be making stuff up just to get her to let him mate with her. Hawkwind had seen matriarchs and what they did to males who tried to force mating or who tricked, slighted, or disgraced them. There usually wasn't much blood, but there was spectacle, screaming, and fur and feather ripping. Sometimes other Linemembers even joined in to defend their matriarch, and the offending male came out much the worse for wear.

"I didn't feel anything like that," she admitted.

"Rainsoft doesn't know how to do it, or that he needs to do it. It's a particular technique," Thornwing explained evenly. "If you'd ask Hawkswift, she'd tell you."

"And if you're lying, she'll help me tear your feathers out," Hawkwind promised.

And in that promise was acceptance. It had slipped out without her really noticing, but her body knew it, and Thornwing heard it, evidenced by the slightest alteration in his posture and the lay of his feathers. He took slow steps towards her until he could, ever so cautiously, reach out and touch her neck, just brushing it with his bill.

"I'll prove it to you," he breathed.

Heart thudding like she'd been fighting, wings quivering, she managed to swallow and take a shuddering breath. "You will."

And with that clear declaration there was no more hesitation. It started the same, though Thornwing was older, bigger, heavier, and his grip was at once both more secure and gentler. It felt just as good, maybe better; she thought he was paying more attention to her, adjusting himself based on her reactions. His style certainly led to upmost repetitive satisfaction.

Then he slowed and leaned forward to whisper to her. "Are you ready? Let me know when you've felt it."

He changed his position, beginning to press hard in one spot.

"I don't know what I'm supposed to feel," she grunted back.

The pressure was becoming intense, making a slight ache. Was that it?

"Probably helps if you relax," he muttered.

She tried to relax, felt the alteration, and a flash of sensation sparked through her. It was part pain, undoubtedly, and part elation and release. It made her shiver and tense.

"Hawkwind?" Thornwing urged. "Was that it?"

The wave of feeling was still crackling through her and, stunned, she couldn't reply.

"Hawkwind?"

Again—sharper this time, making her jerk, gasp, and then hiss out her breath. Thornwing relented.

"That must have been it. Hawkwind, are you all right?" he murmured.

She was shaking as the shimmery sensation, equal parts weakness, joy, and ache, trickled from her deep belly out her limbs, even into each finger and toe. She felt her fur and feathers prickling.

"I suppose," she mumbled, "that was it, or them? You didn't tell me it had two parts."

"Two parts?" he echoed, sounding amused. "Indeed?"

The ability to think and speak was diminishing, thanks to Thornwing, but she tried to put her tongue in motion. "What's funny?"

"I'm sorry, it's not funny, but I am," he breathed, "delighted."

"Why?"

"Two chick-pains?"

"Maybe. So?"

He bit her neck, not hard enough to damage, but hard enough to convey his own passion, and hard enough to spur a peak of delirium.

"Two chick-pains could mean two chicks," he explained after a few more mind-numbing moments.

"How?" she queried, reduced to the simplest of communications.

"Don't ask me," he grunted, "how it works. Just know it can mean that, only if there's two."

Whatever. Hawkwind stopped trying to force herself to think, but rather just gave in, riding the swells until they became waves that crashed at last onto the shore with thunder and fury. And then there was sudden stillness, sudden peace.

"Can I stay with you?" he asked when he'd caught his breath, "the rest of the night?"

"Yes," Hawkwind agreed, grabbing his shoulder to pull him with her.

She led him to the hollow she'd shared with Rainsoft and curled up with him. The rest of the night was hardly restful, but it was deeply satisfying, over and over again, and it was with a bit of sorrow that they both got up, giving each other's feathers a last little nibble, when the morning sun made its presence known.

Hawkwind flew back to the caves, while Thornwing flew off in a different direction, to hunt. She could only hope that what she needed would soon be on its way and her Line would have new life. Now perhaps Swift could answer some of her questions.

Hawkwind's touchdown at the caves brought a variety of reactions from the surrounding griffins. The mating urge was rapidly dwindling now, but young males still dropped whatever they were doing to look towards her. If he had a young female at his side—presumably his mate—it sometimes earned him a hiss or a growl or even a slap to the head. The chicks and fledglings were oblivious to her being any different from normal. The older adults gave her knowing smiles, or confused glances because they knew she didn't have one exclusive mate, or just ignored her altogether.

Thornfire was supervising the flight class, and Hawkwind sensed him staring at her as though he were a sunbeam on a cold morning, which was promptly hidden by a dark cloud. Hawkwind didn't pause to look at him or give him a chance to come confront her. Of Rainsoft she saw no sign. The four children were in the midst of another speaking lesson and waved cheerfully at her, likely oblivious. Joy was actually in the air in flight class and coasting on the warm updraft from the sun-heated rocks where her mother, Swift was sunbathing.

Hawkwind went straight to Swift, who stood at her approach, smiling and nodding without hesitation. She gestured, "let's talk," and Hawkwind followed her away towards a quiet corner of the mountainside.

"Swift, what's chick-pain?" Hawkwind asked immediately.

The older griffin nodded again. "I think you mean," she corrected Hawkwind's terminology; Hawkwind had just combined the hand-words "chick" and "pain" but it seemed there was an actual separate hand gesture for the term.

"I can only tell you what my mother told me," Swift went on. "You have to have the male do it if you want a chick, and by clenching muscles in certain ways you can stop him from doing it if you don't." She

Hawkjoy
first flight

went on to describe how it felt for her, although she used some hand signs that Hawkwind didn't know, and Hawkwind encouraged her to start drawing words in the dirt.

"It doesn't have two parts? One pain and then another?" Hawkwind asked.

Swift eyed her and gurgled a chuckle. "Oh dear. No, it's one pain, but it can happen twice. That means there's a chance of twins."

"Twins? Is that what he meant?" Hawkwind gasped.

"May I ask who?"

Hawkwind felt herself blushing, giddy at the same time. This was almost like having her sister Hawkcall back, to tease and giggle with, except they'd never giggled over such a topic.

"Rainsoft and Thornwing," she admitted, "but it was Thornwing who—"

"I see," Swift gestured. "Rainsoft hasn't been told about it yet. They are both fine young males, each in their own way. Good choices."

"I just hope it works this time."

"With two chick-pains, I'd say it's very likely you'll get at least one chick. Has Thornwing sired chicks before?"

"I don't know, except that he knows how. I can only assume he's had the chance to try. Who can say if he's sired any of the chicks of South-scree? Usually, in griffin Lines, the chicks aren't told who their fathers are, if the matriarch even knows."

"With more than one male, the chances are better, just in case a particular male isn't fertile and doesn't know it," Swift nodded thoughtfully.

Hawkwind shrugged. "I guess we'll see."

"And if it doesn't work, you can try again, but any female that lets the chick-pain happen has a really good chance, to my knowledge."

"I suppose Thornwing knew what he was talking about then."

"I suppose so," Swift agreed. "Take it easy today. Nature needs to take its course. I think sunbathing would be ideal."

"It sounds delightful. I didn't get much sleep, and a warm rock would suit me perfectly."

Without talking to anyone else, Hawkwind went to join Swift on a nice patch of smooth granite, and let the sun bake her into drowsy slumber.

Sometime in the afternoon, Hawkwind was awakened by three children calling her name, and a fourth jumping onto her back.

"Hey now, what's this brutal attack?" she chortled as she sat up, Rikah clinging to her shoulders. "I am defeated."

Taro immediately snuggled himself down between her front paws, using her forelegs as a backrest. "I want more cakes," he whined.

"We want to go back to that house and get more food," Jessika explained, "but I tried to tell them that we maybe can't go back."

"You have been eating only meat again, haven't you?" Hawkwind mused. "Four growing children go through food so fast."

"We can eat just meat again for a while," Jessika declared. "I told them to save some of the stuff, but they ate it all except some salt and herbs and the dried peas."

"We'll go back," Hawkwind decided on the spot, "but not today. I'll plan it, and we'll go see if we can trade another deer sometime in the next few days. Try to make soup with the peas and salt and herbs."

The children exchanged looks like she'd just told them to go compose a symphony.

"I don't know how to make soup," Rikah, the cook, admitted.

"Hawkwind, are we going to live here forever?" Taro asked, twisting around a bit to look up at her.

"No," she answered him. "We might stay here a while longer, but not forever."

Kassandra and Jessika came to sit on either side of her, and she shielded them from the sun with her wings; she knew that human skin could be burned by the sun, unlike griffin feathers.

"When we grow up, we'll take back Northnest and live there again," Jessika whispered.

"I hope so," Hawkwind said simply, not giving voice to any of her doubts or concerns about their ability to do that. The time for that—if it ever came—was far in the future. Finding a safe place to establish the Hawk Line and raise the children now was the matter at hand.

"When can we go get more cakes?" Taro prodded. "Tomorrow?"

"I'll start arranging it," Hawkwind agreed, "but not tomorrow: in a few days."

"I wonder if we can ask for certain things?" Jessika mused.

"What do you want?"

"Blankets and pillows and soap and towels," the girl said. "But I could make the pillows, if I had fabric. I don't know how to make fabric."

"We can get you more fabric in South-scree," Hawkwind assured her.

"And packs to carry all this stuff in," Rikah added. "Now the bags are sleeping pads."

"There's always more things you could use, but this isn't our permanent home, so we shouldn't accumulate too many things. Packs or bags to carry what you have do sound like a good idea."

"Again I could make them, maybe out of canvas," Jessika offered.

"We can try writing a note and leaving it on an offering of venison," Hawkwind said. "We can arrange a price, supplies in return for meat. Swift and Joy will help us."

There was a deep relief in that. She had Linemembers she could depend on for help now. She wasn't alone anymore.

"Joy is funny," Kassandra spoke up with a soft smile. "I like her."

"Wonderful," Hawkwind beamed.

"She's kind of like us, just a little older," Jessika agreed.

Hawkwind took a moment to gaze at the girl, the princess, eyes becoming unfocused as she let herself imagine what the child would be like in a year, two years, five years, ten years. Like Joy, she would grow into an adult. It was pleasantly wistful and scary at the same time; Hawkwind had no idea how to raise a human girl—or a human boy for that matter—into an adult. She hadn't really paid attention while still living at Northnest; raising humans hadn't been her job. It was now.

As Hawkwind was discussing the evening hunt with Swift and Joy she was interrupted when Thornwing landed a few paced away, flopping down a bled buck deer. He gestured at it, the lay of his feathers conveying a degree of shyness she hadn't expected from him.

"For you," he grunted.

Swift beamed at him as Hawkwind tried to find her words.

"Yay, thanks Thornwing," Rikah exclaimed at once, oblivious to the unspoken interaction among the adults. "I'll get my knife."

The boy ran off and Hawkwind gathered her wits enough to yell after him. "Don't run with the knife."

Rikah waved awkwardly over his shoulder as he pelted into the tunnel mouth.

"Thank you, Thornwing," the other children chorused.

Kassandra ran up to him and hugged his foreleg.

"You're very welcome," he said.

"Yes, thank you," Hawkwind nodded as Swift and Joy gestured their thanks as well.

Rikah came back, walking as quickly as he could manage without actually running. The griffins waited until the children, working together, had carved out a hefty chunk of meat from one haunch.

"We're going to go eat," Jessika informed them, giving them a parting wave with a bloody hand.

"All right, don't burn yourself on the Sunstone," Hawkwind cautioned.

"We won't."

The four children scampered back to the tunnel and the griffins gathered around the prey to begin tearing it apart. There was no better way to eat it. Without knives or other culinary preparation, they ate by holding the body down with their fore claws and ripping bits off with their bills, which they then tossed one way or another into the deeper part of their mouths for swallowing whole. Hide and hair went down with the meaty bits. Small bones were broken and eaten in pieces. Larger bones were cracked for the marrow. In the end only the largest bones and the hooves remained. Griffin digestion, including a gizzard that ground the food, would take care of it all.

"How do you feel?" Thornwing asked Hawkwind softly as the four griffins huddled up to preen the blood off each other.

"I feel good," she told him truthfully. "Thank you for," she hesitated, feeling a little embarrassed, "everything."

"My pleasure," he said, and Hawkwind detected the return of his slightly smug and over-confident nature. He gave her a grin and she had to smile back, but shaking her head. She wondered if any chicks he happened to sire would be just as snarky.

"I'll be taking the children back down to that village to try to get some more supplies in a day or two. One child per griffin would make things easier. Can I count on you?"

"Completely," he answered at once.

"I'm going to ask Rainsoft, too," she said. "I'd rather not risk Joy."

"Whomever you like," Thornwing commented without sign of displeasure. "You think it will be dangerous?"

"I don't know," she told him truthfully, "it just feels risky somehow, going down there, hiding, trying to talk with humans. I don't want to keep it up. I want to find ways to provide all the children need wherever we end up living."

Thornwing took his time replying, and when he did, it was hesitant. "You don't think it would be a better idea to help the children find human families to live with, maybe in that village?"

Jessika had wings on her back. She was a princess. She was the heir of Northnest: probably the only surviving member of its royalty. Maybe she'd never take the country back, but those wings did mark her, and the invaders of her country might be looking for her.

"I promised to take care of those children," she said, purposefully not telling him all that had just run through her mind. "They don't want to leave me now. If they ever do, of course I will let them go, whatever makes them happiest."

He nodded, seeming to accept that without argument. "I'll help you, whenever you need me."

The descent of evening darkness had encouraged all the griffins to finish their outdoor activities and retreat to their caves. Hawkwind was one of the last to file in; making sure that none of her charges—children and Linemembers—had been left outside. She almost expected it, but winced nonetheless when Thornfire called her name as she walked past the cave he shared with Thornwing and Starbright. Hawkwind stopped obediently, out of habit, but a part of her mind made the comment that she was, or soon would be, a Linemother, and as a mere male, Thornfire's power over her was diminishing. He was still an elder, and she did still owe him her freedom from the dungeon of South-scree, but the balance of power between them was shifting.

"Hawkwind, a word?" he summoned quietly, and still politely.

She gestured back towards the dark hole that was the tunnel mouth and led him back that way.

"You found some other Hawks among the Snow-in-lee survivors, I noticed."

"I did," she nodded.

"They have," he paused, "inspired you to commit to the position of Hawkmother?"

It was only half question, for his sense of smell and observation of recent activities had surely informed him of the events of the last couple of days.

"Yes," Hawkwind said simply, and waited, letting him put together his words.

"It seems your objectives may be solidifying in new ways?"

This was more of a question. He wanted to know what her intentions were. Well, so did she—want to know his intentions, that is. Thornfire had been shut-beak about how he was intending to work out Hawkwind's future all along.

"I think so," she said, giving nothing else away.

This appeared to inspire him to regard her more firmly. "You still want to become a part of South-scree? I'll no longer need to pressure the Thornmother to take you into her Line, but now a new tactic will be required. All the matriarchs will need to be convinced if you intend to add the Hawk Line to South-scree."

"I wonder what place you've had in mind for me and my children from the beginning," she remarked blandly, "but I was having faith that you would work it out."

"Well, now everything is changed," Thornfire stated, apparently not willing to give away whatever his former plan had been. "You've collected Linemembers, and made another attempt at a chick, I sense?"

"You know well enough," Hawkwind breathed, sternly keeping her voice from becoming a hiss, almost trembling with her own temerity to say such a thing to the elder mage. "I doubt you've missed anything."

Thornfire locked gazes with her, but he didn't look completely angry—more resigned. "I should have realized my brother's impetuous nature would make him brave enough to approach you. I hope he was gentlemanly."

Gripping her courage within, consciously keeping her feathers from flattening with embarrassment or submission—after all, a matriarch felt neither of those things—she kept her gaze even and said, "I wouldn't have welcomed him if he hadn't been, and he did me a great service, one that Rainsoft could not for lack of knowledge. This time, I have a chance of conceiving."

Thornfire's brows did not exactly lower with displeasure, but nor did they fly upward with surprise. Their little dance between the two extremes was almost comical.

"Elder Thornfire," Hawkwind began sincerely, "I have great gratitude to you, for getting me out of the dungeon, for giving me hope, protecting me, and helping to free Rainsoft's family and my new Linemembers. I really mean that."

The flick of his wings and bob of his head conveyed his acknowledgement.

"I'm going to rebuild the Hawk Line," she went on. "I don't know where, but somehow I will find a place. If South-scree won't have us, then we shall have to part ways. You can have the Sunstone, I suppose, if that will dispose of my debt to you."

"Patience," he countered. "There are many griffins here that will need a home. There's no reason that you cannot go wherever they end up going. It may be time for a new griffin settlement. Skycall specified you to bring back the Sunstone and I suggest you do it and hand it over to her. Even if you do not make your home in South-scree, for whatever reason, you will have completed what she demanded for your freedom, and if you do not take a place in South-scree then she will not have repaid her side and the balance will shift slightly to your favor, and if you have a chick by then, she will be forced to recognize you as a Linemother.

"I am sure you are starting to realize some of these facts yourself. Your position in society will change rapidly. You are young, but you will demand respect nonetheless, especially with a retired Linemother in the person of Hawkswift."

Hawkwind nodded absently, trying to process everything he was saying.

"I still want to help you, Hawkwind," he said, and she observed what seemed to be sincerity in his eyes. "And if what you imply is true," he continued softly, "it may be that our Lines will have a linkage in the chick you're going to carry. As an unawakened female you may not have been aware of it, but such linkages between Lines create alliances. Of course the members of the Thorn Line will protect themselves first, but they will also think of the other Lines they have linkages with. If you have a chick sired by a Thorn, it will change how they view you for the better."

Hawkwind chose not to mention that she had the chance of twins, or that it was possible only Rainsoft's blood would mix with hers, that Thornwing—despite giving her the chick-pains—would actually miss out on the conception part. It wouldn't even be completely possible to know after the hypothetical chick was in the world, although its appearance might suggest its sire.

"Thank you, Thornfire," Hawkwind said instead. "I appreciate your continued support."

"You helped me find my brother," he countered. "I owe you much."

They stood for a few moments in the silence before Thornfire spoke again.

"There is something else of some importance," he began. "I found signs that could have been made by talis, some few days of ground travel away from here, back the way we came."

That brought up Hawkwind's neck ruff in an instant. "What does that mean? Are they tracking us, coming for us?"

"I don't know."

"What exactly did you find?" she asked.

"Tracks in an area of soft dirt," he supplied. "I'm no expert tracker and they could have been made by something else, or talis that just happened to be passing through the area and have no interest in us."

"What should we do?"

"I'm going to ask Rainsoft and Wing to do some scouting. They're the ones with resistance to the talis' hypnotism so they're the only ones suitable to do it. I just wanted to make you aware. I'll need to find a way to tell everyone without panicking them, but I'll wait until the scouting turns up more details."

"Thank you for telling me. In a few days I'm going to take the children back down to that village for more non-meat food. We'll have to be careful. I don't suspect that the talis can hypnotize humans, so the children can be my eyes. I'll take Swift with me, and if Rainsoft and Thornwing can't come, maybe Joy, too."

"Be careful," he warned seriously.

"We will, and thank you."

They turned and headed back into the tunnel.

"Sleep well," Thornfire said as he retreated into his cave.

"Good night," Hawkwind responded, feeling considerably more relaxed than she'd felt before their talk, and went to her own cave to chat and groom with her Linemembers and put the children to bed.

Three days had passed and there had been little development in the possible talis risk. Thornwing and Rainsoft had continued to find some small signs of talis in places that held tracks, such as sand and dirt, but most of the nearby area was rock or gravel, and all the scents they'd picked up had been faint. With that hopeful reassurance that talis weren't about to attack the temporary griffin settlement, Hawkwind decided it was time to make a foray to the village and see if they could get some more food and supplies for the children. Swift and Joy would accompany her.

Kassandra had walked over to Joy without being told, and asked the young griffin if she could ride her. Joy and Swift had only recently graduated from their flight training, and Hawkwind was hoping they were up to the task; they'd both been practicing flying intensely for the past days. Joy had agreed to carry Kassandra, and Swift—being the largest—had volunteered to carry Rikah and Karo: that left Jessika for Hawkwind.

"If you need to rest," Hawkwind emphasized, "just call out and head for a clearing."

The others signed their consent and the trio lifted off, heading back toward the village Hawkwind and the children had visited previously. The day was a fine one, warm with some cloud cover to keep the sun from being too harsh, and they had a smooth flight down towards the valley. The children knew by now to keep a good hold and not fidget and neither of the other griffins called for halt, so Hawkwind led them all the way down to the clearing they'd used for landing before, but once they'd touched down and Hawkwind took a look, she saw that they were panting rather more than she was, and were quick to sink down to the ground to rest.

"Are you all right?" she asked.

"Good exercise," Swift gestured.

"We'll have more weight going back," Hawkwind commented.

"We'll be fine," Swift assured her.

"I'm going to go hunt for a buck deer," Hawkwind informed. "I'll be back shortly. Wait here?"

"We'll have a rest in the sun," Swift agreed.

"And we'll look for anything we can gather to eat," Jessika added.

"Just be sure it's not poisonous," Hawkwind cautioned as she headed into the underbrush. "And if anything attacks you, run away."

She felt fairly confident that this close to the village dangerous wild animals, including talis, would be scarce. The human hunters would have seen to that. No human wanted big cats or wolves or anything else that might snatch a defenseless villager to live close to the settlement. She did, however, have to search further from the village to find suitable prey, so Hawkwind kept her ears and eyes and what little olfactory ability she had wide open for any hint that she was becoming prey. Once she spotted a small herd of bachelor bucks, it was hardly difficult to sneak up, launch her body towards them, and catch the slowest runner. What was more difficult was dragging the dead prey animal back through all the underbrush to where she'd left Swift and Joy with the children.

"Look, look, Hawkwind," Karo crowed immediately upon her return. "We found wild strawberries again."

"Not many," Jessika added, "it's still early for them, I think."

"You got a deer," Rikah said.

"Yes," the griffin nodded. "Here's what will happen. Swift and I will take the deer to the riverbank where we left it last time. I am going to wait for the right moment, fly over and land on the roof of their house. From there, I will listen as Rikah goes to talk to them again. Have you all decided what you want to ask for this time?"

The children chorused an affirmative.

"And I memuriz'd—momerzud—mumurizid—I know it all,"

Rikah added sheepishly.

"All right then. Swift and Joy will stay with the rest of you here in the forest. Watch for predators; they might follow the scent of the deer here. Swift, please help me with the deer. Joy, guard the children."

Hawkwind and Swift dragged the deer through the bushes to the edge of the stream. After a furtive look around for anyone watching, they heaved it onto the bank and retreated to the others.

"Rikah, wait until you see me lying on the roof," Hawkwind instructed.

She loped back into deeper forest until she found a clearing and then launched upwards into the air. It was the hardest of hard work to try to get airborne by leaping straight up. Hawkwind labored higher and higher, eventually being able to get a boost from some slightly rising air that took some strain off her burning flight muscles. Once the village below shrunk into tiny toy houses around skinny trails in the dirt, she adjusted the angle of her head to use her far distance vision and check if any villagers were out and about near the house she intended to land on. Griffins were hard to miss. If anyone were nearby she would likely be spotted.

Hawkwind hadn't spent much time high above any human settlements other than the capital of Northnest itself: the castle-palace where she'd lived her whole life. She wondered if the streets were supposed to be empty or busy. The streets of this town looked strangely deserted. The few little human-dots she did see looked like they were urgently scurrying from place to place, not out for pleasure strolls. She widened her examination and noted a set of plain canvas tents and awnings set up on the northern side of the town in a fallow field. A carnival? A fair? There was no crowd of people that would indicate either of those, and she couldn't see what might be resting or living under the canvas. Blue flags with a yellow dot crossed by a red bar flapped weakly from the sides of the tents. She didn't recognize the standard.

The scene felt a little strange, but she didn't detect any immediate threats, so saw no reason to call off the plan. The lack of people on the streets made it easier to dive down to the roof of Judit Rania's house. Hawkwind pulled up at the last second and settled as gently and silently as she could onto the thick thatch, quickly pulling in her eye-catching wings. The house didn't even groan as it took her weight. Griffins were light for their size but still heavier than a human, for example. It was a sturdy house. Hawkwind flattened herself to the thatch. Her coloration helped her blend in a little. If anyone specifically looked at the roof she would still be impossible to miss, but she hoped that no one would have reason to.

After a few moments, she saw Rikah emerge from the forest and cross the stream, heading to the house. He made his way through the vegetable garden and to the back door, disappearing from Hawkwind's view. She heard him knock. A minute passed before footsteps went to the door and then the latch lifted and the hinges groaned a little.

"Oh, you've come back."

The woman's voice did not sound as pleased as Hawkwind had expected. Perhaps it was the voice of the younger woman from last time, who hadn't seemed as friendly as the older lady Judit, but the voice did not sound young.

"Is that all right?" Rikah asked, already with an edge of uncertainty.

"I don't think you should be here. It isn't safe."

"You said you'd help us." There was a quaver in his voice now.

"I'm sorry, truly sorry, but it would be safer for you if you weren't here, and I mustn't be seen talking to any strangers."

What was going on? Hawkwind furrowed her brow with concern. Did this have something to do with the tents with the unfamiliar standard on the outskirts of town? Her neck began to prickle as her fur-feathers started lifting.

"You should go," the woman's voice went on, gentle but firm.

"You even said we could live with you," Rikah argued. "Why won't you help us?"

"I want to, but I could be risking my life to do so, and you're in danger, too." Her voice was a whisper now, and Hawkwind had to strain to hear. "There are people asking after unclaimed children. They might be looking for you. I think you should go away and hide."

Rikah didn't make a reply; Hawkwind just heard and then saw him running for the trees, making no attempt at stealth. Now her feathers were definitely prickling. She could either try to investigate, or follow Rikah's example.

Before she could make a decision, she heard a raspy growl behind her, and then something small and sharp clamped onto her left hind foot.

Hawkwind stifled a shriek of surprise. She kicked back violently, but whatever it was held on. She rolled over on the roof, making the timbers groan, and swung around to take a look. What appeared to be a small, wingless rainbow drake had wrapped itself around her lower leg, but rather than being colorful like its bigger brethren, it was solid black.

Now she did shriek, and thrashed her foot wildly, tearing up patches of thatch from the roof. Below, she heard the women of the house exclaiming with shock. The door banged as they came running out.

"A Feathyr," one gasped.

"I knew it," said the other.

Hawkwind was too preoccupied with the little beast clinging to her to give them any reply. The thing was only about a yard long, nose to tail tip, but its scales were hard and spiny, and it was about as thick as Rikah's forearm at its widest. It had wound itself around her limb three times, its spines and barbs hooking into her fur and scratching her skin. She met its slit eyed gaze as it opened its long, narrow jaws, revealing rows of dense needle-like teeth all pointing backwards down its gullet. Anything it bit would have great difficulty getting free. It growled again, with what Hawkwind would almost have said was gloating triumph as it sunk its claws through her fur into her flesh.

Then she noticed the collar it wore, and recognized it; the drakes at Northnest had worn something similar. The device looked rather like rusted barbed iron wire. Some of the barbs seemed to be digging between the creature's own scales, where old, crusted blood had accumulated. Before her eyes the collar began to glow, turning rapidly red and then red-white. From across the village came a call that sent icy shivers down Hawkwind's back: the hunting cry of a rainbow drake. Was the thing calling them?

"Run," cried the women below.

Hawkwind took one panicked look at them, and then launched into the air with adrenaline-born strength, the spiny drake still wrapped around her leg. One thing she knew: she must not lead the drakes back to the children. As she fled, she saw the beasts rising into the air from the vicinity of the tents she'd noticed earlier: about a half dozen of them, in an assortment of colors.

She started flying south, away from both the children and the drake tent. Three drakes peeled off from the others and headed straight towards her, but then she heard the screams of children and the battle cries of two griffins—the children were also in danger.

Hawkwind would have kept leading the drakes away, the odds might have been better for the others, but she was the only one with drake fighting experience, and maybe she could take on all the drakes, allowing Swift and Joy to escape with the children, if they hadn't been latched onto by a mini-drake yet. She dipped a wing, turning sharply, and dove towards the clearing where she'd left the children. The screams dug into her like spears, worse than the claws of the little beast on her leg.

The drakes were almost within reach of her when she clapped her wings in and dropped like an arrow into the clearing, snapping her wings back out to slow herself only at the last minute. The drakes followed her down, and Hawkwind had only fragments of a second to assess the situation.

Jessika was the center of attention. She was on all fours, holding perfectly still, with the strange paralysis of any animal that fears the slightest movement could end its life. Another miniature wingless drake was wrapped around her torso, it's spines already sunken into her soft skin so blood streaked her sides and stained her makeshift shirt, which the beast had in its jaws. It had ripped away the fabric on her back, exposing the golden wing tattoos there.

Swift, Joy, and the other children were gathered around her, all poised with the need to get the thing off her; all scared that any attempt to do so could make the thing kill her; its sharp tail was hooked around her neck. Then the drakes hit them from above. Hawkwind threw herself over Jessika, straddling her and turning to face the drakes.

"Run," she shouted at the other children, and they scampered into the underbrush.

Swift and Joy went down under the weight of the half dozen drakes.

"Fight," Hawkwind screamed at them next.

Feathers flew and snarls and shrieks ripped the air. Joy managed to wiggle out from under the pile and flop herself over to Hawkwind, fumbling and flailing. A pair of drakes turned towards them and Hawkwind struck out before they could: getting a lucky slash across one's face. It recoiled with a hiss of pain. Joy, showing more fortitude than Hawkwind could have hoped for, followed up the slash with an awkward swipe and scored a slice in its neck. That drake pulled back slightly, but the other snapped forward with sharp jaws. Hawkwind ducked the attack and shot forward a double punch with the wrist joints of her wings, powered by her hefty flight muscles. She heard the drake's jaw break and hissed with satisfaction.

Beside her, Joy reared up and leapt back into the fray before Hawkwind could stop her, but nor could she blame her; her mother was still tangled up with the other drakes. All Hawkwind could do was guard Jessika, slashing and punching every drake that got near. With the distraction of Joy and Swift rolling around with the drakes in the main area of the clearing, Hawkwind was able to keep them off and score a few good hits, but she knew if reinforcements arrived the griffins wouldn't be able to hold them off forever.

Swift and Joy suddenly surfaced, throwing the drakes off except for one, which Swift had gripped in her bill, the point of it buried behind its head. Now with room to work, she pinned the rest of its body and twisted her head. The wet, crunching crack was audible even over the shrieks and hisses. Swift shook her head, dislodging the corpse, and flung it towards the other drakes.

One less drake—but Swift had paid in blood for the kill. There were bloody gashes on her body and good number of her feathers looked broken, but by her posture, Hawkwind didn't think she had any broken bones. Another drake darted at the big female, and Swift slapped it to the ground, stomping down to trap one of its forelegs. It cried out and other drakes jumped to rescue it, but not before Joy punched it in the head with the same wing maneuver Hawkwind had used and stunned it.

Hawkwind couldn't spare her attention to watch the others any longer; another drake was heading for her. She lifted her wings up and spread them to try to intimidate it. When it snapped at her, she dodged and slapped back at it. It dodged, and the exchange of testing blows continued, each fighter taking a little damage but avoiding serious hits until a second drake spun around to take a swipe at Hawkwind. In ducking one attack, another glanced off her shoulder and hit her cheek, making her struggle not to stagger and bump Jessika below her. Another strike hit her upper arm, leaving shallow grooves of blood.

She retaliated, snapping out to catch the hand of the offending drake in her bill. Without hesitation, she bit down, crushing bones and making the drake scream. She twisted and shook her head, getting another cracking sound from a wrist or arm bone. Drakes were fast and vicious, but they didn't have the strength or durability of griffins. Before she could let go, the other drake she faced struck again, swiping out one of her forelegs so that she fell to her elbow. She released the broken drake and tried to get up, but drake jaws suddenly clamped around her skull from above, clenching down, teeth piercing her skin and grinding against her bone.

Another drake bit down on her other foreleg and pulled it out from under her, too. Jessika screamed as Hawkwind fell halfway to the ground, shoving the girl back towards her hindquarters. Hawkwind punched forward with her wing wrists again, hitting the drake that had her head hard enough to make it release her, but the other still held gamely to her forearm, fangs sunk to the gums.

Out of the bushes, Rikah suddenly rushed, carrying a stick thicker than his own thigh. With a warbling yell, voice cracking, he slammed the branch down atop the biting drake's head. It barely noticed him.

"Rikah, get back," Hawkwind commanded.

The boy raised the stick again and smacked the drake a second time, a third time, with all the strength in his little body, but Hawkwind had no doubt that the drakes would make short work of him. Kassandra dashed out of the bushes, too, carrying a short and pointy stick. She skidded to a stop beside Rikah, took careful aim, and jammed her stick deep into the drake's eye. Blood and fluid squirted from the pierced orb and the drake recoiled, shrieking, dropping Hawkwind's arm.

Hawkwind immediately swept out a wing and hooked the children closer, tucking them under her body with Jessika, as she climbed back to her feet, lamed by the drake's bite. She had a moment to survey the scene. Swift and Joy had killed three drakes, but Joy was barely on her feet, leaning against her mother's shoulder. Her wings at least, seemed intact.

"Joy, Joy," Hawkwind called until the battered young female looked up. "Get Thornfire," she ordered.

Hawkwind wasn't sure why he was the griffin she knew they needed, except that the miniature drakes with their glowing, spiky collars that still gripped Jessika and her own hind leg had to be some kind of magic. Perhaps only magic could get them off. The drakes might not stop coming until the mini ones were killed, and if Hawkwind and the others fled back to the caves, it might lead an army of drakes right to them.

Joy half spread her wings, tottering with fatigue and uncertainty. Swift gave her a push, gesturing firmly, "Hawkmother told you to go. Go. Get Thornfire."

While the remaining drakes were still regrouping, Joy turned and stumbled off into the trees. Swift turned her gaze back to Hawkwind.

"Thank you," the older female signed.

Hawkwind was puzzled. Maybe Swift didn't realize that Hawkwind really did need Thornfire. Maybe she thought Hawkwind had given the order so that Joy, at least, could escape. It didn't matter; the drakes were attacking again and Hawkwind had no more leisure to worry about it.

Swift stepped up beside Hawkwind, on her lamed side, and extended a wing to help support her on that side. The three live drakes were all injured, too, and seemed reluctant to continue the fight, but after a moment of shuffling and posturing they advanced nonetheless, slightly spread out so that Hawkwind and Swift would have a harder time defending against them. It was only then that Hawkwind had the leisure to notice that they wore spiky collars, too, just like the mini-drakes, and just like the drakes Hawkwind had faced in Northnest. Theirs were glowing red.

The outer two feinted to try to distract the griffins. Hawkwind recognized it for what it was, but Swift shifted her attention over. The center drake took a swipe at Swift. Hawkwind was already weak with her limb nearest Swift, but snapped out with her bill. The drake dodged. Then the drake on Hawkwind's outer side lunged in. Hawkwind managed to get her wing up just in time, although her attempt at punching the drake only glanced off its chest.

This time, the drake tried something it hadn't done yet. It reached out with both of its own wings, using the hooked claw-like horn on its wrist joints to snag Hawkwind's now-extended wing. It yanked, pulling Hawkwind off balance. Then, a blindingly sharp pain burst in Hawkwind's hind leg and shot up to her back and down to her foot. The shred of her mind not swamped by agony realized that the mini-drake must have bitten her at last.

Hawkwind lost her balance and fell to her side, not crushing the children under her, but leaving them unprotected. The bite burned—a hot coal of pain with shimmering waves of fire radiating from it. The drake above her dropped its jaw open in a grin of conquest and lifted its hooked wings and long claws, preparing to strike. Beside her, Jessika gave a sobbing cry. Hawkwind could feel the girl trembling where her hip touched Hawkwind's belly.

Swift keened a defiant battle cry and adjusted her stance to try to guard Hawkwind and the children as Hawkwind tried to gather her strength to stand back up. The drake above her attacked before she got anywhere. She threw up her free wing and felt the impact of claws rip out some feathers and break others. The drake tried to stomp down on her head, but her flexible avian neck allowed her to dodge and rotate her head right around and clamp her hooked bill onto its foot instead, digging the point of her bill between its foot bones until it screeched.

Meanwhile, the other two drakes attacked Swift with rapid, vig-orous slashes and bites, sensing the end was near for the griffins. Hawkwind heard the exchange of blows and impacts, and then Swift's cry of pain and fury. There was a choking sound, a gasp, and another cry. Hawkwind tried to see over her own body—all she saw was that Swift wasn't standing beside her. She could get a glimpse of a shoulder and a wing tip sticking up with broken feathers.

Hawkwind wrenched her head viciously side to side with a fi-nal burst of adrenaline, getting rewarded for it with the combined sounds of snapping drake bones and drake pain-squeals. The other drakes attacked. They slashed at her. One grabbed her wing in its jaws and pulled. She'd lowered her free wing to cover Jessika, Rikah, and

Kassandra—their last blanket of protection. Now, the drake pulled against the remaining strength of her wearied pectorals.

Hawkwind struggled, but fatigue and numbness was spreading through her body. Her vision was getting blurry around the edges.

"No, no, no," Kassandra screamed as Hawkwind felt her wing dragged up and forward.

The drakes pressed it to the ground. One stood on it. The drake whose broken foot she still held reached down and slashed across her cere. The pain and her growing weakness made her let go of its foot and it tottered away and collapsed.

Hawkwind looked up through fading vision. The drakes were rearing back like snakes ready to strike.

"Help," Kassandra cried out.

A blurred black shape, moving too quickly to be discerned, flashed from the undergrowth behind the children and rammed the drakes. It wheeled about and struck out once, twice, and all was still.

Hawkwind squinted, trying to focus her eyes. It wasn't a griffin. She took a gasping breath, suddenly sensing a fresh, heady breeze, like liquid life: made of all the things that grew and pulsed, from flowers that opened their petals to the sun, to wolves that buried their muzzles in the steaming blood of their prey. The breath restored a fragment of her health and she recognized the creature standing atop the dead drakes, their blood splattered on its hooves, one drake corpse still impaled on its heavy, spiraled horn.

Kassandra stuttered to her feet, took a few stumbling steps, and half fell against the unicorn's bloody foreleg, wrapping her arms around it in a hug. It bent its head down over her, its head almost as long as her whole body, and the drake corpse slid off its horn to join its fellows with a wet thump that sprayed more blood across the torn up clearing.

Hawkwind had seen some horses, though not as many as some. She'd seen sturdy little ponies and lithe runners and middleweight plow horses and knight-carrying war horses and a few heavy draft horses. This unicorn transcended all of them, of course, but was what Hawkwind would have called perhaps a "draft unicorn." It was black, hoary where its coat grew long, with a mixed white and silver mane and tail. Its horn was thick and densely ridged, chipped in places like a mountain ram's horns. Its cloven hooves were near to the size of a human's spread hand, but all but hidden under the gossamer feathers of its long foot fur.

At the moment, its eyes were closed as it bent its head over Kassandra. Wondering, Hawkwind took a glance between its hind legs to ascertain that it was a male: his eyes, then. Around the girl and unicorn, all the drakes were lying still now except for final nerve twitches. Swift slowly straightened up: testing her legs, wings, and tail for damage and stretching her spine. She was coated with quite a lot of blood, but turned calmly to Hawkwind.

"I think I'll be alright," she gestured, "but maybe no flying."

Both Hawkwind and Swift had a number of broken feathers, plus flying when injured was always an extra strain.

"Are you badly hurt?" Swift asked Hawkwind.

Hawkwind tried experimentally moving her legs and wings. Everything hurt, and the sharp, burning bite of the mini-drake on her haunch had not relented.

"Not badly, but not good, either. Jessika, are you hurt?" she called, remembering the girl had a mini-drake of her own wrapped around her chest.

"Hawkwind," the girl sobbed, "help me."

The griffin shoved to her feet above her charge, and then limped around to face her. The drake was still there: spines still digging into the girl's skin and the fabric of her shirt still clutched in its toothy maw. The end of its sharp tail was still wrapped around Jessika's throat.

Hawkwind looked imploringly at the unicorn. "Can you help?" she pled.

The beast opened dark eyes and lifted his head from around

Kassandra
and the
unicorn

Kassandra, who was still tightly embracing his leg. He didn't say anything, just stared.

"More drakes will come, if we don't get rid of these little drakes," Hawkwind went on. "The children will be endangered again."

"We have saved you twice now. I will take her away, and she'll not be in danger again," the unicorn spoke, into her head like the ones she'd seen before had done.

"Take her away?" Rikah repeated weakly. "Kassie? Don't take her away."

"I can't stop you," Hawkwind admitted, "but I swore before you did to protect her. Mine is the prior claim."

"Your priority is there before you, with the golden wings on her back," the unicorn countered with a slight pivoting of one deer-like ear.

At this, Swift seemed puzzled—her wings, after all, were slate grey, not gold—until she recalled the tattoo on Jessika's back, which changed her expression first to one of comprehension, and then to one of more puzzlement. Hawkwind hadn't explained the full significance of Jessika's tattoo.

"I swore to protect them all," Hawkwind countered.

"You swear to protect more than you can handle, Sky-cousin," the unicorn accused.

Offended because he was right, Hawkwind turned away. "Swift," she requested. "Can you kill the drake on my leg?"

She positioned her hindquarters towards the older griffin, and watched as she examined the clingy little wretch. It began growling. It sounded like an angry bee with a sore throat.

"It has already bitten me, it can't do worse," Hawkwind said. "Just bite through its neck."

The mini-drake began to wriggle, digging its spines in deeper, its growl getting louder. When Swift lowered her open bill towards it, it began jerking its head—either trying to rip out a piece of Hawkwind's flesh or loosen its fanged grip. Before it could do either, Swift had chosen a spot to grab it, clenched down, and with a gurgling crack, bit through its body. Hawkwind felt its grip loosen immediately, and sighed as Swift began unwrapping the body from her leg.

"Thank you, Swift. That's one," Hawkwind said, looking towards Jessika again as Swift began prying at the mini-drake head still clamped to her haunch.

The remaining mini-drake hissed threateningly.

"I'm scared, Hawkwind," Jessika whispered. "It hurts."

Hawkwind almost collapsed as Swift finally got the severed head of the little beast to release her leg. She glanced quickly around at the damage. It looked like a chunk of her flesh had been mashed where the beast had bitten into her with all those rows of needle-teeth. Her fur was soaked with blood and her leg felt weak, but it was nothing compared to what could happen to Jessika. She didn't know if the beast would go so far as to kill the girl or not—perhaps it was just a lure for the big drakes, who wanted her alive so they could capture her—but she didn't dare take the risk of trying to hurt it, in case it did drive that sharp tail through the princess' neck.

"I don't know what to do," Hawkwind confessed to Swift as the older griffin stepped up beside her.

"Maybe Thornfire will know," Swift gestured back. "I hope Joy will reach him."

"It will take them time to return. It's a long flight, especially since Joy is hurt."

Both Swift and Hawkwind turned to look again at the unicorn. It was watching them steadily. Kassandra was still wrapped around its foreleg.

"The rest of you are not my business," the unicorn spoke simply, emotionless voice echoing in Hawkwind's head.

"She's the princess of Northnest," Hawkwind said.

"We know. We don't care."

Swift, however, looked sharply at Hawkwind. That hadn't been in the story she'd heard.

"Why Kassandra?" Hawkwind asked.

The unicorn looked down at the little girl. "I can't explain it in a way you would understand."

"Leave her with her friends," Hawkwind ordered. "She's a human girl. How could unicorns take care of her?"

The unicorn stared at Hawkwind, as if saying something without saying anything.

"I'll help you, Jessa," Rikah announced, and before Hawkwind could stop him, he'd seized the mini-drake's tail and was pulling with all his might to unwrap it from her neck.

The mini-drake apparently hadn't foreseen that either, had been watching the griffins instead, and shrieked a growl in anger. It opened its mouth, thrashing its head to try to get the impaled fabric out of its mouth, at the same time that it tightened its coils around Jessika's torso and dug its claws into her flesh. Jessika cried out with pain, but Rikah had pulled enough of the tail away from her neck that Hawkwind didn't think she was in danger of death anymore.

"Swift, help," Hawkwind ordered as she grabbed the mini-drake's head to prevent it from biting.

Swift helped Rikah, grabbing onto the critter's tail above where Rikah had it. With her strength, she managed to unwrap it further. Hawkwind began unwrapping, too. At this, the mini-drake pulled out its claws and slashed for Jessika's neck. Hawkwind snatched at it with her wounded but free arm, managing to deflect the claws. There was no more time for messing about; she bent down and seized its neck with her bill. A sharp twist broke its spine. As soon as it died, the glowing barbed collar it wore went dark, returning to the appearance of plain cold iron.

"Let's unwrap it, hurry," she said.

Jessika collapsed to the ground once the mini-drake was off her. Both blood and tears ran from her, and Hawkwind hurried to check her for major injuries. The spines and claws of the drake had punctured her skin in dozens of places, so that she was peppered with little weeping wounds. It looked like a lot of blood, but none of the wounds were squirting blood, and Hawkwind knew enough to know that meant no major arteries had been pierced.

"See, you do not need my help," the unicorn spoke up suddenly.

Hawkwind had the urge to growl at him, but not the time. "Rikah, Swift, use the remains of this fabric to wrap her up tight. Try to cover all the wounds."

Rikah began taking off the fabric that functioned as his own shirt. "Let's use mine, too."

Hawkwind faced the unicorn. "We're leaving now."

They locked gazes. For a moment, Hawkwind had a disconcerting double-vision of a sturdy young man, dark of skin and hair, in long silver robes, standing where the unicorn stood, with a protective hand on Kassandra's head. She blinked and the image was gone again. Without another word, the unicorn turned and walked off, pulling its foreleg gently from Kassandra's grip. The girl stared after the departing beast in what seemed a stunned silence. Then she burst into tears. Karo made an appearance at last, busting out of some nearby bushes and running to Kassandra, where he threw his arms around her and held her tight.

Chapter 27
Failed Secrets

It was hours later that Joy and Thornfire, with Rainsoft and a few other Snow-in-lee griffins, found them. Hawkwind and Swift had been painfully but steadily walking back with the children balanced on their backs. Thornfire called down through the trees as he flew over, and they met up a ways ahead in the nearest clearing.

"What happened?" Thornfire demanded.

"Rainbow drakes happened," Hawkwind answered as the newcomers helped transfer the children onto their own backs, unburdening Swift and Hawkwind. "And a new creature, like a miniature drake, with spines and lots of teeth, attacked Jessika and me. One bit me, and another hurt Jessika, too." Hawkwind pointed to two bags she'd filled on either side of her harness. "I'll show you the bodies and collars later. The collars glowed when they were on the beasts, but stopped once they were dead, so I thought they would be safe to bring, so you could take a look at them."

"A unicorn saved us," Rikah piped up from where he was perched now on Rainsoft's back.

"Really?" Thornfire murmured, "how unusual. This will be a tale worth hearing, once we're away and safe."

"Take a look at Jessika, please, before we go," Hawkwind asked.

The girl was shivering and panting, still leaking tears and blood, although a lot of the bleeding had stopped.

"We should get her warm, and get some water into her. I brought a water skin for now, and Starbright is brewing some tea back at the caves. Her wounds need washing, and then I can apply the herbs I already sent Starbright to collect, for your wounds, too, Hawkwind and Hawkswift," he said. "Can you fly? We need to get back as soon as possible."

Swift had gone to Joy as soon as the young griffin had landed and

Rikah and Karo had been removed from the older one's back. Joy looked tired and battered, but she was nowhere near as badly injured as Hawkwind and Swift. Thornfire took a few moments to examine all of them for injuries serious enough to warrant immediate magical cauterization, and did some field healing. He promised more thorough repairs once they were back at the caves.

The children were strapped down onto their fresh mounts. Thornfire himself carried Jessika after coaxing her to swallow some water. The sun was westering as Hawkwind and Swift labored into the air behind their rescue party, and Hawkwind could think of little else than getting Jessika safe, warm, and healed.

When at last they landed at the caves, the other griffins crowded around with questions and Joy and Swift made some effort to answer them, but the main focus was getting the wounded into the Hawk cave so they could be treated. Thornwing appeared beside Hawkwind, offering his shoulder to lean on, and she accepted gratefully. He gave her feathers an affectionate nibble—at least the few he could find on her head that weren't bloody, but then he turned and trotted off. In the crowd, she couldn't tell where he went.

Hawkwind, Swift, Joy, Thornfire, and Rainsoft crowded into the Hawk cave. Karo, Rikah, and Kassandra were unhurt except for when they'd gotten some scratches rushing in and out of the underbrush. They all gathered around the cushion where Jessika was placed. She was still shivering weakly. She lay limp on the cushion, eyes closed, breathing soft but rapidly.

"She feels cold," Thornfire observed. "Move her closer to the Sunstone. Rikah, Karo, Kassandra, if you snuggle up to Jessika it will help her get warm." He picked up another water skin from beside the Stone and shook it. "This tea will be quite strong by now. You could all benefit from it."

"Wait," Hawkwind spoke up, "are you sure it's safe for humans?"

"This is a tea we've all drunk before on this journey, including the children. It's just to help warm us up and get some fluids," Thornfire explained calmly.

They helped Jessika sit up and take some drinks of the tea. Though at first she only sipped a little, perhaps because of the bitterness, once the heat of it reached her core, she took deeper draughts.

"That's good," she commented.

When she gave Hawkwind a little smile, the lump of rocky fear in the griffin's chest began to melt. The other children, plus Hawkwind, Swift, and Joy, also had some of the tea. It was strong and hot, and returned a little strength to pained muscles. Once they'd drained the skin, Thornfire immediately set to making another batch.

Starbright shouldered her way into the room with a bag stuffed full of something. "Master, I'm back," she was panting.

"Excellent, Bright," Thornfire greeted her, taking the bag.

The two bent over a flat rock and began messing about with the herbs, the first water skin that held just plain water, and some strips of cloth while Hawkwind made sure the children, Swift, and Joy were comfortable. Hawkwind examined their wounds. Swift had taken the most damage, besides Hawkwind herself, but all the wounds were clotted or cauterized now. That didn't mean they wouldn't become infected, but at least the bleeding had stopped. They could be grateful that drakes were cleaner creatures than snow-screamers and lacked the venom of talis.

Thornfire and Starbright came over carrying bandages smeared with pungent globs of herbs. The sharp scent of the bruised greenery alone brought some clarity to the mind and brightness to the lungs. Starbright attended to the griffins, while Thornfire knelt by Jessika, tenderly laying the poultices onto her wounds.

"These herbs have anti-infection properties," he explained. "They will help keep the wounds clean and healing. Do rainbow drakes have any venom?"

"None that I know of," Hawkwind said. "I've been bitten and

clawed by them before and never had any symptoms of poisoning."

"What about that new creature you mentioned? Did it bite Jessika? It bit you, you said?"

"It did bite me. It didn't bite her, but its spines and claws did hurt her."

"You have one of the beasts?"

"Both of them," Hawkwind confirmed.

She opened one of the sacks she still had strapped to her harness and carefully pulled out the bodies and severed heads. Thornfire put them on another rock, separate from the herb rock, and examined them.

"I've never seen their like," he said. "Exceptional spines they have."

"Look in their mouths," Hawkwind suggested.

"Ah," he exclaimed upon looking. "Once a dried fish showed up at the Harvest Trading Festival in South-scree. It had a mouth much like this, all these thin teeth pointing down the gullet."

"So anything it bites can't get away, right?"

"So is my understanding," he confirmed. "Let me see your leg, where it bit you."

"It hurt," she told him, "so bad."

"All those teeth in close proximity? It mashed your flesh, destroyed its structure; I expect it hurt excruciatingly. This wound will need close watching and attention."

"Thank goodness it didn't bite Jessika," she whispered.

"Indeed," Thornfire said, giving her a serious look. "And why did it not, Hawkwind?"

"I don't know," Hawkwind prevaricated. "Maybe it was because she wasn't resisting."

It was true that she didn't know exactly why, though she suspected it had something to do with the girl being the Northnest princess and her being wanted alive.

"They were trying to kill us griffins the most," she went on.

Thornfire had returned to examining the mini-drake. "This could have killed a human child very easily. I don't see any venom pouches or perforations in claws, spines, or fangs that would suggest a place for venom to be injected, though I can't be certain of course, but it doesn't look like this beast could have poisoned you or Jessika."

"That's good to hear."

"Let's get some more poultices on you all, and then you'll need to rest."

As the injured submitted to having the herbs and bandages pressed to their wounds, Thornwing came back into the room. He had a chunk of raw flesh in his mouth, head tipped up to try to prevent blood from dripping on the floor.

"Wing?" Thornfire greeted, but his brother ignored him, going straight to Hawkwind.

Thornwing nudged her, pointed at the meat he was carrying, then at her, and then finally signed with the language he'd learned from the Snow-in-lee griffins, "for you, eat."

Hawkwind spluttered and blushed. No one had fed her like that since she was a chick, but it was normal behavior for males bringing food to those they felt an obligation to feed. Not giving herself too much time to think of it, she accepted, opening her bill and tilting her head so he could transfer the meat over to her. She swallowed it whole with a few bobs of her head.

Rikah got up from the cushion. "Thornwing, is there more? I'll make food for us."

"There is. Come with me."

Rikah fetched his knife, and as the two left, Swift gave Hawkwind a playful nudge. Hawkwind nudged her back, but despite the embarrassment, the food felt fantastic in her gizzard, and it would feel even better once it moved to her stomach to start getting digested and feeding her taxed body.

It seemed that Thornwing wasn't the only one with the bright ideas.

In another minute, Hawkdash came hesitantly into the cave, bearing a bloody mouthful that he fed to his little niece, Joy. Swift signed to him her gratitude, and he brought her a chunk next. Thornwing came back with another piece for Hawkwind, and Rikah strode in with a steak of whatever kind of meat it was they were eating to place on the Sunstone to cook.

"Thank you, Thornwing," Hawkwind said.

"I'm here to help," he replied. "How do you feel?"

"Better with the food and the poultices, but it was a close thing. I can't remember being more injured," she confessed, "although the escape from Northnest might come close."

"I should have gone with you," he grimaced.

"You had important things to do here. Any more sign of the talis?"

"There are signs here and there, but nothing that has alarmed me yet, and we haven't actually seen any. Don't worry about anything other than healing."

"The tea is ready again," Starbright announced, and the skin was passed around to the injured.

With everyone covered with bandages, full of tea, and either getting fed by Thornwing and Hawkdash or waiting for Rikah to cook the steaks, the room slipped into the calm of resting and recovering adventurers. Only Thornfire, examining the mini-drakes and their collars, and Rikah, prodding the meat, stayed alert. Even Starbright, exhausted from her frantic search for the herbs her master had needed, dozed by the Sunstone. Once Thornwing had brought all the meat he could, he took position by the door, keeping watch. Rainsoft didn't make an appearance, and as she drifted off to sleep, Hawkwind wondered if it was because he was jealous or angry that Hawkwind had accepted Thornwing for mating as well as him.

Too sore and weary to worry any more about it, Hawkwind drifted into an uneasy sleep.

Swift and Joy had gone for a walk, testing sore muscles and taking care of the necessary, while Hawkwind sat, watching Jessika work on standing and moving around a little, with the help of the other children. Everyone's bandages had been changed that morning, and Thornfire had pronounced all the wounds to be healing properly, with no signs of infection.

"So," the master mage said from beside her, making Hawkwind jump a little; she hadn't noticed him approach. "What do the golden wings on Jessika's back mean? I saw them when I dressed her wounds."

"Nothing," Hawkwind lied. "They're just a decoration applied by eccentric parents. It's not unusual in Northnest."

"I don't believe you, Hawkchild," Thornfire murmured gently. "The mini-drake only attacked her? The other children follow her orders—even you follow her orders at times—even though Rikah is bigger and bolder. She shows a confidence and poise that the others lack. There is something about her that is different, special, and not just those golden wings."

"She is a special girl," Hawkwind acknowledged, "but so is Kassandra. The boys are special, too. The tattoos are nothing to worry about."

Thornfire's gaze, patiently awaiting an explanation, did not waver. "I knew when I heard your story that there was the chance those who attacked Northnest could still be hunting you. I knew that could create some risk to anyone travelling with you, but I did not think you were so special that your enemy would make a considerable effort. I did not think it was a personal enemy. Is there anything you need to tell me?"

"I don't know who attacked Northnest," Hawkwind emphasized. "I was a trainee, barely a Feathyr. No one told me anything, although I knew there was some unrest, and that something was going on. Feathyr flights were going out more often but I didn't worry about it. I didn't think it was serious. The attack was shocking to me. All I fought were the minions. I don't know who was in charge."

That was all true, but directly denying Jessika's identity meant lying. She could talk about how she was less than nothing all day, but to touch upon the children would require concealment, and she'd already lied about the wings once. Hawkwind's throat choked of its own will; she couldn't lie. Instead of speaking an untruth, she remained silent. Under Thornfire's heavy countenance staying silent became harder by the minute.

"My feathers may have lost their shine and my bill is indeed dented with use, but I am a mage, a good one. Do you know what kind of mind is required to become a good mage?" he asked.

"I don't," Hawkwind confessed.

"Magery is about more than raw ability," he said. "It requires study and discipline, memorization and willpower, focus and mental agility. I do not flatter myself when I say that it requires a brilliant mind. I can tell, Hawkwind. I know she's different. I know there is more than what you're telling me. What is she?"

Hawkwind's mouth had gone dry. Before she could come up with something, she felt little fingers touch her shoulder, and she turned her head to see that Jessika herself had tottered up behind them.

"I'm a Northnest princess," the girl whispered. "Please keep it a secret, Thornfire."

The mage let out a sigh. "I thought it might be something like that."

"Please don't tell," Jessika repeated.

"I don't care what you are," he said, "as long as you being it doesn't cause problems. I won't tell anyone, but in return I think you had better stay away from human settlements. It's obvious to all of us that the drakes were after you, little one. How did they find you in the forest?"

"I don't know," she said. "We were looking for things to eat, plants and stuff. I was searching, and then suddenly the thing jumped out at me and grabbed me."

"And another grabbed you, Hawkwind. None of the other children or griffins got attacked."

"That's right," Hawkwind confirmed.

"So the drakes aren't just looking for any griffin or any child, but you two in particular, and somehow they know which child and griffin you two are."

"How could they? Those drakes couldn't have ever seen us, been introduced to us, or anything," Hawkwind mused. "There might have been a painting of Jessika in Northnest, but certainly not of me."

"I doubt they are looking for you with their eyes," Thornfire all but scoffed. "Those collars you brought back are magical, although now that they aren't attached to a living mini-drake, they seem to have lost their power source. I'm not certain about everything they do, but I have little doubt that the collars identified you to the mini-drakes, so they knew whom to bite."

"And how would the collars know?" Hawkwind asked.

"The easiest way would be if the mage who made the collars had something of yours—your blood, a hair, a feather—and used it in the spell. They tell the collar to seek something like the item they've given it, and somehow indicate it to the bearer. You told me the collars glowed. That might have been the signal for the mini-drake. Or, the spikes of the collars were digging into the mini-drake's skin, and might have created a conduit directly to the beasts' little brains."

"Magic can do things like that?" Hawkwind marveled, partly revolted.

Thornfire nodded somberly, and his voice dropped even further. "It would be a combination of dark, blood, and earth magic," he muttered. "That's not nice stuff, and it would take a powerful and unscrupulous mage to create such a complex spell. You said that when the mini-drake found you, Hawkwind, it attached itself to you, and then you saw the rainbow drakes rising into the air to hunt you."

"Some went after me. Some headed for the children," she confirmed.

"Suggesting that they were called magically, since you detected no visual or auditory calls," he nodded. "I'll hold onto those collars, keep them safe. As for you two, there will be no more village visiting. It seems that you're wanted by someone. Do us all a favor and stay away from anywhere mini-drakes are likely to be."

"So I can never go back to being with other humans?" Jessika murmured.

"For now," Hawkwind told her. "The situation will change eventually."

"I want to go lie down," she said, and turned and limped back to the cushion by the Sunstone.

"So that's a human princess," Thornfire stared after her.

"Sort of," Hawkwind shrugged. "She had older siblings. If Northnest had never been attacked, she would never have become the heir, and never ruled. She might have married a royal of some other country and been a queen there, although that's not common for Northnest. Probably she would have just supported her siblings in some role in the royal cabinet and married whomever she wanted, or not at all."

Thornfire grinned at her. "Like you, she finds herself assuming a social position she'd never expected."

"So it would seem, but Jessika might never regain the throne of Northnest. Whoever has it now will be difficult to unseat," Hawkwind said.

"That is a problem for the future," the mage commented, "and of no concern at present. I'm glad to know more about your true situation. I'll keep it to myself. Please continue to rest and heal."

Thornfire got to his feet and took himself out of the cave. Hawkwind laid her head down and, like Jessika, partook of some more sleep.

Chapter 28
Reconnaissance Group

Hawkwind, Swift, and Joy were testing out their healed muscles and basking in the early summer sunlight a week later, when a commotion came in the form of a lookout spiraling down from one of the higher peaks where a crude watch tower had been built. Hawkwind went running to see what the problem was, along with Thornfire and Thornwing. Swift followed her at a distance. The lookout gestured his information.

"There are strange griffins approaching," he pointed, "from that way."

"How many?" Thornfire asked.

"Five."

Thornfire grunted. "Five griffins, the exact number of a usual scouting party, coming from the direction of South-scree."

The Thorn brothers exchanged a wry glance heavy with resignation.

"It would seem we have no need to send a party of our own to report on our progress after all," Thornwing commented. He looked over at Hawkwind. "They'll have something to say about the Hawkmother."

"Let them say it," Thornfire shrugged. "It's not like they can do anything about it."

"Should I absent myself?" Hawkwind asked timidly.

"No, you should be here, with us, as a leader of this expedition. Wing, will you go find Rainsoft?"

The younger brother ran off while Hawkwind turned to Swift. "Can you find any elders among the Snow-in-lee griffins that would be interested in meeting this scouting party from an Aerie? These are griffins that might have a hand in determining the future of any griffins that want to join our society."

Swift nodded and trotted away to call on some of the more active Snow-in-lee griffins. Hawkwind summoned Joy with a wave.

"Joy, will you find the children and take them to the cave?"

The younger griffin also nodded and dashed away. Hawkwind squared her shoulders and prepared to meet the scouting party as they circled over and then angled in for a landing. Thornwing returned with Rainsoft and Swift brought over a handful of others just as the newcomers touched down. Hawkwind hid her wince when she recognized Rocksky in the lead: the same big female that had initially captured and detained her in South-scree. Thornfire's group assembled around him, and he and Rocksky exchanged polite if not friendly nods.

"Welcome, Commander," Thornfire greeted. "You have found us."

"Elder," she replied. "The Thornmother prevailed upon the council to send us to ascertain your situation."

"You mean fetch the bodies," Thornwing remarked. His big brother jabbed him with a wing wrist.

"Thornwing," Rocksky gasped. "You are Thornwing, aren't you?"

"Rocksky, isn't it? I do think we've met once or twice," he answered, rubbing his poked shoulder.

"Then you've succeeded." The look of astonishment, like she'd just been doused with a bucket of cold water, was almost comical. "You rescued Thornwing from, from somewhere?"

"From Snow-in-lee, just as I promised," Thornfire smiled in an only slightly smug fashion.

Rocksky's eyes were roving over the group now. "I do not recognize most of these griffins."

"They're from Snow-in-lee, too," the mage told her.

"Other captives? From other Aeries?"

"Not exactly," Thornfire clarified. "These griffins are, like us, descendants of the ancient Snow-in-lee griffins, but they and the generations before them were held captive by the talis. They had never been outside their prison rooms until we freed them. Like Rainsoft, who also came from Snow-in-lee but had escaped on his own, they cannot speak aloud and know little of our society."

Rocksky's wide eyes seemed to be trying to take all of that in.

"And you, the one called Hawkwind," one of the other scouts spoke up, "you, ah," he stuttered to a stop.

"Hawkwind's story is true, just as she told you in the council chamber," Thornfire said, somewhat sternly. "She is the last of her Line."

"And its new Hawkmother," another South-scree griffin that Hawkwind recognized as Skymist, the grey griffin who had been kind to her in the South-scree prison, murmured.

Skymist gave a little bow. Others of the scouting party copied her, and Rocksky gave them a glare, withholding her own bow of respect. Thornfire eyed her, and Hawkwind, too, felt like giving her a look, but after all, it wasn't as though the Hawk Line was a part of South-scree. Maybe bows of respect weren't warranted, and Hawkwind was awfully young and had earned her new status only by coincidence.

"So it would seem your mission has been a success, Elder," Rocksky said. "What of the tasks given to your companions? Surely they have collected the mythical Sunstone and Moonstone." She gave a little chortle.

"Of course they have," Thornfire nodded with simple frankness.

Rocksky blinked. "They, they have?" she echoed.

"Both the Stones are safe and functional," the mage assured her. "Would you like to see them?"

Hawkwind was starting to feel a little sorry for Rocksky. Certainly she could be a bit of a brute, but she was still just trying to follow her orders and if she hadn't believed in the ability of four griffins to free another from a legendary city infested with monstrous finned serpents and retrieve two mythical, magical items, Hawkwind couldn't blame her. Hawkwind herself hadn't believed it could be done, either.

"You'll stay the night, Commander?" Hawkwind spoke up. "There are empty caves for your scouting party. We've cleared the snow-screamers out of a section of the old caves where our armies were once staged for trying to take back Snow-in-lee. We've all been living there for a few weeks now."

"That is resourceful," the big black, grey, and white griffin grunted. "There certainly are a lot of you."

Hawkwind gestured to the Snow-in-lee griffins gathered behind her. "These are Icemoon, Hawkswift, Windnight, and Stormstone," she said. "They are from Snow-in-lee. They're working hard to learn how to fly, fight, and communicate with us griffins that talk out loud."

The four griffins gestured, "hello," at Rocksky.

"They said hello," Hawkwind translated. "They are looking forward to being a part of an Aerie."

At this, Rocksky's visage, which had started to brighten, dimmed again. "The disposition of all these new griffins will cause much debate," she said.

"I'm certain that wise and compassionate minds can come up with a solution," Hawkwind stated firmly.

"I agree with Hawkwind," Thornfire said. "There is room for everyone in this world, if we all learn to get along. I'm sure you've flown far today. Why don't you come to have some rest and food?"

Rocksky was gracious enough or confused enough to go along, and Thornfire led the group, with Hawkwind, the Snow-in-lee elders, and Rocksky's patrol trailing after, to the sunning rocks.

"Should I call you Hawkwind or Hawkmother?" Skymist whispered eagerly as she made her way to Hawkwind's side.

"I still don't feel comfortable with the change," Hawkwind winced.

"Then Hawkwind for now," Skymist grinned. "I'm so glad to see you. The council started thinking you were all dead, and then some of them started regretting being so harsh to you all—not Skycall, of course. Thornmother exerted herself to get everyone to agree to send a search party. I managed to wrangle myself onto the team." Skymist suddenly gasped. "The human fledglings, are they alive?"

"They're fine," Hawkwind assured her. "I just had Joy take them into the caves in case this turned violent."

"Joy?"

"Hawkjoy and Hawkswift are both Snow-in-lee griffins that have joined my Line."

"Really?" Skymist beamed. "How exciting, and are you, I mean, are your planning, or maybe you're already—"

"I don't know yet," Hawkwind cut her off, guessing what she was trying to ask. "I may know in a few days or a week or so, I'm not sure."

"But you've tried? Rainsoft, I presume?" Skymist giggled, nudging Hawkwind with her wing.

A little ahead, Rainsoft glanced back, hearing his name, but then looked away. Thornwing glanced back, too, and winked.

"And Thornwing?" Skymist squealed quietly.

"Hush," Hawkwind growled. "I don't need everyone privy to my, uh, situation." She could feel her nares heating up with a blush. "It's no one's business."

"You're right, I'm sorry, Hawkwind. I'm just happy for you. I don't think I'll ever be Skymother."

"Why not?"

"I'm not high enough rank, but that's alright. It's a lot of responsibility and I don't think I want it anyway. I am happy for you, though."

"Well, it wasn't exactly my choice, but I'm doing it. It's my path now and that's all there is to it."

Skymist smiled at her. "Good luck. I think you'll make a great Linemother."

Hawkwind smiled back. "I appreciate the encouragement."

They took their places on the sunning rocks. Skymist had to sit behind Rocksky with the rest of the scouting party. Hawkwind sat beside and just a bit back from Thornfire, who had Thornwing on his other side. Swift and the other Snow-in-lee elders took places nearby, and Rainsoft got a spot, too, in the inner circle.

"What are you planning to do with all these griffins?" Rocksky asked without preamble.

"That will have to be decided," Thornfire shrugged. "Many of the Snow-in-lee griffins are paired. They might not want to join our society. They might stay here, in the caves, and have their own city."

"They'll end up living in Lines like us," Rocksky shook her head. "Why aren't they in Lines now?"

"They were kept separate from each other, in different rooms, in Snow-in-lee, by the talis."

That shut everyone up for a few heartbeats.

"The talis were keeping them?" Rocksky clarified.

"To power the Stones," Thornfire nodded. "The ancient griffin mages must have known ways to renew the power, but the talis didn't. They discovered that sacrificing griffins on the Stones gave the Stones some power, to keep the heat and the water running. For that, they needed a supply of griffins. A hot place for the talis was apparently more valuable than spending some extra time hunting food to keep the griffins alive and reproducing. Because of our weakness against the talis, they had no trouble managing the families."

Rocksky was staring around at the Snow-in-lee griffins, and then seemed to realize she was staring, and looked down at her claws instead. "Why can't they talk?"

"They were all injured as chicks, by the talis. The talis destroyed their vocal cords. I think it may have been to keep them from calling out to each other or communicating, but over the generations, the population of griffins developed sign language, and it spread among them. I don't know if the talis ever realized it."

"I see." Rocksky seemed to be thinking hard. "They will end up in Lines eventually, you know. That's griffin nature."

"Of course, but some of the families don't understand, or don't care, or don't believe it."

Swift lifted her hand for a turn to speak, and Hawkwind translated aloud for her. "We are splitting into factions," she said. "There are some of us that have listened closely to Thornfire and the others. We recognize the situation you just said. We want to join the society that you have. There is another group that is still confused and traumatized. They can't accept this new way of life, and they are unwell. I don't know what will become of them. A third group wants nothing to do with your world. They accept being out of Snow-in-lee, but they are determined to live as before, to go their own way."

"Thank you, Hawkswift," Thornfire said when she'd finished. "Rocksky, the Aeries will need to know about this exodus from Snow-in-lee. There will need to be a consensus on how to accept the new populations."

"Indeed," Rocksky agreed. "The information will need to be spread. This might even call for a meeting of all Aeries, with representatives from the Snow-in-lee griffins, so everyone can discuss the situation and reach an agreement."

"Until then, I was thinking most of the Snow-in-lee griffins would remain here," Thornfire said. "It seems safe enough, at least during the warm months."

Icemoon raised her hand this time, and Hawkwind translated again. "The factions Hawkswift spoke about are developing rifts between them. This problem has been growing the longer we are out of Snow-in-lee. The confused ones will need help to choose a path. The other two factions are starting to have conflicts."

"What kind of conflicts? I haven't noticed anything," Thornfire said.

"You wouldn't, unless you are paying attention to what we say to each other," Icemoon gestured, "and although you have learned some of our hand speech, I think you do not listen to us much, unless in one-on-one conversation."

For a moment, Thornfire looked slightly insulted.

"I think that's normal," Thornwing spoke up. "It's easy to tune out a language you're not familiar with. It takes effort to understand, so unless there's a need to understand, most people would just not spend the energy to listen to conversations that don't concern them."

The mage shrugged it off. "You're probably right, Wing."

"We—the faction us here are a part of—want to join Lines, or have our own," Hawkwind said aloud for Icemoon. "We have heard and understand that our natural way of life is to end up in Lines anyway if we live in groups. We accept that and will embrace it."

"The others," Hawkswift contributed, "do not want to accept that. They think they can keep their families and that their children can continue living as they do. They don't believe that their daughters will remain asleep, as Hawkwind calls it."

"Maybe they will accept it when they see it for themselves, some years from now," Thornwing suggested.

"But until then, if we cannot convince them, they will need somewhere to live," Thornfire said. "And as long as they are not violent to other griffins, the Aeries will need to know to leave them in peace."

Rocksky rumbled in her chest. "Not all of the Aeries will agree to that. Some of them will see any griffin outside an Aerie as a rogue and a threat."

"But they will have to see that the situation has changed," Hawkwind argued. "Would they really attack a bunch of griffins only recently freed from imprisonment in Snow-in-lee? These griffins have done nothing to the Aeries."

"Not yet," Rocksky countered. "Who is to say that the separatist griffins will remain nonviolent? Besides that, prey must be managed. I don't suppose you know this, Hawkmother, but the Aeries take care of the animal populations on these mountains. We manage our own population size and monitor the wild animal populations to be sure we don't overhunt. If our food source were to decline, so too would we. That is another reason we have little patience for rogues that return to Aerie territory, and these separatist griffins could compound that problem."

"What the commander says is true," Thornfire nodded, while

Hawkwind reeled from being referred to as the Hawkmother by a citizen of South-scree.

Did that mean that Rocksky was acknowledging her status? It must. Did that mean she had a new ally? It could. Rocksky had seemed to hate her before, but maybe the natural tendency to respect and protect the Linemothers was working in the big grey, black, and white griffin. Maybe she couldn't help it. If so, maybe getting the help of Aerie griffins would not be that hard, now that Hawkwind had her new status.

"An all-Aerie meeting will need to be called," Thornfire was saying when Hawkwind focused back on the conversation. "Until then, we'll try to keep all the Snow-in-lee griffins here, unless we can ascertain if South-scree is willing to accept in the ones that want to join our Lines."

Rocksky nodded. "That is the only course I can see, for now."

Just then, a few griffins arrived with some bled prey animals for the tired scouting party.

"Please eat," Thornfire said, getting to his feet. "When you're done, we can show you to a cave."

"Thank you for your hospitality," Rocksky consented.

"This is no developed Aerie," Thornwing rued, "but we'll share what we have."

The scouting party had caused a stir among the Snow-in-lee griffins, but at least Rocksky and the others were being relatively calm and collected about the whole situation, now that the initial shock had worn off. Hawkwind had spent a good portion of the day translating for Swift and some of the others while Rocksky asked them questions. She'd considered calling on Kassandra or one of the other children, as they were much better at the hand-talking than she was, but she hadn't wanted to burden them with some of the complicated topics that were covered, and children were better off playing and—in Jessika's case—healing, anyway.

As dusk fell and the griffins began retreating to their caves, Hawkwind was starting to feel that they might have a tentative ally in Rocksky and her scouts. In a few days the scouting party would return to South-scree, and Hawkwind hoped she could go with them. Thornfire would certainly be going, and Thornwing, too. If Thornfire went, Starbright would probably go, and if Hawkwind also went, that would mean there would be only Snow-in-lee griffins at the cave camp. Some of the Snow-in-lee griffins were quite competent now, but it still gave her an uneasy feeling to leave them without the protection of their rescuers.

The children had already retreated to the Hawk cave with Joy, and Hawkwind saw Swift give her a wave as she, too, disappeared into the cave system. Hawkwind stood a few minutes longer, looking up at the sky as the stars began pricking their way through the darkening velvet of the heavens. The day sentries were going in and the first set of night sentries were coming out to take their places, although stationed closer to the cave entrance. Griffins had poor night vision, though decent hearing; they didn't want to be too far from safety. Rainsoft passed Hawkwind and paused.

"Good evening," she said and gestured, "starting your shift?"

He nodded. "How are you doing? Healing?"

"I'm a lot better," Hawkwind assured him. "My rear leg is the worst still."

"I got to see the thing that bit you. It looked nasty."

Hawkwind extended her wounded leg. It was still well-bandaged, per Thornfire's orders, so she couldn't show him the bite, but she flexed it carefully. Under the wrappings it was thickly scabbed and stiff, and thanks to Thornfire's herbal treatments, no infection had developed.

"I'm sure it will heal eventually," she said. "I just hope it's as strong and flexible as before."

"Me, too. You're going to have a lot of responsibilities." Rainsoft's gaze expressed more than what he said. "I want to help you. I'm just not sure how."

"Your help is always welcome. Your presence is always welcome," she assured him. "Don't ever feel like you don't have the right to," Hawkwind groped for the words even as her nares heated with a blush, "be near me, or help me, or anything like that."

"Do I?" he gestured sadly.

"You do," she stated, and then she asked him something she wasn't sure she should ask. "Do you want to join my Line?"

His feathers perked up.

"I don't know what your family is planning to do, but I don't think the current Rain Line is at South-scree," she told him. "I don't know where it is, at what Aerie, although I assume it still exists. It wasn't at Northnest. I'm going to ask South-scree to let me add the Hawk Line to the Aerie. I don't know what you plan to do, but I think it will be allowed for me to adopt any griffins I want, or you can go seek the Rain Line, wherever it is."

"My parents are confused," Rainsoft gestured. "My little sister wants to join a Line, like me. My brother, his mate, they are a little confused, too, but don't trust the Line griffins. They might separate from the group. I have been trying to convince them to stay."

"I don't know what will happen to griffins who try to separate," Hawkwind said. "There will be an all-Aerie meeting about it. The Aeries will probably not take kindly to them. I don't know how they will feel about Snow-in-lee griffins joining Lines, either, but you and your sister, or any of your family, are welcome to become Hawks."

Rainsoft bowed his head. "I thank you for the offer. I might take you up on it. We will see."

They stood in silence for a few minutes.

Finally, Rainsoft gestured again. "I should take my post."

"I won't keep you," Hawkwind agreed. "May you have a peaceful watch."

Rainsoft began walking into the deeper darkness and Hawkwind headed for the cave entrance, which was slightly lit by a glowing stone Starbright had placed there. Then she heard a scuffle behind her, and turned to see Rainsoft dashing back towards her with wings mantled.

In the oddly still silence, he gestured at her.

"Talis."

Something moved in the darkness behind him as Hawkwind's blood chilled and adrenaline sent vibrant spikes of urgency to her muscles. She couldn't believe it. The night was so calm, so peaceful.

"Talis," Rainsoft signed again, forcefully. "Run. Tell them."

A sharp hiss came from the darkness and something struck at Rainsoft. He wheeled with a shriek, and Hawkwind's body propelled her into motion. She was sprinting towards the cave mouth. She opened her bill and shouted out.

"Talis. Attack. To the caves."

Cries of surprise came from the other griffin sentries. They fled to the cave with her, not trying to turn and fight the hypnotic creatures. Hawkwind shouted out her warning again, and again. She reached the cave and ran right into Thornwing.

"That way," she pointed breathlessly. "Rainsoft's in trouble."

"Run them into the caves, deep into the caves," Thornwing ordered. "Rainsoft and I will hold them back."

Thornwing leapt away and Hawkwind could spare no thought for him, but unbidden came the memory of Hawkcall and Eagleye throwing themselves upon the rainbow drakes at Northnest. Again, Hawkwind was running away.

She stopped to shout into every cave she passed. "Talis are here. Run into the caves, deeper into the caves."

She didn't have time to be sure the griffins obeyed.

"Swift, Joy," she summoned as the cave passages began to get crowded.

The two griffins of her Line waded through to her.

"There are talis attacking. Swift, take the children," she ordered. "Go deep into the caves and keep going. Stay with other griffins: whoever is going the fastest. Keep the children safe. Tell them I will come soon."

Swift nodded and dashed away.

"Joy, try to get these griffins moving. Urge them to go deep into the caves, but if they won't go, leave them. Stay safe."

The younger female was trembling, but she nodded, too, and turned to the nearest griffins, encouraging them to move. Hawkwind ran for the Thorn cave. Thornfire was strapping the Moonstone onto Starbright.

"Hawkwind, get going," he scolded as soon as he saw her. "Take the Sunstone. Go deep into the caves. Bright will go with you. Her magic will keep you safe."

"Where are you going?" she demanded.

"I go to help Wing and Rainsoft. We'll buy you time. Now go. Go."

Starbright left the cave without so much as a farewell. Thornfire followed her example. As Hawkwind stepped back out, she could hear the hissing screeches of talis and the battle cries of Thornwing and Rainsoft. They would buy her time? Did that mean they were sacrificing themselves? Hawkwind felt like a mini-drake had wrapped around her throat and heart, choking her.

"Let's go," Starbright called.

There was no time. As Icefeather had said during the attack on Northnest, they'd made their choice. Hawkwind ran to the Hawk cave. Swift had been true to her name; the children were already gone. Starbright rushed to help fasten the Sunstone to Hawkwind's harness, and they left without a second look. The corridors were filled now with pushing, shoving griffins, although they passed a few caves where griffins looked blankly at them. When Hawkwind shouted at them to come along, they just backed away, frightened.

Despite the pushing and shoving, the griffins were moving along at a good pace. There were many tunnels and no one seemed to know where to go. Hawkwind even heard the shrieks of snow-screamers and the sounds of fighting. She and Starbright had a better idea than the others of how to get through, although they didn't have it memorized. The glow of the Sunstone cleared the way for Hawkwind, and the pair pushed to the head of the pack. There, Hawkwind encountered Swift although Joy was nowhere to be seen.

"Hawkwind," the children cried in unison.

"It's alright, I'm here. Stay on Swift."

Hawkwind took a position in front of Swift, and Starbright came up to stand beside her.

"We need to keep going," the apprentice mage said.

"I know," Hawkwind agreed as she led them deeper. "There's no way of knowing how many talis are out there or if Thornfire, Thornwing, and Rainsoft will be able to stop them."

"If they don't," Starbright whimpered.

"Then there's no telling how far the talis will follow us. We must keep going."

Hawkwind and Starbright, conversing sometimes to agree upon a path, wormed their way through the tunnels. It was days to the other side of the mountain, and they couldn't keep their pace up forever, but neither could the talis. They could only hope to outrun them. The caves were cold; maybe that would slow the talis down.

The chaos of the shuffling, shoving griffins and the sounds of battle reverberating from the walls meant that Hawkwind had little idea of what was going on beyond the dozen or so griffins around her that she could actually see. Surely the griffins were fighting snow-screamers, but had the talis reached the back ranks of the griffins and started fighting? Were the talis fighting with snow-screamers, too?

As they went, Starbright periodically picked up stones from the tunnel floor and lit them with magic. Some she dropped, lighting a path, others she passed to the griffins around her, who in turn passed them on to others. The light would help keep the snow-screamers away, but Hawkwind wondered if darkness might be better for fighting talis. Maybe if it were dark the griffins wouldn't be able to see enough of the talis to become entranced? But then they wouldn't see the talis' attacks coming.

Hawkwind started talking about it, trying to pass the information on. "The light will discourage, keep away, snow-screamers," she repeated, "but let you see the talis. Hide the light stones if you suspect talis. Hide the light stones if you see talis. Use them if you see snow-screamers. Tell others. Pass it on."

It was difficult for the Snow-in-lee griffins to hand-speak while walking, but it seemed they tried to pass on the message. Hawkwind couldn't know how far the message would travel, or if it would get lost in the many passings of it. Most of the Snow-in-lee griffins already knew that snow-screamers didn't like light. Maybe they would remember that, at least.

Hawkwind had to stop talking as they came upon a startled pack of snow-screamers. The beasts winced away from the light of the Sunstone. A few Snow-in-lee griffins leapt courageously over the heads of Hawkwind, Swift, and Starbright, and engaged the animals. The snow-screamers didn't last long. They could see for themselves that there was a crowd of griffins. That, plus the bright light, sent them scurrying away in retreat, and the fighting griffins let Hawkwind take the lead again.

All she could do was lead them on. The talis hadn't reached them after hours of walking, and Hawkwind didn't know when it would be safe to stop. She pushed on, walking so long that soon she wondered if it were day or night. Some of the griffins were falling behind. Surely any talis that were chasing them would have tired as well?

"Let's stop," Hawkwind said finally, when they had reached an extra wide part of the tunnel where it seemed it opened up into a cave and then resumed on the opposite wall.

"Are you sure?" Starbright asked, but she, too, was drooping.

She had been marching as well as making magic, and carrying the Moonstone. Hawkwind had been carrying the weight of the Sunstone, and Swift the weight of four children. Plus, they'd had the pressure of trying to choose the correct route: one that wouldn't result in a literal dead end. All three of them had been plodding on only by dint of will.

"The talis like warmth, right?" Starbright was babbling. "The caves are cold. Maybe they gave up."

"We have to rest," Hawkwind repeated. "This is sort of a wide spot. Let's stop and let others catch up. We'll set a watch behind us and in front of us, and everyone else can rest."

The children got down off of Swift and moved as a pack to a little corner of the cave, where they huddled with skinny arms around each other. Starbright sat where she was. Swift moved ahead, pausing only to gesture, "I will watch the path ahead."

More griffins were already limping into the cave. Hawkwind went to watch the entrance.

"Rest here," she told the arrivals, repeating it as they came in. "Starbright, do you have any magic that would detect a talis approaching, not a griffin?"

"That would be very advanced," she answered. "Thornfire might be able to come up with something, if he had time to think about it."

An idea struck Hawkwind, and she dashed back down the tunnel. Where the tunnel curved, she piled up several glowing stones. When she returned to her post at the entrance to the cave, she watched the shadows of approaching griffins. Having the bright stones all in one spot threw a clear silhouette onto the cave wall. Hawkwind went back to adjust the location of the stones a few times until she had it just right; she could now easily tell from the shadows alone what kind of creature approached. It wasn't much of a warning, but hopefully it would be enough to allow her to shout an alert if the shadow showed a talis-shape.

More and more griffins arrived; including all of Rainsoft's immediate family, and Hawkwind began to be heartened by how many had so far survived. It was also possible that some had gone ahead of Hawkwind's group. Some arrived with wounds from fighting snow-screamers, and Starbright gave more of her energy to magically cauterize the worst of the bites and scratches, since they would be so prone to infection.

Thornfire, Rainsoft, and Thornwing did not arrive. Nor did Rocksky and her scouts, and Hawkwind tried not to worry about them. After all, they had wings. If they had been cut off from the cave entrance, they could have flown to safety. Of course, if they had been cut off from the cave entrance that could mean that talis had entered the cave system, and Rocksky and her scouts were not immune to the talis' hypnotism.

Hawkwind nearly wept with relief when Joy staggered into the cave leading several young griffins, some still unfledged and tottering on baby legs.

"Joy," she cried out, and Swift came running to her daughter.

Hawkwind sent another griffin to take over Swift's post at the other side of the cave.

"Why do you have so many chicks?" Swift asked. "Where are their parents?"

Joy shook her head heavily. "They are chicks of confused ones," she signed. "When I went to the caves to tell the families the talis were coming, the adults looked relieved. They said that was how it should be, that now they could return to their masters. I tried to reason with them at first, but time was short. Some of the chicks followed the lead of their parents, and wouldn't come, but many chicks argued with their parents, and said they wanted to run. I managed to get most of those chicks away, and here they are."

"Bad," said one of the littlest chicks aloud, with its voice, "talis bad."

"Mom and Dad are wrong," whispered another, and then burst into sobs.

That set off the whole group to crying, and the crying of fledglings brought the whole cave of griffins awake. A dozen adults and sub-adults came over to the chicks, gesturing: "come with me. We'll take care of you. Don't worry. I'll keep you safe."

Within moments, the orphans had been absorbed into other griffin families, and Joy was left alone.

"Some of them wouldn't come," Joy signed weakly. She keened softly under her breath. "I had to leave them."

Swift put her wings around her daughter, comforting her as though she were a chick, too, and led her off.

"Perhaps the talis won't have gotten as far as the ones that were left behind," Starbright offered. "Maybe they'll all be safe."

"I'm glad some came at least," Hawkwind said. "Young ones are resilient, and once they were free and saw the world, and began learning to talk and met each other, and saw us flying, they adapted quickly to being like normal chicks. It's some of the older adults who spent decades in four walls that must not be able to feel safe in any other place."

"But if the talis are able to reclaim any of them, they could start their breeding system again," Starbright worried.

"Except that they don't need it unless they recapture the Stones. They sacrifice griffins to power the Stones," Hawkwind reviewed darkly. "If they don't have Stones, griffins are nothing more than food to them."

"We must keep the Stones away from them," Starbright said. "It is the lesser of two evils."

"I agree. Why don't you rest, Starbright? I'll wake you if we need you."

The little mage put her head down and sank into almost immediate slumber. Hawkwind stayed on watch at her end of the cave, examining shadows as they approached, although they came less and less. Someone brushed her lightly with a wing. It was Icemoon.

"Rest," the lady griffin told her. "I will watch for a while. You watch the shadows, right?"

"Yes. You must wake everyone up if it looks like a talis," Hawkwind confirmed. "And we can't rest long."

"Just for a while then," she accepted. "Get a few minutes of sleep."

Hawkwind went to lie by her children, who were already asleep, but instinctively shifted to huddle up against her once she nudged them. She closed her eyes and dropped into blissful darkness for a while that was far too short.

Hawkwind awoke with a start as the sound of running feet broke through her slumber. Cries of alarm followed, and then eight little hands were shoving at her, and four voices called, "Hawkwind, Hawkwind, get up."

She surged to her feet, seeing a group of five panting griffins gesturing, "go, go, they're not far behind us."

Hawkwind didn't need to ask whom they meant.

"Wake up," she ordered, "on your feet, go. Swift, Starbright, start running."

Four random and otherwise unburdened Snow-in-lee griffins hopped over to Hawkwind, gesturing that they would volunteer to carry the children. Hawkwind didn't argue, commanding the little humans to get aboard and sending the four griffins after Swift. Everyone was awake now, and the crowd was pushing into the exit of the cave, away from where they'd started, deeper towards the heart of the mountain.

Hawkwind struggled to get to the front of the pack, since she and Starbright had the best chance of finding the right path. She supposed the talis had probably gotten lost in the caves, too, and maybe that had delayed them. Now, they would be able to follow the big group of griffins if they got within sound, sight, or scent of them.

"Starbright," Hawkwind said, "don't drop anymore glowing stones. Everyone hide your glowing stones, if you have one, and follow by touch and sound. No light, so if the talis attack, we can fight them without seeing them."

"What about your Sunstone?" Starbright replied.

"I'll stay at the front of the pack, and hopefully all these griffins will be enough to block the light coming from it. That's the best we can do without something else to wrap around it."

It took time, but all the griffins got moving into the tunnels again, and Hawkwind led them on as fast as she could go. She had to hope that the talis were getting tired and cold and would soon give up. No one spoke. They encountered snow-screamers from time to time and fought them off.

As more hours passed, Hawkwind began to wonder if it would be safe to stop again. She could see that most of the chicks were being carried. Everyone was exhausted again. They had no food and no water, and soon they would be a two-day journey from the cave mouth. Could talis go that long without warmth, water, and food? Hawkwind feared they could.

Finally, at another large cave through which the tunnel ran, Hawkwind called another stop. Everyone collapsed in piles.

"This can't go on," Swift said, coming to Hawkwind's side.

"I know," she agreed. "It's time to stop running."

"Do you think the talis are still back there?"

"I don't know, but it's time we face them if they are."

Swift's jaw muscles bulged as she clenched her bill. "You're right. Let's get it organized."

Hawkwind went to Starbright, who was possibly the most exhausted of them all. The four human children had gathered around her and were petting her.

"Starbright," Hawkwind summoned, "everyone, listen please. It is time to make a stand."

Kassandra got up and began translating with her hands in the faint light of the Sunstone.

"I want all the chicks and fledglings, with Starbright and anyone who is wounded, to go into a small side tunnel. Find a cave. Put the young ones at the back with the Sunstone and Moonstone. Cover up the Sunstone so no light escapes. Wait in silence. Either the talis will find you, and you fight to the death in the darkness, where you can't be entranced, or the rest of us will come and get you when the talis are all dead or fled."

Cold silence met her words, but around the room griffins began nodding.

"Those who can fight, we turn around, we find the talis in the dark tunnels behind us, and we kill them," Hawkwind concluded.

There were more somber nods. Hawkwind waited a few moments in case there were any objections.

"Let's do it, then," she murmured.

With quiet efficiency griffins began moving. Hawkwind transferred the Sunstone to Joy. The most wounded of the griffins began gathering the chicks and fledglings.

"Jessika, Rikah, Karo, Kassandra," Hawkwind whispered to the children, "I need you to go with Joy."

"You take care of us," Jessika argued.

"I am," she replied. "I'm going to save your lives by killing the talis."

"You'll come back," Karo said.

"If I don't, Joy will take care of you."

Hawkwind locked gazes with Joy, and the little female nodded, but Hawkwind's heart wrenched. She was placing her burden onto another young griffin: one even younger than she was. How long could these children be kept alive? Hawkwind forced herself to breathe through the pain before it overtook her.

"I will," Joy promised.

"If I don't come back, and you survive whatever might come from the talis, Starbright will lead you all to South-scree," Hawkwind promised.

On the other side of the cave, Starbright had gathered her group. "We're ready," she called. "Hawkwind, we will bear to the left. Come find us that way."

"You'll hear me calling once it's safe," she said. "Get going."

Starbright didn't look back as she led the children, youngest griffins, and wounded adults away: that left Hawkwind with a couple dozen relatively healthy adults. Among them were the elders that had spoken with Rocksky, Rainsoft's parents and brother, and others that Hawkwind knew or didn't know, that wanted to join Lines or didn't want to. At the moment, they all just wanted to survive.

The last of the light left the cave with Starbright, and the group was plunged into complete darkness. Hawkwind knew which way to turn, and began walking back the way they had come. In the tunnels, her eyes were now useless. She even relaxed enough to close them some of the time. She felt a griffin at her right and at her left with her partly extended wings. Occasionally another one would bump into her tail feathers. She listened. Everyone tried to make their footsteps silent. Talis had to slide their scaled bodies along the ground. Surely that would make noise? Surely the griffins would hear them coming?

They walked for what must have been an hour or two and encountered nothing. Hawkwind hoped they were still on the main tunnel. It had been relatively straight between the previous resting cave and the later one. Hopefully the talis hadn't turned off, such that the griffin fighting force passed them, and then the talis returned to the main tunnel and continued on, only to find the cave of non-fighters.

Hawkwind would have pricked her ears if she could have when the subtle and constant sound of movement came from ahead of her. It wasn't footsteps, and it wasn't the sound of snow-screamers, which tended to snuffle and huff and grunt as they moved, but it wasn't what she'd expected the sound of snake-like bodies sliding over gritty rock to make. She hadn't actually ever stopped to listen to a big snake moving before, though, so she didn't pause to worry too much; she just set her feet, feeling the others stop, too.

The noise wasn't loud, and over soft dirt or a clean floor it probably would have been silent. Like a soft and steady shifting of sand the source of the noise came nearer. Hawkwind's adrenaline kicked up and her heart began pounding. Any moment now it would arrive: whatever was making the noise.

A wave of stench rolled over the griffin fighters and several sharp hisses came from the tunnel ahead. They had met the talis, and somehow the talis knew they were there.

"Fight," Hawkwind screamed, and then the battle began.

She took a hit immediately as a talis bit into her shoulder, almost too near her neck. She bit back, and reared up to rake her claws along its neck and chest. Perhaps the talis hadn't expected such resistance; it let go. Hawkwind didn't let go. She pressed forward with part of it still clamped in her bill. She pushed down, digging the sharp point into scaly flesh, and grabbed it with her hands, pinning it, walking up onto it with her hand claws and leaving puncture wounds all along its body.

Around her, talis and griffin were engaging, and she could see none of it. She began trilling in her throat whenever she could, to give an auditory clue as to where she was, and right away the other griffins began copying her. That told her that a few griffins had passed her and more were behind her.

Hawkwind began trying to back up, dragging her thrashing talis with her. She heard and felt a couple more griffins clamber over her to engage more talis. She was able to pin her prey down and try to get a better grip with her bill. The talis was bigger around than the neck of a deer or anything else she usually killed, even bigger around than a rainbow drake. Its strength was enormous and it took all of Hawkwind's to keep it pinned.

She felt another griffin stumble and bump shoulders with her. The talis screeched with pain, and Hawkwind suspected the other griffin had done something to hurt it. Hawkwind dug her bill deeper and sunk her claws harder, then lifted one hand and began slashing over and over again at the same bit of talis, until she felt the skin shred and blood soak her fur. She kept slashing, making the wound deeper and bigger, carving out flesh, and the talis writhed with greater urgency. It twisted and she felt it bite her forearm, fangs sinking deep.

Hawkwind had been bitten twice now, and a little voice chimed in at the back of her mind, recalling what Thornfire had once said. Talis were slow. They let their venom weaken their prey. Then they follow and collect the prey when it can no longer run or fight. Hawkwind didn't know how long that would take; she would fight hard for as long as she could.

Her claws dug deeper into the wound she'd made, until a sudden spurt of cool blood hit her chest. The talis shuddered. She kept clawing, ripping the wound larger. Within another minute, the beast stopped struggling. Its grip on her forearm loosened, and the head fell away. Around her, griffins were still trilling. The fighting continued. A piece of talis thumped into Hawkwind's side. She turned and fastened her claws upon it. Like before, she began slashing until she'd made a wound, and then she enlarged it.

Fewer griffins were trilling. Fewer talis were hissing.

Then, a blinding light came from the tunnel ahead.

"Close your eyes," ordered Thornwing in a thundering voice, and Hawkwind obeyed before the light could reveal the hypnotic scale patterns of the talis.

Sharp cold pierced her: Thornfire. The talis stopped struggling.

"Catch that one," Thornwing shouted, but no one could open their eyes to do so without getting entranced.

Hawkwind stretched out her arms and wings to try to stop anything from getting past her, but felt nothing. Then someone went flying over her head; she felt tail feathers brush over her face.

"That was Rainsoft," Thornwing spoke. "He's after it. Griffins, if you can move, turn back the way you came and move away from the battle."

Hawkwind tried to turn, unhooking her claws from her latest prey. She limped up the tunnel. Behind her she heard weak hisses and the sound of slitting flesh. Griffins were bumping against her as they moved away.

"You're beyond them, and I've killed them all," Thornwing announced. "Open your eyes."

Hawkwind did so, but her vision swam. She stumbled. The air was still so cold. Her feet had stopped working. She fell to the floor.

"Hawkwind." It was Thornfire this time. "You're bitten. So are others. Hang on."

"I'm dragging the wounded to this point," Thornwing announced.

"We'll do what we can." That was Rocksky's voice.

Hawkwind managed to look up. Rocksky and Thornfire, and a few others were pulling off blindfolds. They immediately turned them into bandages, but there were so many wounds, and so few blindfolds.

"A talis got away?" Hawkwind slurred.

"Just one," Rocksky confirmed. "Rainsoft will catch it."

"The little ones," she mumbled. "Starbright."

"What about Starbright?" came Thornfire's urgent reply.

"She has them," Hawkwind breathed, feeling drained of all energy. "Ahead. Bear left after the big cave."

"I'll go," Thornwing said. "This is the last of the wounded. The rest are beyond help."

Hawkwind tried to sob. Some of her griffins had died.

"We'll come soon," Thornfire told him, and Hawkwind heard Thornwing run off. "Hawkwind, relax."

She felt him put a hand on her belly. "Yes," he murmured. "I'm going to burn the venom out of you. It will hurt. You would be able to endure while your body fights the venom, normally, but it will hurt your chick if I don't purge it now. Bear it."

Hawkwind's heart lurched and she almost managed to open her eyes. Then she felt her body light on fire. It wasn't real fire, of course, but Thornfire's magic ran through her flesh and blood and bone like lightning, and it lit up her every nerve. She would have screamed if she'd had the energy, but all that came from her was a gurgle of agony as her body arched and quivered.

"Don't worry," she heard Thornfire murmur. "The venom works

slowly. It hadn't reached your core yet. It'll be alright."

He could tell? His magic told him everything about what was happening inside her?

"This is life magic," he went on softly. "It is far more powerful than any other, no matter what the dark mages like to believe."

Hawkwind cracked her eyelids enough to look up. Rocksky and two other griffins were standing behind Thornfire with a hand on his back. Thornfire had both his hands on Hawkwind's head. He gave her a little smile while she watched the waves of magic ruffle through his feathers and fur.

"They're giving me energy," he explained calmly. "I ran out of my own yesterday. Is the pain subsiding now?"

Hawkwind found she could breathe more easily. The burning was becoming sullen and dull. "Yes."

"I'm chasing down the last of the venom. I'm almost done."

Hawkwind relaxed further as the life-fire-magic ebbed and faded. Thornfire said she had a chick. She hadn't sensed it herself yet, but she didn't know what she was supposed to feel, and maybe she wouldn't have been able to sense it herself for more days or weeks. At last, the pain in her melted away, except for the physical damage done by the bites themselves.

She opened her eyes again. "What about the others?"

"There are two dead," Rocksky said gently, "here. There are more in the caves behind you, and more wounded. The other wounded ones here are being seen to. Their bodies can handle the venom; it won't kill them."

"I'll check all the awakened females," Thornfire said wearily, "just to be sure."

The mage walked off with one of Rocksky's scouts following him.

"Up you get, Hawkmother," Rocksky urged. "You said there are others in danger."

The shock of hearing she'd conceived was washed away by the

recollection that her human children were still in hiding. If the talis reached them before Thornwing and Rainsoft could take it down, the young and wounded in the hiding cave would fight for their lives, too. Hawkwind pushed herself to her feet. She swayed and Rocksky caught her.

"This way," Hawkwind pointed. "Swift?"

She looked around, not seeing her Linemember. Her breath got stuck. No. Swift couldn't be dead. Hawkwind needed her.

"She's here, Hawkwind," one of the scouts called, and Hawkwind stumbled over. "She got a lot of venom, but she'll be alright."

Swift looked to be unconscious, stretched out on the floor and bloody with bite marks, but her sides still moved.

"Please, watch over her," Hawkwind begged.

The big female stirred. Without opening her eyes she signed, "Joy?"

"I'm going to get her," Hawkwind stated aloud. "Stay here and heal."

Without waiting for a reply, Hawkwind launched herself down the tunnel, careening off the walls and tripping over her own feet. Rocksky and another scout followed. Rocksky was carrying a glow-stone, so Hawkwind's shadow stretched out black in front of her. She couldn't keep up the running for long, but she pushed herself as hard as she could, only ever slowing to a fast walk to catch her breath. Even wounded, she made better time back to the second rest cave than her fighting group had going out to meet the talis.

From there, she began taking left turns, as Starbright had said she would.

"We could meet the talis at any moment," Hawkwind panted. "Starbright said she would take her group of chicks and the wounded as far left as possible and hole up in a tiny cave where they can defend the entrance. There's no way to know which way the talis went, or where Thornwing and Rainsoft went."

She continued bearing left, always left: only checking right hand passages visually in case there was any sign of talis or other griffins.

Then they heard the screaming fledglings. Hawkwind sprinted ahead and the others followed, making their shadows bob and jerk all over the walls, floor, and ceiling as Rocksky's glow-stone bounced about as she tried to get it into a pouch. They rounded a corner, and another, and then the scene came into view as frigid air bit into their lungs and exposed skin.

The trio skidded to a halt in the near darkness and Hawkwind could barely see what was going on, just the shapes of the creatures before her in the trickle of Sunstone light that escaped from the cave. Starbright was bleeding onto the floor from where the talis had her in its jaws, but her claws were sunk into whatever bit of it she could reach, and her face was tightly shut against seeing it. It was thrashing, but more and more slowly. Hawkwind lunged forward and sunk her claws into it, too, but they didn't go in easily. Frost and then ice was condensing on its body, and it slowed, and slowed, until it keeled over, taking Starbright with it onto the floor slick with ice.

"It's frozen," Hawkwind called out, and Rocksky pulled out her glow-stone just in time for Hawkwind to watch as Starbright froze even its eyeballs solid.

The coating of ice hid enough of its scale patterns that Hawkwind wasn't hypnotized. Her work finished, Starbright relaxed and released her hold on the beast. Then she cried out, and Hawkwind hurried to try to pry the frozen creature's jaws off of her. Rocksky leapt forward to help, too.

"That was the last talis," the commander said over her shoulder, to her scout. "Go find Rainsoft and Thornwing. They'll be in these caves somewhere."

Rocksky handed the other griffin the glow-stone. One of the older young griffins jumped out of the hiding cave and gestured, "I'll go with you, for protection."

"He says he's going with you," Hawkwind translated.

No one argued, and the scout and the volunteer dashed away.

"Uncover the Sunstone," Hawkwind commanded, and in a moment light poured from the cave mouth.

They got the frozen jaws off from around Starbright's chest and shoulder. She was bleeding, but not so badly that Hawkwind thought her life was in danger, except for the venom that must have been in her. The four human children piled out of the cave and ran to crouch by Starbright. They fastened their little hands over the bleeding punctures as the young mage shuddered and groaned.

"Joy," Hawkwind called, and her other Linemember stepped forward. "Your mother is alive," she said. "Go back to the cave where we rested, and then down the tunnel we came from before that. You will find the others and Thornfire. Tell them what happened. Tell them that Starbright is hurt."

"I will," Joy signed back.

Now Hawkwind began to hear the calls of griffin voices echoing through the tunnels. Soon enough the scout, the volunteer, Thornwing, and Rainsoft arrived at the hiding cave.

"The last talis," Thornwing sighed. "It's frozen?"

"Starbright did it," Hawkwind explained, "but she got bit."

Hawkwind, with Thornwing and Rocksky—Rainsoft stood watch—tended to Starbright as well as they could until Thornfire came running down the tunnel to them, with another of Rocksky's scouts: Skymist.

Hawkwind was finally able to step away and collapse as Rocksky and her scouts stood and gave more energy to Thornfire, enough that he could ensure that Starbright would live. When he was done, he, too, fell to the ground beside his daughter-apprentice, curling himself protectively around her. Hawkwind closed her eyes and the world went dark.

Chapter 31
Return to South-scree

The Sunstone was back in place, and it lit up the Hawk cave. Hawkwind blinked against its light, aware that she was awake. She was lying on the patch of sand. Thornfire and Starbright were there, too. Starbright was sleeping, but Thornfire was awake, writing on a thick piece of parchment with an ink quill made from someone's feather.

"Ah, welcome back, Hawkmother," he murmured. "You've been asleep for two days."

Hawkwind's mouth was drier than the sand she lay on. She tried to speak but couldn't even croak. Thornfire looked to the side, at someone out of her range of vision. Skymist walked over to crouch in front of her. She was holding a water skin.

"You'll want some of this," the grey griffin smiled.

With Skymist's help, Hawkwind sat up and drank, and as soon as the liquid hit her insides she felt remarkably better.

"I'll tell the others and they'll bring you food," Skymist said.

Before Hawkwind could protest that she was fine—although she wasn't—Skymist dashed for the door and was gone.

"The total is twenty-seven dead," Thornfire reported without preamble. "Many more are recovering from wounds. You may be saddened to hear that Rainsoft's father died in the attack. He was among the group that went with you to fight. The other of your group that died was a female called Skyblack. The other deaths were mainly among the confused ones who refused to run or fight. Unfortunately, a few of those were chicks and fledglings following their confused parents' lead."

Hawkwind didn't respond. It seemed that she couldn't feel anything; her whole insides were numb.

"It could have been much worse," Thornfire soothed. "You did well in making choices under pressure."

Just then, Rainsoft and Thornwing both came into the room with chunks of meat. Hawkwind accepted hungrily. Thornwing's pet Ferrie scampered down off of Thornwing's back, and darted up to Hawkwind. He extended his arms, holding out a large beetle. Thornwing made some gurgling noises at him and he chattered back.

"I'm trying to tell him that griffins don't eat beetles," Thornwing explained, "but he really seems to want to give it to you. I think he likes you and is happy you're safe."

"I'm happy he's safe, too," Hawkwind murmured.

"I told him to hide when the talis came."

Hawkwind opened her bill and let Ferrie set the wiggling beetle on her tongue. The mountain-ferret looked inordinately pleased when she gamely swallowed it, and ran back up Thornwing's foreleg, chattering all the way. The two males stayed a moment longer to affectionately preen her feathers, and then ran off again, presumably to bring more meat.

"I did not tell anyone what I detected," Thornfire said softly, "although Rocksky and the scouts with her at the time may have heard. They have no reason to speak of it. Thornwing and Rainsoft do not know, to my knowledge."

He meant the knowledge that she was carrying a chick. Hawkwind gave him a nod.

"Congratulations," Thornfire told her with a little smile. "There will soon be no one that can rightfully deny the existence of your Line."

Thornwing and Rainsoft came in again with more mouthfuls, and left again once Hawkwind had accepted them.

"Rocksky took one scout and left to report to South-scree what has happened here," Thornfire went on.

"Do you think that's wise?" Hawkwind spoke to him for the first time since waking up.

"Commander Rocksky is on our side," the mage assured her. "She will report the facts. The final decision is not in her hands at any rate.

Once we are well, we will move ourselves closer to South-scree, to a safe place, and a delegation including yourself will go to South-scree, and we shall see what will come of all this."

Starbright groaned and shuddered. Thornfire placed a gentle hand on his apprentice's back, and in a few moments the young female opened her eyes.

"Water magic, Bright?" Thornfire chortled, eyes brimming with pride. "You used water magic on that talis, and the results reinforced what I always knew: you can master every element you put your mind to. Once you're healthy, I'll begin teaching you how to blend magic."

Starbright trilled like a little chick and closed her eyes again. "It fought back, Master, with its own water magic," she mumbled. "I felt it, but I had to overcome it. I had to stop it, and it bit me, but I won."

"You did win, and you saved all those chicks. Your bite has been taken care of. You'll be fine, and you'll be a fine mage," he murmured, stroking her head.

Skymist came back into the cave with a fresh water skin for Starbright. Hawkwind curled back up, feeling wounds pinch and twist but not break open. Swift and Joy were next to visit; the word of Hawkwind's recovery must have been passed on. Her Linemembers sat on either side of her, preening her battered feathers.

A few minutes later, Hawkwind's human children came running into the room, calling her name, and restrained themselves from jumping on her with happiness. They cuddled up with her, and Hawkwind tucked them under her wings: Jessika with her golden tattooed wings, Rikah with his cooking knife, Kassandra with her strange little pink forehead bump, and Karolan with his magical potential. Hawkwind tenderly nibbled their ears with her bill, making them all giggle. Perhaps now she would have the power to make them a home where they could be warm and safe.

Two weeks had passed. The Snow-in-lee griffins had moved to the other side of the mountains, closer to South-scree, by flying, not navigating the long and dangerous path through the tunnels. Everyone who could recover had. The new settlement was divided into two sections and located in another series of caves. In one section were the griffins who wanted to join Lines or start Lines of their own. The other section was made up of the separatist griffins, who wanted nothing to do with the griffin society of the Aeries. Most of the confused ones had died in the talis attack. A few remaining confused ones had just left one day and no one knew where they'd gone. A few more confused ones had finally accepted their situation and chosen a side.

As for the orphaned chicks of confused ones, Thornfire had exerted himself, and simply taken them away from any separatist griffin that had wanted to raise them, not that there had been many, as they were more focused on their own family unit. He'd found homes for the chicks with griffins of their own Line among the Snow-in-lee griffins who wanted to be in Lines. Of course, even though the Line griffins felt the best thing for all the chicks would be to join Lines, they hadn't tried to take any chicks born of the separatist griffins. They would learn in time.

Now, Hawkwind stood before the South-scree council again, without any restraints this time. Rainsoft, Thornfire, Thornwing, Starbright, Hawkswift, Rocksky, Stormstone, and Windnight were with her. Icemoon and a few other elders had remained at the settlement to keep an eye on things. Joy had come also, but she was waiting outside the council chamber with Jessika and the other children. Hawkwind and Rainsoft were both carrying what they had been tasked to bring back: the Sunstone and the Moonstone.

Eldest Skycall was looking off-balance.

"So you see the situation, Eldest," Thornfire was saying. "We have accomplished what we set out to do, as well as potentially unseated the talis from Snow-in-lee, and saved a great number of our people."

He'd spent the last half hour recounting the basics of what had happened since he had left South-scree with his party of four griffins and four humans. Of course, some things that everyone didn't need to know had been left out.

"We bring our news here," Thornfire went on, "to put the situation before the council. There are many griffins that need homes, and others still that do not want homes with us."

Skycall straightened. "We'll have nothing to do with—"

"Fire, we cannot make a decision for all the Aeries," Thornmother interrupted, "as we all know."

"An all-Aerie meeting must be called," agreed another matriarch whose name Hawkwind didn't know. "That is the clear path, before any decision can be made."

The gathered matriarchs and elders chimed their agreement. Hawkwind thought Skycall might have ground her bill a little, but she did not object. "Then we shall send out messages at once, and an all-Aerie meeting will be arranged."

"Until then I ask for asylum for the freed Snow-in-lee griffins," Thornfire said smoothly. "They are, technically, beyond the borders of South-scree. I will ensure that they watch the prey animal population."

"And what of chicks?" Skycall challenged. She suddenly pointed her wing down at Hawkwind. "That one has awakened and could kindle at any moment, maybe already has."

Muttering fluttered around the room. Hawkwind could sense it now, and had been able to for a few days. There was new life in her, and it would cement the legitimacy of her Line. She forced herself not to bristle at Skycall.

"We can all tell, Eldest," said one of the other matriarchs, "and there's nothing to be done."

"We'll not be adjusting our quota because of this," Skycall retorted. "And any griffins not of South-scree will not be tolerated hunting in our territory."

"If South-scree agrees not to have the compassion to take in griffins who have suffered much and have no home, you'll not be forced to, by my estimation," Thornfire spoke firmly. "You'll also do without the honor of taking in Lines that have been absent from our society for generations. The Hawk, Eagle, Ice, and Snow Lines, once thought gone forever, or perhaps merely a myth, are back. Reject them if you will, but they are here. If South-scree does not take them in, some other Aerie will, and that Aerie will have the benefit of its blood being strengthened by them."

There was more muttering.

"Eldest Skycall," Hawkwind put in, "you told me if I brought back the Sunstone my place in South-scree would be considered, and likewise for Rainsoft. We have the Stones. You see them. What say you now?"

Thornmother stood up. "It is thanks to Hawkwind and Rainsoft that Wing has returned." She spread out a hand. "We are not overpopulated here, and indeed for several years now the mothers have been unable to make the quota of chicks the council seems to think we need. Eldest Skycall, we have the space."

"You propose adding a Line to our Aerie?" Skycall retorted, bill open with astonishment. "There are only five seating sections in here."

"That's your excuse?" another matriarch scoffed.

"Perhaps younger mothers would do better at meeting the quota," Skycall said next, ignoring the accusation.

"Excellent," one of the other matriarchs smiled. She pointed at Hawkwind. "Here we have quite a young mother. Surely she will be able to help."

A few griffins chuckled.

"I call for a vote," someone shouted out.

"Wait, what about Rainsoft?" Hawkwind interrupted. "What's the fifth Line here? I know about the Thorn, Star, Sky, and Rock Lines, but I've never been told what the fifth is. Is it the Rain Line?"

"I'm afraid not," said Thornmother. "It is the Water Line." She nodded towards one of the sections of the seating. "However, I would be more than happy to adopt Rainsoft into the Thorn Line, if he wishes it."

All eyes turned to the charcoal grey griffin. He lifted his hands to begin speaking.

"Rainsoft cannot speak aloud," Hawkwind explained. "All griffins held prisoner in Snow-in-lee were injured by the talis as chicks. The talis destroyed their vocal cords."

Rainsoft lifted his head so his feathers parted on his throat, showing the scar.

"I can translate for him," Hawkwind concluded.

"Rainsoft, is that acceptable to you?" Thornmother asked. "Nod for yes?"

Rainsoft nodded and began speaking. Hawkwind spoke aloud for him.

"I appreciate your kindness, Thornmother. If I were alone, I would accept at once, but I have a little sister, and a mother. They both are asleep, so there is no problem there yet," Hawkwind explained for him, noting to herself that he did not mention his brother and his brother's mate. They had joined the separatists. "We have decided that we would like to stay together."

"I see," Thornmother said. "Are you considering seeking out the Rain Line in the Aeries and asking to join? I will tell you that the Rain Line is a part of the Aerie called In-the-wind. I can send a special request there. I do not know the Rainmother personally, and the Aerie is a two day journey from here, but I will do all I can for you, if that is your desire."

"Thornmother," Hawkwind added. "I, too, have volunteered to adopt Rainsoft, his mother, and sister into the Hawk Line."

"You are hardly a Line and already think you can adopt others?" Skycall interrupted.

Grumbles came from the assembled griffins.

"Eldest Skycall," sang out the matriarch Thornmother had identified as Watermother, "I see the tides of this council turning against your voice."

Thornwing shifted nervously beside Hawkwind. "Hold onto your feathers," he whispered.

The hall fell silent. Skycall wasn't gaping, but rather scowling.

"I call for a vote," one of the other matriarchs stated, crest lifted.

The matriarchs looked between themselves and even down at Hawkwind: who could only look back with genuine puzzlement.

"I second," a different matriarch said.

"A vote it shall be," Thornmother confirmed, when Skycall said nothing.

The mothers turned to their elders and began speaking quickly and quietly. Thornfire flew up to join Thornmother.

"Hawkwind," Thornwing said flatly, "the matriarchs are going to vote out Skycall and put in a new Eldest. They might ask for your vote; they seem to like you. You'll need a yea or nay vote for Skycall. To vote, you'll be offered a basket of white and black stones. A white stone is yea; a black stone is nay. You reach in and secretly select your stone. Keep it hidden in your hand. Then, you drop it in a box that will be brought to you. A majority of white stones means Skycall stays. A majority of black stones unseats her."

"I understand," Hawkwind whispered nervously.

"If Skycall is unseated, a new Eldest will be elected. That won't happen today. Today, each Line will nominate one of its elders. Everyone will get to think about who they want and voting will happen tomorrow."

"What exactly does the Eldest do?" Hawkwind asked.

"The Eldest doesn't technically have any extra power to make decisions that regular Elders don't have, and in a way, he or she has less, although Skycall has been known to abuse her position," Thornwing explained. "The Eldest is required to help moderate discussions and remind griffins of any laws they might have forgotten in their passion. The Eldest needs a thorough understanding and knowledge of all our Words. He or she acts like an encyclopedia of them, ready to recite any bit of them needed at any time."

"What are the Words? I remember Thornfire mentioning them before."

"They are a combination of our history, our laws, our beliefs, and our ethics, that we in South-scree try to live by," Thornwing told her. "The other Aeries have similar Words, but some minor differences. Wherever your Line is accepted, you will need to read and learn the Words of that Aerie."

"I think I understand."

One by one, the matriarchs were returning to their position at the head of their seating section. Once all had returned, one said, "I think it is time for the stones?"

Someone fetched a basket and someone else a box. The basket and box were carried around to the matriarchs who voted just as Thornwing had said they would. Thornmother looked briefly at Hawkwind, but no one suggested bringing the box to her. The box was taken to Skycall, who removed the stones one at a time. They were all black. Hawkwind was a little surprised; even Skymother had voted out her own Linemember. Skycall seemed even more shocked.

After gaping at the room for a few breaths, she seemed to gather what little dignity she had left. "I will step down," she said to the room, and then did just that, leaving her collar of office on the podium and gliding down to the council hall floor. She looked straight ahead, although Hawkwind had half expected her to glare at her.

The matriarchs all stood ready at the front of their sections. They looked to their right to the matriarch farthest from Hawkwind. That one nodded.

"The Star Line nominates Starkind," she said. Hawkwind sought out the elder who had straightened to attention at those words. So that was Starkind, Starbright's mother according to Thornfire and his good friend. She was something of a tarnished gold in color, with darker wings and lighter feet.

The next matriarch nodded. "The Rock Line nominates Rocktall."

"The Thorn Line nominates Thornfire."

"The Sky Line nominates Skywhite."

"The Water Line nominates Watercloud."

Only after all the names were announced did muttering and soft comments run around the gathered griffins.

"Until tomorrow, when a new Eldest is chosen, we will adjourn, in accordance with the Words," Thornmother said, and all the other matriarchs nodded in agreement.

"We'll have to come back," Thornwing shrugged.

"Are you happy?" Hawkwind asked him. "Your brother might become the Eldest."

"That would be a mixed blessing," he said frankly, as they turned towards the exit. "Thornfire's time needs to be devoted to his apprentice, to training future mages of our Aerie. He'll also need to devote time to studying the Stones and those drake collars you got."

"And what would the benefits be?"

"Status. Being the ranking mage already, and then becoming the Eldest would put him with nearly as much status as a matriarch. With that status would come power and influence."

Hawkwind and the others passed out of the council hall, joining up with Joy and the children, and Thornwing led them back to Thornfire's home. His own home had been uninhabited for years now and was in need of repair and cleaning. For the time being the group was squishing themselves into Thornfire's domicile, except for Rocksky who had her own home to go to. Hawkwind figured it was also likely that Starbright would go stay with another Linemember, to make more room in her master's house, but for now she went with the others.

They snuggled in, almost shoulder-to-shoulder, and Hawkwind

set the Sunstone into the fireplace for safety. Ferrie ran out from where he'd been hiding among Thornwing's feathers and curled up by the Sunstone to nap.

"What happened?" Rikah demanded.

"Can we stay?" Jessika asked, the two younger children nodding beside her.

"We don't know yet," Hawkwind answered them. "What do you think will happen, Rocksky? Thornwing?"

"Elder Thornfire is well-liked by most," Rocksky answered, "but there are others who would question passing him so much power in addition to what he carries already. He is also considered a radical by certain griffins," she said this last with a sheepish grunt.

Hawkwind knew that Rocksky and Thornfire rarely saw eye-to-eye on matters of policy.

"I believe he would make a good Moderator," the commander went on, "but Thornwing made some excellent points, and I think many others will see them, too. It would be a controversial appointment. The only thing that might swing it in his favor is that he has brought us the Stones, and potentially regained us Snow-in-lee."

"I wouldn't go that far," Thornwing argued. "We may have taken the Stones, the Snow-in-lee griffin prisoners, and killed many talis, but they will not give up the city. There was always a natural spring there, just a smaller one. The talis will stay."

"It's also Thornfire's fault that we have this new problem—all these Snow-in-lee griffins that need homes," Rocksky went on. "Some will dislike him for that." She shook her head. "As much as some may like it, I don't think he will be elected."

Thornwing was nodding. "You are probably right. Who then?"

Rocksky went silent to think, only looking up when she'd made a choice. "Thornfire, we can agree, is out of the running. The same Line almost never holds the seat of Moderator twice in a row and Skymother knows it, so she nominated Skywhite, who is unremarkable enough that she won't draw votes from other candidates. Watercloud is a steady, gentle griffin, but too gentle for a time when an all-Aerie meeting is about to be called. That leaves Rocktall and Starkind. There it is a hard choice. Tall is one of the youngest elders. He is fit and strong and would bring a solid presence to the all-Aerie meeting, but I am thinking the matriarchs will want someone more like them, and more likely to follow their direction, more predictable. For that, I think Starkind will be victorious. She is past her years as Starmother, but still sound of mind and not so old that she will appear weak."

Starbright perked up and ventured to speak. "Starkind-mother is smart and fair. I think she'd be a good choice."

"Then you know where to cast your vote," Rocksky nodded at her. "I should go now, and hear what the Rock elders have to say about it. I'll see you all tomorrow."

The rest of the group gestured or said their good nights and Rocksky took her leave, making a bit more space in the room.

"Everyone in the Aerie votes for the Eldest?" Hawkwind clarified. "Not just elders and matriarchs?"

"All fledged Linemembers may vote," Thornwing confirmed. "Most will vote the way their matriarch and elders council them to. Depending on the Line, the matriarch may be more or less firm about whom the vote for. As you have just observed, it is not always—in fact not even usually—the case that Linemembers vote for the candidate from their own Line; the situation is often more complicated than that."

"You will vote, too?"

"I'll vote with the others, in the morning."

"And whom will you vote for?" Jessika asked.

"I will probably cast my vote for Starkind," he shrugged, "but I'll sleep on it. Many griffins will discuss it with an elder in formal or informal meetings, but I was there, I heard the announcing of the candidates myself, and I am known for keeping my own counsel."

"So Thornfire won't be back for a while? He'll be in meetings with Linemembers?" Hawkwind guessed.

"Probably. We should go ahead with getting a meal ready and settling sleeping arrangements."

Starbright took herself off to find a spot to sleep with a Star Linemember and offered her room to Hawkwind's children, as it would be more comfortable than the floor. They accepted, and that meant Hawkwind would get the room, too. Thornwing announced that he would make his brother share his room with him. That left five adult griffins to share the main room, which would be snug but not impossible. The remaining group set about organizing their accommodations.

Chapter 32
The Thornmother

As Hawkwind retreated to Starbright's room with the children she felt a slight sense of relief. Starbright's nest of worn leather and canvas cushions stuffed with plant fibers would be far more comfortable than the floor. The children started claiming cushions and Hawkwind let them; they soon enough tired of it and ran back into the living room. She lay down for a few moments. She wasn't tired, and didn't know if she should be. Swift knew of course, but hadn't given her any precautions yet—

"So."

Hawkwind startled. Thornwing had come through the door. He let the leather curtain fall down behind him.

"You're going to be Hawkmother, aren't you?" he said, voice low so his words wouldn't carry beyond them. "You haven't told anyone?"

"Everyone will be able to tell, eventually, by scent?" she asked. "I'm not sure. I've never really paid attention."

"Unawakened females won't know, and won't care. Other matriarchs might be able to tell; I've never really asked. Males will just know you're awake but not in heat. Of course, everyone will know once you start showing. I only know now because I know when you last, uh, and we," he trailed off.

"Yes," she admitted. "Thornfire could tell, with his magic. After I was bit by talis, he burned the venom out of me, after he checked, and said there was—that I—"

Thornwing leaned forward and preened her neck feathers. "I'm happy," he said simply, through a mouth of feathers. "Are you happy?"

"Sort of," she whispered. "I won't rest easy until I have a place for my Line. Then I will probably be happy."

"If you tell the matriarchs, they will be more inclined to help you, and more forced to help you, which would be good and bad; they don't like having their hands forced."

"I thought about that."

"I can tell Thornmother for you." He stopped nibbling her feathers and sat back. "If we knew I was the sire, I could tell her that, too, and she'd be even more inclined."

"I can't tell. I don't know who," she paused and took a breath, "but there are two."

He tilted his head at her. "Two?"

"Two chicks," she managed. "I can feel two. I just know there are two, but I don't think Thornfire could tell."

Thornwing's bill had dropped open a little. "It, it's not unheard of," he stuttered. "That explains," he went on in a soft whisper, "why I thought maybe there had been two chick-pains. Now you know what it feels like, you should only let there be one. Twins are difficult, I've heard."

"Difficult?" Hawkwind repeated, hackles rising slightly with concern.

"Don't worry," he hurried to reassure her, "not fatal or anything. The chicks just might be early, and small, and the birth could be complicated, but with Linegrandmothers to help, and a mage or two just in case, it will be fine."

"We never had mages at Northnest," Hawkwind reflected, "but I suppose the Linegrandmothers helped. I don't remember there being any twins at the castle."

"Because they're rare," Thornwing nodded. "It's usually an accident. I guess it was sort of an accident this time."

"I didn't have a Linegrandmother to advise me. I hadn't asked Swift anything."

"Does she know?" Thornwing asked.

"She knows I'm pregnant. I haven't told anyone there's two yet, except you."

He preened her neck ruff again, briefly. "Hawkwind, my loyalty is to my Line, but I still want to help you, at least until your Line is established, and you're safe, and you have enough Linemembers to keep you safe." He shuffled his feet against the floor. "Plus, you saved my life, freed me, and it might be that we made a chick or two together."

"I wouldn't have these chicks if it weren't for you," she admitted.

"You'd have gotten some eventually, just not yet," he assured her.

"I suppose."

"So, should I say anything to anyone?"

Hawkwind shook her head. "No, but thank you. I'll tell people as I want to."

Rikah suddenly burst into the room, throwing the curtain aside with boyish enthusiasm. "Hawkwind," he panted. "There's someone here to see you, a big griffin."

Thornwing spun and slipped smoothly past the boy.

"Thank you, Rikah," Hawkwind told him, and followed in Thornwing's wake.

The Snow-in-lee griffins had crammed themselves into one corner together and were engaged in mutual preening while chatting fluidly with their hands. Hawkwind took a brief moment to realize how convenient that was. They could keep talking even while their bills were in use. The children had plopped down next to the hearth where the Sunstone was warming them, with laps full of fabric, following Jessika's directions in sewing more clothing, but taking frequent breaks to pet Ferrie.

Thornwing was showing in a large female griffin, with much head bobbing, his feathers slicked flat in subservience. Hawkwind recognized her, although she hadn't seen her up close before.

"Welcome, Thornmother," Thornwing was saying. "May I present: Hawkmother."

"I thought as much," the matriarch said with a smile. "You really were the last of your Line."

Thornmother was a dark chocolate brown with a white underside dusted with gold. The golden color was in her flight feathers, too, and her upper coverts were black. She had a black crown and eye-stripe, as well. She was also nearly double Hawkwind's size. Daintily, she found a scrap of empty floor, and sat. From there, she eyed Hawkwind.

"So, I'll be blunt. Do you have a chick yet?" she asked.

Behind Thornmother, Thornwing twitched.

"Yes," Hawkwind admitted.

The matriarch's sharp bill swung like a compass needle to the male behind her. "Yours, Wing?"

"Maybe," Hawkwind said, before he could speak. "I don't know whose."

"You're a quick one," Thornmother remarked.

Rainsoft had also twitched at Hawkwind's admittance, and his gaze was now steady on her. The Thornmother noticed.

"Or yours? Rainsoft, aren't you? From Snow-in-lee?"

He bowed his head with somber assent.

"You are correct," Hawkwind said, calling the attention back to herself. "I don't know whose. Either or both could be the sires."

"Both?" The matriarch's feathers flicked with surprise.

"Twins," Hawkwind confirmed.

For a long moment Thornmother stared at her, and she stared back. "Your manner may be modest, but I see more behind it. I want you for South-scree. Will you stay?"

"If I am granted permission to stay, I will stay," Hawkwind agreed.

"Understand; this settlement has as many problems as any city. Not every griffin is kind and understanding. Not every griffin will welcome a new Line. There are even griffins here who disobey the Words, and the council deals with them."

"Whenever people live together, there will be difficulties," Hawkwind responded, lifting her bill. "It was so at Northnest. There were troublemakers, even an occasional evildoer. That is the way of society."

"We understand each other," Thornmother nodded. "We work

THORNMOTHER

hard: the council, the matriarchs, the elders, and the Eldest. You will join us in that?"

"I will do my best. I have a lot to learn. I am young."

"We will help you, if you do as you say, and do your best."

Hawkwind struggled internally against the fragile flutter of hopeful butterfly wings.

"I can't guarantee anything," Thornmother said swiftly, as if able to see inside her to that delicate glimmer of relief. "Tomorrow we will count the votes for a new Eldest and then I will bring the matter to the council. It may be that we can agree to induct you right away, but others may want to wait for the all-Aerie meeting, and settle the matter of all the new griffins at once. Messengers have been sent off to the other Aeries. It will take weeks to organize the all-Aerie meeting. Until then, you would have to return to your caves in the mountain, where the rest of the Snow-in-lee griffins currently reside."

"I understand," Hawkwind was quick to assure her.

"Good." The Thornmother got to her feet. "I once had twins. I was young and stupid and trying to fulfill the quota. I vowed to never do it again, and listen to my Linegrandmothers, whatever the quota might say. Expect to be very uncomfortable before the end, and I was larger than you at the time."

The matriarch laughed. "That's why I'm only doing one this time, again." She patted her own belly, and then reached out to put a hand on Hawkwind's head. "I know you have friends and even a couple Linemembers to help you, but if you need anything, you can come to me."

The frail little butterfly fluttering in Hawkwind's chest almost turned into drips of teary relief, but she held onto her composure. The Thornmother looked over at the four children. After the novelty of a new griffin in the room had worn off, they'd returned to their sewing, happily ignorant of the adults' conversation.

"Most curious creatures," the Thornmother murmured. "They will be living with you?"

"They are in my charge. I have sworn to protect them," Hawkwind answered levelly.

"Fear not. I won't try to take them from you," she promised. "You should make them Linemembers, so they have legitimacy."

"Even though they are human, not griffin?"

"There is nothing in the Words that say all Linemembers must be griffins," the matriarch shrugged.

Hawkwind stared at her.

"So, you're a Linemother, as long as the Eldest does not object—and he or she will have no legitimate reason to—you can bring them into your Line. Do that, and no one can question their presence here, and they'll have full rights, but please, Hawkmother, do not add to them."

"I won't," Hawkwind agreed. "Thank you for that information."

"I should be on my way. There are still members of my Line I haven't spoken with." She turned to go and paused before Thornwing. "You've already made up your mind about the voting, I presume, Wing?"

"As always I am eager to hear your guidance, Mother," Thornwing bowed immediately.

"Cheeky. Not that what I say will matter to you, but I am counseling voting for Starkind."

"I came to the same conclusion."

"Luckily, and even if you voted for someone else, I wouldn't know, so do as you like."

He bowed lower.

"And thank you for establishing a connection between the Thorn Line and the Hawk Line."

He shook his head. "Thank the Hawkmother for taking pity on me."

Hawkwind almost laughed. Thornmother looked over and shared a wry glance with her.

"He is charming, isn't he?"

"In a slightly arrogant and annoying way," Hawkwind said. "I do owe a great debt to the Thorn Line, for the assistance of both Elder

Thornfire and Thornwing."

"Don't go around proclaiming debt like that to anyone," the matriarch countered. "As a Linemother, you can't afford to admit debt any time except for when you're backed into a corner and have no other choice. Considering that Fire took advantage of your situation to manipulate you into going with him on a fool's errand that returned to us a missing Thornson, and that the Thorn Line has gained both a link of alliance with and the status of being the favorite of the Hawk Line due to Wing's actions, I'd say we're equal. We don't owe each other anything yet. Let's try to keep it that way, and not take on debts that aren't there."

Hawkwind winced, chastised. "I understand. I am still learning—"

"And I'm trying to teach you. I am a most impatient teacher."

"Rather like Fire," Thornwing commented with a snicker.

"You could try listening, for a change, too," the Thornmother scolded. "I'll go now. See you tomorrow in the council hall."

"Thank you," Hawkwind called after her as she left.

As Thornwing's back was turned as he watched the Thornmother leave, Hawkwind saw Rainsoft gesture rapidly: "you said I was your favorite."

Hawkwind gestured back: "she said it, not me. You are."

And as she looked at him, at his serious orange eyes with sincerity shining soft like moon glow from them, tension melted from her, and she knew she hadn't lied. Thornwing was indeed charming and useful, but Rainsoft was special and important. She still didn't know what would become of him. Would he go to join the Rain Line at In-the-wind? Would he and his sister be willing to become Hawks instead? What of his mother?

As the group settled down for the evening—with Thornwing slipping out to go fetch food—Hawkwind found herself stuck in pondering possibilities, which stayed with her and followed her into her dreams that night.

Ice-peak had been chosen as the site for the all-Aerie meeting. Every matriarch from every Aerie with the exception of a few who were too pregnant to make the journey and had sent Linegrandmothers instead, each with an elder, and the Eldest from every Aerie had arrived and been accommodated. Hawkwind and Swift, with Jessika along, had also come to Ice-peak. Rainsoft and Windnight had been chosen to represent the Snow-in-lee griffins. They had asked Jessika to be their translator.

Young though she was, she was more skilled at their language than anyone except Kassandra, and Kassandra had been judged too shy to stand up and talk confidently in a room full of strange griffins. Hawkwind hoped they'd made the right choice; Jessika, too, might be too intimidated. Regardless, she'd felt that Jessika, as the largely unknown princess of Northnest, most deserved to be there, of the four children. Giving the Snow-in-lee griffins a non-griffin translator who was not officially part of a Line had been a move to indicate impartiality.

The morning of the all-Aerie meeting dawned cold and crisp like fresh ice on a pond. Ice-peak's council hall was filled to capacity. Each Linemother had a prominent seat, with her elder beside her, grouped around the Aerie's Eldest. Hawkwind—who had not been officially taken on by South-scree because the council as a whole had wanted to wait—with the Snow-in-lee delegation were seated centrally, as they were the whole reason for the meeting.

Thornmother had brought Thornfire with her, for obvious reasons. Thornwing had been left behind; there just hadn't been room for him in the delegations, according to the regulations. Starkind had been elected Eldest, as predicted, and sat at the head of the South-scree group. Most of the griffins were staring curiously at the Snow-in-lee group: perhaps mostly at Jessika; none of them had seen a human before. The girl was wrapped in layers of fur to keep her warm, but her head and hands were still clearly visible and strange to the griffins.

There was no single moderator for the meeting. The Eldest griffins were all expected to work together to maintain order, but Thornmother had said it was likely the Ice-peak Eldest—as the host—would be the most vocal. Now that everyone was seated, they were looking between each other, judging when to start the meeting. Slowly, the volume of conversation in the room decreased. Almost as one, the Eldest griffins each raised a wing straight up, attracting attention and signaling for quiet. The last of the talking faded and died away and the Eldest griffins lowered their wings.

Starkind stood up. "South-scree has called this meeting," she began. "Everyone has agreed to it. Ice-peak has graciously hosted it. South-scree thanks you all for your efforts to make this meeting happen."

She paused and many griffins gave small nods of acknowledgment.

"You have all been told, briefly, what this is about. Please allow South-scree to give you all the details of the extraordinary events that have brought us here."

After some curt muttering, each Eldest griffin lifted both wings straight up and open, showing all their wing feathers forward. Hawkwind assumed that was a signal for yes, and Starkind nodded, lifting her wings the same way. Then she began to speak.

Clearly, Thornfire had told her almost everything about their journey, and Starkind must have spent copious time memorizing it all. She spoke with a strong, clear voice, without dramatizing anything. Hawkwind listened as she recounted the past when Thornwing went missing. She told of Thornfire's hopeless efforts to get a rescue party from his own Aerie—which got some indistinct muttering from the crowd in return. Next, she spoke of Rainsoft's discovery near the Aerie, and then Hawkwind's, and the eyes of many griffins turned onto each of them. When Starkind explained about the human children, it was Jessika's turn to endure the stares, but she smiled and waved at everyone, getting some chuckles and even croons of delight in return.

Starkind went on to tell of the bargain the disgraced Skycall made with Thornfire and his party. From there she recounted the journey Thornfire's group made, through the mountains, to the camp near Snow-in-lee. Hawkwind tried her hardest not to blush as Starkind mentioned—in the simplest and most straightforward way possible—how Hawkwind awoke, and how it was evidence that she really was the last of her Line. Rainsoft's history also had to be explained, because it was relevant to how the party approached Snow-in-lee.

By the time Starkind was describing the exploration of Snow-in-lee, the theft of the Stones, and the fight to free the prisoners, the whole room was hanging on her every word. Coos of relief and astonishment filled the air when Starkind told of how the prisoners escaped to the safety of the camp. After that, Starkind had to tell how the group of griffins moved to the caves, began to learn how to communicate and hunt and fly, and then how they were attacked by a group of talis trying to recapture the Stones.

As Starkind was wrapping up, explaining how South-scree felt the need to call for an all-Aerie meeting, most of the griffins were nodding and muttering with acknowledgement. They seemed to Hawkwind to understand the situation.

"So, the disposition of these griffins freed from Snow-in-lee must be addressed," the Ice-peak Eldest summed up. "We cannot ignore them."

"There are two factions, however, among the freed Snow-in-lee griffins," Starkind informed. "To describe them, I would turn to our Snow-in-lee representatives themselves, Windnight and Rainsoft. The human child, Jessika, is their interpreter."

All eyes turned to the Snow-in-lee delegation. Windnight raised her hands and began to gesture. Watching her carefully, Jessika began to speak.

"Greetings all griffins from all Aeries," the girl translated as well as she could for having known the language only a couple months and being only six years old. "We griffins freed from Snow-in-lee thank you for letting us come here. We are grateful also to the ones that freed us. Everything is different out here. We don't know how you live, but many of us want to join you. We learned that you live in Lines. We didn't. We lived in pairs with chicks of our own. We learned that griffins don't normally live that way. We want to live the normal way.

"However, not all of us want this. Some of us don't understand. Some of us want to keep our mates and chicks and keep living like we did in Snow-in-lee. He, Rainsoft, and I, Windnight, want to join Lines. We think that's the right way. We don't know what to do about the others that don't want to join Lines. We think they're wrong, but we can't change their minds. Will you let us, who want to join you, be in your Lines?"

Rainsoft patted Jessika on the back as she finished. She smiled at him, and all three of the little group looked around at the gathered griffins. The Eldest of Ice-peak raised a wing to speak.

"What do you think should be done with the griffins who don't want to join Lines?"

Jessika translated even though Windnight and Rainsoft were both good at understanding spoken language. In another moment, she was translating their answer for the griffins that had no hope yet of reading their hand signs.

"We don't know," the girl announced. "If griffins naturally live in Lines, with one matriarch, then they will see the truth in time. They will experience it."

Everyone muttered and nodded in acknowledgment.

"What should we do about them for now?" the Ice-peak Eldest asked.

Jessika translated. "We don't know. Maybe let them alone?"

This time the mutters were louder, and Hawkwind heard clearly over and over again "the prey, the prey, the prey." The prey would suffer without the careful monitoring that the Aeries did. The In-the-wind Eldest griffin raised a wing.

"None of these—what should we call them? These griffins that don't wish to live in Lines?" he asked first.

Thornfire raised a wing and spoke. "We have been calling them separatists."

"None of these separatists wished to come here and speak for themselves?" the Eldest went on. "Do they realize how the Aeries view outside griffins, how we view rogues?"

The room waited while Jessika translated. "Us good Snow-in-lee griffins have tried to talk to them," she said, and there were a few chuckles at her word choice. "They don't want to listen. We tried to tell them about the Aeries and how it's important to live in Lines and take care of the animals. Some of them did listen, but not all."

"Thank you, Windnight," the Eldest nodded.

Starkind raised a wing for a chance to speak, and everyone looked to her. "It seems that there are two issues to address. One: will we, the Aeries, take in the Snow-in-lee griffins who want to join us? Two: what will be done about the Snow-in-lee griffins who don't want to join us?"

A chorus of agreement met her words, but an Ice-peak matriarch raised her wing amidst it. "What about this other, Hawkwind, the last of the Hawk Line? She is not of Snow-in-lee. She is not of the Aeries. She comes with a Snow-in-lee griffin called Hawkswift that she has already considered to be a Linemember, and as we heard from Eldest Starkind, there is another, Hawkjoy, that she calls Linemember."

Into the muttering that followed her words, Thornmother called out, "and she carries new life. Some months from now, with a live birth, there will be none permitted to call her other than Hawkmother, matriarch of the Hawk Line. She will lead a Line without a home. Hawkwind?"

"I seek an Aerie that will welcome the Hawk Line," she called out, struggling to keep her voice even.

"And you bring with you four human children, including this one," called out one of the South-scree elders. Hawkwind thought it was the elder from the Rock Line.

Some more muttering flitted through the room, some curious, some concerned. One of the In-the-wind matriarchs raised her wing.

"Legend tells that our Lines split after a great war. Some Lines, including the Hawk Line, left us to ally with humans. If what we are told is true, those Lines, except the Hawk Line, are now dead, because they allied with humans," she proclaimed.

"To my knowledge," Hawkwind called out before anyone else could speak, "I am the only griffin survivor from Northnest. There could be more, but I honestly do not know. By your logic, we could say that the humans of Northnest suffered as much from the allegiance. The four children I escaped with might be the only survivors of the attack on the capital; there were more towns with many more humans, but I don't know what kind of casualties they sustained."

"Your point is taken," Eldest Starkind welcomed. "The laying of blame in the past is of no concern now. The past should not be forgotten, but we are here to plan the future."

"Association with humans doomed some of our Lines," the same In-the-wind matriarch reemphasized. "Who is to say it won't do it again?"

The under-the-breath comments turned more ominous, and Hawkwind wasn't sure what to say to assuage them. Thornfire stood up.

"Hawkwind," he summoned, "what are your plans for these humans?"

"Uh, well, they are people, just like us," she began awkwardly, "but I have seen a city attacked and decimated. I have seen everyone I know killed. I have seen drakes tear apart my Linesisters and Linebrothers, chicks, and humans both adult and young, right in front of me. Have any of you?"

Silence met her words.

"If you think I would do anything that would bring that kind of death to any city, you are seriously mistaken. I have seen it. I lived through it." Hawkwind fought a sudden lump in her throat and tried to ignore her rising pulse and adrenaline. "I saved these human children. It was all I could do. I will soon have chicks of my own. I would never put any of them in that kind of danger again."

She looked over at Jessika, who was watching her with a trembling jaw, tears rolling down her cheeks. The girl had her hands over her mouth to keep from making noise. Hawkwind felt bad about describing what had happened at Northnest, but it had to be mentioned; she hadn't wanted to make the girl cry.

"These human children will grow up in an Aerie," Hawkwind went on. "They will have each other, and many more griffin family members. The Aerie will be their home. I believe they are all kind, bright young ones. I'm sorry I couldn't bring them all to this meeting, but ask the other South-scree and Snow-in-lee griffins who have met them; they'll tell you about them. Elder Thornfire knows them well. With an Aerie to raise them, I believe they will grow up to want nothing but peace and safety for their home. They, too, saw their city, friends, and families destroyed."

Thornmother swiftly raised a wing, interrupting Hawkwind. "I have asked Hawkwind not to add to their numbers. She has promised it will be so."

"Then what when these human chicks grow up? Will they want to have chicks of their own?" an Ice-peak elder asked.

"It may be that these children, once they are grown and able to take care of themselves, will want to return to a human city," Hawkwind shrugged. "If they want to make their own families, then it may be they will need to find a home in such a city, and merely visit their Aerie, or perhaps Aerie griffins will wish to visit them. They might become an intermediary for trade between human and griffin cities—something that the Aeries have never had, to my knowledge.

"Here is how it stands," Hawkwind summed up. "When I fledged, I swore on my life's blood to protect the people of Northnest. These four are all I have left. I am the last of the Hawk Line. I will become Hawkmother. I swear now to honor both my responsibilities. I promise to never allow these responsibilities to fall upon any who are not willing to bear them. I promise to do all in my power to never allow them to hurt others.

"If the Aeries turn me away, I will take my children and my Line and find a place to try to build a home on my own, far beyond your borders. I realize these featherless chicks are a departure from the norm, but I will vouch for their harmlessness, and take responsibility for all of their misbehaviors. I ask you to welcome back the Hawk Line."

Most of the South-scree griffins smiled down at her, and some of the others did, too. Thornmother gathered the heads of the South-scree delegation to her and spoke rapidly with them. Some of the other griffins were talking urgently among themselves, too. Hawkwind wished she could comfort Jessika, but she was too far away. She met Rainsoft's gaze, not having to say anything, and he reached out to give the girl a little hug. Jessika turned and wrapped her arms around his neck, drying her face against his fur.

Eldest Starkind suddenly stood up and flared both her wings for silence. She looked around at the room and then down at Hawkwind.

"South-scree welcomes the Hawk Line," she declared, "and asks the Hawkmother to establish her Line with us."

Elation flared in Hawkwind's chest, making her feel like she had floated up a half a foot into the air. She could barely keep herself from crowing. "Yes, the Hawk Line accepts your offer."

Beside her, Swift was beaming. Jessika had stopped hugging Rainsoft and was laughing through her tears. Some of the other gathered griffins were making sounds of approval. A few weren't smiling, but none of them booed or hissed, at least.

Hawkwind's heart and mind were bubbling over with mingled relief and joy, like she'd drunk a gallon of the fizzy sugar water a brewer back at Northnest had made for the children. She hadn't been able to taste the sweetness of the sugar, but she'd felt its jittery effects on her body. The Ice-peak Eldest promptly moved the meeting on to other business, oblivious to her ecstasy.

"That takes care of the Hawk Line. What of the Snow-in-lee griffins who wish to join our established Lines?"

"There is precedence for adopting griffins into other Lines," someone commented; Hawkwind wasn't paying as much attention as she should have been and didn't know who had said it.

"But those cases were when there was an irresolvable conflict between a griffin and other members of its Line, and the mothers and grandmothers were upset by it," someone else said.

"That's right. It's usually a young male or female that hasn't broken any laws but for whatever reason cannot live peaceably in its birth Line, or sometimes even in its own birth Aerie."

"That's what the petition process is for; this is different."

Hawkwind, though her body still felt full of crackling elation, forced herself to look up and focus, knowing how important the meeting was.

"These Snow-in-lee griffins haven't done anything wrong," Thornfire spoke up.

"But they don't know our ways," an Ice-peak elder countered.

"They will learn. They want to learn," the mage rebutted.

"Are you suggesting the petition process?" an In-the-wind matriarch asked.

"It could be done that way, but that would probably be tedious. I am more inclined to wish that first each Aerie would decide if they are willing to take in refugees. If they decide to allow it, then each Line within the Aerie would decide if they will accept the Snow-in-lee griffins of their same Line," Thornfire explained.

"That makes logical sense to me," an Ice-peak matriarch nodded, and others seconded her.

"What if an Aerie or a Line decides not to welcome new Linemembers?" another elder asked.

"Then, other Aeries and Lines would state whether they are willing to adopt Snow-in-lee griffins of other Lines. Only those that need adoption would petition," Thornfire suggested.

Some griffins were nodding, but others were holding still, not expressing their opinion. Only a few seemed to be against the ideas, evidenced by slightly shaking heads or looking away. Hawkwind approved of the process in general, but she'd spotted a problem that Thornfire appeared to have forgotten. She raised a wing to speak, and got acknowledgement.

"This would work for most of the Snow-in-lee griffins, but the Eagle, Ice, and Snow Lines were at Northnest, and all were killed, but I know there are Eagle, Ice, and Snow griffins among the Snow-in-lee survivors. I've been told that those Lines are not among the Aerie Lines anymore. If those griffins are adopted into other Lines, those three Lines will be no more."

"She makes an excellent point," someone said.

"Thank you, Hawkmother," Thornfire called, "I had forgotten about that."

"Then Aeries will need to take in those Lines, the same as has been done for the Hawk Line," the Ice-peak Eldest realized.

"Is it just those three?" someone asked.

"We have a list of names," Thornfire announced. "If everyone is interested, let it be passed out to all."

The chorus of assenting voices was enough to get the parchment scattered around the room. Hawkwind shared with Windnight, and she glanced quickly down the list. She guessed there were about five-dozen griffins there. They were grouped by Line. Beside each name, the sex and age of the griffin was written, and in the case of females, whether they were awakened or not.

"Some of these females are awakened," an Ice-peak elder objected, right on cue.

"The Linemother will need to dominate them," Starkind said. "They should go back to sleep."

"That's not certain," someone else worried.

"If they don't, then the current Linemother will go to sleep instead," Thornmother spoke up. "There can be only one mother of a Line."

That statement got waves of conversation rushing through the hall. An In-the-wind matriarch stood up and flared her wings for silence.

"That would not be a bad thing," she began, and almost got shouted down. "No, listen to me. These griffins have been separated from us for a long time, while we have been breeding with each other for ages and they have been breeding with each other. They must have different blood from us and we from them. Mixing blood makes blood stronger. We know this and have seen it. Having a different mother for a decade or two will not ruin a Line; it will improve it."

Now the waves of conversation turned varied. Some griffins clearly agreed with her. Others stubbornly refused to.

"If we bring in any of these Snow-in-lee griffins, the males will mate with our matriarchs," the Watermother of South-scree pointed out. "Their blood will mix in that way. Who is to say a female chick we bring in from Snow-in-lee won't grow up to become a mother? The chick of a union between an Aerie mother and Snow-in-lee male may become a mother. If we have any contact with the Snow-in-lee griffins, their blood will find its way into ours."

An In-the-wind elder stood up. "The Watermother is right. And remember, nature selects the female who is the best for the Line at the current time to become the next mother when the old one gets tired. If an incoming awakened female from Snow-in-lee is not put back to sleep by the presence of the current Aerie Linemother, but rather the

Aerie Linemother goes back to sleep—then the Snow-in-lee female is the best choice for the Line. We all want what is the best for our Lines, right?"

Some voices tried to shout over the elder's last words, but others called out in support of him. Hawkwind waved her wings to get attention.

"From what I have seen, I think it is unlikely that a Snow-in-lee female, even one who is physically fit and strong, would dominate an Aerie Linemother," she told everyone. "The mature Snow-in-lee griffins are self-conscious of their inability to speak aloud. In addition, they don't understand many of our customs, so they're cautious and reserved, keeping to themselves while they observe from a distance. I would be surprised if any were confident enough to overcome one of you. I think it is more likely that a chick from Snow-in-lee, if raised in an Aerie, might one day become a mother.

"On a related point, I'm not sure what to expect from the mature males," Hawkwind went on. "If the talis placed them with a mate, and that female awakened, the male will have been used to mating only with his one female. When she goes back to sleep, he'll be confused, and she might be sad. Both the griffins of the pair will need to adjust to their changing feelings for each other and their situation. The males might not want to mate with other females, or they might become tormented when they discover they want to mate with a Linemother who is not the mate they've lived with—and even had chicks with—for years."

Thornfire waved his wings next. "That's another issue that must be addressed. The pairs of griffins are mostly of two griffins from different Lines. Many want to stay together. That would involve one half of the pair being adopted, probably the male being adopted, because the chicks will bear their mother's Linename, so the female and chicks would more easily go together into the same Line."

Grumbles of exasperation came from many of the assembled griffins.

Thornfire waved the parchment of names. "You'll see after the sex and age, and a note of what Line the griffin wants to go into."

Starkind raised her voice over the continuing hubbub. "I suggest that each Aerie consider whether they will allow new Linemembers at all before we continue with this discussion. If we don't wish to allow it, then we can stop talking about it now, and decide instead how to keep the Snow-in-lee griffins out of our borders."

"Show of wings for agreement: take time to decide if Aeries will allow new Linemembers," the Ice-peak Eldest cried out.

Nearly all of the gathered griffins raised a wing.

"Passed. Take time now."

Chapter 34
Consensus

Starkind waved at Hawkwind, beckoning her to come join the South-scree matriarchs. Heart pounding, Hawkwind made her way to the group, Swift following her. Windnight and Rainsoft sat together, separate from the rest of the gathering, hands moving rapidly as they conversed.

"Let us take an initial vote," Starkind was saying as Hawkwind reached them. "Let us all give our yea or nay opinion on if South-scree is willing to accept at least some new Linemembers from Snow-in-lee. If the consensus is yea, then we'll work out the details of in what circumstances we'll approve a transfer, but if the consensus is nay, then we can stop discussing it now."

"Agreed," the matriarchs and elders said, and Hawkwind added her own voice just a breath behind them.

Starkind hefted a bowl of black and white stones onto the table between them, and then put an empty bowl beside it.

"White for yea, black for nay," the Eldest said. "Conceal your choice or not."

Hawkwind knew what she would vote without having to think further. She reached into the bowl with other early voters and fished out one of the small white stones. Beside her, Swift—as the Hawk Line elder—reached into the bowl, too. Hawkwind transferred her stone to the empty bowl, her vote anonymous among all the other hands dropping stones in the bowl. When all were done voting, Hawkwind saw that the voting bowl had a neat pile of white stones. There were only two black ones.

"Majority says we will allow at least some transfers from Snow-in-lee into our Aerie and Lines," Starkind proclaimed. "Those against it, do you wish to argue your position, or do you forfeit to the majority position?"

No one spoke. Starkind waited for several breaths before she poured the stones back into the selection bowl.

"South-scree will allow the option for Lines to accept transfers of Snow-in-lee refugees," she declared. "Individual Lines may still refuse some or all transfers, but all Lines are granted the option to accept."

Hawkwind found herself wondering who had dropped in the black stones. Who didn't want the Snow-in-lee griffins joining South-scree? It was Hawkwind's Aerie now, and she would have to live with dissenters. No one was meeting her gaze, and no one gave visible evidence of being angry; there was no way to tell who had voted nay.

"It seems the other Aeries have not made their decisions yet," Starkind said. "Shall we look at the list of who might want to transfer to South-scree?"

Everyone bent over the list, and Hawkwind worked hard to read everything that was written in Aerie text, which she'd only learned to read a few months ago. She counted four Sky griffins, four Star griffins, three Rock griffins, and two Water griffins; however, there were griffins of other Linenames that wanted to join their mates in South-scree Lines. There were also five Eagle, three Ice, and three Snow griffins to be settled somehow.

"Sorting this out is all going to be tediously complicated," the Skymother groaned.

"And there are more Snow-in-lee griffins that don't want to join Lines," Thornfire said, "but who might change their minds in a few years."

"We'll face that when it happens," Starkind shrugged. "We have agreed as an Aerie to allow transfers. Each Line can decide to accept or reject the griffins that say they want to join. It doesn't need to be decided now, either. Many of us may want the counsel of more elders before making a decision."

"Agreed," several South-scree griffins confirmed.

There were no Snow-in-lee griffins among the South-scree Lines who had written that they wanted to join the Hawk Line, but they wouldn't have really known it was an option. Even griffins who knew Hawkwind hadn't known at the time of writing if the Hawk Line was going to officially exist. She decided then that if there were any griffins who were rejected, she would accept them into her Line.

Hurriedly, Hawkwind searched for the Rain griffins. There were only three names written: Rainsoft, Rainsharp, and Raincloud. By the sex and ages, Rainsharp was Rainsoft's little sister, and Raincloud was his mother. It seemed that Rainsoft's brother had not added his name to the list; he and his mate would remain separatists.

Breath held with apprehension, Hawkwind read what the three Rain griffins had requested for their transfers. For Raincloud: In-the-wind, Rain Line. For Rainsharp: In-the-wind, Rain Line. For Rainsoft: South-scree, any Line. Hawkwind felt like she'd been punched in the chest. Rainsoft wanted more to be in South-scree than he did to be with his mother and sister in his birth Line. When had he changed his mind? Gentle warmth spread through her; some Line would take him—Thornmother had already volunteered—so he would be close by.

Hawkwind looked over at him, but he was half turned away from her, still talking with Windnight. She searched out Windnight's name. The older griffin had put down In-the-wind, Wind Line, as her preferred choice. Her body had gone back to sleep, and her mate was dead, but she had one still-living chick, a female who was awake and had been placed with a Star male. The pair did not have a chick yet. Interestingly, Hawkwind saw that Windcold, Windnight's daughter, wanted to join the Wind Line, but Starclaw, the male, wanted to join the Star Line in South-scree. It seemed the two hadn't developed much of a bond.

"I suppose every Snow-in-lee griffin will have his or her own story," Hawkwind commented to Swift, who was reviewing the list with her.

"Skycall was right about one thing," Starkind spoke up. "This will affect our quota of births. We will have to adjust it for the next few years, or we'll get over-populated."

"I don't think us mothers will mind," Starmother chuckled. "We've been being pressured to meet the quota for some time now. It really isn't that pleasant to be making chicks as fast as possible."

"It will certainly make the males happier if you're not," the Sky elder chuckled.

For a moment, Hawkwind didn't understand, and then her brain connected the dots and she had to fight the blushing of her cere. If the mothers weren't pregnant all the time they would be coming into heat once a month—and the males would enjoy that.

Everyone looked up at the sound of a bell. The Ice-peak Eldest had flown over and rung one that hung at the head of the council hall.

"Have the Aeries all made their decisions?" she called out as she flew back to her seat.

The other two Eldest called out in the affirmative.

"Ice-peak has decided to allow transfers on an individually addressed basis," the Eldest went on. "What of In-the-wind?"

Their Eldest stood up. "We will allow them, again on an individually addressed basis."

"South-scree?"

Starkind stood. "We also, will accept transfers with the same condition."

"Excellent," the Ice-peak Eldest praised. "We are in agreement."

The In-the-wind Eldest remained standing. "It was mentioned earlier that perhaps each Line would like to decide what griffins it will accept at a later date. However, I have noticed that some Snow-in-lee griffins have specified a second choice next to their name. If we do not decide now, many messengers might have to be sent between Aeries to sort out the transfers, which will delay them."

"You are proposing we decide now, without the benefit of additional elders to help make the decisions?" a matriarch called out from the other side of the room.

"Ideally, the Snow-in-lee griffins in question could be present to talk to about it, but that's not possible either," another matriarch mentioned.

"Deciding now would be expedient," an Ice-peak elder said. "The South-scree delegation could carry the decisions back and directly dispatch the transferred griffins with a guide to their new homes."

"There are two Snow-in-lee griffins here," said the In-the-wind Eldest. "We can ask them about their fellow survivors, can we not?" he asked directly to Windnight and Rainsoft.

The two griffins gestured and Jessika translated. "Ask us anything you want."

Everyone looked around at each other for a moment until someone said, "well, then shall we get to it?"

The chorus of replies was not uniform in eagerness, but at least overall affirmative. The three Aerie groups put their heads together again, and Hawkwind joined back in with the South-scree group.

"Let's start at the top," Starkind directed firmly. "Skymother, there are four Sky griffins who want to join. One is a juvenile male, another is a female chick, another an older female who is asleep, and another an adult male who does not seem to be bringing whatever mate he might have had."

The Sky elder nodded with a smile as the Skymother glanced at him for his opinion.

"We'll take them," she confirmed.

"Excellent," Starkind grinned and made a note next to them. "Next are four Star griffins, ah—but one would rather join the Stone Line. That's an Ice-peak Line."

"I'll check if they've noticed," said the Rock elder, who hopped over to the next group.

"The other three are two males and a female, the female is awake, but there's no mention of a male associated with her."

And so it went. Hawkwind didn't need to say much, as no griffins were asking to join her Line. She was relieved to see that the South-scree griffins had a welcoming attitude towards the Snow-in-lee refugees. A few snags came up, like when one of the Rock griffins wanted to bring her mate, a Fire griffin, to join the Rock Line, and he was requesting the Rock Line, too. She was awakened, but they had no chicks. Windnight was summoned to tell more details about the situation and it was revealed that the pair both wanted to live in an Aerie and stay together, as they seemed to have true affection for each other.

"There are times when a true pair bond does occur among us," Thornfire commented. "We all know it is rare. I think I know this pair, too. They spend a lot of time together, but they are also intelligent and adjusted quickly to being outside of Snow-in-lee. We have had paired griffins living happily in Lines before. They cause no trouble. The female remains asleep and the male doesn't sire chicks, but they still serve their Line well."

"You think this female will go back to sleep?" the Rockmother worried.

"You are afraid you cannot quell her?" Thornfire challenged with a raised eyebrow. "Look how young she is."

"If she has a true pair bond with that male, she'll not go quietly. It will be a scene at least, and a fight at worst. She won't win, however."

"Our nature selects against pair bonded females becoming matriarchs," Thornmother put in. "Such females refuse to mate with anyone other than her bonded male. It's not healthy for the Line. It is exceedingly rare that such a female awakens, in the normal course of things."

"If she doesn't go back to sleep, she'll need to be removed from the Line," Rockmother said flatly. "If she does go back to sleep, she and her mate may mourn what they've lost, more so than other non-bonded but mated pairs in this situation."

"Perhaps the Fire Line would take them both," Starmother suggested with a shrug.

So began a discussion between South-scree and Ice-peak regarding this unique pair of griffins. The Firemother was particularly sympathetic. In the end, it was agreed that Rockmother would meet the pair and evaluate them. If it didn't look like it would work out, Firemother agreed to have them sent to Ice-peak, and she would try to work it out. No one could decide what they should do if that didn't work out either.

One of the Water griffins was a male, a juvenile, who Windnight explained had come from one of the separatist families. Although his parents were holding tight to his younger sibling and refusing to consider the Aerie way of life, he'd already decided to join a Line and split from them. Watermother accepted him without hesitation. The other was an older female, apparently the grandmother of the juvenile male, who had gone back to sleep. Watermother accepted her, too.

It was hours later that a plan had been established for every griffin but a few. It took longer to sort out griffins of other Linenames who wanted to join different Lines. Someone posted a master list at the head of the room, and as transfers were settled, notes were written on the list and names checked off. Hawkwind saw that Windnight and her daughter Windcold had been accepted by In-the-wind, and likewise Rainsharp and Raincloud. She was happy for them all, although she liked Windnight and would be sad to see her go.

Finally, the issue of Rainsoft came up among the South-scree griffins.

"I offered to bring him into the Thorn Line initially," Thornmother said, "and my offer still stands, although perhaps he would rather join the Hawk Line? The Hawk Line is rather short of males."

Hawkwind took a minute to think about how she would like Rainsoft in her Line. The children were terribly fond of him, and he would be an excellent provider since he seemed to like Hawkwind so much. She clenched her bill. Actually, no, that wouldn't be that good of a situation. Rainsoft did like her a lot, an awful lot. She liked him, too, but having him in her Line would mean having him around all the time, especially while the Line was still so small.

Hawkwind wanted a strong Line with strong and varied blood.

She would be mating with many different males from many different Lines—she'd already decided that. Having a, well, possessive male around when she would be wanting to welcome and choose among many would be a frustrating complication. No, as much as she liked Rainsoft, there was a good chance of him getting in the way. He could still take care of her from a different Line.

Unlike females, who usually stuck close to their sisters, nieces, and aunts, males normally spent a lot of time visiting other Lines. There would be nothing wrong with Rainsoft bringing Hawkwind food or dropping by to visit with the children. Moreover, giving him to another Line would show Hawkwind's own impartiality and generosity. He knew Thornfire and Thornwing and they could read a little of his sign language. If he went to the Thorn Line he would not be among total strangers. The Thornmother was willing to take him. The whole Line would look favorably upon him for helping to rescue Thornwing, and he was a partial celebrity for fetching the Moonstone.

"The Thorn Line has received no new members tonight," Hawkwind began slowly. "The Hawk Line will have males of its own in good time, and is not in desperate need. No Aerie lets a chick starve."

Some of the gathered griffins smiled at that last. It was an Aerie saying that Hawkwind had heard and tucked away in her mind for future use.

"The Thorn Line was the first to offer him a place. If that is still how it stands, then that is how it should be," Hawkwind finished.

Thornfire was giving Hawkwind a look that suggested he knew exactly what was going through her mind, and approved of it. Thornmother's expression was similar, and she nodded at Hawkwind's words.

"Let it be so, unless any other Line contests my claim," she said.

No one objected, although there were a few little sighs and shrugs, and Hawkwind wondered it if was because the Thorn Line had attracted so much notoriety of late, and would now have another notable griffin to show off.

Thornfire went to the master list and wrote down the decision by Rainsoft's name. From the corner of her eye, she saw Rainsoft notice and look at what had been written. He showed little reaction except for a relaxation of the muscles in his shoulders. It could have been a sign of relief or disappointment, or possibly a mix of both.

When every griffin had been sorted except for the Ice, Eagle, and Snow Lines, attention went back to the front of the room. The Ice-peak Eldest looked pleased.

"The only question remaining is the fate of the griffins in the Ice, Eagle, and Snow Lines," she summed up. "As pointed out, they are the last of these Lines. To absorb them into other Lines would end them." She consulted the list. "There are four Ice griffins, including an awakened female. There are three Eagle griffins, with an awakened female there, too. There are five Snow griffins, with two awakened females. All of these Lines have the potential to be viable. Are we willing to make room in our Aeries for new Lines, not just new griffins?"

There was grumbling around the room.

"The issue is not just our kindness," an In-the-wind matriarch said. "The issue is the supply of food."

"Nightmother makes an excellent point," Rockmother agreed. "South-scree has taken in the Hawk Line. Our numbers are slightly low right now, and we are glad to have the Hawk Line, but in the long run it will mean fewer births per matriarch and lower individual Line populations, unless the hunting improves somehow, but our records show a fairly steady trend in prey over the last few decades."

"Perhaps what is needed is a new Aerie, in a new location, far enough away to provide enough game for the new Lines," an Ice-peak elder suggested.

"Starting a new Aerie is no easy task," a different Elder argued, "and not something for a dozen griffins with no experience living in an Aerie—or even in the open world, on their own—to undertake."

"Indeed," Starkind said. "It is hard enough for experienced griffins."

Everyone went quiet, likely thinking the same thing.

"Lines from our Aeries would have to go," Thornfire voiced. "The Ice, Snow, and Eagle Lines would take their places in the current Aeries."

"A new Aerie hasn't been made in generations," called out another matriarch. "Where would we go?"

"We would have to scout a location," Thornfire shrugged. "It could be done."

The sound of dozens of griffins thinking hard was deafening.

"Fire Line will not go," announced the Firemother abruptly.

"Moon Line will not go." That was the Moonmother, fast on the heels of Firemother.

More matriarchs spoke up, raising their wings urgently for attention.

"Wind Line will not go."

"Thorn Line will not go."

"Star Line will not go."

"Rain Line will not go."

Hawkwind's hopes sank. Perhaps no one was brave enough. Perhaps she should volunteer? No, she did not have any experience running an Aerie either, and without being a large Line, she needed the help of other large Lines in a safe and established Aerie.

"Hawk Line will not go," she added to the tally, as others called out their intentions, too.

But then, into a breath of silence: "Storm Line will go."

Everyone turned and stared at the Stormmother; her advising Elder stood firm and tall behind her.

"Claw Line will go."

Now everyone was staring at Clawmother, too.

"Sky Line will go."

The entire South-scree delegation gaped at Skymother. Hawkwind could hardly believe it; a Line from South-scree was volunteering, too.

"Sun Line will go."

That was four. Four was plenty. The room broke out into conversation.

"Will we take on one of the new Lines?" Starkind asked the South-scree matriarchs, firmly and rapidly.

"No," said Thornmother, and the others echoed her, so Hawkwind did, too.

"South-scree will not welcome new Lines," Starkind declared to the hall as a whole.

"In-the-wind will welcome the Eagle Line," announced the In-the-wind Eldest.

"Ice-peak will welcome the Ice and Snow Lines," the Ice-peak Eldest proclaimed.

So it was settled.

Hawkwind gazed around the room, dazed by the sudden flurry of decisions at the end. Every Snow-in-lee griffin that had wanted to join a Line now had either already been accepted or had a plan with a backup plan for acceptance. It was done, and relief drained Hawkwind of the last of her anxiety like fluid from a cracked egg. Her legs trembled and she sat down.

"It is decided," the Ice-peak Eldest said, sounding rather surprised by it herself. "Does anyone have any objections?"

Hawkwind couldn't wait to go back to the Snow-in-lee survivors and report on the results. She imagined their faces when they heard the news. They would be in Lines; they would have a place in society. In the case of the Eagle, Ice, and Snow griffins they would found their own Lines. One of their females—already decided in two cases, but still uncertain for the Snow griffins—would become the first matriarch. A couple of those females had mates of other Lines who wanted to stay together, but it would probably be fine for them to join the Lines.

No one objected to the settlement, although everyone was looking around as though they feared someone would speak up with a new point that would undo all their work.

"Then it is confirmed," the Ice-peak Eldest crowed out. "May the matriarchs of Sky, Storm, Claw, and Sun meet to discuss their scouting and Aerie-founding plans on their own. Ice-peak will host them until they are ready to depart."

For a few moments, babble ran around the hall like a circling wind, until someone called out. "What of the separatists?"

"There's nothing we can do," proclaimed Nightmother.

"They are not welcome," came a voice from the back of the room, hidden from view.

The chorus of agreement was undeniable.

"When they want to live like proper griffins, then we will consider them," Moonmother stated.

Another chorus of agreement rocked the walls.

"It seems we have a consensus," the Ice-peak Eldest nodded, although she looked a little disappointed to Hawkwind. "Does anyone wish to dissent?"

The room went absolutely silent. Hawkwind wanted to speak up, but she knew there was little that could be done. Griffins that wouldn't follow the Words and the Aerie councils' guidelines on hunting could not be tolerated. They would endanger the entire Aerie with the risk of starvation.

"Let the record show that none have spoke in favor of welcoming the separatists," the Ice-peak Eldest concluded. "They must remain outside our borders. Our work here is done. Thank you all for your cooperation and wisdom. This all-Aerie meeting is adjourned."

Something not quite a cheer but still joyous erupted from the crowd. Griffins began standing up to leave or shuffling about to talk with each other. The Thorn, Rock, Star, and Water matriarchs stood together facing the Skymother. They were saying their good-byes. Hawkwind looked over at Windnight and Rainsoft. The two were making their way over to the South-scree group. Jessika ran ahead of them and jumped on Hawkwind, giggling and wiggling.

"Hawkwind," Windnight gestured, "I will return with you to my fellow survivors, before gathering those that will come to In-the-wind and leaving with them, but now I wish to go greet Windmother. I will return, and thank you for all that you've done on our behalf."

"You're very welcome," Hawkwind told the older female.

Jessika transferred to Windnight's back so the elder griffin would be able to speak with the Windmother, who knew no Snow-in-lee sign language. Windnight took herself off, and Hawkwind faced Rainsoft.

"I'm glad you will be staying in South-scree," she told him.

"Me, too. I will still be able to visit my mother and sister whenever I wish," he replied by hand, "but I wish to be closer to you and Thornfire, and the children, and the others."

Thornmother stepped up beside Hawkwind. "The Thorn Line welcomes you," she said. "Will you accept us, and join us?"

Rainsoft stood tall, his long ebony wings folded back and crossed at the tips. He bowed his head slowly in agreement.

"The Thorn Line will need to learn to speak with our hands," Thornmother said. "All of South-scree will. I hope you will teach us." She leaned forward and preened the neck feathers of her newest Linemember. "Welcome, Thornsoft."

Epilogue

The passing of the months had brought the seasons past midwinter to the fiercest cold of the year. South-scree huddled under a thick coating of sharp and gritty snow wherever screaming winds failed to scour it away. The griffins had dug tunnels through the snow and avoided going topside as much as possible. During the winter they spent much time sleeping and crafting, living off preserved foods except for on the rare days when the weather cleared enough for intrepid hunting parties to make a quick trip down the mountain.

On one of the days that the winds were raging their hardest, Hawkwind rested, panting, in a deep room of her Line's home under the stones of South-scree, while Joy and Swift saw to her comfort and gently cleaned the two weak and struggling chicks she'd just brought into the world. They were a little early, but big enough.

Starbright had been on hand for the delivery. It was she who kept the room warm and properly lit. Thanks to her, the birthing had not been fatal for mother or chicks, despite the potential complications that came with twins. The babies were blind, naked except for a fine coating of fur and wet downy feathers that would fluff up and keep them warm once they were dry. Swift was overseeing their care, checking their breathing and severing their umbilicals. Joy offered Hawkwind fortifying tea and adjusted her cushions.

"Hawkswift says, 'nicely done,'" Starbright translated.

From Hawkwind's position, she couldn't see Swift, and she tried to turn around.

"Stay still," Starbright said. "We'll bring them to you."

Fresh towels, the softest the Aerie could make from the coats of mountain sheep, were put down over the cushiest cushions in front of Hawkwind's chest. Swift and Joy each carried over a trembling chick. Hawkwind had to catch her breath again as she saw them.

"They're perfect," she whispered.

Swift gestured, "yes, they are."

Four legs, two naked wings, oversize head, and stubby and feather-less tail: griffin chicks were called ugly by some, cute by others, but to Hawkwind they were exquisite miracles. The one on the left opened its bill and chirped a soft little chick-chirp. The other heard it, turned its head towards its twin and chirped back. Hawkwind leaned forward, nestling her head between the two of them, and chirruped in reply, the same way she remembered her mother and grandmother and great-grandmother chirruping to her. The chicks immediately chirped again, and she chirruped back, nudging them gently. Their baby toes curled against the towels. Their naked wings twitched. They couldn't yet hold up their heads; they had a lot of growing to do.

"Bring the light up a little," Hawkwind whispered, and Starbright touched a glow-stone set into the wall.

With brighter light, Hawkwind could tell their fur color, although they would be white and downy where their feathers would be for sev-eral months. One had dark grey-brown fur, lightening to slate grey on its belly and feet. The other was rusty red-brown, with light brown underside.

Swift smiled at her. "One of each," she gestured.

Hawkwind shook her head slightly. It would always be impos-sible to know for sure, and chicks did not always resemble their sires, but it was hard to deny Thornwing's rusty red and Rainsoft's—now Thornsoft's—charcoal grey in the fur of the two chicks.

"What are they?" Hawkwind asked, knowing Swift would have checked, although in their current positions the bits in question were hidden.

Swift held a hand over the grey-brown chick. "Male," she gestured.

Hawkwind nodded with relief. The Line would need males to protect and feed the future chicks. This chick would be the first of them, and would hold the position of eldest male for as long as he lived. He would also probably be in high demand by other matriarchs, as he would be South-scree's first chance to get Hawk Line blood into the other Lines.

Swift moved her hand to hover over the rusty-brown chick. "Female," she gestured.

Elation flowered in Hawkwind's chest. Female: Hawkwind had an heir. Joy might yet awaken in some years and take over the position of Hawkmother, but in case she did not, this chick would be right in line, raised and ready to assume the position.

Of course, Hawkwind intended to have more chicks, and when she did the importance of these two would dim a little, but for the moment, their presence told Hawkwind that she was safe. Her Line was legitimate.

"Can we see now?"

Hawkwind looked over at the leather curtain in front of the doorway. Four sets of little human feet were visible in the gap below it. Jessika, who had called out, was already starting to stick her head through.

"Come in, but don't touch them just yet," Hawkwind said, "and keep your voices down, please."

The four children tiptoed in with obvious restrained excitement. They gathered around the cushions and sat down.

"They're not very pretty yet," Hawkwind smiled, "but they will be."

"I saw kittens born once," Rikah whispered. "They weren't pretty at first, either."

"What will you name them?" Kassandra asked breathlessly.

Hawkwind leaned her head to one side, softly brushing her male chick with her cheek feathers. "Hawknight." She tipped her head the other way, to nudge her female chick. "Hawkday."

The children smiled.

"I like them," Kassandra grinned.

"Me, too, but I like my name better," Jessika boasted. "Hawkwings."

Hawkwind had taken Thornmother's advice and inducted the children as actual Linemembers. For that they had received Hawknames. Hawkwind had worried that the name Jessika had chosen was too suggestive of the stylized wings tattooed on her back, but the girl had insisted, and Hawkwind had acquiesced.

She had, however, guided Rikah away from certain of his initial choices, like Hawkblood, Hawkkiller, and Hawkman. He'd eventually settled on Hawkdare, which Thornwing had helped him choose. Kassandra had taken a long time to think about hers, and had picked Hawksky in the end. Little Karolan hadn't known what to pick, so Hawkwind had sat down with him and Thornfire, each of them coming up with names, until Karo had agreed on Hawkrain, perhaps in sympathy of Thornsoft losing his birth Linename.

The other griffins of the Aerie were happier calling them by their Linenames, and the voiceless griffins especially preferred them, as there was no easy way for them to sign their human names. The children called each other by either name interchangeably. Hawkwind found that she used their Linenames more for light, casual topics. If there was something serious she needed to talk with them about, especially something from the past, she often reverted to their human names.

The twin chicks were starting to give hunger chirps and struggle to lift their heads, and Swift sent Joy to fetch some food, which Hawkwind or Swift or any Linemember would tear to bits and feed to them. As Hawkwind and Swift helped the little ones take their first nibbles, Hawkwind felt her thoughts drifting forward, imagining the chicks in a year, in two, five, ten, twenty. They'd have personalities. They'd talk and fly and hunt and maybe make more chicks. They'd take their places in the Hawk Line.

She transferred her gaze to her human children. What about them in a year, two, ten, twenty? They would grow, too. Jessika, Hawkwings, noticed her gaze and met it. Might she be seven years old now? Hawkwind supposed she must be. The girl's gaze felt far older than that, and in it Hawkwind read her thoughts.

The griffin turned her head away, tired from the birth, and burdened from her long fight to achieve this security for the children. She was Hawkmother now. Snow-in-lee was emptied of griffins; they had been absorbed into the Aeries and the separatists exiled. Thornfire had the Sun and Moonstones hidden in his possession. Hawkwind had won a safe home for Jessika, Rikah, Kassandra, and Karolan, but the girl's gaze said that wasn't enough.

The Princess of Northnest still wanted her kingdom back.

To be continued...

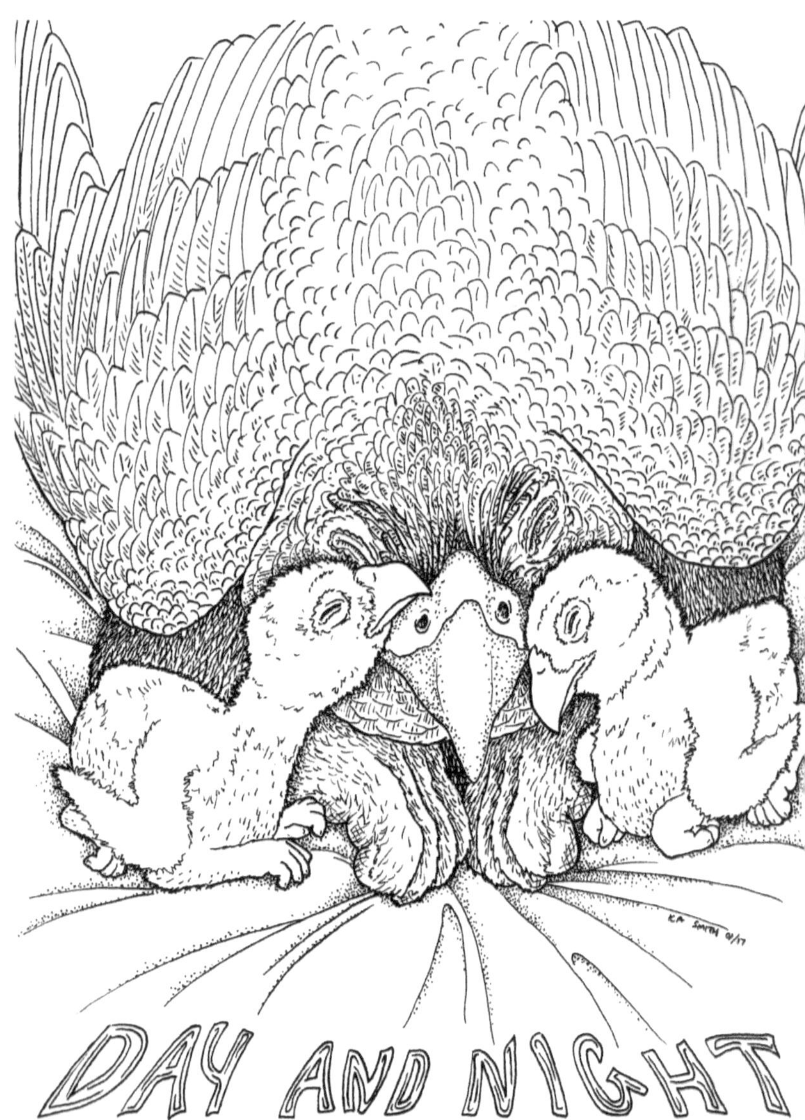
DAY AND NIGHT

Appendix of Names

Warning: this section contains spoilers for the story.

Griffin settlements and their Lines

- Northnest Lines: Hawk, Falcon, Eagle, Ice, Snow, and Cloud
- South-scree Lines: Sky, Rock, Thorn, Star, Water
- Snow-in-lee Lines: Rain, Ice, Star, Sky, Eagle, Rock, Snow, Stone, Storm, Wind, Fire, Hawk
- Ice-peak Lines: Stone, Storm, Fire, Sun, Owl
- In-the-wind Lines: Rain, Wind, Moon, Night, Claw

Humans

- Jessika – female, 6 year old human
- Rikah – male, 5 year old human
- Kassandra – female, 5 year old human
- Karolan "Karo" – male, 5 year old human
- Rikan – male, Rikah's father, a blacksmith
- Judit Rania – female, a villager

Griffins of Northnest

- Hawkwind – female, a young Feathyr
- Eagleye – male, Hawkcall's friend, a Feathyr
- Hawkcall – female, Hawkwind's full sister, a Feathyr

- Icefeather – female, retired Feathyr trainer
- Hawkmoon – female, Hawkwind's great-grandmother
- Hawkbright – female, Hawkwind's mother, matriarch of the Hawk Line
- Hawkbrave – female, Hawkbright's grandmother

Griffins of South-scree

- Starsun – female, a scout Captain
- Rocksky – female, a scout Commander
- Thornfire – male, a mage, Elder of the Thorn Line
- Thornwing – male, Thornfire's younger brother
- Skycall – female, Eldest and moderator of the council
- Skymist – female, a scout
- Thornmother – female, matriarch of the Thorn Line
- Starbright – female, an apprentice mage
- Starkind – female, Eldest and moderator of the council
- Rocktall – male, Elder of the Rock Line
- Skywhite – female, Elder of the Sky Line
- Watermother – female, matriarch of the Water Line
- Watercloud – female, Elder of the Water Line
- Rockmother – female, matriarch of the Rock Line

Griffins of Snow-in-lee

- Rainsoft – male
- Icemoon – female, an Elder
- Skystrong – female, a chick
- Eaglesong – female, a chick
- Hawkdash – male, Hawkswift's younger brother
- Snowstar – female, Hawkdash's mate
- Hawkswift – female, an Elder
- Hawkjoy – female, a juvenile, Hawkswift's daughter

- Windnight – female, an Elder
- Stormstone – female, an Elder
- Skyblack – female
- Rainsharp – female, Rainsoft's younger sister
- Raincloud – female, Rainsoft's mother
- Windcold – female, Windnight's daughter
- Starclaw – male, mated to Windcold

Other named griffins

- Firemother – female, matriarch in Ice-peak
- Stormmother – female, matriarch in Ice-peak
- Nightmother – female, matriarch in In-the-wind
- Moonmother – female, matriarch in In-the-wind
- Clawmother – female, matriarch in In-the-wind
- Windmother – female, matriarch in In-the-wind

- Icecloud – a mage of ancient Snow-in-lee, created the Moonstone
- Starflight – a mage of ancient Snow-in-lee, created the Sunstone

- Featherfire – the wild griffin that made the Northnest pact many generations ago

About the Author

Thank you for reading!

Katherine A Smith grew up on the Mendocino Coast in Northern California. She started drawing and writing stories as soon as she could hold a pencil. This is her fifth published novel. Her hobbies, besides writing, include drawing and painting, sewing, hiking, video games, board games, reading, and dance. As of the time of this writing, she lives in Los Gatos, California. (She's been known to move around quite a bit.)

Under the Kasmith Art & Books imprint, Katherine produces books and artwork for the love of it.

Visit the Kasmith Art & Books website:
www.elucidationimages.com

Find Kasmith Art & Books on Facebook and Google+.

Katherine's artwork can be acquired on a variety of products through her Kasmith Art & Books CafePress and Zazzle stores.

Please leave reviews of this book on Amazon, Goodreads, and any other site you use to tell others what you thought. Reviews and ratings make a big difference! Thank you!